The NOUGHTY *Spy*

LUCY LYONS

Published in the UK in 2025 by Twist House Books
Copyright © Lucy Lyons 2025
Cover Art by Spiffing Covers

lucylyonswrites.com

This is a work of fiction. The characters contained within its pages are wholly imaginary. Any resemblance to actual persons, living or dead, is entirely coincidental. All locations, although loosely based on real places, have been re-imagined to suit the convenience of the story. The opinions expressed are those of the characters and should not be confused with the author's own.

Paperback ISBN: 978-1-7393079-4-3
eBook ISBN: 978-1-7393079-5-0

"If you want to find the secrets of the universe, think in terms of energy, frequency, and vibration."
Nikola Tesla

1

— · —

AUGUST 2000, BIRMINGHAM

'This is a bad idea.' Antony taps the steering wheel. He checks his watch and fiddles with the stainless steel clasp, clearly in two minds over whether to put his precious Breitling in the glove box or keep it on. The problem is, this neighbourhood isn't somewhere you want to be seen with an expensive watch. Or a nice car.

'The place isn't as bad as it looks,' I say. The knot inside my stomach grows larger.

I peer through the windscreen across a crumbling expanse of tarmac to the Clydesdale Tower, a thirty-one storey building that casts a long shadow across the car park. Another identical block looms in the distance. Together, the towers are called The Sentinels which is apt as I can't help feeling we're being watched.

Antony has parked his pristine Audi TT in view of the main road, between a BMW with lowered suspension and a battered Ford Sierra with its bonnet and half the engine missing.

He turns the engine off and the air conditioning cuts out. The car's interior swiftly becomes stifling.

I lower my window a sliver. The ceaseless drone of traffic from the A38 rushes in, along with blaring drum and bass beats from an open window above, screaming children, and barking dogs. On the far side of the car park, kids form a disorderly line at the window of a Mr Whippy van, coming away with rocket lollies and 99 ice creams with chocolate flakes stuck in them.

Opposite the ice cream van, a group of youths stand around a concrete pillar, giving each other fist-bumps and kicking an empty bottle around on the tarmac. Despite the sweltering weather, they're dressed in dark jogging bottoms and hoodies. I reassure myself it's standard teenage jinks. They're not as bad as they look.

Somewhere in that tower block is Fred, a pedigree brindle Pug belonging to my friend Beverley. We struck up a friendship during our weekly aerobics class, and meet for coffee whenever she can snatch time from her job with Birmingham City Council. Beverley has a string of failed relationships behind her and Fred is the one constant joy in her life.

Ever since he was snatched from her back garden she's not been sleeping, and her mojo has gone.

'This shouldn't take long.' I unstick my hair from the nape of my neck and twist it into a messy bun, securing it with a hairgrip.

Antony chews his lip. 'How much do you like Beverley? I mean, for real? Why can't we tell her the dog's here and let the council do the rest?'

'We've been through this. Bev works for the housing department.' I lift my rucksack onto my lap. 'She can't do anything about stolen pets except ring the RSPCA, and they won't act without a police warrant.'

'Then it's the police's problem.'

'Do you really think a missing Pug is high up on the police's priority list? Seriously?'

Beverley cried again in front of me this morning, her eyes puffy and red-rimmed. I can't sit back and do nothing when I have the means to help.

Antony throws his hands up. 'Maybe Fred likes it here?'

But his voice falters as he surveys the stark, brutalist tower block with its mean strip of grass between the car park and certain death from a never-ending stream of traffic.

'Tell you what,' I say. 'Once we get Fred back I'll treat you to a 99.'

'No thanks.' Antony stares at the ice cream van. 'Mr Whippy's probably dealing drugs on the side. Let's just get the dog and get out of here.'

'Deal. But please stop looking at your watch. You choose your own hours, remember?'

Last year, Antony worked stupid hours for an unscrupulous employer before he came to his senses and quit. He barely had two seconds to himself let alone me. But now he's part of a friendly design cooperative with flexible hours.

He sucks air through his teeth. 'I've got back-to-back meetings in an hour and I'm already cutting it fine. It's not a good look if I crash in late.' He glances at me. 'Have you signed Saskia's card?'

I brandish a red envelope with a grin. My thoughts on his stunning work-colleague Saskia are significantly less murderous than last year, especially now she's getting married. 'Who's the lucky guy?'

'Some posh bloke from Kensington. They're made for each other.' He opens the glove box and chucks the card inside. 'Saskia's off to Crete with him and left me to hold the fort. I have to brief the designers this afternoon, then head off to the Edinburgh Expo tomorrow, so we need to get a move on.'

'No problem.' I unzip my rucksack, remove Fred's photo, and show it to Antony. 'Isn't he cute? Look at his big, soppy eyes and snuffly nose.'

'That dog has a face like a squashed potato,' Antony says.

'You have no heart.'

Reaching inside my rucksack, I turn on the finding machine, feeling the chill slowly pulsing from the side-vent. For once, I welcome its cold.

The display shows a green dot. Dad's dot. That part of the machine is the same as ever.

I unfold the two antennae from the recessed groove at the top and position them upright, before inserting Fred's photo between the soft clips at the ends.

Last year, the Turing-Tesla League upgraded my machine with a shiny new case. The plexiglass square at the centre of the console, which previously protected the electronic components, has been replaced by an LCD text screen that displays not just location co-ordinates, but also addresses.

52.474133, -1.900744

Clydesdale Tower, Birmingham, B34 6HQ

Five LED indicators run in a line above the screen. One is solid red and the second is flashing. When we're close to Fred all five lights will turn red.

'I'm ready.' Taking a deep breath, I reach for the door-release latch.

My mobile vibrates in my pocket.

I pause to check the display, hoping it'll show *JPP_TTL*, short for Jonathan Prudente-Poulton, Director of the Turing-Tesla League. Jonathan asked if I'd like to work for the League back in January. I said yes, but it's come to nothing.

The thought of working for my late father's mysterious organisation has kept me going all these months, but my patience is running out. I turned down a job offer from Hertfordshire Constabulary to find people using my machine, and now I can't help wondering if I made the wrong decision.

UNKNOWN NUMBER

Antony peers at the screen. 'Don't answer it.'

'It might be important.' I press the green button to accept the call.

A man with a South Asian accent says, 'Hello, am I speaking to Miss Alexandra Martin?'

'Yes...who is this?' I ask warily.

'Miss Martin, I'm Sanjit Manhar, how are you today?'

'Well, I—'

'Miss Martin, you are a lucky lady! We are offering you a free vacation to Disneyla—'

I swiftly end the call and shove my phone away.

'Let me guess? Another cold call?' Antony gives me a pitying look. 'How many's that now?'

'Loads.' I sigh. Since the first telemarketer called a few weeks ago, I've been flooded with once-in-a-lifetime opportunities to purchase a new kitchen, time-share apartments in Spain, personal liability insurance, and prize draw tickets.

'My advice, block 'em,' Antony says. 'And don't answer if you don't recognise the number.'

'Got it.' I lean over. 'Kiss me. For luck.'

Antony draws me in for more than a simple peck on the cheek. I reluctantly pull away before we attract unwanted attention. I zip up my rucksack, sling it over my shoulder, and step from the low-slung car into brilliant sunshine.

I delve into my pocket for a lanyard with an ID card and slip it around my neck. I created a fake ID from my Birmingham City library card and an old passport photo, and completed my masterpiece by adding the council logo, a phoney identification number, and random date.

I crane my neck to look up at hundreds of open windows, many with net curtains hanging limp in the breezeless afternoon. Heat radiates from baking tarmac onto my bare legs. It's another day for shorts as England basks under a hallelujah heat wave.

Antony double-checks the windows are up before locking the car. His dark umber skin contrasts with his garish tropical shirt and beige chinos. The ensemble would be great for a Hawaiian-themed party but it's glaringly out of place here.

'Hang on.' He whips his sunglasses off and examines the ID card around my neck. 'What's this?'

I squirm. 'We need to look the part if we're knocking on doors.'

Antony drops the lanyard, looking pained that I've blundered into his field of expertise – graphic design. 'Let's hope no one looks too closely. What did you use to do this? Microsoft Paint? I'd get a better result if I fell asleep on my keyboard.'

'Thanks.'

He steps back, looking over my Quiksilver T-shirt, denim shorts, and tennis shoes. 'And you don't look anything like a council worker.'

'It's Casual Monday.' I sling my rucksack over my shoulder and stride towards the swing doors at the main entrance to Clydesdale Tower. Scaffolding surrounds the tower's southern face. High above, builders are fitting new cladding and replacing the windows.

A vaguely threatening atmosphere hangs over the place despite the ongoing refurbishment. The Sentinels often feature in the local papers for the wrong reasons. This is Birmingham's troubled heartland, populated by isolated old people, low-income and unemployed council tenants, bored teenagers, and well-known troublemakers.

We take a wide line past the youths. One kicks a lager can in our direction. I'm about to kick it back when Antony moves gang-side, keeping himself between them and me, and fixes the ring leader with a long, hard stare.

'Keep walking,' he says from the corner of his mouth.

The kids jeer and make rude gestures. My heart picks up along with my pace until we reach the main entrance. An elderly lady with hair in rollers, pulling a tartan shopping bag on wheels, approaches the doors the same time.

Antony strides past a discarded shopping trolley filled with bricks, bottles and other junk, and opens the battered swing door for her. The old dear gives him a suspicious stare as she walks through, gripping the strap of her handbag extra-tight.

'You're welcome.' Antony sighs.

The old woman hurries to the lift and repeatedly jabs the button until the graffiti-covered doors open. She wheels her bag inside and stands by the control panel, eyes fixed on Antony until the lift doors close.

The foyer is solid concrete lit by caged, lozenge-shaped lights. A CCTV camera is mounted in the corner.

'Big Brother's watching,' Antony mutters, and turns his face from the camera.

A dubious puddle in the corner gives off an unpleasant, acrid smell. I skirt around it, covering my nose.

As council blocks go, this isn't the worst I've seen. There's a working lift and the 'Urban Boom!' wildstyle graffiti shows a modicum of artistic talent. I'm tempted to take a photo for my next painting, but there isn't time.

Without knowing what floor Fred is on the lift is no use to us.

Antony heads for the stairs. I fall in behind him as he hurries to the first floor landing. I join him, peeking inside my rucksack to check the finding machine's reading.

Two solid reds.

I re-check on every floor to the sound of barking dogs. Any one of them could be Fred.

Antony ascends the stairs without breaking a sweat. By the seventh my thighs are burning and I'm praying Fred's not at the top of the building. My exercise regime of aerobics and gentle jogging definitely needs an overhaul.

By the tenth floor, I stop to pound my complaining thighs and get my breath. Antony peers into my rucksack.

'Three lights. Fourth is flashing. We're getting close.'

Somewhere above us, a dog barks. It sounds a lot larger than a Pug.

I force myself up to the eleventh, through another set of swing doors and onto the landing. The rectangular space is inadequately lit by a single plastic light and meagre daylight filtering through the swing doors' glass.

A cacophony blares behind the row of doors. Reggae music, thrash metal, and hip-hop clash with daytime TV. More dogs bark nearby. I walk from door to door.

My best reading comes from a tatty blue door with the number 91 in white plastic.

Four solid lights and one flashing. I walk past and lose the flashing light.

'What do you think?' I return to number 91. 'Good enough?'

'It'll have to be.' He gives me a worried glance. 'You sure about this?'

'As sure as I'll ever be.'

I fix my rucksack over my shoulders and press the doorbell.

2

I can't hear the doorbell over all the noise coming from the flat. I ring the bell again, then lift the letterbox flap and peer through the slot. Inside, a dimly lit hallway with a brown linoleum floor leads to a kitchen. The roar of a crowd comes from a room down the hall accompanied by commentary from a famous football pundit whose name eludes me.

'Hello! Anyone home?' I call through the letterbox. 'Hello!'

A shape appears in the darkened hallway. I jerk back and drop the flap.

Antony raises his clenched fist in a gesture of solidarity. But it's impossible not to think of the consequences if the occupant challenges my shoddy ID. They could get me arrested for impersonating a council officer. That is, if they don't punch my lights out first.

The door opens, releasing a bluish haze of smoke. I cough into my hand as a scrawny woman with sunken cheeks looks me up and down. She raises a cigarette lodged between yellow-stained fingers to her lips. Her blonde, frizzy hair is black at the roots and scraped back into an untidy pony tail. She wears fluffy pink slippers, a denim skirt, and dingy white T-shirt with palm trees under the slogan: *Aloha!*

The woman's gaze drops to the ID around my neck, making my heart thump louder than the *doof doof doof* beats coming from next door.

Wrinkles frame her lips as she drags on her cigarette. 'What's this about?'

'I'm Jane White from Birmingham City Council.' I put my hand out but she ignores it.

'You from the social?' She puts her hand on her hip. 'Took you long enough.'

I swallow. 'I'm s...sorry, Mrs...?'

'Sharon. Lawler.' The woman casts a glance down the hall. 'Any news on a new flat? My Keith's been on your waiting list forever.'

'Well...erm...I'll look into that once I'm back in the office. I'm actually here on a different matter.'

Sharon's gaze turns flinty.

Her hand grips the door. Before she can slam it in my face, I say swiftly, 'We've received a report of a dog in your flat. Your tenancy agreement prohibits pets, so I have to carry out an inspection.'

Beverley mentioned the no-pet council tenant policy ages ago, but it's seldom enforced. I brace myself for a torrent of abuse or laughter. Instead, Sharon frowns, her sparse eyebrows drawing together.

'What you on about?' Smoke streams from her nostrils. 'How am I going to look after a dog on my money?'

'We need to confirm it.' I peer past her shoulder.

Sharon's mouth tweaks into a wily smile. She opens the door wide. 'Come in, then. See for yourself.'

She retreats down the hall and halts by the room with the blaring TV.

I whisper to Antony. 'Check the reading?'

Antony unzips the backpack and looks inside. 'No change,' he whispers. 'Fred's not here.'

'He might be!' I whisper back.

Sharon beckons me into a red-carpeted lounge which is stiflingly hot even with the window open. Stains from water damage form large brown blots across the ceiling.

Sharon follows my gaze. 'That charmer upstairs, his washing-machine leaked for days. There's water still trapped up there. It won't dry even in this heat.'

Within moments, sweat trickles down the back of my neck. Photos of grinning children in school uniforms clutter the mantel. A football match blares on the TV. Birmingham City — in their blue-striped kit — play some other team I don't recognise.

A portly man in his fifties who must be Keith watches the match from a sunken armchair with a roll-up in one hand and a can of Carling in the other. His bandaged leg rests on a footstool. Beside him is a walking frame.

Sharon raises her voice. 'This is wotzername from the Council. They think we got a dog.'

'We had Shammy, but that was years back,' Keith says.

'Told you.' Sharon crosses her arms with a tight smile. 'Keith's the only one with fleas.'

Keith rolls his eyes. 'Cheeky.' He catches Antony's eye and points his can of lager at the screen. 'What do you think of City's chances with Paul Furlong out front?'

Antony cocks a brow. 'Didn't the club pay one-and-a-half million for him? For that amount, he should put them in the back of the net every time.'

'You're a Londoner?' Keith raises a brow. 'Not a City fan, then?'

Antony shakes his head. 'Hammers.'

'Bad luck, mate.'

'Tell me about it,' Antony says.

I look around but Fred is nowhere to be seen. I wrinkle my nose at the damp mixed with fag ash. 'May we check the other rooms? Then we'll be out of your hair, Mrs Lawler.'

A gleam comes into her eye. 'Look all you want.'

I follow her across the hall into a tiny galley kitchen with wonky doors on the units. In this heat I'm looking for a water bowl but there isn't one. Neatly stacked plates and matching floral mugs dry on a drainer by the sink.

I give Antony a pointed look. 'My colleague will check the other rooms if that's okay?'

Sharon gives a terse nod.

Antony crosses the hall and looks into the bedroom and the bathroom.

'See that?' Sharon points to an ominous dark patch of mould covering one side of the ceiling. 'You could grow mushrooms on it. And now my daughter won't visit coz little Jimmy's got asthma. Council promised Keith a ground-floor flat. I've called this number and that one which costs me an arm and a leg but all we get is the bleedin' runaround. The way things are, Keith'll die first and then you can cross him off the list.'

I open the kitchen cabinets that work, looking for tins of Pal, bowls, brushes, or a lead. No dog food. I can't understand it. The finding machine never lies.

After closing the last drawer I walk to the window. The view is dominated by Cleveland Tower. In the distance, Birmingham's industrial heartlands give way to forest.

A deep woof draws my gaze upwards. A flurry of high-pitched yapping follows it.

Pointing at the ceiling, I ask, 'Sharon, who owns those dogs?'

She crosses her arms. 'Don't ask. Nasty bit of work, him upstairs. Knows all kinds of lowlifes. I wouldn't go up there if I were you.'

Antony appears in the doorway. 'Thank you for your time, Mrs Lawler.'

'What about my flat?' Sharon asks, following us to the door. 'What shall I tell me husband?'

'Tell him the council will be in touch,' I say. 'Thanks again.'

Sharon stands in the doorway. 'Ta-ra, then,' she says, reaching in her pocket for another cigarette.

Antony pushes through the swing doors to the landing and flaps his shirt. 'I smell like an ashtray!'

I peer over the railing, shivering at the sheer drop.

'You heard what she said about the guy upstairs.' Antony puts his foot on the stairs. 'We're not messing with him. Let's go.'

I put my hand out to stop him. 'Why don't we take a quick look upstairs and make a note of the door number? Beverley can take it from there.'

Antony sighs. 'Promise me, after that, we can go?'

Raising three fingers, I say, 'Scout's honour.'

I run upstairs to a pair of swing doors smeared with grime and shoulder my way through. The twelfth floor has an identical layout to the floor below. I count the doors to the flat directly above Sharon and Keith's.

To my astonishment, the front door is wide open. A child's safety gate shields the gap. Behind the bars, a small Pug is stretched out on the floor, panting in the heat. Although the dog is missing his collar, his unusual brindle colour and distinctive white-tipped front paw is enough to identify him.

Fred is the spit of his photo. He gets to his feet, snuffling in my direction.

I unsling my rucksack to double-check the reading.

Five solid reds.

3

—·—

Fred stands on his hind legs, trying to stick his muzzle through the safety-gate's bars. Beyond him, the dark hallway leads to a closed door.

In one swift move, I lean over the barrier and scoop Fred up in my arms. He wiggles his warm body and lets out a string of excited yaps.

'Ssssh,' I whisper into Fred's ear. He whines and licks me.

A low rumble comes from the dark hall. The sound sends ice trickling through my guts. My breath catches as a bulky silhouette moves in the darkness. Dull pinpricks of light shine in its eyes.

It's a Rottweiler. The largest I've ever seen, with a barrel chest and broad tan-and-black head. The beast is all muscle and easily weighs more than me.

Antony takes my hand. 'Walk away slowly and quietly,' he whispers, tugging me towards the stairs.

Claws scrabble on lino. The black monster barks loud enough to make the walls vibrate.

My legs turn to rubber as a voice bellows from inside the flat. 'Oy! Where's me dog, you bastard!' The stairgate rattles. 'Get 'em, Buster!'

A black shape crashes over the stair gate.

'Run!' Antony shoves me towards the stairwell doors.

I push through, onto the concrete landing. The doors swing closed behind us.

'Buster won't be able to open them,' I say breathlessly.

'You're joking!' Antony hisses. 'Give Fred here!' He tucks the Pug under one arm and races down to the eleventh floor with me hot on his heels.

Hinges squeak above. The swing-doors nudge open. A black muzzle appears, slicked with slobber and baring formidable teeth. Buster forces his bulk through the doors with a growl.

'Oh, God!' I call in horror.

'Run!' Antony yells.

We hurtle down to the tenth floor as Buster barrels down from the eleventh. The dog makes an ungainly descent, misses its step and crashes into the landing. It releases a spine-chilling growl and pushes off the wall.

'He's still coming!' Antony yells. Fred whines in his arms.

He waits a beat for me to catch up and we run on together. Terror spurs me to leap the stairs three at a time, my breath escaping in panicked huffs. I trip and lunge to catch the hand-rail before I fly head over heels and break my neck on the concrete landing.

My spine prickles at the thumping and scrabbling behind us.

I dare a look back. The Rottweiler, despite its awkward and clumsy descent, is gaining. Barely ten steps separate us and the dog.

Acid burns in my throat as I leap recklessly down the stairs, counting each landing until we finally reach the ground floor.

Antony gives me an ungentlemanly shove through the main doors and into the glaring sunlight. I shield my eyes, desperate to collapse to my knees and kiss the ground.

'Keep going!' Antony yells.

He grabs the abandoned shopping trolley and rams it against the doors.

Antony dashes after me with Fred bobbing up and down under his arm. The finding machine bangs painfully into my spine as I push myself faster but there's no time to tighten the straps. I dodge around a wide-eyed child with ice cream smeared around his mouth. The gang of hoodies glare as we race past.

The Audi looks miles away.

I cast a terrified look back as the main doors to the Clydesdale Tower judder open a fraction. The wheels on the shopping trolley swivel. The trolley rolls away enough for Buster to force his way through the gap.

The Rottie charges across the tarmac.

'Get 'em boy!' one of the hoodies laughs.

The dog streaks past the lads. Drool whips from its jowls as it heads straight for us.

Antony holds his key fob in front of him and presses it like a man possessed. Twenty feet away, the orange indicators flash. He yanks open the driver's door and jumps behind the wheel.

I skid around the other side, one hand on the bonnet to propel myself around to the passenger door. I jump in and engage the lock.

Antony dumps Fred unceremoniously on my lap as he fumbles to get the key into the ignition.

The Rottweiler's face smashes against the driver's window.

I scream. 'Go! Drive!'

Antony fires the engine, throws the gearstick into first and guns away without securing his seat belt.

Buster disappears from the window. Twisting in my seat, I glue my eyes to the dog as it gives chase.

The Audi screams up to the junction. Antony barely glances at the road before hauling the steering wheel hard left to join the busy dual-carriageway. We skip onto the road inches from an articulated lorry. Lights flash and a horn blares.

Antony's expression is grim as he switches lanes. I keep an eye on our backtrail, looking for swerving cars, chaos and flying fur. But there's nothing but the normal flow of traffic and The Sentinels looming in the background.

'It's okay, you're safe now,' I say to Fred. He shivers on my lap, his cute little face peering up at me. I stroke him and he gives me a warm lick. When I think how close we came to being mauled by Buster, I want to throw up.

My mobile vibrates in my pocket. I ignore it.

Antony closes the gap with the car in front until we're nearly touching bumpers.

I press back in my seat. 'Please slow down.'

'He peed all over my Calvin Klein's!' Antony hisses, glaring at the dark stain spreading across his chinos. 'I'm late for work and I smell like a fag packet. And that hell-hound scratched my car!'

'I'm really sorry, Antony.' I pause. 'Please can you drop me at Beverley's? She works from home on a Monday.'

Five minutes later, Antony pulls up on the kerb, leaving the engine running. 'Just so we're clear, I'm not doing this again. I'm a graphic designer.'

'Antony, I promise you, we won't.'

He shoots me a less-than-friendly look. 'How many times have you said that?'

I clutch Fred close. 'I swear I won't ask for help again.'

'Good. Because this is it. I'm done. Got it?' He cuts the air with his hand. 'Done!' His brow creeps upwards. 'This is taking years off me.'

'I get it. I'm sorry.'

Antony's tone softens slightly. 'If you want my advice, stick to painting. You're great at it and people want to buy your art. And the best bit is you won't end up dead.'

'You're right.' I offer a weak smile. 'I love you.'

Antony sighs. 'Love you, too. Gotta go.'

I grab my rucksack, cradle Fred under my arm and step from the car.

I watch Antony drive away. I pushed him too far. This time he's out for good.

'It's okay,' I tell Fred. 'You're home.'

I walk up Beverley's front path. Her house is a Victorian terrace, a few roads from me in Digbeth.

Beverley opens the door. She bursts into tears when she sees Fred.

'Oh my God, Alex, I can't believe you found him!' She takes Fred in her arms. The Pug's brown eyes shine as he leaps up to lick her chin. 'Where was he?'

'In a tower block near to the Chinese Quarter. Luckily for us, my friend who lives there saw him.'

Beverley blinks her tears away. 'Come in and tell me everything.'

She leads me into the lounge and sinks onto the sofa, smiling through her tears at Fred who turns in crazy circles on her lap.

I tell her about turning up at the wrong flat and how we heard barking, before giving her a brief summary of Fred's rescue.

'I was so glad to get out of there,' I say.

'I can never thank you enough for what you've done. Coffee and cake are on me for the rest of the year!' She hugs Fred tight. 'If there's anything I can do for you, and I mean anything, you only need to ask.'

'Actually...there is something.'

4

Once we're settled on Beverley's sofa with a cup of tea, I explain how I knocked on Sharon and Keith's door by mistake and Sharon gave me an earful about the state of their flat. Just thinking about the mould makes me shudder.

'Sharon and Keith can't stay there,' I say. 'There's mould in every room, the kitchen is falling apart, and Keith struggles with his mobility. If the lift packs up the poor man will be trapped on the eleventh floor. Can you get them a ground-floor flat?'

Beverley sits Fred on her lap and runs a flea comb through his coat. 'I'll do my best to get them bumped up the priority list. It won't happen overnight but I promise to personally oversee their case.' She pauses to examine the comb. 'Oh, God, there's another one. I'll have to buy some medicated shampoo. The Rottie must have passed them on.'

I rub my arms, feeling imaginary itches and tickles all over my skin. I'm definitely not telling Antony about the fleas.

'Can you do anything about Buster? One of these days he's going to eat someone.'

Beverley says, 'I'll report him to the dog warden. Honestly, the way some tenants behave they should be kicked out, but we haven't the resources to keep tabs on them.' She pauses. 'Are you sure you and your friend won't make a statement? I want the man who stole Fred to get his just desserts.'

'I'm sorry. It'd be my word against his, and besides, I don't want any comeback. My friend feels the same.' I chew my lip, hoping she doesn't push the point.

'That's a shame.' Beverley frowns.

'Look, I had a run-in with dognappers before,' I say. 'The police told me that kidnapping a dog is the same as nicking a bike. They treat it like property theft. Unfortunately, scumbags like that rarely get their comeuppance.'

'It's ridiculous he'll get away scot-free considering what he put me through.' Beverley clips a lead onto Fred's collar and grabs her handbag. 'Come on. Let's get some fresh air.'

She treats me to lunch at The Shack, our favourite deli, which is a converted stable overlooking the canal. By the end of the meal, she's laughing and back to her old self with Fred conked out on her lap.

I walk home with a spring in my step, buzzing from returning Fred to his owner, and hopefully getting the Lawlers the ground-floor flat they desperately need.

Halfway home, my mobile vibrates in my pocket. I check the screen. Three missed calls, and one from Mum:

UNKNOWN NUMBER
UNKNOWN NUMBER
UNKNOWN NUMBER
MUM_AGH!

After today's thrills and spills, talking to Mum should be a piece of cake. I press the button to accept the call, determined to keep it brief for the sake of my sanity.

'Hello? Can you hear me, Alexandra?'

'Just about!' Wherever Mum's calling from, it's somewhere noisy. Her loud Irish lilt competes with children's happy shrieks and a booming tannoy announcement in the background. 'Are you at a festival?'

'We're at Our Lady and St Ignatius's Summer Fête. Isn't the weather grand? I hope you're getting some sun on your face and not listening to the UV police. They'd have you walking around in a potato sack rather than let you go brown.'

I glance at my bronzed arms. Once the weather turns, my tan will be a lovely reminder the heatwave was real and not a dream.

'Was there a reason you called earlier, Mum?'

'I wanted to tell you, Father Egan's running a fundraiser for a car park extension so we're doing our bit to raise some money. I've emailed you a flyer for a sponsored silence. There needs to be a group of you so you can all watch each other. You can put one up in your church.'

Mum has a habit of volunteering me for church stuff, even though I don't attend church and live in a different country. The sponsored silence is a new one. But, like all her other flyers, it will end up in the same place. The trashcan on my desktop.

'Are you doing the sponsored silence?' I have a sneaky suspicion she sent it to me because she wouldn't last thirty seconds.

'I've already done my bit,' Mum says. 'I've bought a cake, won a bottle of Campari in the tombola, guessed the sweets in the jar, and had my face painted. I told the face-paint lady "you can do what you like with me. Give me a bit of everything if it's for the car park." It's very good, some mish-mash superhero thing, but I can't for the life of me remember which ones they're supposed to be.'

'You have more than one?' My mind boggles.

'I've two Marvels, but don't ask me. It was either superheroes or a butterfly princess, and you know how I feel about pastels.'

I cast a nervous glance around the sunny street, hoping nobody's listening in.

'Moira said I looked a crazy mess, but Pierce said I was adventurous. He asked Nuala Doherty to take a photo for the parish newsletter.'

'Who's Pierce?' I ask.

'Haven't I mentioned my new friend? Pierce recently moved into the area. We met at Feeney's Garden Centre by the desperate plants for sale. Moira nudged me in the ribs and said, "Who's the film star?" Next thing I know, Pierce is asking our advice on reviving pelargoniums. He treated us to a drink in the coffee shop. It was frappuccinos all round.'

My antennae prick up. 'And now he's at the church fête?'

'Why wouldn't he be?' Mum tuts. 'Just because he's not Catholic doesn't mean he can't help raise funds for the car park.'

'He's not Catholic?' I miss a step and almost fall off the kerb.

'Pierce is going through an internal struggle. He has a lot of questions about his faith. It's my God-given duty to help him find answers.'

Your answers, you mean. My mother's interminable lectures about the path to redemption used to drive me loopy. Pierce must be a tolerant guy.

'What does Moira think of him?'

'I wouldn't know. Moira and I are having a little break from each other while I help Pierce find his way.'

Alarm bells go off in my head. Mum and Moira have been inseparable since Mum moved back to Ireland seven years ago.

'What does Pierce do for a living when he's not rescuing plants?'

'He's an accountant and a very fine one, too. He's taken a keen interest in Father Egan's fundraiser and the new car park.'

I wonder why this man who has no connection to the church is asking about church finances and grilling my mother.

What concerns me most is Mum's lack of tact. She can't be trusted with any type of secret when she's on transmit, whether it's spoilers for the latest episode of *EastEnders* or nuclear codes. If Pierce is trying to gain her confidence for some shady reason she'll tell him where she hides the front door key, her bank details, everything.

'What else do you know about him?'

'What is this, the Spanish Inquisition?' Mum's tone loses some of its warmth.

'I'm just interested, that's all. Where does he work?'

'Here and there. He has clients all over and is always travelling around.'

'Do you know where he lives, whether he has a family?'

'Would you stop now with the questions?' Mum shrills. 'If you visited me you'd see how things are. Pierce is a good man.' She leaves a long pause. 'And you never know. He might be more somewhere down the line.'

I fall into stunned silence.

'It's strange, Alexandra, but after your father died I didn't think there would be another man in my life. But Pierce really is one in a million. He cannot do enough for me.'

Where has all this come from? After Dad died, Mum gave the impression she was relishing her freedom in Ireland with family and friends.

Mum says, 'Pierce bought me a meal at Eala Bhan. We had steak and wine, no expense spared. And with the weather so fine he bought me a barbeque for the garden.'

'As opposed to a barbeque for the lounge?'

'Don't be smart with me, young lady. As I said, if you'd only get on a plane you would see how things are for yourself.'

Perhaps I should get a flight over.

'Alexandra, I have to go. They need me for the penalty shootout.'

'Hold on, Mum. Do you have a photo of Pierce?'

'Nuala snapped him on her digital camera. She's emailing me the picture from the presbytery, so I suppose I could forward that on to you.'

'Please do it as soon as you can.'

'Very well. I have to go now. Bye!'

She hangs up on me. Another first. I stare at my mobile in disbelief. I wonder what Moira thinks about Mum's new mystery man. Pierce must have looks and charm in spades if she mistook him for a film star.

He sounds nothing like Dad. Maybe that's what's bothering me.

I give up trying to work it out, shove my phone in my pocket and keep walking. Whatever she's doing with Pierce is none of my business. Let Mum enjoy herself. She has her good points, even if

I often struggle to see them. She's living her best life, out to coffee, garden centres and fêtes, scoring goals and running here, there and everywhere.

My life pales by comparison. I check myself.

No way can I be jealous of my own mother.

My route home takes me past turn-of-the-century terraces. Humming to myself, I turn onto the private road leading to my flat. Rose bushes line the wrought iron fence, surrounding me with sweet aroma.

Key in hand, I skip to my front door.

Before I slide it into the lock, a dark shape moves alongside me, a finger pressed to his lips.

I stifle a yell and drop my key.

'Inside, now. We need to talk.'

5

'Marshall!' The air escapes my lungs in a rush. 'You scared the bejeezus out of me!'

Marshall, the Turing-Tesla League's head of security, retrieves my key from the doorstep and pushes it into my hand. He's an imposing figure in a dark suit and loosely knotted tie. Silver stubble coats his dark teak chin. It looks odd as I've only seen him clean-shaven.

I unlock the door. Marshall doesn't wait for an invitation and heads inside. He stands in the narrow airless hallway, dabbing sweat from his brow with a handkerchief.

On the doorstep, I glance back at the empty visitor bays before closing the door behind me.

'Where's your car?'

'Next street down.' The American holds up his mobile and waggles it. 'Don't you ever answer your phone? I've been calling you for two days.'

'All I've had is unknown numbers. And my mum.'

'Those unknowns were me. I changed my phone.'

'I thought you were a nuisance call. I've had so many recently I've stopped answering them. Why didn't you text me?'

'I didn't want to compromise you. Texting, voicemails, they leave a trace.'

I wave him through to the lounge. 'Take a seat.'

'Can I have a glass of water?' Marshall unbuttons his jacket and sinks onto the sofa with a sigh. Judging from the bulge under his shirt, he's put on a few pounds since I last saw him. 'Have you guys ever heard of air conditioning?'

'What's the point? We're usually shivering in this country, not boiling.'

I carry my rucksack through the open archway into the kitchen and tuck it out of sight beside the bin before pouring two glasses of water.

Marshall downs his in three long gulps. 'May I have a refill?'

'Here. Have mine.' I pass him my full glass and perch on the coffee table opposite him. 'I'm guessing this isn't a social call. What's going on?'

Marshall sets his empty glass on the table. 'We've had a security breach at the League. Me, TJ, and Carmen are using burner phones. I've shut down the entire operation until we get to the bottom of it.'

My eyebrows shoot up. 'You've shut down the League?'

'Suspended it.'

'Okaaaay.' I stall for time, worried about what's coming next.

Marshall clears his throat awkwardly. 'Jonathan's gone AWOL.'

'What?' I can't imagine the Director of Operations going missing. The League is his life. 'Can't you ring him?'

Marshall gives me a pitying look. 'Come on, Alex.'

'Sorry…but I don't understand. You have your own finding machine…I mean, Drive.' The technical term for my machine is the Turing-Tesla League Human Drive, or the Drive for short. 'Why can't you find Jonathan yourself?'

Marshall clasps his hands and glances up at the ceiling. 'Our Drive has gone, too.'

I shoot to my feet. 'What! How could you be so careless?'

'We weren't.'

I pace a tight circle in the restricted space of the lounge, brushing past the dragon tree, the TV, then back to the coffee table. 'Jonathan could have taken the Drive to help out MI5 or another top bod—'

'Jonathan would never have left without notifying me.' He stares me down.

Marshall's unflinching loyalty to Jonathan has left him with one hell of a blind spot. I run through different scenarios, each one worse than the next. The League is an ultra-secret organisation with connections to powerful forces in the UK government and overseas. The idea that someone has breached it terrifies me.

One idea above all keeps returning. Jonathan is the man at the top. But who is he, really? He gives nothing away. He's an enigma.

I take the glasses into the kitchen and rinse them in the sink, giving myself time to think. An outlandish idea occurs to me. I drink some water to alleviate a sudden dryness in my throat before returning to the lounge.

'Marshall,' I say from the doorway. 'Could Jonathan have betrayed you?'

'No way.' His brow furrows. 'Jonathan has given his heart and soul to the League. His first priority has always been to keep our operation secret.'

I take Marshall's point. Jonathan was extremely reluctant to let me join the League even as an honorary member.

'What about Carmen and TJ? Can you trust them?'

'Carmen is like family. When I joined the League, she was my mentor. And TJ...' Marshall rubs his chin. 'TJ is incapable of hiding anything. What you see is what you get. Out of the three of us, he's struggling the most. Whoever's responsible for Jonathan's disappearance hacked into the server and locked us out. TJ ran those systems.'

I rub the tension knotting my forehead. 'What about the plans for the Drive?'

'Those are safe.'

Releasing a breath, I ask, 'What happened the day Jonathan went missing?'

Marshall leans back, resting his head on the sofa cushion. 'Jonathan stayed overnight at Red Croft Lodge like he often did. In the morning he was gone. We didn't think anything was wrong at first, as the perimeter warning system wasn't triggered. TJ tried to access the CCTV footage but the hard drive had been wiped. That's when we realised we'd been hacked. Our automated back-ups have been corrupted and our tracker's gone.' He takes a breath. 'Details of our members and confidential projects are on those computers. It's bad.'

'How can you be sure Jonathan's not behind this?' I push him. 'He knows all your systems inside out.'

'I'm telling you, it wasn't Jonathan. I'd bet my life on it.' Marshall hangs his head, hollows evident below his eyes. 'We need you to find him.'

'Give me a moment,' I say, a sudden lump forming in my throat. I turn my back on him and seek refuge in the kitchen.

Leaning on the sink, I remember how Jonathan Prudente-Poulton assured me the League would use the clone Drive for the good of the country. Foolishly, I thought he could keep it safe.

The kitchen window overlooks the communal car park. Through the blinds, everything looks peaceful. Yet, a crawling sensation runs down my spine. Whenever Antony warned me about the risks of owning the finding machine I accused him of being paranoid. He suspected sinister agencies would eventually come after it.

Turns out he was right.

Yet, Marshall needs my help. As does Jonathan. Finding him should only take a few minutes of my time, and then I can pass the problem back. And if it helps Marshall recover the clone Drive I'll sleep more easily.

I return to the sofa. 'Okay, I'll do it.'

'I appreciate it.' Marshall reaches into his inside jacket pocket and passes me an envelope. 'Here's a recent photo.'

I open the flap on the unsealed envelope and pull out the picture of Jonathan. It's a professional work shot, the kind you see in a boardroom. He's the quintessential English gentleman in an exquisitely cut Savile Row suit, gold cufflinks, pink tie, and matching handkerchief. Silver streaks add a touch of elegance to his ash-brown hair.

Jonathan appraises me with a neutral expression, softened by the barest hint of a smile.

Grabbing my rucksack from the kitchen, I retrieve the finding machine from my rucksack and set it on the coffee table. Marshall's one of the few people I trust around it.

I switch it on. My skin prickles as the green dot appears. 'All right, Jonathan. Where are you hiding?' I mutter.

Marshall leans forwards on the sofa, eyes fixed to the display.

I insert Jonathan's photo between the clips. Nothing. The LCD screen remains blank.

Frowning, I toggle the on/off switch. Still nothing. That can't be right.

Marshall glances at me. 'What's wrong? Is it glitching?'

'I used it today. It's working perfectly.' I shake my head. 'This is the first time I've had no reading. This makes no sense. Even if you're dead, it finds you.'

All you need is a photo.

My theory is the machine locks onto part of your soul. Maybe Jonathan has no soul.

'Try another photo,' Marshall suggests.

I grab a picture of Antony from the mantel, slide it from the frame, and replace Jonathan's photo with his.

11-15 Berkeley Street, Birmingham, B1 2LB

I feel a rush of relief. 'That's Antony's work address.'

Marshall closes his eyes and puts his head in his hands.

'This is even worse than I thought.'

6

— · —

Marshall sits forward on the sofa and runs his fingers through his short, greying crop.

'Looking at this logically, if the Drive's working properly the problem's got to be with Jonathan. I guess there could be scenarios where the Drive doesn't give a reading. Problem is, we haven't done extensive testing so we don't know what they are.'

I pluck Jonathan's photo from the coffee table. 'Maybe he's somewhere deep underground surrounded by thick concrete, where he can't be traced.' I shrug. 'He could be on a plane. Or, in outer space.'

'He could be anywhere.' Marshall interlaces his fingers. 'Thing is, the Drive is crucial for our investigation. How would you feel if I borrowed it?'

'Are you kidding?' I swallow a terse breath. 'You lost your Drive. I'm not letting you lose mine, too.'

Marshall gives me a penetrating stare. 'Apart from Jonathan, we're looking at two persons of interest who might be linked to his disappearance. We need to know what they're up to. With your Drive we can get to the truth. Please think about it.'

'I'm not sure that's a good idea.' I rub my arms, feeling an inner chill despite the stuffy heat inside. 'If Jonathan was abducted the bad guys might come back for it.'

'No one knows about your Drive.'

'You sound very sure about that.'

'I am. You're off the grid, too. Officially outside the organisation. I made sure of it.'

I don't see how Marshall can be sure of anything. With Jonathan gone everyone's a suspect. Yet, his cause is worthy, and I've been waiting since January to work for the League. Here's my chance.

'I want to help.' I sigh. 'But I can't give you the Drive.'

Marshall glances down. 'There's another way we can do this. How about you come to the Lodge? Bring the Drive and help us out. Hopefully, we can get to the bottom of this thing in a few days.'

He makes it sound so easy. Maybe it will be.

'I'll have to let Antony know. I can't just up and disappear.'

'Fine, just don't mention the League, Jonathan, or me,' Marshall calls after me as I head for the hallway. 'Pack some things. I'll ring Carmen and tell her you're coming.'

'Got it.'

I cross the hallway into the second bedroom Antony and I use as a home studio. Inside, it's a squeeze, with desks, chairs, computers and blank canvasses. We really need to find a bigger place.

I grab my mobile to call Antony when my phone buzzes with a text.

`I emailed you the photo. LOL Mum x`

Mum certainly knows how to pick her moments. There's no way I can leave without seeing her mystery man. I have to know if she's deluded about Pierce or they're a match made in heaven.

I turn on my computer and speed-dial Antony's mobile while it's booting up. His voice message cuts in:

You know the drill. Only your Gran leaves voicemail. Text me.

I ring the office but no one picks up. I guess the team is still in meetings. It could be hours before Antony gets out and Marshall needs a decision now.

Sinking into my swivel chair, I grab a pencil and notepad. Only a few hours ago I told Antony I didn't want to use the finding machine again, yet here I am helping to look for Jonathan. The best course of action is to say as little as possible so he doesn't worry.

I fold the letter and leave it on Antony's keyboard, then head into the bedroom to pack.

I stuff clothes inside a gym bag along with a jumper, my tartan snood, an umbrella, and a cagoule in case of a cold snap. You can never over-pack where English summers are concerned.

After dumping the gym bag in the hall I return to the office to check my emails.

Subject: The Man Himself!

Mum's email has two attachments. The first is the sponsored silence form. I open the second, steeling myself for disappointment. Mum's idea of handsome is Val Doonican.

I push back in my chair in horror at the photo that pops up. Half of Mum's face is soaked in blood.

My heart spikes before my rationale kicks in. It's red face paint. I take a deep breath. Face paint.

The black strokes on top meant to resemble a spider's web look more like the feathering on a Bakewell tart. The other side of her face is bright green. Incredible Hulk green. Mum looks ridiculous clutching her sensible handbag yet her smile is broad and genuine.

Mum stands in line with five others. My eyes skip from Father Egan, dressed in black with a white dog collar, past Moira and two women I don't recognise, to the man in question.

Pierce is tall, athletic, and handsome. He's smart but casual in a blue polo shirt, one hand in the pocket of his chinos. I guess he's in his early sixties, slightly younger than Mum, with jet-black hair thinning on top.

With his generous smile and eyes crinkling attractively at the corners, his good looks only accentuate how ridiculous Mum looks. Their pairing is so odd it looks like she won him in a raffle. One thing stands out above all else, and it isn't Mum's facepaint or Pierce's film star looks.

It's Moira.

Mum's best friend and constant companion isn't looking at the camera. Instead, she shoots a suspicious glare in Pierce's direction.

Consumed with questions, I crop the photo so only Pierce is in the frame, shove a sheet of photo paper in the printer and print off a copy to take with me. If I wasn't rushing off to help Marshall, I'd be calling Aer Lingus to book a flight to find out about Pierce for myself.

I grab my pop-up phone book and press the M tab. The lid flips up.

Matt Martin, Mane Attraction Hair Salon, Mazz Motors, Moira.

I'm scribbling down her number when a knock comes at the door.

Marshall peeks his head in. 'How are you doing?'

'All good!' The printer chugs away. 'Just a sec.'

Marshall follows my gaze to the folded sheet on Antony's keyboard. He walks over, opens the letter and scans the contents.

'Do you mind?' I ask.

'Sorry, I need to check,' Marshall says, replacing the note. 'It's fine. Nice touch about self-destructing. I'll wait in the hall.'

He ignores my glare and leaves. Once the photo's finished printing I shut down my machine and check the flat one last time. After tucking the photo into my notepad and slipping it inside my rucksack, I grab my gym bag and follow Marshall outside.

We walk to the next road. A sleek, black Lexus sits under the shade of a London plane tree.

Marshall walks up to the car and pauses, keys in hand. 'Is the Drive switched off? Remember, every signal leaves a trace.'

'It's off.'

'Do the same with your mobile. In fact, you'd better take the battery out until you return home.'

I hesitate. 'But I need to speak to Antony.'

'We'll give you another phone to use while you're with us.'

'All right.' I reach into my rucksack, double-check the finding machine is off, then remove my battery from my mobile phone. 'Everything's off.'

'Good.' He opens the boot, takes my bags and places them inside before getting into the car.

Marshall turns on the ignition. The powerful engine rumbles to life. The air-con pumps frigid air through the car, sending goose-bumps up my arms The leather seat creaks as I lean forward and switch off the air vents nearest me before sliding down the electric window to allow warm air inside.

'That kinda defeats the purpose,' Marshall says with a sigh.

As we pull away from the kerb, scattered clouds cover the sun. After two weeks of unbroken heat the city looks unusually sombre. The grass verges, parks, and gardens are brown and parched with many flowers drooping.

Marshall sticks to the speed limit through the residential streets. He checks his mirrors constantly until we join the ring road and leave the underpass and the city behind. Business units and blocks of flats give way to open countryside in multiple shades of yel-low, brown, and green. The sun returns, bathing fields filled with swaying hay, golden barley, and sunflowers. Oak trees cast welcome shade over sheep and cows chewing the cud.

'So, how've you been?' Marshall asks. 'I saw you had an exhibi-tion at the Ikon Gallery.'

'You know about that?' I check myself. 'Of course you do.'

'I look in on you from time to time to make sure you're okay,' Marshall says. 'I feel I owe it to your dad.'

I touch my fingers to my cheek, thinking about my father. I know so little about his involvement with the League. Hopefully, staying there will give me the chance to find out more.

The engine purrs as we join the busy M6, powering south-east to join the M1.

My mind drifts off in that semi-somnolent state that long-distance driving induces until we reach a green sign with white letters: *Welcome to BLETCHLEY, home of the Codebreakers.*

The last time I came to the League it was dark and I slept for most of the journey. This time I take in everything. I feel a swell of pride to be in the town where Alan Turing spearheaded a project to crack the German Enigma code, helped end the war early, and saved so many lives.

Marshall drives past the train station. Passengers emerge from gloom beneath the station's concrete overhang, squinting against brilliant sunshine. We dogleg down quiet residential streets before turning onto a narrow lane called Church Walk.

We pass large detached houses set back from the lane with dense verges opposite. Unruly hedges brush against both sides of the car. The houses stop and the road narrows until it looks like we can't possibly continue.

A ten-foot-high red-brick wall blocks the way. Two mature sycamores stand like sentinels either side of imposing gates. The gates look more suited to guarding a maximum-security prison than the elegant Victorian villa standing behind them.

Marshall slows to a crawl and presses a button on his key fob.

The gates to Red Croft Lodge slowly swing open. A camera mounted on top of the brick pillar points in our direction. I don't remember the camera from my last visit, or the gates.

Marshall drives through the gates and parks beside a yellow VW Beetle. He turns off the ignition and smiles.

'Welcome back.'

7

—·—

I step from the Lexus and stretch out my back. Marshall grabs my bags from the boot, locks the car, and crosses the sunlit driveway towards the tiled porch.

Behind me, the security gates swing shut with a resounding *clang*. The high wall and trees dampen the sound of the distant motorway to a barely noticeable hum. Above me, a blackbird sings, perched in the sycamore tree. Leaves rustle in the warm breeze.

Marshall stares at a spot above the black panelled door. The door clicks and opens automatically.

I run across the drive and over the threshold before it swings shut.

Marshall hands over my rucksack and drops my gym bag by the curving staircase. 'I'll take that up later,' he says.

The entrance hall's black and white chequered floor leads to two passageways at right-angles. In the far corner, a grandfather clock marks time with a loudly ticking pendulum. An oil painting hangs beside the clock, depicting a galleon caught in a storm with grey waves spewing over her decks.

The hall smells of musty fabric and polished wood. The only difference from the last time I was here is the radiators are cool to the touch.

The old-fashioned *bringg-bringg* of a rotary telephone carries through from a nearby room. It rings three times before cutting out.

36

'Isn't your receptionist here?' I ask, hoping to meet the lady with the cut-glass voice who answers the landline like a 1940s BBC broadcaster. In my mind's eye, she exists in black and white.

'We suggested Cecilia take some time off. She's on paid leave.'

'Oh. Why did you send her away?'

Marshall shrugs. 'I'd rather not have her mixed up in this. The fewer people who know about the situation, the better.'

'You don't trust her?'

'I do. Absolutely. Cecilia used to work at Bletchley. You couldn't find anyone more trustworthy. TJ is fielding our calls for now.'

The phone rings again.

'That's probably another disgruntled League member,' Marshall says. 'They want to know why they can't access their files. The cover story is the server's down for maintenance. That should buy us time to sort this mess out.'

I follow Marshall across the hall into a drab corridor with bare floorboards and yellowed skirting boards. A Constable print of 'The Hay Wain' hangs on the wall down the end. Two recessed doorways stand next to each other.

Marshall retreats into one of the recesses and gestures me to do the same in the other. I peer around the architrave, grinning in anticipation at what's coming next. On the strip of wall between us is a box switch with masking tape stuck across the top with the word *FIRE* handwritten in pen. A compact fire extinguisher hangs on the wall opposite.

Last time I was here, Marshall pressed the *FIRE* switch. This time he opens the box switch by hinging the front-plate upwards, revealing a glowing pad inside.

'It's a fingerprint scanner,' he says, and presses his thumb against the pad.

As he closes the cover, a *clunk* comes from below our feet. A large rectangular section of floorboards drops away to form a staircase. Even on second viewing, the engineering marvel leaves me dumbfounded. When the secret staircase is down it looks permanent, yet when the passageway returns to normal you'd swear the staircase couldn't possibly exist.

'This is so cool,' I say, following Marshall down the stairs to a reinforced metal door with a keypad. He inputs a security code, and the door unlocks with a *click*. The high-tech security measures are a far cry from the locked desk-drawer where I keep the finding machine at home. I'll have to rethink that when I get back.

'After you.' Marshall sweeps his hand forward.

I step into the underground vault. The shelves are full to overflowing with old and new tech – rotary phones, oscilloscopes with green screens, microchip circuit boards, manual typewriters, beige video display units, power adaptors, bulky transformers, and black boxes sprouting wires. Photos of the League's founders and key members hang on the wall. My father's picture hangs alongside Nikola Tesla and Alan Turing, whose inspired ideas formed the basis of the League.

I meet Dad's warm smile with my own. Seeing his picture next to other great minds sends a warm tingle through me.

Carmen and TJ sit behind a large table in the centre of the room. Behind them is an rack of computers. Monitors display live-feed CCTV from the main gates, front door, and back door leading to the garden.

Last time I was here, the screens were alive with information. The servers hummed and the console lights were lit up like a Christmas tree. Now, only one computer is on and most of the lights are dead.

'Alex, welcome!'

Carmen walks over to greet me. She's an elegant lady in her early sixties with a perfect silver bob. She wears a cream silk blouse, freshly-pressed linen jacket and smart green trousers — the kind of outfit I'd immediately squirt ketchup over by accident if I was wearing it.

Her eyes crinkle as she leans in for a hug. 'When the Drive went missing I said we have to let Richard's daughter know. It's only right.'

'I'm glad you did.' I hug her back.

'Hey, Alex.' TJ, the League's teenage computer whizz, puts down the receiver on the switchboard phone. He raises a hand in greeting, his tousled blond hair flopping over his eyes. His Scooby Doo T-shirt and frayed, slouchy jeans make him look like a grungy hippy.

I wave back but he doesn't return my smile. With his slumped shoulders and doleful expression, he looks like he's had the stuffing knocked out of him.

I look around the room. 'Are we safe here?'

'Right now, the Vault is the *only* place I feel safe,' Carmen says.

'I know you trust each other, but what about everyone else in the League?' I set my rucksack on the table. 'Professor Feldman saw my Drive at Christmas. And the old man who met Nikola Tesla. I think his name was Lazar something.'

'We've discounted both men as a security risk,' Marshall assures me. 'Feldman's on a round-the-world cruise with his wife, and Lazar Stovanović is currently at Mount Sinai Hospital following a fall.'

'Is he all right?' I ask, remembering the old man with a twinkle in his eye.

'Yeah, he's doing well.'

My eyes go to the security door. 'What if the bad guys come back?'

Marshall says, 'We don't know for sure they were here.'

'There's no evidence of intruders,' TJ adds. He doesn't look directly at me, but that's his way. 'In all probability, the system takeover was done remotely.'

Tingles race up my spine. 'How could anyone tamper with the system if they weren't here?'

'Easily, with the right know-how,' TJ explains. 'Every system has its vulnerabilities. They used master codes to get into ours. Only me, Marshall and Jonathan know them.'

Marshall raises a finger. 'Jonathan wouldn't have given up the codes unless he had no other choice.'

I raise a brow. 'Are you absolutely sure about that?'

TJ places an ansaphone on the table and rewinds the tape, watching the counter dial back. '14715. This is it.' He glances at Marshall. 'A call came in two hours ago. You need to hear it.'

Marshall frowns. 'You should have mentioned it earlier. Go on.'

TJ presses 'play'. A man's distorted, robotic voice comes through the tiny speaker:

'To the good people at the Turing-Tesla League. Do not panic. Normal service will resume shortly. Your Director of Operations is currently our guest and is in good shape. No harm will come to him providing you stay out of my business. Once my work is concluded he will be released unharmed. However, if you interfere or involve the authorities I guarantee you'll never see him again.'

The tape runs a few more seconds before TJ presses the 'stop' button.

I break the silence. 'So, it's true. Jonathan was kidnapped.'

Marshall closes his eyes for a second. 'TJ, any luck tracking the caller?'

TJ shakes his head. 'These guys are serious phone phreaks. They've used multiple redirects to fake their location and bounced the signal all over the place. I lost track of it in Mumbai.'

'What about stripping out the distortion?'

'I ran the recording through a demodulator but there are too many layers. These guys are good.'

'Anything else you can do? Marshall asks.

'Not until they ring again,' TJ says. 'The more they say, the better the chances of them slipping up.'

'If Jonathan's been kidnapped we need to call the police,' I say.

A long silence follows.

Carmen beckons me to sit beside her. 'The problem is, we don't know who we can trust. Jonathan was working with agencies all over the world. Any one of them could be responsible. It would help immensely if we could recover our systems data but our backup tapes contain nothing but gibberish. TJ has tried every workaround he can think of.'

'Whoever did this is streets ahead of me,' TJ says dolefully.

I lean across the table. 'But you're a hacker. One of the best.'

TJ's shoulders slump further. 'You'll have to revise your opinion.'

'Don't you have a back door? Isn't that something programmers use?'

TJ's mouth turns down until he resembles Eeyore. 'Whoever kicked me out patched my key access points and used next-level encryption to keep me out. If we can't restore from backups we'll have to wipe these machines and start again from scratch.'

'We'll find out who did this, TJ,' Carmen says. 'Don't you worry.'

The phone rings again. TJ turns away to answer it.

Marshall looks to me. 'We don't know how long these people had access to our servers. They could have seen our members' personal information and details of our projects. If this information has fallen into the wrong hands, it could be weaponised.'

'We have to stop them.' Carmen presses her lips together. 'It's vital we preserve our work for future generations and ensure it is used for the betterment of mankind. That's the premise on which the League was founded.'

Carmen's impassioned plea hits deep. A molten core of resistance burns within me.

'Will you help us, Alex?' Carmen asks.

I glance back at my dad's photo, sensing his eyes on me. How can I walk away when everything he achieved in his lifetime could be lost forever?

'I will.'

8

Marshall opens a drawer, removes a Motorola flip phone and charger, and slides them across the table.

'We can't make any outgoing calls from the landline. Use this while you're here.'

Carmen adds, 'You mustn't use your card to withdraw money from the cash point, Alex. No purchases from shops unless you're paying cash.'

'But I've only got twenty pounds on me,' I say in dismay.

'Anything you need, we'll get it for you,' Carmen assures me. 'We have a well-stocked kitchen. I'm not a bad cook.'

I grip the edge of the table as a terrible realisation hits me. 'Whoever took Jonathan can use the clone Drive to find anyone. Including me.'

'We're aware of that.' Marshall hangs his head.

'You said I was off the grid,' I remind him. 'Are you absolutely sure?'

'We've shredded everything on you.'

I wish I could have seen my file before Marshall shredded it. Then again, I shudder to think of the problems I caused and how he covered up for me. If I knew everything I did wrong I might never turn on the finding machine again.

'Your past's gone.' Marshall retrieves a manilla folder from a drawer. 'We've only kept one photo of you.'

My heart starts racing. 'Why? Get rid of it.'

Marshall flips open the folder, extracts a photo, and places it on the table.

The woman in the picture is about my age, bathed in sun on a beach with palm trees. She's grinning, her long blonde hair wet from a recent swim. The location is nowhere I've ever been. The woman is someone I've never met.

'Who's she?'

'She's you. Alex Martin, daughter of Richard Martin. Currently working with an environmental group in the Antiguan rainforest.' His eyes twinkle. 'You're an eco-warrior.'

My mouth falls open.

Marshall says, 'Anyone who wants to hunt you down will have to trudge through uncharted rainforest looking for a woman who doesn't exist.'

My eyes are glued to the other me. 'Who is she?'

'She's nobody. I created her.' TJ speaks up. 'We thought in your case disinformation would be safer than no information. If you put your decoy's photo in the Drive you get nothing.'

Marshall says, 'You're untraceable which puts you in a unique position to help us.'

'How?' I squeeze my fingers into a ball, bracing myself.

'We're working on that,' Marshall says, slipping the photo back in the file.

'You have lots of photos of Jonathan,' I say. 'Why can't the Drive find him?'

'We don't know.' TJ shakes his head. 'If we had more Drives we could test if it was a problem with Jonathan or the technology.'

'Why don't you have more Drives?'

The phone rings.

Marshall tips his chin to TJ. 'You'd better show her the problem. I'll take this call.'

'Follow me.' TJ unwinds his lanky frame from his computer chair and leads me to a door at the other end of the room with a green light above it. He presses his thumb against a sensor pad and pushes the door open. Inside, a glass wall separates a preparation area from the clean lab.

He pulls plastic shoe covers and hair protectors from boxes on the wall. Moving to the steel sink opposite, he operates the tap's long lever with his elbow and washes his hands.

Following the teenager's lead, I cover my hair and shoes, then soap and rinse my hands. I catch my reflection in the glass divider as we walk into the lab. The blue cap makes me look like a dinner lady and TJ looks even more ridiculous.

Not for the first time I wonder what the appeal of this isolated villa is to a bright teenager.

'TJ, how did you end up working for the League?'

'I joined the Turing Programme at Bletchley Park the summer after my A levels,' he says, leading me into the lab. Fluorescent strip lights illuminate white workbenches with microscopes and futuristic looking lab equipment, including a robotic arm. 'I came top in the programme, found it easy. I got bored and thought it would be fun to hack into Bletchley's servers.

'Once I was in, I patched a clip of Tom and Jerry racing across the top of every page the staff loaded. It tied the team up in knots. That's how the League found me. Jonathan asked if I'd like to put my skills to better use. And here I am.'

I wonder why TJ wouldn't prefer to hang around people his own age instead of a woman old enough to be his grandmother and a middle-aged American.

'Don't you miss being around young people?'

He shakes his head, making his cap rustle. 'I'm not good in groups. I like it here. Carmen and Marshall understand my triggers.' He opens a white cupboard and drags out a large, plastic tub. He removes the lid. 'This is what your Drive's made of.'

The tub contains tangles of wires, green circuit boards, and old-fashioned calculators.

'We used Olivetti accountancy calculators to house the Drive,' TJ informs me.

The black plastic wedge-shaped cases are the same as my finding machine, although they're missing the antennae, LCD screen, and proximity lights. Delving deeper into the box, I find a plastic bag of metal antennae and crocodile clips, a stack of plexiglass squares, and a roll of thin gossamer fabric that feels smooth as velvet.

'Is this the stuff that goes around the antennae?'

TJ nods. 'It's a conductive polymer which acts as a signal insulator. We call it polycon, for short.'

I open a small cardboard box. Inside, sixteen microchips nestle in perfect polystyrene hollows.

'Those are the CPU and GPS address system upgrades,' TJ explains. 'These parts are off-the-shelf.'

Sitting back on my heels, I blink at him. 'So, what's the problem?'

'*Problems*.' TJ turns the plastic lid upside down. Taped to the underside is a plastic box. He unpeels the tape. Beneath the see-through lid is a vial and two medical slides taped together.

The vial contains a cloudy solution within which is a strip of black tape. The tape reflects the light in an iridescent sheen like a blue-bottle fly. I turn the vial this way and that. The contact strips on my finding machine also shift from green to blue.

'Is this the same as the strip that runs down the Drive's antennae?' I ask.

'Yes, and that's our last fragment,' TJ says. 'It's a prototype static tape that doesn't require 'erase', 'record', or 'playback' heads to record or re-record data. It is weatherproof and scratchproof, but the downside is its inflexibility. The tape can't be fed around a spool which means its data storage capacity is extremely limited. But it's perfect for your Drive.'

I hold the slides up to the light. Tiny white particles, tinged icy blue, are trapped between them.

'And this?' I ask.

TJ runs his fingers through his goatee. 'It's a rare mineral. A form of silicon dioxide.'

'How rare?'

'Very.'

'What does it do?'

TJ holds his silence.

'I suppose it doesn't matter,' I sigh, staring at the meagre contents of the vial and the slides. 'How much more tape and silicon dioxide do you need to make more Drives?'

'Far more than we can hope to get. We were lucky to have enough to build the clone. Your father sourced the original tape and silicon dioxide. We don't know how.'

I stare sadly at the remnants of Dad's great experiment. After he died, Mum cleared out his garden workshop in Sudbury before she moved to Ireland. Any static tape or silicon dioxide he stored there is long gone.

'We'd best get back to the others.' TJ replaces the lid on the plastic tub and tucks it away.

After throwing our protective gear into the bin, we leave the clean lab and rejoin Carmen and Marshall at the table.

I sit and place my hand on my rucksack, reassured by the chill seeping through the canvas.

9

On the table is a small red diary open to the month of July, a sheet of paper containing a hand-written note, and two slim bundles of paper held together with paperclips.

Marshall shows me the diary. Five of the days contain annotations in pencil.

He says, 'I've gone through my work diary noting every place I drove Jonathan and everyone he met. On the fifteenth of March he visited two League members, Okada Atsuko and Grigor Volodin. He made return visits in July. Jonathan always catches up on calls and paperwork in the car. But after the July meetings his mood was off. He stared out the window muttering about "the cost." I don't think he meant money.

'The day after Jonathan went missing, we searched his study and found a torn-out page from a notepad with faint impressions on it. There were charred scraps of paper in the fireplace, but we couldn't salvage them. We had a stab at deciphering the impressions on the pad.'

He nods to Carmen, who reads out Jonathan's note: *'GV & OA: Q: Once the genie is out of the bottle, can we control it? Q: Should we destroy a power that could do good out of fear it will be used for profit or political gain?'*

I wonder if Jonathan was referring to the finding machine, as I have had those very same thoughts.

'The initials match the two people Jonathan met,' I say. 'Could they be the key to unlocking this mystery?'

'We think so.' Marshall slides the papers across the table to me. 'Ms Atsuko's a League member, but we can't access her files.'

TJ shifts uncomfortably on his chair. 'I found this on the internet. It's not much.'

The photograph clipped to the first folder is a portrait of an Eastern-Asian woman in her twenties with reddish shoulder-length hair. She's smartly dressed in a navy-striped silk blouse with a red scarf tied around her neck and has a neat, white smile.

Marshall says, 'Ms Okada Atsuko heads up the product development team at Yoioto Corporation. It's a Japanese company with a subsidiary in Leighton Buzzard.'

I flick through pages full of technical information, dates and corporation history. 'Says here, Yoioto are world leaders in LTO tape storage, whatever that means.'

TJ informs me, 'Linear Tape Open, or LTO tech, is a reliable method of storing data backups, archives, and data transfer.'

'Why was Jonathan seeing her? What was she was working on?' I ask.

'We don't know,' Marshall says. 'Ms Atsuko hasn't checked in since Jonathan's disappearance. She hasn't asked about him. It may mean nothing—'

'Or, she already knows about Jonathan,' I say. 'Maybe she had something to do with it.'

Marshall runs his hand over his stubble. 'Carmen and I agree we need more intel. Someone on the inside.'

I swallow hard. 'Who were you thinking of?'

Carmen raises an eyebrow. 'Oh, we have a few ideas.'

I give her a wary look before moving to the second file. This photo is the polar opposite of Ms Atsuko's — a full-length image of a man built like a lumberjack. He's wearing a red and white checked shirt, toolbelt, and cargo trousers. His dark, scraggy eyebrows overhang piercing blue eyes and a large, crooked nose. A grizzly beard completes his rugged look.

'Grigor Volodin,' says Marshall. 'This photo is eighteen years out of date but I can tell you firsthand Grigor hasn't changed that much. He hasn't checked in with the League, either.' He taps a manilla folder. 'One good thing. Grigor's been with the League so long we've got a physical file on him. He's a Russian mineralogist who worked for the KGB before defecting to the UK during the Cold War. His father worked for a Russian mining company called Sovmineral until the late '70s.'

I say, 'It seems odd that Jonathan trusted Grigor enough to accept him into the League if he used to bash heads for the Russians.'

'The British government considered Grigor on the level,' Marshall says. 'They gave him a passport.'

Carmen adds, 'The government valued his expertise in minerals and gemstones. Grigor shared research and donated samples of his rarest finds to museums. His fieldwork has contributed to technologies including micro-encapsulation, crystal batteries, and cold energy.'

My mind spins with the scientific terms. To say I'm out of my depth is an understatement.

'Alex, are you okay?' Carmen's hand touches my shoulder and I blink back to the present. I must have zoned out from information overload.

I knead my forehead. 'I'm sorry, it's a lot to take in. I still don't see how I can help.'

'We're the ones who should be sorry.' Carmen leans forward and squeezes my arm. 'We shouldn't have tried to dump everything on you in one go. It's easy to forget not everyone's a scientist.'

I flash her a grateful smile.

'You look about ready to crash. Why don't you take a break?' Marshall suggests as he collects the files. 'You can settle in upstairs while we plan our next steps with Grigor and Ms Atsuko.'

Carmen waves me to the Vault door. 'Come on, Alex. I'll show you to your room.'

'Thank you.' I grab my rucksack and follow her from the Vault, up the secret stairs, and into the chequerboard hall.

Carmen holds tight to the wooden handrail as she ascends the staircase. Sunlight falls through an ornamental window, throwing patterns on the Persian carpet. The carpet is threadbare at the centre of each tread, a testament to all the comings and goings over the years. Farther up, the dark eyes of long-dead men and women stare at me from gilt frames. An Oxford varsity oar hangs on the wall with the names of the crew of 1938 hand-painted on the blade.

'There's Dad!' I exclaim, pointing at the name *Richard Martin*.

Carmen stops and turns. 'You know, you look a lot like him when you smile.'

'I've heard that.' Sometimes when I look in the mirror I see him looking back.

I follow her to the first-floor landing which splits in two. Carmen heads down the left passage and pauses by a door near the end. 'The bathroom's through there. I've left fresh towels. Watch out for the hot water, it can be rather temperamental.' She goes to the door at the end of the landing. 'This is your room.'

The door opens into a light and airy room with an iron-framed bed at the centre complete with bed knobs and a patchwork quilt. An original cast iron fireplace gives the place a homely feel. A table, chair, and simple pine wardrobe complete the furnishings.

I look through the open sash window overlooking the garden. Closing my eyes, I breathe in summer air heady with the aroma of English roses. It's impossible to believe that only this morning Antony and I were racing across a car park pursued by a slavering Rottweiler.

Below me, a gnarled apple tree spreads its branches. The garden has run wild with unpruned shrubs and the fruit trees are heavy with swelling apples, pears, and plums. Daisies, red clover, and sow thistle run amok through high grass, topped with swaying seedheads. The English cottage garden is straight out of an Enid Blyton book.

I release a sigh. 'This is lovely.'

'I thought you'd like the room.' Carmen smiles. 'Your father did, too. He stayed here whenever he had business at the Lodge.'

'Really?' I smile to think of Dad standing in this very spot. 'You worked with him, didn't you?'

Carmen nods. 'I considered it a privilege. Richard was one of those rare people who had an extraordinary mind. He was a wonderful person too.' She walks to the bed and straightens the pillow, a wistful smile on her lips. 'Your father always pushed beyond what was possible. I should have known he would build something incredible like your Drive.'

'Why didn't he share it with you? It sounds like you two were very close.'

'I think that's the reason why. He knew me too well. I would have encouraged him to use the Drive for more than just finding his sister, and he wanted to keep it secret. That's why I'm so proud of you. You're using his invention for good.'

'I wish everyone thought the same.'

'Fear shouldn't stop us from using the Drive,' Carmen says gently. 'We can't let them win.'

'You're right.' I stifle a yawn.

'Why don't you have a little nap while we work on?' Carmen says. 'We'll have supper in the garden at seven o'clock. Nothing fancy, just some sandwiches and a slice of cake.'

10

Leaning on the windowsill, I close my eyes and enjoy the sun's warmth on my face. A lost bumblebee crawls on the windowsill. I usher it onto my hand and release it into the garden before collapsing on the bed with my burner phone.

My eyes droop as I enter Antony's number into the address book and hit the call button. The phone rings four times, five, before his voicemail kicks in. I kill the call and send a text:

```
Hey, its me. Got new phone so save this
no. Will B at TTL a few days. Sleeping in
Dads old room!! How amaze is that? Call
me! XXX
```

I'll have to be extremely careful about what I say to Antony. I don't want him fussing over the whys and wherefores. The situation's complicated enough.

Yawning, I add Moira's number to my phone and call her. After five rings, her ansaphone kicks in with a curious mash-up of a robot and Moira saying her name: *"Moira Mooney" is not in. If you want to leave a message for "Moira Mooney," please do so after the beep.'*

I leave a message, then text her with a request to call me when it's convenient.

The curtains sway in the late afternoon breeze. Sparrows chirp outside. My eyes close.

A weird zinging in my fingers jolts me awake. My burner phone buzzes in my hand, its screen lit up blue. Outside the window, the low sun tinges the furniture orange.

ANT_MOB

I sit up and press the answer button. 'Hey, it's me.'

'Hey, you!' Antony says. 'So, what's going on with the League?'

'It's a long story. I'll tell you later.' I swiftly change the subject. 'How did your meetings go?'

'Great! I had to sit through them with a massive damp patch on my trousers. They must have thought I was a right weirdo.' In the background, I hear electronic beeps and trills. 'What happened to your old phone, you lummox? You didn't drop it when we were running from the Rottweiler, did you?'

'I'm not that clumsy. Marshall doesn't want me using my mobile here. He's being extra-cautious.'

'Why?' Antony asks.

'Just because.' I cringe at my lame response.

More electronic squealing.

'What's that noise? Are you standing too close to the radio or something?'

Antony laughs. 'No, it's a Tamagotchi.'

'A Tama-what?'

'Come on, Alex. You must have seen the commercials. Tamagotchis are virtual pets.'

Images of pink elephants skipping through the clouds come to mind.

Antony says, 'One of our clients brought in a box of samples. I nabbed the Rancor. You have to feed it Gamorrean guards and give it a bath once a day.'

'I wish your clients would bring you something decent,' I interrupt. 'It's always stuff like dongles, keyrings, and pens with company logos. Why can't they give you chocolates and champagne?'

'Speak for yourself! This is great!' A musical trill rings out. 'Hold on, I have to clean up some Rancor poop.'

'Wouldn't you rather have a real pet? A warm, cuddly animal that loves you back like Fred?'

'Nah, this is way better. When I've had enough I switch it off.' The sound cuts out. 'Like that. So, dish the dirt. What's going on?'

'Just a small hiccup at the League.' I watch my words. 'Jonathan has gone AWOL, and Marshall wants me to use the finding machine to locate him.'

After a short silence, Antony says, 'Why? The League has their own finding machine.'

'Here's the thing. It's not working properly.' I cringe at my lie.

More silence.

'Are you sure you want to get involved? You barely know anything about the League.'

'It's perfectly safe.' I scrunch the bedcovers. Antony hasn't met Marshall, Carmen, or TJ. He doesn't know they're regular people doing an extraordinary job. 'I'm staying in Dad's old room overlooking the orchard. Everyone's made me really welcome and Carmen made a cake! Please don't worry about me.'

'It's hard not to. What happens if Jonathan's been taken by goons with guns?'

'I don't know. Marshall sends his goons in with bigger guns?'

'This isn't funny, Alex!'

'Stop catastrophising, then!'

'You can hardly blame me. Remember when Henry Longhurst asked you to pop down to Hertford to go through some old files? That sounded nice and safe, too. You ended up staring down the barrel of a gun with Henry half-dead on the floor!'

'This is nothing like that. Marshall used to work for the U.S. Secret Service. If he needs help, he'll call in Special Branch or a SWAT team. I won't be involved.'

'God, I hope not,' Antony says. 'I know what you're like. It'll start off with cake and end in carnage.'

'As if!' I can't help laughing.

After chatting a while longer, Antony makes noises about catching up on work. As soon as I'm off the phone, I realise I forgot to ask him about the photo of Mum and Pierce. I send him a text, keen to have his take on it.

Faint conversation and rattling crockery drifts through the open window. I slip the phone into my pocket, stash my rucksack in the wardrobe and pad downstairs. Instead of returning to the Vault, I explore the terracotta tiled hall with white wood panelling.

The first room I come to is a comfortable lounge with a brown Chesterfield sofa and matching armchair. A modern flatscreen TV rests on a wooden storage unit. The next door leads to a dining room with a polished, oval table.

Opposite, is a study with a grand walnut desk inset with green leather. A modern switchboard phone sits in pride of place. I wonder if Cecilia works here. Farther down is a plain door set into the panelling, most likely a cupboard or a cellar.

The aroma of baking drifts from an open door at the end of the hallway. I follow my nose and cross the threshold into the kitchen. Inside, a yellow table contains a tray with sugar, a jug of milk and a platter of sandwiches cut into neat triangles with the crusts removed. An iced chocolate cake is covered by a glass dome. A roaring, rattling sound followed by a loud click comes from an electric kettle chugging steam from its spout.

'Is that you, Alex?' Carmen calls from the adjoining pantry.

'Hello.' I poke my head through the pantry door. Carmen is two steps down, rummaging among stone shelves laden with pans, Pyrex dishes, and various kitchen utensils. Flower-patterned cups and saucers with gold frilly edges and matching plates are stacked by her feet.

Carmen says, 'I'm trying to find a larger teapot. You'd think I'd know where everything is by now. Would you be a love and take out the sandwiches?'

'Of course. Where are the others?'

'Marshall's just finishing up and TJ's taken his supper to eat on his own. He finds company at mealtimes difficult.'

I carry the sandwiches through the back door, past a log store, and into the garden. Some enterprising soul has mown a path through long grass to the apple tree under my window.

Beneath the tree's knobby branches is a plastic patio table covered in a polka dot oilcloth, weighted down by vases of summer flowers. I set down the sandwiches and follow the mown path to the end. Beyond it lies an inviting wilderness.

I high-step through long grass, ducking beneath overhanging fruit tree branches and around patches of stinging nettles. An abandoned garden roller lies tangled in the undergrowth, its handles pitted with rust. I catch glimpses of the boundary wall through hawthorn, bracken, and rampant brambles.

A low building is concealed by shade close to the old wall. Sweet chestnut trees tower above the corrugated roof, their prickly fruits hanging like small green grenades ready to drop. The top of the roof is barely two feet above ground level. A set of concrete steps lead down to a recessed door.

I descend and try the loop handle. The door shudders open on stiff hinges.

The interior is windowless, gloomy, and filled with musty air. I fumble around with my phone until the torch comes on and venture inside.

A long bench runs along one wall. On the dusty table beside it is a pack of playing cards swollen by damp and a dial radio. A coal-fired stove is set inside a brick arch on the back wall. A rusty cast iron kettle rests on the hot-plate. Scraps of yellowing posters cling to the walls and litter the floor. I shine the torch on them:

ERSONS MAY SHELTER HERE AT THEIR OWN RIS

AIR RAID WARDENS WANTED! A RESPONSIBLE JOB FOR RESP

DON'T RUN. DON'T SCREAM. PREVENT DISORDER. OBEY ALL INSTR

I close my eyes, drinking in the atmosphere of this World War II time capsule. The Lodge's inhabitants must have huddled on the bench when the air raid sirens sounded. They must have masked their fear playing cards, drinking tea, and listening to the radio, silently praying the enemy bombers would pass over without releasing their deadly loads.

More posters are scattered in the corner beside the hearth alongside a large metal lid that sits flush to the floor. I lift the lid, releasing a strong smell of coal and a puff of dust that makes me cough. Inside, is a deep bin, stained black after years of storing coal for the stove.

'Alex, are you down here?' Carmen calls from outside. 'Alex?'

'Coming!' I drop the lid and leave the shelter. Closing the door behind me, I run up the stairs and brush coal-dust from my hands.

Carmen waves from the shorter grass. I head back to the dining table where wasps buzz around the chocolate cake. Marshall smacks them with a fly swat.

'We wondered where you'd got to,' Carmen says.

'Sorry, I was exploring.' I take a seat. 'I found an air raid shelter.'

'I can tell,' Marshall whacks another wasp into oblivion. 'You have soot on your nose.'

'And your hands.' Carmen passes me a serviette, then pours tea. 'There used to be a proper path leading there but now it's completely overgrown. Once things are back to normal, we'll bring in a gardener to tidy it up.'

'It's perfect as it is,' I say, savouring the beauty of the untamed wilderness within the old walls.

Marshall slides the sandwich platter over. I help myself to egg mayonnaise, smoked salmon, and cucumber with cream cheese.

'We've finalised our plans for the next few days,' he says. 'Are you ready to head out into the field and help us find Jonathan?'

'I guess so.' Antony's words of caution circle in my head. 'You won't be sending me out alone, will you?'

'Of course not.' He cuts three slices of chocolate cake. 'Eat up and get a good night's rest. The real work starts tomorrow.'

11

I wake the following morning to my phone beeping. Bleary-eyed, I check the text from Antony:

```
Sprayed coffee everywhere when I saw your
Mum. She looks like Princess Fiona from
Shrek. Half of her anyway! She's done well
with Pierce - proper silver fox ;)
```

With a text limit of 160 characters including spaces Antony can't say much, but I get the impression the unlikely match is fine by him. I double-check my phone for voicemails or messages from Moira but she hasn't responded. I tell myself everything's fine and to stop worrying.

After a swift wash, I get dressed and head downstairs, following the aroma of coffee to the kitchen.

Marshall sits at the small table, eating thickly-buttered toast and flicking through his red diary.

'Hey, Alex.' He looks up and waves me over. 'Sleep well?'

'Like a log.'

'Help yourself to coffee. Cream and sugar are on the table.'

I head to the fancy coffee percolator on the counter, pour myself a mug and sit opposite Marshall. He gestures to a half-full toast rack, butter dish, and selection of miniature jams.

I take a deep sip of flavoursome coffee and sigh. 'I needed this. There was so much to take in yesterday I could barely think straight.'

'You're pretty much up to speed,' Marshall says. 'My advice is to avoid too much tech talk with TJ. His deep dives can fry your brain.'

'I'll try to remember that.' Grinning, I butter my toast and open the strawberry jam.

I'm finishing my toast when Carmen comes in from the garden with an armful of pink dahlias.

'We're just about to head down,' Marshall tells her, taking our plates and mugs to the sink.

'Let me put these in water and I'll follow you down,' she says, fetching a large vase from the pantry.

I collect my rucksack from my room and bring it to the Vault. TJ sits at the one working computer. Marshall stands by his shoulder. On screen is a different geolocation website to the one I normally use, but the input fields are the same.

'Find out where Grigor is,' Marshall says, handing me the Russian's picture.

I remove the finding machine from my rucksack, place it on the table and slip Grigor's photograph between the crocodile clips.

51.981651, -1.544501
Chipping Norton
'That's not much to go on,' I mutter. 'Not even a postcode.'

TJ clicks the keyboard, entering the co-ordinates into boxes on the website. A green block fills the screen with a straight grey strip running through the middle.

'Grigor's on an unmarked road between Great Rollright and Little Rollright,' TJ says.

'Okay. Let's check back in a minute, see which way he's going.' Marshall nods. 'In the meantime, we'll try Ms Atsuko.'

I replace Grigor's picture with Okada Atsuko's.

51.285483, 0.759807
15 Eden Way, Chartmoor Road, Leighton Buzzard, LU7 4WG

'Okay, that's the Yoioto Corporation,' Marshall says, before TJ can type in the location. 'It fits with her weekday routine. Check Grigor's location again.'

I swap the photos back.

51.97597, -1.57017

Rollright Road, Little Rollright, Chipping Norton, OX7 5QB

'He's heading south-west,' says Marshall. 'Let's wait five minutes and check again.'

When I check the reading again, the numbers have barely changed; Grigor hasn't travelled far.

'He's about fifty metres away from his last location,' TJ confirms, after inputting the co-ordinates. His monitor fills with green.

'Mark the location in here.' Marshall opens his AA Big Map at the correct page.

TJ leans over the table and marks a pencil cross on Marshall's atlas, close to the boundary between Oxfordshire and Warwickshire. 'He's heading into a field.'

Marshall glances at his watch, then the map. 'Little Rollright is about an hour away. Thanks TJ. Can you get back on the network? We need it up and running a.s.a.p. Carmen, go through Grigor's background again. See if you can dig deeper.'

'What about me?' I ask.

'We're taking a drive.'

• • • • • • • • • •

Back in the Lexus, Marshall drives us through Bletchley to join the A421, a dual carriageway heading west towards Buckingham. The finding machine is tucked inside my rucksack and the AA Atlas is open on my lap. The familiar tingle of excitement shoots through me, mixed with nerves.

It's another sunny day and Marshall has the air conditioning on full whack. Whenever he's not looking, I turn it down a notch and continue by tiny increments until the hairs lie flat on my arms.

Marshall glances my way. 'That thing you're doing. With the air-con?'

'Uh-oh. Busted.' I cross my hands in my lap, grinning.

'My daughter used to do the same thing.'

My brow shoots up at this rare snippet of personal information. 'You have a daughter?'

'Yeah. Marcia.' He smiles and drums his fingers on the steering wheel. 'She's about your age, thirty-two. My son Wade is two years older.'

'I guess you don't see that much of them now you're over here?'

'Not as much as I'd like. I flew back in February to cuddle my grandchildren and catch up with family. I'd like to see more of them. I'm not getting any younger.'

'What made you leave them and move here? America's got the weather, the customer service, the great food. Everyone's so friendly.'

'In Disneyland, maybe!' A brusque laugh escapes him. 'In my old line of work people were the opposite of friendly. They'd shoot you rather than look at you. A few years of that makes you reassess your priorities. I wanted to stick around for my family, not end up in the morgue.'

I stare at Marshall's ring finger, and the paler indentation there. 'Was there a Mrs Marshall?'

'A long time back.' He glances away. 'We're divorced.'

'I'm sorry. I didn't mean to—'

'It's fine. I was working long hours. She wanted more of my time. I couldn't give it to her so she shopped elsewhere.'

'Oh.'

'It's all right. I've gotten used to it. I like being a one-man-band, living on my terms. The League pays me well which helps, especially with the IRS demanding their pound of flesh from me every year. I don't even live in the States yet they still want a cut. It's nuts.'

Silence settles in the car for the next few miles. Sunny wheat-fields and trees stretch to the horizon.

'What do you think Grigor's doing out here?' I ask.

'He's a mineralogist. Maybe he's digging for minerals.'

I study the atlas. 'There's a quarry down this road. He could be going there.'

'Maybe.'

The roads skirting Buckingham are gloriously empty and the traffic gods stay on our side as we breeze down sunlit lanes free from roadworks and bottlenecks of traffic. Marshall turns off the main road, following signs to Over Norton. A low stone wall forms a boundary along one side of the road. On the other, open parkland stretches into the distance.

'Check your machine,' Marshall says, as we pass a sign for Little Rollright.

Placing the rucksack on my lap, I fold down the front flap for ease of access, and slip Gregor's photo between the clips. He's still in the same spot. I check the five proximity LEDs but they're unlit.

'We're in the right area, but no lights yet.'

Fifty yards further down the road the first red LED flashes.

'Got one!' I announce. 'We're nowhere near the quarry, though.'

Marshall slows the car and drives past a layby with several parked cars.

'The light's gone off. We've gone too far,' I say.

'I'll make a turn,' Marshall says, checking his rear-view mirror. He brakes sharply and makes a swift three-point turn before returning to the layby. He pulls into a wide gap in front of a minivan and turns off the engine.

He studies the map and taps TJ's cross. 'Grigor's close by. We'll go the rest of the way on foot.'

I grab my rucksack and step from the car.

Marshall gets out and locks the Lexus. We cross a grassy verge to an open gate leading into a field. The only signs of modern life are the occasional car zipping by and aircraft vapour trails crossing the blue sky above.

The finding machine's display glows within the rucksack. 'The red light's back.'

'Good. We're on the right track,' Marshall says.

'Grigor's ex-KGB, right? What's the plan when we find him?'

'Don't worry. For now, we just find him and watch him.'

A wooden arrow with *Rollright Stones* painted in white, points towards a footpath running through long, swaying grass. We follow the path over the field, through a corridor of trees, and back into the open.

Marshall looks seriously out of place in his freshly-pressed suit and tie. His dark forehead shines with sweat. With his shades on he looks like an extra from *Men in Black*.

'Don't you ever wear anything casual?' I ask.

Marshall raises a brow. 'This is casual.'

'Can you at least take off your jacket and tie?' I unzip my rucksack. 'We can put them in here.'

'Everything I need's in my pockets.' Marshall pats his jacket. 'Tell you what, I'll lose the tie.' He unknots his tie, rolls it up carefully and puts it inside his pocket before unbuttoning the top button of his shirt. 'There, happy now?'

'Oh, yes. Huge difference.' I raise a hand. 'Grigor will smell a rat as soon as he sees you. He'll probably do a runner.'

'Where's he gonna run to?' Marshall puts his arms out to the soft breeze and turns 360 degrees. 'I suggest you stop worrying. That's my job.'

The silhouette of a dog walker appears on the horizon before disappearing over a ridge. The field ahead is an open vista, scattered with ragged-looking stones that form an enormous circle.

Ahead, a group of seniors is gathered inside the circle. The women wear long summer dresses and flip-flops, or T-shirts and shorts like the men. I spot packaway cagoules clipped to the men's belts despite the fact there isn't a cloud in the sky. None of them look like Grigor.

The closer we get, the more I realise how massive the circle is. Close to one hundred weather-bitten stones of all shapes and sizes make up the ancient ring. Many are full of holes and resemble worm-eaten wood. Others have worn down over the centuries to stony nubs.

In the distance, three stones lean on each other as though they're huddling together. They must have been here for thousands of years. The thought makes me feel tiny and insignificant.

'Give me an update on Grigor,' Marshall says as we amble up behind the group.

I peer inside my rucksack. 'Two solid lights and one flashing.'

The day-trippers' group leader puts his arms out to the stones and projects his voice. 'The legend of The Rollright Stones has held strong through the centuries.'

'Let's get past,' Marshall urges, mopping his brow with a handkerchief.

'Wait a second.' I touch his arm to stop him striding off. I'm a sucker for a legend or a ghost story. 'I want to hear this. It'll help us blend in.'

Marshall rolls his eyes.

The tour leader continues. 'It is said that in ancient times the King and his army marched over the Cotswolds and met a witch who turned them to stone. He points out an unusual 'S' shaped stone encircled by metal railings. 'Here stands the eternal King.' He sweeps his arm around the circle. 'There are his men.' Lastly, he nods towards three huddled stones. 'The Whispering Knights, plotting treachery.'

Marshall leans close. 'This is cute, but it doesn't help us find Grigor.'

'He came this way for a reason,' I say. 'The rocks might have something to do with it.'

The tour leader waves towards hedges and wooden copses forming a line at the field's boundary. 'The witch transformed herself into an elder tree which still stands over there...somewhere.'

An excited murmur goes through the group. Everyone except Marshall stares at the shrubbery as though the witch will spring back to life if they wait long enough.

'The legend ends with a promise,' the tour leader says. 'If anyone chops down the elder tree, the stones will turn back into men and the King will take his rightful place on the throne once more.'

'I think The Queen might have something to say about that,' Marshall speaks up, raising a laugh from the group.

I place one hand on the nearest sun-warmed rock and imagine the knight trapped inside. What tales he could tell.

The tour leader pats the nearest stone. 'Sadly, I think the legend will outlast the stones. Centuries of wind, rain and frost have wrecked the porous limestone. In another thousand years there'll be nothing left where we're standing.'

I wrap my arms around my rucksack, taking in the ancient circle one more time.

Marshall taps my shoulder. 'I saw movement.'

He tilts his head towards the trees.

12

— • —

'What can you see?' I ask, dragging my gaze from the standing stones.

Marshall stares into the trees adjoining the field. 'A big guy heading into the woods. It's got to be Grigor. Come on.'

He nonchalantly walks away from the tour group, picking his way through the straw-coloured grass towards the trees.

I mouth, *'thank you,'* to the tour guide and follow Marshall, picking my way over stones and rock fragments hidden in the grass. On the way, I check the read-out inside my rucksack.

Three solid lights. The fourth is flashing.

Closer to the trees, I spy movement. A man in a green and brown checked shirt roams through the woods collecting sticks. No one else is in sight.

'Four lights,' I say.

The man leans over to add a slim branch to his haul before walking away from us. I lose another light.

'It's him.'

Marshall lengthens his stride, passing two immense oaks encroaching onto open land.

I secure the rucksack over my front like a baby sling so I can read the display without stopping. Pushing past bracken, I follow him in. The temperature drops as we enter the woods. Without a visible path or obvious route in, I doubt many visitors come this way.

Marshall moves from tree to tree, tracking Grigor.

The spongy forest floor dampens my footsteps as I hurry to catch him up. The air is heavy with the astringent smell of pine needles.

'Grigor will see us if we get too close,' I say breathlessly, pressing my back to a tree trunk.

'Trust me,' Marshall whispers.

The canopy blocks the sunlight as we push deeper in. Whichever way I look the view is the same; columns of tall pine trees stretching into the distance. I glance over my shoulder but the sunny field has vanished. It could be behind me or ahead of me. I'm completely turned around.

I follow Marshall past huge ants' nests, the type I used to poke with a stick as a child. Apart from Grigor, the ants are the only signs of life I've seen. Even the birds have stopped singing.

My breathing sounds loud in the eerie quiet as I shadow Marshall from tree to tree, watching my step. The distance between us and our target increases until only two lights remain on the machine. I catch the odd glimpse of Grigor's earthen-coloured shirt in the distance.

Marshall stops short a few feet from a sunny clearing. He presses his finger to his lips and points to Grigor, who skirts the clearing and heads further into the trees.

'I've got two lights,' I whisper.

'Doesn't matter. I see him,' Marshall whispers. 'This is as far as you go. Wait here while I assess the situation.'

Then he's gone, moving from tree to tree until I lose sight of him.

The clearing stretches about thirty feet in diameter. A stone stands at the centre with moss covering its base. A tiny shiver goes through me. The stone's surface is riddled with holes just like the King and his army, yet this solitary knight has ended up far away from its fellows. It's isolated, an outcast.

There's no sign of Marshall or Grigor, no footsteps, no voices. It's like the forest swallowed them up. The reading on the machine still shows two lights.

I shift my weight from foot to foot, wanting to be useful instead of cowering behind a tree. Staring into the clearing, I spy an elastic strap wrapped around the stone's base, connected with a snap clip to a black plastic box. I creep towards it with every sense on high alert.

My throat tightens as I see the box more clearly.

Knobs and dials run along the top. Tiny holes drilled into the main face form a circle. The pattern reminds me of a radio speaker.

I follow the wires from the plastic box to a cassette recorder resting on a tree stump at the edge of the clearing. The recorder's shiny black plastic is emblazoned with the symbols for *Dolby B, C,* and *Autoreverse*. A cellophane-wrapped stack of TDK C-90 cassettes rests on top.

At the edge of the clearing is a fold-out camp chair containing a rectangular foil package with an apple on top. Sandwiches, probably. Beside the apple is an Ian Fleming novel, *Thunderball*. With Grigor's background, I'd have expected *From Russia, with Love*.

The tape-reels slowly rotate inside the recorder. Listening hard, I hear the faint sound of the tape mechanism. What on earth is Grigor recording? Invisible breezes around the rock? The conversations of passing ants?

I jump at a distant shout. It sounds like Marshall. I stare in all directions but can't see him.

I check the finding machine. Three lights with the fourth flashing.

A branch snaps close by.

I whirl around but can't pinpoint the source of the sound.

Four solid lights. The fifth flashes.

Oh God oh God.

I back out of the clearing, glancing in every direction.

Five lights.

A dull thud behind me.

I turn and scream.

A man charges me. Beneath the navy baseball cap shadowing his eyes and his unkempt beard, his expression is thunderous. Coarse black hair covers his broad forearms. He's built like a bear, with huge clenched fists.

Grigor runs up to me and comes to an abrupt halt inches from my face.

I shriek, stumble back, and crash into a tree. The finding machine smacks against the bark, grinding painfully against my spine.

Grigor towers over me, a beam of sunlight striking the top of his faded blue baseball cap.

'You stupid girl!' he snarls, voice thick with a Russian accent. 'You ruined my research. Now, I must start again!'

My heart thumps so hard it's fit to burst from my chest. I throw up trembling arms in a gesture of surrender.

'I didn't touch anything, I swear!' My voice shakes.

'You did not need to touch!' His fingers hook upwards like claws to rend the air. 'You made noise. Your breathing is like earthquake!'

Grigor turns away abruptly, drops to his knees by the cassette recorder and examines his equipment. He checks the wires and the connecting strap, then presses a button that stops the tape.

Sweat trickles down my neck as I slump against the tree, overcome with light-headedness. I can't believe I'm still standing.

As I'm counting my lucky stars, Marshall stumbles into the clearing with twigs caught in his collar. One cheek is scraped raw and there's a lump on his temple. He makes his way unsteadily towards me, placing himself between me and Grigor.

'You okay?' he mouths.

I raise my thumb even though I'm far from okay, my heart thumping in my ears. Compared to Marshall, it looks like I got off lightly.

Grigor gets to his feet. Although his breathing has slowed, his eyes are hard and flinty as he looks down on Marshall.

Marshall puts his shoulders back, standing his ground. 'Grigor, wait. We're on the same side. We both work for the League. I'm a friend of Jonathan's.'

Grigor removes his baseball cap and stares at Marshall. 'I don't like people following me.' He tilts his head towards me. 'Who is she? Why are you here?'

'She's a friend,' Marshall says. 'We need to talk about Jonathan. You heard what happened?'

'No.' Grigor slowly raises his head, his mouth tight.

'He's missing. We need to find him.'

'I know nothing.' Grigor folds his baseball cap in his big hands. He mops sweat from his brow with his sleeve.

'You were one of the last League members to meet him in July. Then he disappeared. What did you talk about? What did he want?'

Grigor's shoulders tense. 'That is League work. I cannot talk about it.'

'Normally, I'd agree with you, but things have gone too far to worry about protocol. I'll be honest, Grigor, I'm really worried about Jonathan.'

A muscle jumps in Grigor's jaw. 'I cannot help you.'

'Whatever you tell me is in confidence,' Marshall pushes. 'You have my word on that.'

Silence descends.

Marshall sighs and blinks up into the sunlight. 'Look, Jonathan's not the only issue here. League projects have been compromised including whatever you're doing here.'

Grigor resolutely holds his silence. He strides to the cassette recorder, ejects the tape and shoves it into one of his cargo trouser pockets.

Rubbing my sore spine, I step towards Grigor but stop short when he turns his powerful glare on me. I move around the standing stone, keeping it between us just in case.

'What are you recording, Grigor?' I ask boldly. 'What sounds can you get from a stone?'

He crosses his arms and glares at me.

'Are you doing this for Jonathan?' Marshall asks. 'Did he ask you to record the ston—'

'Enough questions!' Grigor tips his chin up, staring both of us down. 'Leave me. I have work to do.'

Marshall meets his gaze a long moment before saying, 'Have it your way, Grigor. Thanks for your time.'

I shoot Marshall a puzzled look before following him from the clearing.

'Just like that?' I say once we're a safe distance away. 'You're not going to press him for information?'

Marshall feels along his scraped face, wincing. 'There's more than one way of finding out what he's up to.'

'Here.' I rummage in the front pocket of my rucksack and pull out a blister pack of paracetamol. 'These should help with the pain. Take two with water.'

'Thanks.' Marshall presses out four tablets and swallows them dry. 'Hey, I'm sorry about what happened back there. Are you okay?'

I nod, adding, 'I don't think Grigor liked your suit.'

'No, I don't think he did.' Marshall flicks dust and twigs from his jacket. 'You saw how he reacted when you went near his stuff.'

'He's a monster.'

'I don't think he's a monster. Someone's putting pressure on him.'

'Who?'

'That's what we need to find out.'

We re-emerge into the sunlight and retrace our steps through the field of standing stones, rejoining the path that leads back to the car.

'Aren't you worried about Grigor's next move?' I ask. 'If he tells the bad guys what happened here, they'll come after us.'

Marshall shows me the display on his mobile. 'No signal. We've got time. Besides, he's got all those ninety-minute tapes to fill up. If I'm right, he'll be here the rest of the day and probably into the night.'

'Are you sure?' I glance back at the dark woods.

'Grigor's got a sleeping bag and he's built a fire. He's not leaving anytime soon.'

Marshall has a point. Grigor's the outdoor sort. I can imagine him catching a rabbit with his bare hands and cooking it over the fire.

'What was he doing with that stone?' I ask.

'No idea. I've seen a lot strange stuff in my job but nothing like this.' Marshall shrugs. 'Carmen's a mineralogist. We'll ask her.'

We return to the layby. Marshall walks along the row of parked cars. He glances inside a sporty BMW coupé, a silver Ford Mondeo, a gold Citroën BX estate, and a VW minibus, before returning to the Lexus.

He unlocks the boot and lifts the carpet, revealing a spare tyre, jack, locking wheel-nut, and a line of unusual-looking tools neatly stored in foam slots. He removes a long strip of metal with a hook at one end.

He smiles. 'Meet my friend, Slim Jim.'

13

Marshall tucks the Slim Jim under his jacket and walks back to the Citroën. The estate car is shabby around the edges and sits low on its wheels.

'This has to be Grigor's,' Marshall says.

I cup my hands around my eyes to block out the sun's glare and peer through the windows. The rear seats are folded down and the load-area is fit to burst with tool boxes, an extendible ladder, a spade, overalls, a folded-up tent, an inspection lamp, and a portable stove with gas canister.

Empty Red Bull cans, cheese and onion crisp packets, crumpled Golden Virginia pouches and multi-coloured disposable lighters clutter the passenger footwell.

'Give me a heads up if you see anyone,' Marshall says as he works the Slim Jim between the window and the rubber seal on the door frame.

I put my back to the car, keeping an eye on the path as Marshall pulls the Slim Jim sharply upwards.

The door catch pops up.

'That looked easy,' I say, taking the Slim Jim from him.

Marshall opens the door. 'Right tool, right car. It's not so great on newer vehicles with automatic locks.'

The smell of stale tobacco drifts from the car's faded interior. The driver's seat is split at the seams and patched with duct tape. Marshall sinks into the low-slung seat which is fully reclined and so far back from the pedals I'm surprised Grigor can see anything when he's driving.

Marshall opens the glove box, drags out a handful of papers and sifts through them. 'Let's see, petrol and MOT receipts, a fixed penalty notice...five years old. A Burger King receipt for a Double Whopper and large fries. This is all trash.'

He stuffs everything back in the glove box, checks the sun visor and storage bins in the doors. He kneels on the driver's seat and stares at the junk in the back. 'I'm not wasting time on this mess. Let's go.'

Marshall locks the driver's door. He crouches by the rear tyre and unscrews the valve cap, then pulls a pen from his pocket and inserts it into the valve. Air hisses out. Once the tyre has deflated, Marshall replaces the cap and we return to the Lexus.

'Was that for the face, or to slow him down?' I ask, climbing into the passenger seat and securing my seat belt.

Marshall laughs, then winces. 'A bit of both.' He passes me his open diary and points to an address. 'That's Grigor's place. I made a note when I drove Jonathan to meet him. He lives in Tingewick, about forty minutes away. Can you check the route on the map? I have a hunch we'll find something there.'

'Jonathan?'

'No, I don't think so. But we might find clues to his where-abouts.'

'How good are your hunches?'

'After forty years, pretty good.' Marshall pops on his shades and starts the ignition. He pulls out of the layby and puts his foot down.

As the car surges forwards, I open the AA map and cross-check the location with the address in the diary. 'You want to take a right onto the A3400, then follow the signs towards Banbury.'

Marshall follows my directions onto the A-road. 'You made a good start today. It took guts to approach Grigor and ask him questions. You have the makings of a good investigator.'

I smile. 'Henry Longhurst said that.'

'If two people you trust say the same thing, it must be true.' Marshall passes me his mobile. 'Call Carmen as soon as we get a signal. We need to update her and TJ.'

The signal bars don't appear for several miles. When I have two bars I scroll to her number and hit dial. Marshall presses a button on the dashboard and the phone rings through the car's speakers.

'Hello, Marshall,' Carmen answers. 'How are things going?'

'We found Grigor but he wasn't cooperative. He's working on an experiment with an old stone. It looked like he was using a cassette-recorder to tape sounds from it.'

'Grigor was taping stones?' Carmen's voice rises.

'I'm no expert but that's what it looked like.'

'But...why would he...this shouldn't be happening. Not after all this time.'

'Carmen, are you okay?' I ask. I've never heard her rattled.

'Forgive me, Alex. Grigor's experiment reminds me of a League project from years ago. It was a failure and we abandoned it. I don't understand why Grigor or anyone else would pick it up again.'

'What was the experiment?' I ask.

'We were trying to capture ancient resonances. But we ran into all kinds of technical difficulties.'

'Can you check through the paper files? There might be some-thing on the project,' Marshall says. 'We're heading to Grigor's house to see if we can find out more.'

'I...I'll do my best.'

'Good. We'll talk later. Take care.' Marshall ends the call.

I catch his eye. 'That was interesting. What does 'capturing ancient resonances' mean?'

Marshall rubs his neck. 'I think it's something about EVPs. Electronic Voice Phenomena. They come from rocks and trees, and the land around us.'

'That's a thing?' I screw my face up.

'Carmen's the expert.' Marshall shrugs. 'It sounds like Grigor's opened up a can of worms.'

The Lexus purrs as we speed down country roads. Powerlines stretch between pylons through the fields on one side. On the other, a combine harvester gathers wheat and propels it into a trailer driving alongside. We pass the villages of Swerford, Deddington, and Croughton before coming off the A421. Marshall takes the second exit off a flower-filled roundabout towards Tingewick.

A long line of traffic forces us to slow. Marshall says, 'Do me a favour and check Grigor's location.'

I unzip my rucksack and switch on the finding machine.

'He's still in the woods,' I say with relief.

'Good.'

Marshall follows the lane through the village, passing barns and cottages. On the high street, the post office, pub, and village store operate from timber-framed houses. Marshall weaves past parked cars and turns up Church Lane.

The houses on the corner are modern. Farther up the steep road, whitewashed cottages with iron cross-braces are topped with thatched roofs that have slumped with age.

Marshall continues to a grey church at the top of a hill. Past the church, the road splits in two. He creeps down the right-hand fork.

'We're looking for The Old Croft.'

I read the house names outside the gates. The Old Croft sits back from the road at the end of a grassy track. The thatched roof brushes the tops of the upstairs windows, giving the place a sleepy look.

Marshall drives past an old man tugging a scruffy terrier on a lead before pulling up on the opposite verge. He removes his shades and checks his mirrors. A car goes by, puffing black smoke from the exhaust. Twenty yards away, builders unload MDF boards from the back of a panel van into a house.

The old man walks past the car, the dog stopping frequently to cock its leg on the verge.

Marshall unclips his seatbelt. 'I should tell you, what I'm about to do isn't strictly legal.'

'And breaking into Grigor's car was?'

'The point is, you come with me or wait in the car. I don't mind either way.'

'Aren't I already guilty by association, simply by being with you?' I cock a brow.

Marshall shakes his head. 'Like I said, it's up to you.'

The old man and his dog shuffle further away. The builders have disappeared. Grigor is miles away. There's no slavering Rottweiler. This should be a breeze.

'I'm coming.'

'Okay, I'll I grab my stuff, and you go ring the bell. Check no one's home.'

'Sure.' I step from the car, cross the road, and walk down the driveway to Grigor's front door. I peer through the diamond-shaped leaded window into a narrow hallway. If anyone's in, I'll say I've lost my cat.

The iron handle of a bell-pull is mounted beside the door. I pull on the handle and a bell shrills inside.

I give it thirty seconds then ring again. After a final glance through the window I run back to the road and give Marshall the thumbs-up.

I wait for him in the shade of an overgrown walkway leading along the side of the cottage. Marshall appears carrying a navy holdall. He directs me down the garden path to the back of the house.

Pink petals cover the path like pastel snow. I push past over-crowded brambles and duck under rambling roses that have clambered onto the thatched roof. The garden has run riot, with knee-high grass and bindweed everywhere.

The windows are metal-framed. Cracks run through some of the smaller panes.

The cottage must be freezing in the winter. No wonder Grigor doesn't mind living outside.

I examine the back of the cottage. No alarm.

Marshall follows my gaze. 'No cameras, no sensors, no alarm,' he confirms. 'Grigor's a Luddite when it comes to security.'

He hands me a pair of latex gloves and dons a pair himself. He rattles the back door handle before trying a set of French doors further down. Drawn curtains block the view inside.

I point to a cracked windowpane in the back door. 'You could break the glass.'

'I might not need to. Let's look for a key.'

Marshall hunts around a cluster of weed-filled plant pots. He lifts a terracotta one brimming with couch grass. A startled toad blinks and leaps away.

I pick up an upturned pot. Fat, green slugs cling to the underside. Gagging, I hurriedly place it back and reach for another. An eruption of woodlice scramble in all directions. I drop the pot, brushing dust and cobwebs from my hands.

'Maybe I should look for a key round the front.'

Marshall glances up. 'The front drive is too visible. This is the natural place to hide it.'

I lift a faded mat.

'Got it!' I raise a dark iron mortice key and grimace. An enormous wolf spider crawls up my fingers. I shriek and shake my hand with such force it must look as though I'm trying to detach it from my body.

'Seriously?' Marshall raises a brow. 'You should see the yellow sacs we have back home. They're something to scream about.'

The spider scuttles into the grass. I can still feel it crawling on me. I shudder, rubbing my arm to make the hairs go down again.

I hand over the key and keep my distance as he unlocks the back door.

Marshall cracks the door open. A solitary bluebottle buzzes out.

I take a steadying breath then follow him into a low-ceilinged kitchen that's stuck in the 1960s. A dark loaf sits on a breadboard by the toaster. Brown stains and rust-red wine rings cover the chipped Formica countertops, along with unopened tins of tuna, beans, potatoes, plates and mugs, and clothbound books with daunting titles on the spines: *Rutley's Elements of Minerology,*

Advances in Geochemistry, Fission Track Dating, Thermogenic Gas Extraction.

Housekeeping is clearly not top of Grigor's list.

Dismantled kitchen gadgets including three toasters with their insides on display and a rusty waffle maker sit in the corner. Red canisters of Calor gas line the back wall. Water drips from the taps into the ceramic butler's sink, hitting ketchup-smeared plates and bowls with food stuck to the sides.

A wall calendar hangs behind the door, open to August 2000. Most of the daily squares are empty apart from a dentist's appointment on the third and a boiler service on the tenth. The last calendar entry is on the twenty-eighth, three days from now.

N.H.M. Archives 2 pm.

'Date for your diary,' I say.

Marshall pulls a digital camera from his inside pocket and takes a picture. I squeeze my eyes shut as the flash goes off.

'How about you take a look down here while I check upstairs?' he says. 'We're looking for anything relating to Jonathan, League documents, references to stone experiments, anything unusual. Shout if you find anything.'

Marshall heads upstairs. I leave the kitchen and enter the dark, musty-smelling lounge. The drawn curtains cut out much of the light.

'Jonathan? You here?' Marshall calls out.

I flick on the wall switch. A single bulb surrounded by a frilled lampshade comes on. A worn leather sofa covered in orange antimacassars takes up the back wall. Opposite the sofa is a crazy-paving fireplace with an old cabinet TV in the corner. A cheap sideboard displays mismatched glasses alongside a delicate, mother-of-pearl tea set. Probably an heirloom.

A black and white photo on the mantel draws my attention. A young Grigor stands by a lake holding an enormous pike. His broad grin is in complete contrast to the angry man I met earlier.

The stairs creak. I go to the lounge door and peek out.

Marshall descends the stairs, brushing dust and cobwebs from his jacket.

'Anything?' I ask.

'No chance. Upstairs is a mess.' He heads to the room beside the front door. 'I'll check out the study. How are you doing?'

'Nothing yet.'

As I return to the lounge, an uncomfortable sensation settles in me at prying into another person's private life. Marshall's acting on a hunch, but Grigor's done nothing wrong as far as I can tell. Somewhat reluctantly, I rifle through out-of-date newspapers on the coffee table before moving on to the sideboard. Inside the drawers are cork placemats, coasters, and a prayer book. An old record player sits on the bottom shelf. In the drawer below is a collection of Russian long-play records, including 'The Voronezh Russian Folk Chorus,' and classical music vinyls.

On the shelf above are classic videos including *Some Like it Hot* and *North by Northwest*. Two videos with hand-written labels catch my eye:

AVEBURY 1969

STONEHENGE 1970

As I slide them out, Marshall calls from the hallway. 'Alex, get in here. We have a problem.'

<h1 style="text-align:center">14</h1>

I take the video cassettes from the lounge and follow Marshall's voice to the tiny study at the front of the house.

I step inside, squeezing myself between the desk and a sideboard. Piles of books and stacks of papers cover every surface.

Marshall stands at the desk, examining the receiver of a rotary-dial phone. Beside him, his open holdall contains a head torch, pliers, screwdrivers, wire strippers, and electrical tape.

I brandish the videos. 'Grigor's got old videotapes of Stonehenge and Avebury. What's that about?'

'No idea,' Marshall says without looking up. 'Put them in the bag. We'll look at them later.'

I slot the videos into his holdall and look over his shoulder, somewhat miffed he's not more impressed by my great discovery. Marshall peers into the phone's unscrewed mouthpiece and examines the insides with a loupe magnifier pressed to his eye. My dad used loupes for precision work.

'You said there was a problem?' I say.

Marshall pulls a silver disc with multiple holes from the receiver. 'See this? It looks like a standard microphone element. But it's a bug.' He turns it over, revealing green letters and numbers stamped on the underside.

'Who put it there?'

Marshall shrugs. 'Could be the Russians or Americans. It could be the League. This technology dates back to the '60s or '70s. Way before Jonathan hired me.'

'They're not listening in now, are they?'

'No. I've disconnected the phone. Sometimes, surveillance teams install a backup battery inside the phone but there isn't one here.' Marshall screws the mouthpiece cover back on and replaces the handset.

I watch him with growing confusion. 'Aren't you going to remove the bug?'

'Uh-uh. We want anyone listening in to think it's business as usual.' He slips the loupe into his pocket. 'Take a look at this.'

Beside the telephone, a Dictaphone is set to 'play'. A wire from the Dictaphone is connected to a modern Sony tape recorder which is set to 'record'. The mini-cassettes in both units are turning.

'I haven't a clue what's going on here,' I say.

'Grigor's been taping his calls, so I'm making a copy of his tape. He may suspect someone's listening or be trying to collate intel himself.'

I frown, staring at the bugged rotary phone, Dictaphone, and Marshall's tape recorder. 'Have you listened to Grigor's tape?'

'Some of it.'

My brows rise. 'And...?'

'This would be a good time for you to tell me you have a talent for languages.' Marshall turns up the volume on two men conversing in gruff tones. One of them sounds like Grigor.

"Skazhi svoemu nachalniku, shtoby on ostavil menya v pokoye. a nevo uzhe yest moy isladovania."

"Dai nam kamen, ee me otstupim."

'Russian?'

'Sounds it. I don't speak it and neither does Carmen or TJ. We'll have to find a workaround.' Marshall turns the volume down. 'If someone's bugging Grigor we need to monitor his calls. So I've bugged his phone, too.'

'How?' I stare at the handset, wondering how he could have squeezed another bug inside.

'You're looking in the wrong place.' Marshall follows the phone line back to a white box — the phone jack — above the skirting board. He reconnects the phone line then peels the carpet away, revealing a slim black wire spliced to Grigor's phone line and secured with black insulating tape. The adapted double-wire continues along the wall and disappears behind the cabinet.

'Where does it go?' I ask.

Marshall stands on a chair beside the cabinet to show me where the phone line terminates: a small, beige box tucked out of sight.

'I've wired the line into a GSM wireless bug. The moment Grigor picks up the phone, the bug sends me a message.' He waggles his burner phone. 'We can listen in with this.'

'Wow.' I pause. 'On a scale of one to ten how illegal is this?'

'Depends. This is my bread and butter.'

'So, eleven, then.'

Marshall shakes his head. 'Look, we vet all League members before they join. They sign a contract that gives us the right to monitor them using whatever means we deem necessary, should we suspect misconduct. I'm just doing my job to keep the League safe.'

The news doesn't come as a complete surprise. Although I haven't formally joined the League, Marshall has kept tabs on me. He probably put me through the same vetting process as other League members without me even knowing.

Marshall shakes his head. 'I expected better of Grigor, especially considering he's one of us. His blind spots regarding security could have compromised the League for years, if not decades.' He takes out his digital camera. 'There must be thousands of pages of research here. I can't photograph it all. Can you give me a hand? Look through his papers and see if anything jumps out.'

I rummage through pads of lined graph paper full of diagrams, scientific terms and handwritten annotations. The writing is in English and elegantly scribed. If it's Grigor's, he must have hidden depths behind the brutalist exterior.

I flick through the first pad. 'Strata Analysis.'

'Nup.'

'Rock formation during the Devonian Period.'

'Uh-uh.'

I pick up a notebook and flick through the pages. I freeze. 'EVPs. Electronic Voice Phenomena.' I turn the page. 'There's a quote from Thomas Edison. Something about using spirit phones to record the voices of the dead, and how sensitive recording devices might better connect with the spirits than a Ouija board or a medium.' I hand the notebook to Marshall. 'Is this for real?'

Marshall flicks through. 'Looks like it. There are auditory test results and charts on analogue sensitivity versus output waves. I'll take pictures.'

He vetoes 'Ore Deposits Coast by Coast,' and 'Further Thermogenics.'

I pick up the next pad. 'GQ and Tunguska. How does this help us find Jonathan?'

Marshall's head whips round. 'I don't know yet. Let me see that.' He turns to the first page of the document. 'This is good.'

He photographs each page.

I hunt through physics, maths, and electronics reference books and riffle through loose papers, hitting Marshall with technical terms and snippets of data so he can make the call on whether to take pictures or not.

Next, I search the cabinet. Inside are stacks of box folders. The first three boxes contain technical papers on the same subjects I found earlier. Underneath is a blue box file. I open the lid.

Papers spring out. The topmost page is crisp white with blue ruled lines.

STONE TAPES

Notes cover the pages. Further down, the papers turn mottled yellow and brown.

'Take a look at this.' I hand the file to Marshall.

He reads the title. 'Good work. I'll photograph it, then we'd better leave. We've been here long enough.'

· · · · ● · ● · ● · ·

Marshall puts on Classic FM on the way back to Red Croft Lodge. 'Do you mind? This helps me think.'

'Fine by me.'

Harpsichords and violins fill the Lexus's cabin with a lively tempo. I think it's Bach. My mind's awhirl with our discoveries in the woods and at Grigor's house.

I'm starting to feel like a bona fide investigator.

I check my phone and open a text from Antony. He sends his love and hopes my day is going well. My pulse picks up at a missed call from Moira, reminding me of Mum and her mystery man. After today's excitement, discussing Mum with her best friend should be easy street. And, I won't be spending my hard-earned money on the overseas call. I'll let Marshall pick up the tab on my burner phone.

We pull into the Lodge's drive. Marshall grabs his grey holdall, I take my rucksack, and we head down to the Vault.

Carmen's mouth drops when she sees Marshall. 'What happened to you?'

Marshall gives a rueful smile. 'I had a disagreement with a tree.'

She rushes over to examine his scraped and swelling face, gently pressing his skin. 'When you said Grigor was uncooperative I had no idea you meant this! I'll fetch the first-aid kit. Then you can tell me what happened out there.'

'Don't fuss, it's fine.'

Flashing lights dance across the bank of computers on the back wall. There's a lot more activity than earlier.

'Hey, TJ,' I say, approaching the teen. 'Have you rebooted the system?'

He nods, his tangled hair bouncing. 'There's a caveat. I've restored the system from the first of March. I couldn't get any of the later back-ups to work.'

'At least we're in! Excellent job.' Marshall goes to clap him on the shoulder without thinking.

TJ flinches.

'Sorry.' Marshall draws his hand back. 'How did you manage it? Scratch that, just tell me you've got access to our members' files and projects?'

TJ's mouth tweaks down. 'That's the other problem. I managed to log on as an administrator but a lot of the data is compartmentalised. I can't access the sensitive files for Jonathan and Ms Atsuko.'

'Shame,' Marshall says.

Carmen gives him a stern look. 'It's a good start. TJ has worked marvels to get this far.'

'Sure, he has.' Marshall removes the SD card from his digital camera and passes it to TJ. 'I need printouts of every photo on here.'

'Not a problem.' TJ inserts the card into a slot on his PC.

Marshall removes the two video-cassettes and slides them over to Carmen. 'Look what Alex found.'

Carmen's hand flies to her mouth. 'I thought these were lost forever.'

'What are they?' I ask.

'They're video recordings of an old stone tape experiment. The League had high hopes it would work but it never went anywhere. Jonathan must have passed the videos to Grigor to aid his research.'

Sidling closer, I ask, 'What was the experiment about?'

Carmen sighs. 'Thousands of years ago, many ancient cultures held the belief that places could store memories. The League was following that theory.'

I take a seat, opening my mind to concepts that are bound to strain my rationale. The finding machine was a big enough leap. But I have a feeling stone tapes will tax me further.

'The idea took off in England in the 19th century,' Carmen continues. 'Theorists expounded that sudden, violent, or traumatic events would be imprinted on stones and stored there indefinitely. The concept went by different names like 'Residual EVPs' or 'Electronic Voice Phenomena'. Famous scientists like Thomas

Edison bought into the idea. He experimented with wax cylinder recordings in an attempt to communicate with the dead.'

I'm almost frightened to ask. 'Did it work?'

Carmen shakes her head. 'If it did, I guess we'd have wax cylinder recorders in every graveyard.'

'That's creepy.' Marshall chuckles uneasily. 'The stones have ears.'

'I've heard that ghosts haunt the place where they died,' I say. 'They won't leave until someone hears their story.'

'If I might point out, ghosts don't exist,' TJ breaks in. 'Carmen's simply talking about stones as a recording medium.'

'And you find that easier to believe than ghosts?' I raise a brow.

'There's more to it.' Carmen clears her throat. 'It's true that elements of the stone tape experiments cannot be proven by science. But science cannot explain many things. Alan Turing was fascinated by the interaction between science and the spirit, especially after death. He envisaged a future where Bletchley's code-cracking bombes might be re-engineered after the war to create sophisticated computers that might one day unlock the secrets of the soul. He wasn't alone. Many scientists were fascinated with the afterlife.'

'Is that why the League ran with the stone tapes?' I ask. 'Because of Turing's interest?'

'I like to think so,' Carmen says. 'Nikola Tesla believed vibrations and waveforms connected the universe like an invisible web. Charles Babbage, who developed the world's first computer, also believed words floated in the air forever. TJ, can you find the quote?'

He slumps forward over the keyboard. 'Do I have to?'

'Yes please.' Carmen taps her finger on the desk.

TJ types into the Netscape Navigator search bar. He clicks the mouse a few times, then reads from the screen. Despite his monotonous, sceptical delivery he can't entirely remove the wonder of Babbage's words:

"The air itself is one vast library on whose pages are for ever written all that man has ever said or woman whispered."

Carmen raises her hands, palms upwards. 'Imagine if we could capture those words? We could hear our ancestors' voices, centuries before their words were written down. How incredible that would be!'

'But *how* can you hear voices from a rock?'

She shrugs. 'Grigor may have an answer to that. We can only hope.'

Marshall comes alongside. 'I have some things to discuss with Carmen. Would you mind breaking for lunch while we debrief? It's been quite a morning.'

'No problem.' I take my rucksack, jumping at the chance to be free of mind-blowing theories and experiments and change out of my sweaty clothes. I'll also be able to call Moira.

Carmen leads me to the Vault stairs. 'Help yourself to soup and bread in the kitchen. I'll come and find you later.'

I dash upstairs and leave the rucksack with the finding machine in my wardrobe. In the bathroom, I have a wash in the sink and change into a clean T-shirt, shorts and flip-flops. I hang my old clothes over the heated towel rail before heading down to the kitchen.

A large saucepan ticks over on the hob. My stomach growls as I lift the lid and inhale the rich aroma of simmering chicken broth. Taking a bowl, I ladle soup into it, cut a slice from a crusty farmhouse loaf and butter it generously.

I carry my tray outside and place it on the patio table before sinking into a chair and stretching my legs in the sun.

After eating my lunch, I call Moira. The long, international dial tone sounds.

'Hello?' answers a woman with a strong Irish accent. 'Moira Mooney speaking.'

'Hi, Moira, it's Alex Martin. Brigid's daughter.'

15

— • —

'Alexandra!' Moira exclaims. 'It's great to finally speak with you! Your mum's always going on about your art and exhibitions. She's ever so proud of you.'

'She is?' This is news.

'Indeed! Although between you and me, she can't see the appeal of vandalized trains and rusting boats. Or is it pollution and litter? Forgive me if I can't remember.'

I laugh, spewing crumbs from my mouth.

'Alex, are you all right?'

'I'm fine! Contemporary art's not really Mum's bag.' I leave it at that rather than attempting to explain the appeal of nature in contrast to the modern urban landscape.

'So, you're a modern artist? I'll be sure to tell your mum when I next see her. Whenever that may be.'

'That's why I wanted to speak to you. Mum said she has a new friend called Pierce. They seem quite close.'

'I don't know what's going on with her.' Moira's tone darkens. 'Today, I suggested she come over for lunch. But Pierce got in first and took her for a picnic by Lough Gill. To be fair to Brigid, she did ask me to come along but no one likes being a gooseberry.' She groans, and something creaks like an old ship.

'You okay, Moira?'

'Just trying to get comfortable in my deckchair. Brigid and I like to sit out when the weather's fine with a lager shandy float.'

'A what?'

'It's lager lemonade with a scoop of ice cream on top.'

I make a face. 'Sounds lovely.'

'It is lovely. But now I'm drinking my shandy float alone and looking at a big old space where your mother should go.'

The news gives me pause. Moira and Mum are such great friends. 'Pierce must have really turned her head.'

'I wouldn't mind, but Pierce isn't just schmoozing Brigid. He's charming female parishioners left, right, and centre. Luckily, I'm immune to that old nonsense.'

'Mum told me Pierce is interested in joining the church.'

'You know men. They say one thing when they mean another.' Moira huffs. 'You should have seen everyone fighting to sit next to him at Mass. The eternal spinsters in pew five went into convulsions. Nan Byrne elbowed me in the ribs so hard she left bruises. I've never seen so much looking around since Seamus Finn's pet rat escaped during the sign of peace and someone shook hands with it.' She pauses for breath. 'Did you know he's a divorcé?'

'Who, Seamus Finn or the rat?'

'No! Pierce!'

'I didn't.' A non-Catholic *and* divorced. It gets better and better.

Moira goes on. 'I can't arrange any outings with Brigid. She's always putting me off in case *he* turns up. The man comes and goes at a moment's notice. I'll bet he's up to no good.'

I wonder what Pierce could be after if not Mum herself. She hasn't much in the way of money, lives in a modest two-bedroom house and doesn't drive.

'Are you the only one who thinks this way?'

'Dervla O'Hara says he has a shifty look about him and she wouldn't trust him alone with the church silver. Mind you, she hasn't a good word to say about anyone since her husband left.' Moira pauses. 'I think we should do something but I don't know what.'

The fact Moira's at a loose end gives me an idea.

'Why don't we find out where Pierce is when he's not with Mum? That would tell us if he's on the level or not.'

'I suppose it would. But I don't see how—'

'If I told you where he's spending his time could you check up on him?'

'That's a grand idea, but how would you know where he is?'

'It's amazing what you can do on the internet these days.' If Moira's anything like Mum, she's clueless where technology is concerned. The first time Mum used a mouse, the cursor bounced around on screen like she was playing Pong.

Moira says, 'I'm not sure. I don't want Brigid to think I'm sneaking around behind her back.'

Her backpedalling isn't surprising. Venting your suspicions about someone is one thing, but acting on them is another entirely.

'You're the best friend Mum could wish for. She's always talking about you,' I gush. 'All we'll do is check everything's above board. It will probably turn out to be an enormous fuss over nothing.'

'I suppose you're right.' Moira pauses. 'Does she really talk about me?'

'Every time she calls.' It's the truth, even if it's mainly Mum passing on Moira's laughable notions as fact.

'So, I'm to be a spy?' Moira asks, her voice dropping low. 'Shall I take binoculars and a newspaper to hide behind when I'm tailing Pierce in my car? He knows what I look like so I'll need a disguise.'

'There's no need for that,' I assure her, as if I'm an espionage expert. 'I'll find out where Pierce goes and then you can check him out. Once we know he's on the level it's happy days and we can stop worrying.'

Moira's voice wavers. 'I won't have to do anything illegal, will I?'

'Course not.'

'All right, Alexandra. You be the spymaster.'

'Okay. Just promise me you won't take any unnecessary risks.'

'I'll be the soul of discretion,' Moira says. 'Pierce won't know I'm there.'

'Great! Let me build up a picture of Pierce's movements, then I can set you in motion.'

'Standing by, Alex.'

'Over and out, Moira.' I end the call and clap my hand to my mouth. What am I doing?

After washing up my lunch dishes, I slip upstairs to my room and insert Pierce's photo between the finding machine's clips.

54.260107, -8.314707
Lough Gill, Kilmore, Co. Leitrim, Ireland

This is my first target outside the United Kingdom. My breath catches knowing the finding machine works overseas. Pierce is where Moira said he'd be, picnicking with Mum on the shores of the Loch.

Mum's probably having a lovely afternoon.

So why can't I stop worrying about Pierce drugging her sandwiches and throwing her into the Loch? My dealings with a serial murderer last year have coloured my thinking.

Pierce is probably a good man. Probably.

·•••·•••··

I lie on my bed and stretch out, closing my eyes with a blissful sigh. I'm close to nodding off when a knock comes at the door.

'Sorry to disturb you, Alex.' Carmen's voice is muffled through the wood. 'Marshall wants to talk to you in the Vault.'

My eyes snap open.

'Coming!' I call out, jumping to my feet. It's three p.m. The others must think I'm bone-idle.

I rush outside and head for the stairs, passing Carmen who is stacking freshly laundered towels in the airing cupboard.

'You go on. I'll join you in a bit,' she says.

Downstairs in the Vault, the videotapes I took from Grigor's house are stacked on the table. The laser printer next to TJ spews out paper. Marshall stands by the printer, holding a bag of frozen peas against his cheek. He arranges the printouts into piles and awkwardly staples them one-handed.

The landline rings. TJ answers it.

I rush over to offer my help, my cheeks flushing. While I've been eating, chatting on the phone, and nodding off, the others haven't come up for air.

Marshall looks up as I approach the table. 'Hey, Alex. How do you feel about putting your administrative skills to good use?'

'Sure. How can I help?'

He gestures towards the paperwork. 'There's more than enough here to keep the rest of us busy. We were thinking you could help us by—'

'Sorry to interrupt.' TJ holds the receiver with his hand cupped over the end. 'It's Ms Harman from Human Resources.'

Marshall gives me an apologetic look. 'Let me take that. I've been expecting her call.'

He walks to TJ's workstation still holding the peas. He turns his back on me to take the call.

I amble around the table. Grigor's paperwork consists of rough notes, field studies smeared with mud and grass-stains, photocopies from technical books, pages of diagrams and formulae, and random printouts including one of his wall-calendar.

I re-read it. *28ᵗʰ August. N.H.M. Archives 2 p.m.*

Perhaps N.H.M. is a person. It could be an organisation. I run through a few ideas: National Hub Meteorite, Nuclear Horizon Mission. I haven't a clue. It could stand for Nuns Hate Marmite for all I know.

I turn my attention to the *GQ and TUNGUSKA* pile. Marshall's eyes lit up when he laid his eyes on these papers, but I've never heard of Tunguska. While he's on the phone, I flick through the pages. From the typed overview I learn Tunguska is an area in central Siberia.

In 1908, the area suffered the largest impact event in recorded history. The scientific consensus is that it was caused by a meteor burst that exploded five to ten miles above the ground. Complicated formulae and diagrams fill the following pages. Some of it's in Russian. The rest might as well be Russian for all the sense it makes. Halfway through, Grigor has left a handwritten annotation:

"GQ sample likely formed before our sun and billions of years before any other star."

I take the papers over to TJ. He's re-orienting and enlarging Marshall's photographs on screen before printing them out.

'Hey, TJ.' I smile. 'Do you know anything about the Tunguska event or what GQ might mean? Grigor's papers are hard going. If I could see a picture or get a layman's explanation, I might understand it better.'

'Hold on.' TJ pushes his tangled hair from his face and uses an elastic band to tie it up in a man bun. He brings up the AltaVista search engine and types in 'Tunguska'. Several results come up including an episode of 'The X-Files' from 1996 and articles on the Russian 2K22 Tunguska anti-aircraft gun, 'The Explosion that Rocked Siberia', and 'Tunguska, Alien Spaceship Fragments Found.'

TJ clicks on the penultimate entry. A blue screen with white text and tiny images pops up.

'Here's a summary,' he says, the azure rectangle reflecting in his glasses.

I read over his shoulder. 'Event' seems far too mild a word. The force of the meteor burst registered a thousand kilometres away, reaching the UK and America. It lit up the skies from western Europe to east Asia.

'The blast was the force of one thousand nuclear bombs!' I say in awe.

'Yeah. If it had happened over the UK we'd have been toast.'

Carmen enters the room and takes a seat at the table. I smile before returning my attention back to TJ.

I lean forward to see the tiny picture better. 'It must have left one hell of a crater.'

He double-clicks on an image. A new page opens with a photo of an irregular circle of green surrounded by forest. 'There was no crater, but the shock wave toppled eighty million trees and left a large clearing that's still treeless today.'

I stare at the enormous circle of downed trees. 'What was left behind, apart from fallen trees?'

TJ hits the 'back' button and scrolls down the page. 'An abundance of inorganic, extraterrestrial material.'

'Extraterrestrial?' Green aliens with long, glowing fingers pop into my mind. 'As in alien rocks?'

'Yes, but it's nothing to do with the 'Russian Roswell' conspiracy or crashed alien spaceships. The debris contained rare carbon minerals including nanodiamonds, lonsdaleite, troilite and schreibersite.'

'Diamonds? There's treasure lying around the place?'

'*Nano*diamonds.' TJ gives me a pitying look. 'They're so small you can't see them with the naked eye.'

'Shame. Anything else?'

'Only that Tunguska's so inaccessible it took Russian mineralogists over ten years to get in there and research the site. Even then, the government kept their research secret.' His mouth tweaks up at the corners. 'The Kremlin isn't famous for sharing.'

I show him Grigor's handwritten annotation. 'Do you know what GQ stands for? The only thing I can think of is the lad's magazine.'

TJ hesitates. 'Carmen knows more than I do.'

I thank him for his help, and approach her.

Carmen glances at the papers in my hand. 'Helping us out with research, Alex?'

'TJ filled me in on the Tunguska Event. Do you know what GQ means?' I show her the same page.

Carmen beckons me to take a seat. 'GQ stands for Ghost Quartz. It's an extremely rare stone that's only been found around impact sites like Meteor Crater in Arizona. From our research it appears that scientists recovered fragments at Tunguska. Grigor must have a sample if he's analysing it.'

'How did he get his hands on it?'

'We don't know. Yet.' Carmen flicks through the papers. 'The League used to have links to the Russian Academy of Sciences. One of our members researching Tunguska could possibly have passed the quartz to him and asked him to smuggle it to the UK when he defected.'

'Why did the League want ghost quartz? Was it for the stone tape experiment?'

'Hopefully we'll find answers somewhere in here.' Carmen peers at the stacks of paper over her glasses. 'When Richard and I ran our stone tape experiments, I'd never heard of ghost quartz. This could be a potentially groundbreaking development.'

I look up with a start. 'Hold on. Did you just say Dad worked on the stone tape project?'

16

Carmen taps the Avebury tape. 'Richard was extremely protective about these recordings. I always wondered where they went.'

'Those were Dad's? Why didn't you say?'

'It never occurred to me. They're not your typical home video.' She places her hand on the Avebury videotape. 'The camera was aimed at the stones almost all the time. As I recall, the audio recordings were a painful listen.'

My gaze goes to the videotapes. I straighten in my chair. 'I'd like to watch them, if that's okay?'

Carmen slips the tapes into a drawer. 'Let me go through them first.'

I nod reluctantly, my heart clenching. Even though the videos are probably a dead end I'm desperate to find out if Dad's on there. It's been over seven years since I've heard his voice.

Marshall puts down the phone and comes over. He gives Carmen a nod. 'It's all arranged.' He turns to me. 'Do you remember Ms Atsuko, our second person of interest?'

'The Japanese lady?'

'Japanese-American. Carmen and I had a chat about it and we're agreed. That is, if you're amenable to helping us.'

I eye them warily. 'What do you want me to do?'

Marshall's words come out in a rush. 'We'd like you to start work at Ms Atsuko's office tomorrow morning at nine.'

'What?' I shoot to my feet. 'Are you crazy? That's not what we agreed. I'm using the Drive to help you find Jonathan. That's it!'

TJ winces and hides behind his monitor. Carmen drags her gaze from her paperwork and gives me a sympathetic smile. 'You're the perfect choice, Alex. You're an outsider, ideal for the role.'

'Why can't TJ go? He knows all that technical stuff.' I give Marshall a pointed stare. 'Or you?'

Marshall lowers the bag of peas. 'Ms Atsuko saw me with Jonathan in July. TJ's interpersonal skills aren't up to it. It has to be you.'

'Don't look at me,' Carmen adds with a shaky laugh. 'I'm far too old.'

'Yoioto Corporation is League friendly, we've placed people there before,' Marshall says. 'You'll be in Ms Atsuko's office, perfectly placed to find out what she's up to. 'We don't expect you to do it for nothing. We'll put you on the pay-roll.'

I raise my hand to put a stop to this nonsense. 'Look, I appreciate you asking me but I'm really not interested.' The day I stopped temping was one of the happiest of my life.

Marshall asks, 'What can I do to persuade you? Without your help, we're pretty stuck.'

I throw up my hands. 'Don't you get it? I'm not a spy. I don't know how to hack into networks or bug phones.'

'You don't need to do any of that,' Marshall says. 'You're going in as a short-term temp. Just be friendly and gain Ms Atsuko's trust. If the opportunity arises, go through her files or poke around on the computer. It's worth a shot.'

Carmen speaks up. 'You can still touch-type?'

'Ye-e-ss,' I say.

'And take dictation, Pitman shorthand?'

A laugh escapes me. 'No one does shorthand anymore unless they're over seventy.'

I close my eyes, feeling a wave of inevitability wash over me. Being a temp is bad enough without the added danger of being caught spying or searching through confidential files.

I meet Marshall's eye. 'Tell you what. Make me a member of the League and I'll do it.'

Marshall lets out a sigh. 'Give me a second.'

He withdraws to confer with Carmen. After a few minutes' hushed discussion Carmen folds her hands on the table, her eyes gleaming.

'It's a deal.' Marshall extends his hand across the table. 'Welcome to the League.'

A thrill goes through me as we shake on it. 'Do I get a badge?'

'Don't push your luck.'

'I have a question. How do I casually slip Jonathan, ghost quartz, and stone tape theory into the conversation?'

'You don't,' Marshall says. 'Just see what shakes loose.'

'What if nothing shakes loose?'

'We'll amend our approach if it's a no-go,' Marshall says. 'This could take a little time so be patient.'

I stare down at my casual T-shirt, shorts and flip-flops. A glimmer of hope rises in me that this might not be possible, after all. 'I don't have anything suitable to wear.'

Carmen gives me a motherly grin. 'Don't worry, we have a wardrobe full of clothes you can choose from.'

'Modern clothes?' It's a question worth asking, considering most of the contents of the house predate the war.

'Classic clothes, which are even better,' Carmen says. 'They never go out of fashion.'

Somehow, I doubt Carmen and myself are on the same page regarding fashion. She probably came into the world dressed in pearls and a twinset.

Catching Marshall's eye, I ask, 'What if I get into trouble? How do I send up the Bat-Signal?'

'Call me.'

I eye the slight bulge in his tummy, remembering all the cake he's eaten and his lunchtime plate piled high with sandwiches. Marshall left his youthful metabolism back in the '70s. If I need help, he should arrive...eventually.

Marshall adds, 'It'll be fine.'

'You saying it'll be fine doesn't make it fine.' I glower.

'It'll be fine.' He forms an 'o' with his forefinger and thumb.

Carmen raises her brow. 'I'll take those peas if you've finished with them, Marshall.'

She holds the packet of defrosting peas between finger and thumb and walks to the door. 'Why don't you come with me, Alex? We can sort out your outfit for tomorrow.'

I follow Carmen from the Vault and up the secret staircase. At the top, she presses her thumb on the switch to restore the passageway before continuing to the entrance hall.

I wait by the grandfather clock and lean on the swirly banister while Carmen deposits the peas in the kitchen. The clock chimes on the quarter hour.

Carmen returns and slowly climbs the main staircase. At the first-floor landing she turns away from my bedroom and walks along a hallway clad in mahogany wood panelling.

She halts by a narrow door with a brass doorknob set into the panelling. 'You go first. I'll follow you up.'

I twist the knob and pull the door open. A narrow staircase is sandwiched between the walls. I ascend the steps to a stuffy attic. Sunlight from two dormer windows falls onto dusty floorboards. Wooden trunks, a broken clock, sunken leather suitcases, and old rugs lie under the eaves.

I walk over to the dormer windows, brushing old cobwebs aside. The handles are stiff and make a creaking sound as I unlatch them and push the windows open. Tilting my face to the breeze, I look out over the driveway, perimeter wall, and closed entrance gates.

Carmen reaches the top of the stairs and flicks a switch. A security light screwed to the rafters illuminates the farthest reaches of the attic. She points to an elegant walnut wardrobe with curved doors.

'You should find everything you need inside. Scarves and belts are in the drawers.'

I throw the wardrobe doors open, hit by the pungent smell of mothballs. Coughing, I sift through outfits crammed on wooden hangers.

'Where did all this come from?'

'Our visitors often leave this and that behind. Over the years, we've built up quite a collection. I'm sure you'll find something to suit you, if you'll pardon the pun. I'll be in the kitchen if you need me.'

She slowly clomps down the stairs.

Carmen's blasé conviction doesn't match the reality of the musty outfits hanging in the wardrobe. One side is full of diamanté ballgowns and men's suits in brown velvet, cyanide green, and funereal black. The trousers are absurdly baggy, made from corduroy or velvet or patterned with hideous checks and flecks.

My hopes for a fashionable women's section die as I slide the hangers along.

There's an A-line tweed skirt made from miles of material, a golfing outfit complete with Plus Fours, an Aran knitted jumper, polyester shirts that give me a static shock when I touch them, and a crimson and pink cape that feels like it's made from Fuzzy Felt. Carmen's recollection of the wardrobe's contents is so far off the mark I wonder if she's been up here in the last ten years.

If I had it my way I'd wear jeans, trainers and a T-shirt tomorrow, but Japanese workplaces are known for their smart dress code. I have to come up with something.

After much griping I settle on the tweed skirt. It's a winter garment which starts boiling me alive from the waist down the instant I try it on. The waistband gapes a little, but the upside is it allows air to circulate. With that settled, I turn my attention to my top half. There are six tops but only two are my size. The first is a pink and white striped shirt that looks like New Romantic wallpaper. The second is a flowery Laura Ashley blouse. I take both.

I slip on a natty royal blue blazer which is the same colour as my primary school uniform. The huge pockets might come in handy.

A pair of shiny court shoes with a low sensible heel completes my mismatched ensemble — the same style of shoes my mother wears. They're a size too big. I stuff a pair of tights in the toes to ensure they stay on my feet.

My reflection in the wardrobe mirror makes me cringe. I look like Nancy Drew trying out as a 1960s air hostess, only without any panache.

I have an exploratory clomp around the attic, and adjust the stuffing in my ill-fitting shoes until I'm satisfied they won't fly off at an inopportune moment.

Returning to the wardrobe, I open the bottom drawer. A bundle of colourful scarves spill out, revealing a glint of metal beneath. I pull out an old-fashioned brown satchel secured by two large buckles. The letters GPO are imprinted on the front. General Post Office, I presume. I unfasten the buckles and remove ration books and war coupons, and a comical poster of Hitler wearing swastika underpants: *'Let's catch him with his Panzers Down!'*

Beneath the poster is a folded sheet of yellowed paper and an envelope containing two black and white photos dated 1943 and 1944.

The first shows two uniformed motorcyclists smoking cigarettes on the front porch of Red Croft Lodge. Fifty years have gone by but the porch looks the same. The lads wear goggles pushed back on their foreheads and military-style jackets with double rows of buttons. The motorbikes, leaning on their kickstands, have saddlebags slung behind the seats. The lads must be dispatch riders.

In the second photo a woman grips the handles of a sit-up-and-beg bicycle and smiles for the picture. Her dark lipstick and glamorous curls contrast with her utilitarian trousers, canvas jacket, and postal satchel which is identical to the one I'm searching through. Her felt cap also has GPO emblazoned on the front.

The Lodge may have operated as a sorting office or postal sub-branch during the war. Either that, or post office workers were billeted here and rode to work on their bicycles or motorbikes.

I unfold the sheet of paper which is an Ordnance Survey map of the local area, including Bletchley Park's mansion and the lake. The nearby train station is a rectangle with black and white lines running from it. The area was a lot less built up back then with green spaces surrounding the town, and farms and cottages with names such as *Bramblebank* and *Forshawes Farm*.

Red Croft Lodge is marked near the bottom of the map. Church Walk has only three houses marked on it along with a church and a general store. A faint grey path leads from the Lodge to a place called Wilton Hall before continuing to The Old Rectory and St Mary's Church. The final stretch enters Bletchley Park and stops outside the mansion.

I remember reading that large houses were requisitioned by the government during the war. The Lodge was probably one of them. With all the housing developments, roads and offices that have sprung up in the intervening time, it would be impossible to walk the path now. Still, it's a fascinating piece of history.

When I look up from the map, the light has faded outside the window and shadows are lengthening in the attic. I glance at my watch, surprised how long I've spent here. I return the photos and the map to the satchel, close the windows, and brush myself down before changing back into my clothes.

I return to my room and dump my work outfit on my bed before checking my phone.

I have a text from Antony:

`Missing you. The Rancor is doing my head in. Thinking of yanking out the batteries. U were right. Let's get a dog xx P.S. how was the cake?`

My heart swells. I wish Antony were here so we could cuddle up. Something about this room, knowing Dad stayed here, makes me extra-emotional. I text back:

`Cake was lovely and no carnage! We found 2 old videos Dad made. Carmen says they're`

just rocks and noise but I want to watch
them.

Within seconds, I get a reply:
Course you should watch them. It's your
dad xx

I omit the big news.
I've joined the League.

17

For dinner, Carmen serves up fish fingers, oven chips, and un-surprisingly, peas. TJ takes his meal downstairs to the Vault.

I hadn't realised how hungry I was until I take the first bite, but Carmen only picks at her food. She says no to the tinned peaches and ice cream Marshall offers for dessert.

'More for us,' Marshall says.

The last time I ate peach slices in sickly sweet juice, Kool & the Gang were in the charts. I scrape my bowl clean.

Carmen leaves the table to rummage in a cupboard. She swallows two white pills with water.

'Alex, I need a favour,' Marshall says. 'We were hoping you could leave us the Drive tomorrow. We need to track Grigor's movements and I want to keep trying Jonathan's photo.'

I set down my spoon. 'I was going to take the Drive to Yoioto.'

'That's not a good idea. Ms Atsuko will wonder why you're lugging that thing around. I promise we'll take good care of it.'

'It would really help us,' Carmen adds. 'The chances of finding Jonathan decrease with every day that passes. We must follow every lead and the Drive is our one advantage.'

'And theirs,' I'm swift to add. 'If the bad guys who took Jonathan are tracking Marshall and catch him in the field, they'll end up with two Drives for the price of one.'

Marshall stretches back in his chair. 'What if we promise to keep the Drive locked in the Vault at all times?'

It makes sense, and there's no point in me lugging the finding machine around for no reason. The goal is to find Jonathan.

'All right. I agree, on one condition.' I push my bowl aside. 'I want you to track someone for me. His name's Pierce. He's latched onto my mother in Ireland and I don't know why. I want to know where he goes during the day.'

Marshall raises a brow. 'Sure, we can do that. Okay with you, Carmen?'

Carmen fills the sink with hot water. 'That's not League work. But I suppose we can make an exception under the circumstances.'

'Thank you,' I say.

'It's settled, then.' Marshall smiles.

I clear away the dishes and bring them to the sink. Carmen stands with her hands under the water, staring into the bubbles.

'Penny for them?' I peer at her glazed expression.

'What? Oh, sorry.' Carmen shakes her head. 'I was miles away.'

'Let me wash up,' I offer. 'You've done so much already.'

'If you insist. I do feel rather tired.' Carmen wipes her hands on a tea-towel and says goodnight before leaving the kitchen.

I wash up while Marshall dries.

'Thanks for offering to help,' he says. 'Carmen's struggling. I don't know if it's the workload or the stress over Jonathan.'

She's not the only one. Tremors play around my stomach as I consider my assignment. If I were at home I'd go for a long walk by the canal to get my thoughts together. But I can't do that here. I'll have to stew in my room.

'By the way,' Marshall says, reaching into his jacket for a sheet of paper. 'Here are the details for tomorrow. Background information on Yoioto, Ms Atsuko, and other stuff.'

'Thanks.' I slip the paper into my pocket. 'I might head up myself.'

'Sure, big day tomorrow. Remember to leave the Drive in the Vault. See you in the morning.'

I hang the damp tea towel over the oven door and leave Marshall setting up the coffee percolator for his evening caffeine fix. I dash upstairs to get the finding machine and am about to unzip my rucksack when an idea comes to me. Hooking the strap over my shoulder, I return downstairs and along the passageway to the Vault.

I run down the secret stairs, narrowly avoiding a collision with TJ as he comes up with his dinner tray. He stops short, cutlery rattling.

'Sorry!' I put a hand out. 'I've brought the Drive. Is it okay if I leave it on the table?'

'Sure. I'll wait up top.'

'Won't be a sec,' I assure him, dashing into the Vault. I unzip the rucksack and place the finding machine on the table, telling myself it will be safe and this is for the best.

My eyes skip to the drawer where Carmen hid the video cassettes. I hurry over, slide open the drawer and remove them, feeling a rising sense of proprietorship. Carmen helped with the experiments but they're also Dad's legacy. That makes the recordings partly mine. Besides, I consider it my duty to find out about Dad's work. At least, that's how I justify it to myself.

I slip the cassettes into my rucksack and head out.

At the top of the stairs, I flash TJ a grateful smile.

As he presses the FIRE button to elevate the staircase, I sneak down the terracotta tiled corridor into the TV room and close the door behind me.

The elegant room boasts a brass standard lamp in one corner, velvet draperies, pelmets and picture rails. On closer inspection, the lamp-shade is moth-eaten, the draperies are faded and the leather Chesterfield is flaking. I unhook the tasselled tie-backs and draw the curtains closed to cut out the setting sun's glare.

I switch the TV and VCR on at the mains. Snowy interference dances across the curved TV screen.

Nostalgia blooms in me as I get to my knees and press my nose up to the screen. Static crackles against my nose as I smell the distinctive electrical charge. I thought peaches and cream was a trip down memory lane, but the old television set takes me back to when Dad built our TV in the '70s. The Lodge's set is a similar size but not half as grand.

I slot the video labelled *AVEBURY 1969* into the VCR and rewind it to the start. Ensuring the volume is turned down, I press 'play,' and hug one of the mismatched sofa cushions.

Interference turns into wavy grey and white bands. A colour picture emerges — a summer countryside scene with trees in full leaf. The colours are as artificial as icing on a child's birthday cake with every tone punched to the max. The grass is virulent green and the sky is a band of intense orange where it meets the horizon.

The picture jolts as the camera operator pans around to a grass-filled circular clearing. Birdsong rings out in the background. Sheep graze around a spectacular group of rocks. I guess this is Avebury.

The ancient stones make me think of the summer solstice, pagan rituals, burial rites, and celebrations. I wonder if the legends surrounding Avebury are as good as the petrified King's Men at the Rollright Stones.

'We're lucky no one's around,' a man says off-screen, pointing the camera across empty fields. 'Let's make the most of it.'

My throat tightens. I increase the volume. Shivers travel through my spine and clench around my temples. Even though the recording is over thirty years old, I recognise Dad's voice instantly.

I lean forwards hugging the cushion tight, wanting to catch every word.

'Did you set the gain the way I showed you?' Dad says.

'You don't need to go on, Richard!' a female voice chastises him with a laugh.

A young woman appears, wearing a denim dungaree-skirt with large amber bangles on her wrists. She looks around my age, somewhere in her mid to late twenties with a waist as slim as a whippet.

'You're supposed to be filming the rock, not me,' she protests, setting down a large black box with dangling wires next to a standing stone far taller than any of the Rollright Stones. She adjusts the controls on the box, which is twice the size of the box Grigor was using.

The camera rises and the screen shakes. I presume Dad is securing the camera to a tripod.

'Testing, testing,' Dad says, moving in front of the lens.

My breath catches. He wears a short-sleeved shirt that shows off his sun-tanned arms. If my maths is correct, Dad would be fifty years old. He sports a decent thatch of hair and his trademark chunky sideburns. On screen, he appears surprisingly handsome and rugged, like Oliver Tobias or Olly Reed in their prime. I'd never acknowledged that about Dad before. Why would I? To me, he was only ever Dad.

I was born in 1969 so I don't have memories of him from back then. He never told me or Mum about Red Croft Lodge or his fieldwork.

Dad wears black padded headphones around his neck. Wires run from the earpiece to a large tape recorder hanging from a thick canvas strap across his shoulders. The picture quality isn't the best, but I can make out a row of silver knobs along the top.

Dad twiddles the knobs. I wince at a high-pitched squeal that escapes into the lounge.

'We're supposed to be recording noise, not making it!' the woman laughs.

I scrabble for the TV volume control. After a moment, the squealing stops and I restore the volume.

The woman bends over and attaches bungee cords to metal hoops on either side of the box. She stretches the cords around the base of the rock and interlinks the hooks to hold it in place, before raising a slim, brown cigarette to her lips. She flicks open a metal lighter. One strike, and a flame appears. Casually, she lights her cigarette, one hand on her hip.

It can't possibly be...can it?

In place of the stylish silver bob, the woman on screen has flowing, golden locks. Golden lashes fringe her eyes. I never noticed them before because of the spectacles. I struggle to connect the lithe young thing on screen with the rather prim woman who served up fish fingers for dinner.

I'm transfixed by Carmen's inherent grace and the way she moves balletically on bare feet. I feel a pang, remembering how she gripped the stair banister earlier and how slow she was.

Dad places the headphones over his ears, making adjustments to the equipment. He plugs an audio cable into the box by the stone, then follows it back to a bulky tape recorder a few feet away. He moves in front of the lens making final checks.

Behind him, Carmen raises her face to the sun and uses her fingers to comb her hair away from her face. Wisps of bluish smoke stream from her cigarette. Her nonchalant manner is strikingly different to the sensible, motherly attitude she has now.

'Okay. Stone Tapes Project, subject number twenty-two,' Dad says. 'We're at the village of Avebury in Wiltshire. Our subject is one of the outer sarsens, farthest from the village.'

Dad slides off the headphones, places them gently on the ground by the rest of the equipment and says quietly, 'I've made those adjustments you suggested, Carm. Fingers crossed they work.'

'Have faith. We'll strike it lucky. I know we will.' She creeps towards him on bare feet. 'Once we get a result, you won't care how long it took.'

'I wish I had your confidence. We still have thousands of variables to try.'

Carmen closes the gap to Dad. A curl of smoke escapes her lips. 'Things would go a lot quicker if you could keep your hands off the equipment.'

A peculiar feeling settles on me at her soft, come-hither tone.

Dad's voice softens. 'You're right. That's always been my trouble.'

Carmen passes behind the camera and out of sight. I hear a giggle.

Heat rushes up my neck to my cheeks. My forehead pulses. My dinner sits like a stone in my stomach.

Birdsong rings out in the background, along with a low hum of background interference from the video tape. Dad says something I can't quite catch.

It sounded like, 'Over here,' or 'Come here.'

The camera goes black.

18

A barrage of sound erupts from the black TV screen. I squeeze the cushion tighter as the hypnotic chorus wraps around me like a blanket.

In the background, crackling, electrical interference clashes with a roar like amplified wind. Both sounds waver in and out of audible range as though crossing vast distances in moments. At the top end of the sound spectrum is a high-pitched noise like someone whistling through a blade of grass. Beneath the whistling are low arrhythmic booms like irregular heartbeats.

The overall sensation is like an experiment conducted by the BBC Radiophonic Workshop, transporting me to another planet.

I stare into the TV, my mind leaping from stone tapes to ghosts to what Carmen was doing with Dad off-camera. I beg the logical side of my brain to step in but it refuses to come up with an acceptable explanation. Dad continued with the experiments for years despite constantly failing to achieve meaningful results.

Maybe he and Carmen spent time together for reasons that had nothing to do with the League.

My mind replays the hot, lazy day by the Avebury stones. Dad and Carmen alone while Mum was in Sudbury, her hands full with a toddler whilst heavily pregnant with me.

Someone yanks back the curtains. Sunlight pierces my eyes. I blink the glare away, the spell broken.

'What the hell's going on?' Marshall strides to the VCR and stops the video. 'It's a miracle that racket didn't wake Carmen.' He

112

jabs his finger at the empty video cassette sleeve. 'Did she say you could watch these?'

My frozen larynx and spinning head strangle my reply.

'They're Dad's videos, too,' I force the words out. A nagging pain grips my temples as I struggle to stand, my knees stiff and aching.

Marshall glares at the video recorder, struggling to keep his tone level. 'That VCR is old and the heads need cleaning. It could have chewed the tape. The recordings are irreplaceable and need analysis in the clean lab before anyone else looks at them.'

'You won't get anything from them.' My voice rises. 'The picture quality is terrible and you heard the sound. There's no technology in the world that could make sense of that.'

'Technology has advanced since 1969. We can do things they could only dream of.' Marshall ejects the cassette from the VCR and checks it for damage before slipping it into the cardboard sleeve. He spots the other videotape sticking out of my open rucksack and picks it up.

I should protest but I can't find the words. My mind keeps replaying Carmen shimmying over to my dad. Was this the reason why she was so distracted after dinner and took pills? Were they sleeping pills? Maybe the sight of the videos brought it back.

'—said, are you all right? You've gone pale.'

'Sorry.' I shake free of my thoughts and pick up my empty rucksack. 'I'm going to bed.'

Marshall steps aside to let me through the door. 'Look, no harm done, just ask me next time.'

TJ waits outside in the corridor. 'What did you hear? Could you make out any voices?'

I blink up at him. 'No, it was a mess.'

'All right, TJ, save the questions,' Marshall intervenes.

Squeezing past, I run upstairs to my room and lock the door. My ears ring in the silence.

I throw myself onto the bed and stare at the ceiling.

How could he? An insistent voice whispers in my ear. It has an Irish lilt. It sounds like my mother.

I swallow the lump in my throat. Poor Mum. While she stayed home, Dad was away pursuing empty projects for the League and gallivanting in the countryside with Carmen.

Carmen must have known Dad had a young family but for some reason she didn't care. I remember her saying she was in awe of Dad. Maybe she fell for him in an adulating, hero-worshipping way. She was the young, hot thing and he was the experienced mentor. It's hokey enough to be a second-rate Mills & Boon plot.

Remembering the tone of Dad's voice on the tape sends a nasty sensation winding through me like a parasitic worm. I don't remember him ever speaking to Mum that way. He wasn't physically affectionate in public. Nothing beyond a peck on the cheek and a brief hug before he went to work.

The gloom of my unlit bedroom matches my mood. I shiver on the blankets as cool air streams through the open window. Picking up my phone, I bring up Antony's number then drop the phone on the floor. None of this makes sense. How can I possibly explain it to him?

Weariness sinks into my bones and with it comes doubt. No one wants to think of their father as a cheating Lothario.

At the end of the day, what did I actually see? Carmen laughing and sharing a cheeky joke or two with Dad. It could have been harmless fun.

It's not like I haven't been guilty of misinterpreting things before. Last year, I suspected Antony of cheating and he gave me more reasons to suspect him than a suggestive laugh and a double-entendre. I turned out to be wrong on all counts.

The fact is, my parents' marriage wasn't great. Mum thought Dad was obsessed over his missing sister Lilian and she felt sidelined. Their views on religion differed and they often argued. God knows, I hated the way Mum used to force her opinions on me. If Dad wasn't happy perhaps he sought happiness elsewhere.

I force him from my mind and go through my bedroom routine. After putting on my pyjamas I slip into bed. A lump settles between my ribs like a stone. If I don't get a grip and deal with this I won't be able to look Carmen in the eye.

I should man up and simply ask her what the deal was.

But I can't. The truth is, I don't want to hear the answer.

19

I wake with a start to my beeping alarm and a knot in my stomach. It's a miracle I slept at all after last night's revelations.

Groaning, I roll out of bed and dress in my terrible tweed skirt, pink striped shirt and old woman's shoes. I tie my hair back in a simple pony tail, hoping that will be smart enough for my new boss. I'm actually glad I'm temping today. I need some distance from Carmen. Hopefully the work will keep my mind off her shenanigans with Dad.

I creep downstairs towards the aroma of coffee drifting from the kitchen, hoping I won't run into her.

To my dismay, Carmen is at the yellow table, buttering toast. Marshall sits opposite with jars of peanut butter, honey, and marmalade open before him. He's dressed in a button-down shirt and tie with a napkin tucked into his collar, his jacket over the back of the seat.

I force a smile. 'Good morning.'

'Morning.' Marshall licks peanut butter from his thumb. 'Coffee?'

'Please.'

'You look smart, Alex.' Carmen appraises me with a tilt of her head. 'Ms Atsuko should be impressed.'

'Really?' I say, examining her expression for any hint of sarcasm, but she looks and sounds sincere.

'Richard would be proud.' Carmen smiles. 'I'm looking forward to analysing his video tapes. Hopefully, we can glean new information from them.'

Taking a seat, I look at Marshall. He shakes his head ever so slightly.

It doesn't look like he told Carmen I watched the Avebury tape. And, she doesn't seem concerned about watching the tapes in front of Marshall and TJ. Perhaps she's forgotten what Dad filmed. Or maybe, she never saw them.

Marshall hands me a mug of coffee loaded with whisked, frothy milk and a dusting of cocoa. It's a struggle to eat with everything on my mind, but I manage a buttered toast triangle.

'Before I forget, this is for you,' I say, placing Pierce's photo on the table.

Marshall examines the image. 'This the guy you want to track? What's the story?'

'He's moving in on my mother and I'm not sure I trust him. I'd like to know where he goes, that's all.'

'All right. Leave it with me.' He glances at my discarded toast. 'If you're finished we should head out.'

I drain my coffee, say goodbye to Carmen and follow Marshall outside. 'You didn't tell her I watched the videotape?'

Marshall unlocks the Lexus. 'Did you want me to?'

'No.'

'That's what I figured.'

'I appreciate it. Thank you.'

Putting Carmen to the back of my mind, I sit in the passenger seat and place my feather-light rucksack containing pens, paper, tissues, a spare pair of tights, and my phone in the footwell. Little panicky moments go through me.

Without the familiar weight of my finding machine, it's as though part of myself is missing.

I put my sunglasses on and stare out of the window. 'How far away is Ms Atsuko's office?'

'About eleven miles.' He pauses. 'It was in the notes I gave you.'

'What notes?' I stop short, remembering the information sheet Marshall handed me after dinner. I put it in my jeans pocket. With all the chaos surrounding Dad's video tape it completely slipped my mind that I was supposed to read it.

I clench my fists in my lap and say nothing. Marshall's counting on me. I don't want to seem incompetent.

Marshall drives to the end of Church Walk and heads through town to join the A4146.

'It's going to be a warm one today,' he says. Sunshine breaks through the trees in flashes of intermittent golden light as we cruise along the dual-carriageway.

Memories of old temp jobs flood back. I once turned down an assignment with a Japanese bank because of the long list of rules including wearing my hair in a chignon, reciting the company motto, and joining in with morning Radio Taiso exercises. In the end, the chignon was the deal-breaker.

'You okay?' Marshall asks, passing me a box of Tic Tacs. 'Here, have a mint.'

I pop the mint in my mouth and tuck a lock of stray hair behind my ear. 'I feel I'm going in blind. What if I make some dreadful cultural faux pas?'

'Don't worry. The Yoioto Corporation is international. Everyone speaks English.'

'Yeah, but Ms Atsuko's a scientist. She'll suss me out as a fraud and then what?'

'It's a work placement, not an interrogation,' Marshall says, as we pass a sign for Leighton Buzzard. 'Ms Atsuko isn't expecting a technical genius, she's expecting a temp. If she blindsides you with a question you can't answer, be honest and say you don't know. Think back to the times you turned up for a new assignment. You put on a brave face and showed willing and it always worked out, didn't it?'

'I suppose.'

Marshall's right. Employers don't tend to expect much from temps. A high percentage of my previous bosses bemoaned the fact their favourite PA or secretary was ill, off on holiday, had broken a leg skiing, or gone on maternity leave. The upside was they never expected me to fill their kitten heel shoes.

'Just keep your eyes and ears open. Don't overthink it.'

'Can you run over what you know about Ms Atsuko again? Just to cement things in my mind.'

Marshall gives me a sharp look. I tense, waiting for an accusation I've not done my research. Instead, he gives a resigned sigh. 'All right. Okada transferred from the U.S. two years ago to head up Tape Storage Solutions.'

'Are tape storage solutions things like tape cassettes and videos?' I chew on my fingernail. 'All mine are in boxes. I've barely looked at them since CDs and DVDs came along.'

'Interesting you say that. I have a hunch it's the retro tech we're interested in.' Marshall flips down the sun visor as we round a turn into bright sunlight. 'The sample of ghost quartz is old, the Stone Tapes are old, and the Drive's tech is old.'

'What does that have to do with Ms Atsuko? Or Jonathan, for that matter?'

'TJ's been digging into Yoioto. The company was a world leader in magnetic tape technology back in the '60s and '70s. They had a fully funded research lab making prototypes for major organisations like NASA and IBM.'

'But that old stuff is obsolete. They've probably chucked it out.'

'Maybe, maybe not.'

For the remainder of the journey I stare out of the window, feeling clueless. By the time we reach Chartmoor Road, a country road with industrial units dotted along its length, I'm twisting my hands in my lap and jigging my legs to quell growing nausea.

Marshall turns the Lexus into a car park past a large silver display plaque: YOIOTO CORPORATION. He parks in the bay farthest from the entrance.

I stare at the two-storey brick building with the number 16 on the front in enormous orange digits, and consider making a run for it. I wonder how far I'll get down the road before Marshall catches me.

Marshall asks, 'Do you want me to hang around a while?'

'No, you should go.' I smooth out my skirt with sweating hands.

'Tell you what, I'll wait twenty minutes until you're settled in. Call me if there's a problem.'

'Thank you.' I open the car door.

'One more thing,' Marshall adds. 'Remember your pseudonym?'

'What?'

'Your name, while you're working here.'

My mouth drops open. 'God, I'm sorry. It's completely gone out of my head.'

Marshall rubs his forehead, squeezing his eyes shut. 'Susan Moore. Remember?'

'I'm sorry. Really sorry. Susan Moore, Susan Moore, Susan Moore. Got it.'

Marshall retrieves a muesli bar, a banana, and a twenty-pound note from his jacket pocket. 'Snacks and money for lunch. You've got your phone for emergencies.'

'Thanks, Dad.'

Marshall smiles. 'I'll pick you up at five, Susan.'

I clamber from the car onto the warm asphalt and hobble to the entrance in my uncomfortable shoes while muttering my new name to myself. The path crosses a formal garden with a bench and a pond before arriving at the entrance.

The main doors slide open at my approach, releasing a delicious blast of cool air. The interior is modern and light with a white tiled floor and chrome and black furnishings. Classical music plays softly in the background.

The receptionist is a handsome guy in his twenties dressed in a crisp blue suit. He looks up as I head towards the gloss-black reception desk.

'Good morning,' I say. 'My name's Ale—' I cough into my hand. 'Susan Moore. I'm working for Ms Atsuko.'

'Sign here.' He slides over the visitors' book before picking up the phone. 'Hello, Ms Atsuko? I have a Susan Moore for you down in reception.' He pauses. 'Yes, I'll send her up.'

My pen hesitates over the signature box. I write my fake name in block capitals which I can easily replicate. The receptionist prints out a label with my alias, sticks the label onto a visitor's pass, and inserts the completed badge inside a laminated sleeve.

'Wear this at all times, please. You want the second floor, room C46.' He points out the staircase as I clip the ID badge onto my lapel.

The walk will give me time to prepare myself. And delay the inevitable. My cursed shoes resound on the tiles as I ascend the stairs with one hand firmly on the rail. I'm having as much trouble getting up them as Carmen.

Technicians in lab coats and men and women in business suits pass me going down.

The first-floor doors begin with the letter B, followed by numbers. I continue to the second floor. The layout is identical, but the door numbers start with C. Room forty-six is at the end of the corridor.

Straightening my skirt, I push my shoulders back and knock three times.

'Come in!' a bright voice with an American accent calls from inside.

I step into a large office with a floor-to-ceiling window. Potted plants fill the room. Exotic climbers twine up a lattice of bamboo rails attached to the back wall. The lush greenery softens the modern boxy space and adds a tropical feel.

An elfin, petite woman in her thirties, who must be Ms Okada Atsuko, sits behind a pale beech desk that contains in and out trays and an A4 desk diary. She has the office phone pressed to her ear.

'Sorry, my new temp is here,' she says. 'Give me half an hour and I'll come down and check on progress.'

Ms Atsuko shoots up from her desk and skips out to greet me. I find myself in the rare position of being able to look down on another adult.

Her dead-straight black hair has a reddish sheen and falls below her shoulders. Her smile is perfect, her skin flawless. The grey pinstripe suit she wears must have been personally tailored. I curse Carmen and her fuddy-duddy collection of mothballed clothes.

'Hello Susan!' She shoots out her hand, looking me up and down. 'I'm Ms Atsuko. You can call me Okada.'

'Very pleased to meet you, Okada.' Her handshake is firm. I'm relieved we don't have to bow to each other.

'You are so welcome!' she says with an openness that reminds me of Marshall.

'I love all the plants,' I blabber. 'It's like being outdoors when you're indoors.'

'That's down to my mother.' Okada tips her head to one side. 'She's a pot plant fiend. Heaven help me if the soil's too dry or I'm not misting the leaves enough.'

I smile, remembering Marshall's instructions to be friendly. 'My mum's like that, always pointing out ways I should improve.'

'I get that.' Okada rolls her eyes. 'Mom's been staying with me, but I think we're both ready for her to move back to America.' She pauses. 'So, what kind of experience do you have?'

The question lands like a cannon ball. 'Um...Microsoft Office, Lotus Notes, database querying...that kind of thing.'

'I understand you have experience working for tech and software firms.'

One cannon ball becomes two cannon balls. A nervous laugh escapes me. Marshall must have bigged me up to Human Resources to get me the job. I rack my brain, pull old jobs from the archives of my mind and fling them at her. 'Fujitsu, Seagate and...uh...Toshiba. They all made me sign NDAs.'

The last bit is to stop her digging deeper, as my technical know-how is limited to working the fax and photocopier and unjamming dodgy printers. Even so, I count seven more knots in my stomach until Okada finally smiles.

'That's good. I can use an all-round administrator. Let me show you where you'll be working.'

She waves me over to a small desk nestled by a pillar with a computer, printer and franking machine. 'Please, have a seat.'

The chair's flexible back support springs back and forth as I sit and adjust the height via the lever. A chrome company logo — a large Y within three interlocking circles — slowly rotates on the black screen.

'Let me show you where everything is. It's really straightforward.' Okada leans forward to wiggle my mouse. The Yoioto logo is replaced by the home screen. The desktop contains Word, Excel, Outlook and yellow file directories in a neat column to one side.

The familiar Microsoft icons have a calming effect. I'm keen to search through the computer files but it will have to wait until my new boss isn't looking over my shoulder.

'Any questions?' Okada asks.

'Am I right in thinking that Yoioto used to lead the way in tape storage?' I ask.

'We still do.'

'My father worked with reel-to-reel tapes in the seventies, but I've never seen them working in real life. Only in pictures.'

'Umm.'

The office phone trills.

'One second.' Okada raises her finger, rushes to her desk and picks up the receiver. 'Hello? Oh, hi, Mom.'

She swivels her chair away to face a giant potted palm. The garbled stream of incomprehensible words erupting from the other end spurs her to retaliate with short exchanges in Japanese.

'*Okāsan, ima chotto isogashikara atode ne!*' She reverts to English. 'Mom, I'll have to call you later, okay?'

A flow of words follows, so rapid-firing it sounds as though her mum has pushed the fast-forward button. Mrs Atsuko Senior sounds just like my mum when she's on a mission.

I turn my head to catch Okada's whispered reply. 'I told you not to worry. I'm dealing with that.'

I dare a look around. Okada has her hand cupped over her face. A suffusion of pink stains her cheek. 'Yes, *Katsudon* is fine. I've got another call coming in, Mom. I have to go. Great, bye then, bye, yes bye bye.'

Okada puts the phone down, looking shell-shocked. I think she could do with a hug. My new boss glares at the phone as though daring it to ring again.

'Where would you like me to start?' I ask.

'I've got a mailing to go out, but that can wait,' she says. 'HR would normally give you the tour but as I'm going to the lab I can do it myself. Follow me.'

20

I follow Okada out of the office and towards the stairs. She points down the corridor. 'Our meeting rooms, HR, accounts, and admin are on floors B and C. There's an auditorium downstairs for presentations and visiting speakers.'

She takes swift and dainty steps down the stairs, giving the illusion she's gliding. I lose one of my old lady shoes on the landing trying to keep up. Okada glances over her shoulder. I mutter an apology and stuff my foot back inside.

We reach the ground floor. Okada points out the staff lift tucked away around the corner.

'The company encourages walking,' Okada says, quashing my hopes of using the lift to save my feet.

I pause by a grey metal door labelled, 'Private.' Through a small observation window, a set of stairs lead down. 'What's through there?'

'Security, and our server room. They're both down in the basement.'

The toilets are opposite. Farther along, Okada stops at a scuffed red door with a metal fingerplate labelled 'Push.'

'You'll be using the mailroom.' She gestures me inside.

I shoulder through the heavy doors. A radio atop a filing cabinet plays the *Capital Radio* jingle. Parcels and letters cover a large table with trays on the end. Two male workers give me uninterested glances before returning to work, sorting mail into pigeon-holes.

One worker drags a grey sack through double-doors at the back of the room into a covered loading bay. I catch a glimpse of panel vans with Yoioto emblazoned on the side neatly parked within yellow-lined bays.

'Shall we move on?' Okada waves me out.

I follow her past the main reception desk to a large library at the front of the building. Large windows overlook the formal garden I walked through earlier. I look for Marshall's Lexus in the main car park but he's long gone.

Bookshelves line the walls with freestanding shelves taking up much of the floorspace. The shelf nearest me contains such gripping titles as: *Bit by Bit: An Illustrated History of Computers* and *The Complete Hypercard Handbook.* I flick through the nearest volume. The scientific formulae, incomprehensible diagrams, and dense blocks of text make my eyes cross. I think it was Socrates who said, 'I know one thing: that I know nothing.' The ancient philosopher could not have described me better.

Okada walks to a table at the centre of the room containing two computer terminals and a colour photocopier.

'The digital catalogue is regularly updated with our latest scientific papers,' she says. 'Employees use them for research.'

I return the book and casually glance at the computer screen. If I could search the computer catalogue for references to ghost quartz or static tape I might find what I'm looking for.

The system looks old with orange text on a black screen. *Dynix Scholar ~ Automated Library System* runs along the top. Two boxes contain flashing cursors awaiting a user name and password.

'We have the same system at my local library,' I say, casually pressing the space bar.

'This isn't a public library. The computers are for employee use only,' Okada says sharply.

'Sorry.' I pull my hand away.

Our next stop is at the farthest end of the building. Swing doors lead into the staff canteen, full of the sounds of clattering utensils, hissing steam, and sizzling. Staff wipe down tables and the stainless steel serving counter. The smell of chicken and chips makes my stomach growl.

'If you're still here on Friday I recommend the chicken Katsu,' Okada says with a smile.

'I'll remember that.' I smile back.

We leave the canteen and turn into a side passage with a glass door at the end. An illuminated card reader with an integrated keypad is mounted beside the door.

'Last stop on the tour,' Okada trills, swiping her security pass through the reader.

The red light changes to green. The door opens inwards with a sucking sound.

I step into a grey tiled corridor smelling of antiseptic pine. A technician in a white coat walks past with a clipboard in hand. The laboratory inside takes up the full height of the building, exposing the metal struts that support the roof. Silver ventilation ducts snake overhead, joining at square grills that emit a low and steady hum.

The temperature is markedly cooler in here. I fold my arms around myself. For once, I'm grateful for my layers and heavy tweed skirt.

Technicians in white coats work at long tables separated into individual booths by six-foot plexiglass screens, installed with standard power and modern CAT-5 sockets. Okada leads me past banks of analytical and diagnostic machines. Computer monitors and electronic panels display data in charts and waveforms, while a dot matrix printer churns out a concertina of paper.

She halts beside a female technician who is studying the readouts from two visual display units. Jagged lines and scrolling data fill the screens.

'This is where we analyse the long-term performance of our magnetic storage tapes,' Okada says.

'Sounds fascinating.' I nod along.

The female technician turns from her work. She smiles at Ms Atsuko.

I read her name-badge. *Audrey Luft-Beutelspacher*. She sounds like a James Bond technician.

Audrey says, 'Thanks for coming by, Okada.'

'This is Susan, the new temp,' Okada says. 'I'm showing her around.'

Audrey gives a brief nod before pointing to a printout full of graphs. 'These are the latest results on our linear tape experiments.'

Okada peers at the line. 'Awesome. What about the LTFS? Have you tested it?'

'I'll show you what we have so far.' The ensuing conversation is techno-heavy, involving words like 'compression' and 'LTO dri-ves.' It's double Dutch to me but even if TJ were here to translate it wouldn't help. None of it's ghost quartz or static tape related.

Okada and her colleague pore over printouts without inviting me to join the conversation.

My attention drifts to a roll-down shutter set into the back wall, presumably for transporting large items in and out of the lab. In the far corner are a pair of fire doors. One is propped open with a cardboard box. A technician smokes a cigarette outside by a parked car. The sun baked tarmac ends at a chain-link fence.

Along the internal wall are three grey doors with viewing win-dows.

I leave Okada deep in conversation and wander over. The first door leads to an empty meeting room with a whiteboard and projector. The next door is labelled *Stores*. It's dark inside.

I peer through the last door's observation window, into an old-fashioned laboratory. Industrial-sized reel-to-reel tape ma-chines from decades ago sit alongside lumps of beige and grey metal. Tape reels turn. Lights flash. Shelves stacked with boxes, multimeters, soldering irons, plugs, wires, and reels of lead solder run along the back wall.

The old technology reminds me of Dad. He was always sur-rounded by bits of metal and machines with their insides spilling out.

A technician in a beige lab coat sits with his back to me at an L-shaped wooden workbench. He wears grey headphones with padded ear pieces over a mop of thick, dark hair, and stares at a piece of lab equipment with a glowing screen.

From the back he looks a bit like Dad. A lump comes to my throat. I place my palm on the doorplate, filled with a sudden urge to go inside and tap him on the shoulder. Then I come to my senses. Dad died in 1993.

'Miss Moore!'

Oh, crikey, that's me! I turn with a start.

Okada beckons me away from the door with her lips pressed together.

I give her a disarming smile. 'I hope you don't mind me having a look around. This old lab looks amazing. They have an old reel-to-reel machine.'

Ms Atsuko's eyes flick to the retro lab door. 'That's Yoioto's hardware archives. Melvyn's retired, but he likes to keep our old technology working. I suppose it will be useful for future generations to see how far we've come.'

'Will the public ever have a chance to see inside?'

'At some future date, possibly. We'd better get back and make a start.'

Okada shuts down the conversation and moves with military speed out of the lab.

I take a last glance at the retro lab door before hurrying after her.

21

For the rest of the morning I work on a PowerPoint presentation. The slides show the Tape Storage Solution department's
performance over the last six months. It's all fiscal this and pro-
jection that. It's one of the driest documents I've ever seen and I
should know — I'm the poor sod who once had to transcribe five
hours of meetings on the subject of rotten concrete.

I coax my rusty skills back to life, determined to do a good job in
record time. Okada might entrust me with greater responsibilities
if I prove myself efficient and reliable. With any luck, she'll leave
me to my own devices or send me around the building on errands.

My desk is angled so my back is to her. She can see my screen
over my shoulder, so it's impossible to start searching through
computer files.

I mull over my next steps while I work on the presentation.

Okada's earlier abruptness made it clear she didn't want me near
the retro lab which only increases my desire to see inside. But unless
I can sneak in via the open fire door I'll need a swipe card to get past
the security pad on the main lab door. Either way, entering the lab
without proper authorisation will throw up massive red flags.

The library computers may hold clues to Yoioto's retro tech, but
I need a login and password to access them. Okada may have that
information written down somewhere, which reminds me, I need
to look in her diary.

I ask Okada questions about her preferred format for the presentation and play the ideal employee. She keeps her answers brief

and her eyes on her computer, barring further conversation. While I work I listen in on her phone calls. The one-sided conversations are mundane, concerning timescales and meetings. Between calls, she works on her PC. I hear multiple mouse clicks and rapid-fire typing.

I'm beginning to wonder if she'll ever leave me unsupervised.

An hour later, I show Okada the finished presentation.

'Nice,' she says, before suggesting some minor amendments. 'Once you've made the changes, print them out and frank the ones that need posting.' She hands me a batch of pre-printed labels with internal, UK, and international addresses.

'Wouldn't it be more efficient to email them?' I ask, hoping this could be a route into the computer mailboxes.

'Absolutely,' Okada rolls her eyes. 'But the older executives are dinosaurs. It's easier if all the presentations go by post.' She hands me an 'Internal' stamp. 'For the in-house labels. Keep them separate for the mailroom.'

I check my watch. Eleven-thirty. I'm starting to think that Marshall has sent me on a fool's errand.

The mindless, repetitive admin requires little mental input from me. I stuff envelopes and read labels. None of the names, titles, or addresses jump out. At twelve-thirty on the dot I frank the last envelope.

'Well done, Susan.' Okada goes to the door and holds it open. 'Why don't we break for lunch? Bring the post.'

We head downstairs to the mailroom. Okada lets me go inside alone. I push through the door, relishing the freedom of not being in the same room as her.

A middle-aged man with a jowly face looks up from his sandwiches.

'Excuse me, where does the post go?' I ask, lifting the pile of envelopes.

Still chewing, he grunts and points to two large trays with paper labels.

'Thanks,' I mutter, chuck the post in the correct trays, and leave.

Okada takes me to the canteen which is bustling with employees on their lunch break. She passes me a tray. 'Lunch is on me. Have whatever you want.'

'Thanks.' My stomach's a yawning chasm. The lunch options are colourful and healthy: salads, fresh fruit, yoghurt, and a Japanese dish called Yakisoba. Maybe tomorrow. Today, I go for chicken, chips, baked beans and a cup of tea.

Okada scans her card at the till and checks her watch. 'Will you be all right if I leave you? I have a meeting with the other department heads.'

'I'll be fine, thanks,' I assure her.

'Good. I'll see you back at the office in an hour.'

Alone at last, I search the tables for the retro lab man but he's nowhere to be seen. The only free seat is beside two young secretarial types with glossy talons and hoop earrings. Perhaps they can tell me more about the retro lab or the password to the library computers.

One girl picks cucumber slices from her salad and stacks them on the side of her plate. 'What did Jase say?'

Her companion frowns. 'He's got feelings for Shell but sez he fancies me.'

She glances at me as I place my tray on their table.

'Do you mind if I join you?' I ask with a smile. 'It's kind of busy in here.'

Cucumber girl gives me a desultory nod. Her friend sips a can of Diet Coke between spoonfuls of yoghurt.

'I'm Susan,' I say brightly. 'I started in Tape Storage Solutions today. How about you?'

'Accounts.' Yoghurt girl stares into her half empty pot as though her will to live is somewhere inside. Cucumber girl says nothing. An uncomfortable silence falls between us.

The women huddle across the table. I abandon all hope of getting anything useful out of these two and eat my meal.

'You should break up wiv him first,' Yoghurt girl whispers loudly. 'Then he'll come crawling back.'

'I can't. I love 'im!' Cucumber girl gives me a narrow-eyed glare. 'Let's 'av a fag.'

The girls push up from the table and walk off, leaving their mess behind. They're one of the reasons I gave up temping.

I quickly finish lunch and glance at my watch. Forty minutes left. I blot a puddle of spilled Coke with a serviette and stack the girls' lunch things on my tray.

Underneath Cucumber girl's plate is a white card.

My heart jumps. It's a Yoioto swipe card with a black strip running down it like the one Okada used to enter the main lab. After checking no one's looking, I slip it inside my pocket.

I return my tray, leave the canteen, and head for the lab. There's no guarantee the swipe card will work but it's worth a try.

To my dismay, three technicians are in the corridor beside the lab door having a jovial conversation about summer holidays. I veer aside at the last moment before they spot me and detour into the library. I'll give it ten minutes, then try again.

Two employees sit at the computers with folders and paperwork, engrossed in note-taking and searching the catalogue. Maybe one will leave without logging out. The bookshelves are arranged by subject. I search for Quartz, Ghost, and Minerals and flick through the table of contents in two reference books on the Lewisian Gneiss Complex and British Minerals. Neither mention ghost quartz. The second book is authored by a Natural History Museum curator.

A flag goes up. Natural History Museum. N.H.M – the abbreviation from the wall calendar in Grigor's kitchen.

I search for books on tape but there are so many on the subject I end up bamboozled: *Advances in Bidirectional Tape Heads, Transfer Rates and Volumetric Efficiency, Tape Recording the New Revolution.* And those are only four titles out of dozens.

Ten minutes has gone by and the employees are still on the computers. Leaving the library, I return to the laboratory. The technicians have gone. After checking the coast is clear I walk to the door and swipe Cucumber Girl's card.

The light blinks and remains red.

I reverse the card and swipe again. Still red.

Damn. I daren't try again in case another failed attempt triggers a lock-out or alarm. Thrusting the card into my pocket, I turn and leave the building. I need headspace.

I wander to the formal garden area. The smell of cigarette smoke drifts from a curved stone bench beneath a cherry tree that overlooks a fountain. The girls from lunch are sitting there, smoking. Pattering water masks their conversation, thank the Lord.

I walk to the far side of a covered bike rack before they see me. With no one else in sight, I take out my phone and call Marshall.

'Hey, Susan,' Marshall says carefully. 'How's it going?'

'All good so far. Listen, I found an old lab on the ground floor. Yoioto stores its old tech there like a museum. I want to take a closer look.'

'Only if it's completely safe,' Marshall warns. 'It's better to stay under the radar gathering information than blowing your cover on your first day. We can discuss what you've found tonight.'

'I am being careful,' I assure him. 'If anyone asks, I'm the newbie who doesn't know her way around. Speaking of museums, I worked something out about Grigor. That meeting he had on his calendar? N.H.M. I think that stands for the Natural History Museum.'

'We're ahead of you. Carmen worked it out this morning. But well done.'

'Oh.' I thought I'd made a breakthrough there. 'What's Grigor going there for? Does he want to steal a dinosaur?'

'I wish he did,' Marshall laughs. 'We think he'll head for the Hall of Minerals. It contains the world's largest chunk of ghost quartz, which was recovered from Tunguska.'

'By recovered, do you mean stolen?'

'I prefer the term, 'liberated,'' Marshall replies. 'Our guess is Grigor's going to steal it.'

'So, what's the plan? Intercept Grigor and take him down?'

'We'll discuss that later, not on the phone.'

I switch subjects. 'How are you getting on with the videotapes? Any luck?'

'None so far.'

'Carmen looked so young on tape, didn't she?' I push.

'I didn't see her,' Marshall says. 'Just the stones along with that godawful noise. There was nothing of research value.'

'That's a shame.'

'The other thing,' Marshall says. 'I've been tracking that guy, Pierce. You want me to text over his location? Looks like he's at a regular residential house'

'Sure.'

'See you at five.'

'Okay then, bye,' I say and hang up. Shortly after, my phone buzzes with a text message.

10:25 am, 12:45 am 53.722764, -7.792784 11 Kennedy Drive, Longford, N39 Y4A9

If 11 Kennedy Drive is a normal house on a regular street, there can't be any harm in Moira checking it out from a distance. I forward the address to her with a warning to be careful, before putting my phone away.

I feel the swipe card in my pocket with Marshall's warning ringing in my ears. The old me would be a good Samaritan and hand it in to Reception. The new me slips the card into my wallet. I'll ask TJ about it later.

Pondering my options, I follow the footpath that runs along the front of the building.

At the corner, I peer round. An access road passes through an open security gate. A CCTV camera is mounted to the side of the building, aimed at the road. If I stick close to the wall, I should be in the camera's blind spot.

Hopefully, the fire-door around the back is still propped open. As long as there are no technicians smoking outside, I could sneak inside and head for the retro lab.

I pick up my pace as much as my clumsy shoes allow and reach the open gate. I'm about to cross the Rubicon when a voice calls behind me. 'Excuse me? Lady, can I help you?'

I whirl around. An old Japanese man in a grey suit hurries up to me, car keys in hand. His eyes flick to my visitor's pass while mine zero in on his: *Taro Matsuoka: Senior Vice-President.*

'Susan Moore,' he reads from my lapel, his voice heavily accented. 'This gate is for deliveries. Not staff.'

'Sorry.' I clamp my hands to my head. 'I'm so lost. It's my first day.' I add a hapless shrug.

The man leans closer, his eyes boring into me. 'Where you trying to go?'

'I just wanted to stretch my legs after lunch,' I say. 'The main road's too busy with all the cars flying past.'

'Why don't you walk around the garden?' He points back the way I came. 'It's a nice day. There is a bench to sit down and enjoy when you have finished walking.'

'Yes, thank you.'

He dips his head and walks away. Now that he's seen me, I can't try the same trick again.

I turn away from the gate with my plans foiled and hurry back to the office before Ms Atsuko comes looking.

My time has run out.

22

Upon my return to the office, my hopes that Okada will give me something interesting to do are instantly dashed when she points to a wodge of handwritten reports which need typing. It's a mammoth undertaking that consumes the whole afternoon.

After I've finished typing the reports, I take a break to stretch my back and rub my tired eyes. I'm ready to ask Okada for my next assignment when a bell shrills in the corridor outside.

I jump from my chair. 'Is that the fire alarm?'

'No, the home time bell.' Okada points to the wall clock. Five o'clock on the dot. 'It's one tradition we've kept from the Japanese branch.'

The sound takes me back to my school days. I look from the window, half-expecting to see a horde of uniformed children exploding out of the doors, shoving each other and kicking footballs around. Instead, a few employees appear with briefcases and bags, walking sedately to their cars.

Okada stands. 'Thanks for your help, Susan. You've had a productive first day. I'll see you in the morning at nine.'

I take a moment to tidy my desk and fiddle with my rucksack on the off-chance Okada will leave before me but she continues typing at her desk.

'Bye then.' I give her a cheery wave, grab my rucksack and join the stream of departing workers on the stairs. I go with the flow of people through the main doors.

Outside, I break free from the crowd. There are several Lexuses in the car park which shouldn't come as a surprise, this being a Japanese company. Three are black. I head for the one farthest away.

Marshall gives me a wave from the driver's seat. I open the passenger door and slide into the cool, air-conditioned interior.

'Good day?' Marshall asks, leaning towards me.

'Long, hot, and boring. My mind's full of market share projections and pie charts.' I unbutton my jacket and kick off my hateful shoes. 'You should be proud of me. I've found two areas of interest within the building.'

'What about Ms Atsuko?' Marshall asks, as he starts the engine and cruises out of the car park.

'Okada never left me alone in the office so I had no chance to check her diary or search the computer files. She gets edgy whenever I stray from her side.'

'Anything else?'

'I found a retro lab with a technician whose job is to keep old tech alive. It's strange, because if Yoioto's all about the future why do they keep their old equipment working?'

'That is unusual,' Marshall says.

'I also nabbed a security card but it won't allow me access to the main lab.'

'You're there to observe, not take company property,' Marshall warns. 'I said to be careful.'

'I am being careful. I need to be a little bit sneaky or I'll never find anything out.' I pause. 'Oh, and I need TJ's help to access the library's computer catalogues.'

'We'll discuss that later. We've had a development regarding Grigor.'

'Oh?' I straighten in my seat.

'Before you ask questions, it's better if I show you.' Marshall refuses to say more until we get back to the Lodge.

He holds the front door open and I enter the hall.

'Can I have ten minutes to freshen up?' I ask, desperate to change out of my frumpy work clothes.

'Sure. I'll put coffee on.'

Shoes in hand, I pad upstairs in stockinged feet to the bathroom. I'd give anything for a shower but the bath only has a hose attachment with plastic suction cups that fit over the taps. The water won't run hot, only tepid. I settle for a shallow bath, running the water up to the black line still painted on the enamel from the war. After my bath, I change into jeans and a T-shirt before joining the others in the Vault.

My finding machine sits on the table with Grigor's photo in the clips. Lying next to the machine are pictures of Jonathan and Pierce.

'Marshall tells me your day went well?' Carmen says, gesturing to a tray containing mugs, a coffee jug, sugar and milk.

'It was all right,' I give her a smile as I pour myself coffee. Spending the day away from Carmen has given me time and space to calm down. If she wants to pretend nothing happened with Dad, I'm happy to go along with it for now. 'What's Grigor been up to?'

'Remember how we set up the tap to monitor his landline?' Marshall says.

I nod, recalling him rejigging wires in Grigor's messy studio.

'Grigor received a phone call this morning. Take a listen.' He nods to TJ, who presses a key on his computer.

An electronic buzzing sound breaks the quiet, followed by a gruff voice.

'Da?'

'I only have a second. Listen carefully.' My heart leaps into my throat. The smooth voice and upper-class accent are unmistakeable. It's Jonathan Prudente-Poulton.

Jonathan speaks swiftly. *'They will ask for the stone. Whatever they threaten, do not get it for th—'*

I hear a clunk before a new voice comes down the phone line. An American.

'Now you know he's alive, Grigor. We need to talk business.'

'*I want proof he is unharmed,*' Grigor demands. '*Send me his picture.*'

'*He's unharmed. How long he stays that way is up to you. This will all be over as soon as you get us the stone.*'

'*Put Jonathan back on the line. I follow his instructions, not yours.*'

'*Not from where I'm sitting.*'

Grigor's voice deepens. '*You stole my research tapes. You stole many months of work. That is enough.*'

'*I'll tell you when it's enough. Jonathan's relying on you.*'

'*You kill him, I kill you.*'

I want to cheer Grigor on, but dread settles in my bones. The consequences for Jonathan could be dire.

'*You're in no position to make threats, Grigor. I've been speaking with my contacts in Moscow. The Russian intelligence service has a long list of KGB defectors they want to...how shall I put it...question. Guess what, buddy? You're on that list.*'

'*The UK government will keep me safe,*' Grigor says.

'*Not anymore. Now Jonathan's our guest, no one's looking out for you. Thing is, Grigor, the Russians don't forgive and forget. You should know that. I'd hate for you to spend the rest of your natural life in a gulag.*'

Grigor hisses, '*You make trouble for me if I get you the stone or not! What if I can't get it?*'

'*Make sure you do. When it's in my hands I'll forget you exist. What do you say?*'

Cursing in Russian follows. '*Da. I do it.*'

'*Atta boy. We're watching and listening, so don't do anything stupid like contacting the League.*'

'*Grigor, don't help him!*' Jonathan Prudente-Poulton shouts in the background. '*They'll sell our secrets to ev—*'

With a click, the line goes dead.

Dizziness washes over me. I lower my head into my hands. 'Oh my God. Poor Jonathan!'

Carmen's voice wavers. 'His worst fear was the League being compromised. I can't bear to think how he's suffering.'

'Can you trace the call?' I ask.

TJ shakes his head. 'They used a re-router like last time.'

'What about the American? Any idea who he is?'

'It's tricky. He's careful not to give too much away.'

Marshall says, 'Whoever he is, he can't acquire ghost quartz through his usual sources. Kidnapping Jonathan and blackmailing Grigor is a pretty desperate move.'

I say, 'Wasn't Grigor recording his calls? The ones we heard in Russian? Did you have any luck with those?'

'A trusted contact is translating them but we haven't heard back yet.'

'I've been tracking Grigor.' Marshall taps the finding machine. 'He's been back to the Rollright Stones. We can assume he's re-recording the stone tapes the American stole from him. We've got two days before he heads to the Natural History Museum.'

'Two days is a long time,' I protest. 'Can't we contact the rest of the League and ask for help?'

Marshall says, 'Alex, we've been compromised. We can't trust anyone in the League. Until this thing is over, it's me, you, Carmen, and TJ. There's no cavalry coming over the hill to rescue Jonathan. It's just us.'

'Have you kept trying Jonathan's photo?' I push him.

'Of course.'

I sip my coffee, my mind racing. Maybe there is another way to find Jonathan.

In any other situation I'd deal with this alone but I need TJ's computer, email, and scanner for it to work.

'I have an idea.' I reach in my pocket and pull out my wallet, removing the scrap of paper I carry around like a talisman.

Miriam, Spirit Reader, available for all messages from the nether to the NOW! Have you lost someone you want to contact, was there something important you needed to say? Do you need to know if someone has passed over peacefully? Miriam can help you,

Clearing my throat, I say, 'I want you guys to hear me out no matter how weird this sounds. Okay?'

'Sure.' Marshall shrugs. Carmen peers over her big glasses as I pass the scrap of paper to TJ.

'There's this psychic—'

'Are you kidding?' Marshall rolls his eyes.

I throw my arms up. 'You promised to hear me out! I never thought much of psychics until I phoned Miriam. I've contacted her a couple of times and she's really helped put me on the right path.'

'Mystic Miriam claims she can contact the dead.' TJ tweaks his goatee as he reads her advert. 'That's impossible and unscientific. Psychics rely on confirmation bias, cold readings, and the gullible. There's no reliable evidence to support the paranormal and whenever they're tested under controlled conditions, they fail. They're no better than spoon benders.'

'This isn't spoon bending!' I clamp my hands to my head. 'Look, I'm sure some psychics and mediums are frauds. Maybe most of them. But Miriam's different. I can't explain how, but she has amazing insights.'

Carmen speaks up. 'Even so, contacting this lady breaches protocol and could pose a security risk. "Mystic Miriam" is an alias. Who is she, really?'

'Don't you think it's worth a shot if it brings us closer to Jonathan?' I plead.

A long pause follows. Carmen is first to relent. 'If Miriam can find Jonathan, maybe we should give it a try.'

'All right, have it your way,' says Marshall. 'TJ, can you email Jonathan's photo over to her?'

'If you insist.' TJ stares at his mug. 'We'd have more luck trying to read my tea leaves.'

23

— • —

'Can you take me to Yoioto first thing tomorrow?' I ask Marshall through a mouthful of homemade steak pie, buttery mash, and broccoli. Carmen has outdone herself with dinner and there's still apple and blackberry crumble with custard to come. 'I was thinking before seven, if possible.'

'That shouldn't be a problem.' Marshall wipes his mouth with a napkin. 'What's your cover story for being so early?'

'The same one I always use. I'm new. I'm lost. I didn't know.'

Carmen places the crumble on the table. The blackberry filling oozes over the golden crust as she scoops generous portions of dessert into three bowls and passes the custard jug around.

'I worry about you, Alex,' she says.

'Please don't.' I pour a pool of custard into my bowl. 'The fact I'm a temp is a good enough excuse for almost anything.'

Marshall's brow shoots up. 'How does that work?'

'It's easy. If anyone stops me I'll say I'm lost or the manager next door said it was fine. Or Dave said it was okay. There's always a Dave in every office.'

'And there I was thinking you were a person of integrity.' Marshall takes a large bite of crumble.

'I am,' I mumble through a mouthful of dessert.

Marshall scrapes his bowl clean, stretches back, and pats his stomach. 'You should come and stay more often.'

Carmen raises an eyebrow.

'I mean, now you're in the League,' he hurriedly adds.

143

'Carmen, that was delicious,' I say, rising from my seat. 'Do you mind if I take a bowl down to poor old TJ? I don't want him missing out.'

'That's a lovely idea,' Carmen says, taking plates to the sink.

I descend the stairs to the Vault with a tray and call TJ's name until he lets me in.

'I'm not disturbing you, am I?' I place the tray on the table. 'I brought crumble and a cup of tea.'

'Great, thanks.'

I hand him the white swipe card. 'Oh, I found this in the staff canteen.'

TJ flips the card, examining the security strip. 'Found?'

'Sort of. It looks the same as my boss's but doesn't allow access into the main lab. Can you do anything with it?'

'Maybe. Although the card's probably been deactivated if the owner reported it missing.'

'Damn.' I click my tongue. 'So, it's useless?'

'Not necessarily. I can try to re-encode the card to give you open access privileges. If that works, you'll be able to get past any swipe card reader. The system will log each access back to the original user.'

That means Cucumber girl. 'Sounds good.'

TJ strokes his sparse beard. 'Problem is, if you're caught out of bounds with an open-access card you could be in serious trouble.'

'I'll be careful.' I push my worries to one side. 'I also need access to the library catalogue. The computers use a program called Dynix Scholar.'

'Let me look it up.' TJ goes to his computer and accesses a green text menu on a black background.

As he's typing, I lean across the table. 'TJ? Do you mind if I ask what your initials stand for?'

TJ's mouth twists. 'It's an inside joke from my intern days. Jonathan gave me the nickname when he caught me hacking into the Bletchley servers.' He puts on a posh accent. '*You must think yourself quite the joker.*'

I laugh at his spot-on impersonation. 'So TJ...The Joker? I didn't think Jonathan had a sense of humour.'

'He doesn't. Marshall was the one who ran with it. TJ stuck.'

'So, what's your real na—'

'Right. Dynix is old and uses dumb terminals which is good news, as it may allow for external access. I'll do my best to find a way in, but no guarantees.'

'Just do your best,' I say in earnest. 'I really appreciate it.'

'No worries.'

I leave the Vault and escape into the garden as the sunset paints the sky with glorious orange streaks. After a day in an office it's wonderful to close my eyes and soak up the fading warmth. A pang goes through me thinking of Antony. I miss him.

I head back to my room and call him.

'Hey you!' I say as soon as he picks up. 'How're things?'

'Mad busy. I'm flat-out juggling two separate ad campaigns, but it's good money so I can't complain.' Antony pauses. 'The place is empty without you. When are you coming home?'

'It should only be a few more days.' I hear a series of beeps in the background. 'Are you still playing with that Tamagotchi?'

Antony groans. 'I'm *this* close to yanking out the batteries. Whoever said Tamagotchis are fun should have my Rancor. If I don't keep him regularly fed he goes ballistic. And I can't just feed him fat guards as he prefers shapely women as treats. He got sick this morning from binge-eating so I pressed the button to send in the medic. He only bloody ate him.'

'Poor you!' I try not to laugh.

He yawns. 'Sorry. How are things with you? Any luck finding Jonathan?'

'Not yet, but we've got some leads.'

'And Marshall's keeping you safe?'

'Everyone's looking after me. Please don't worry.' I daren't tell him about Grigor, swiping security cards and sneaking around Yoioto.

'I'm working late to clear my diary,' he says. 'Once you're back, we should go abroad for a week or two. What do you think?'

'I'd love that. Why don't you go to the travel agents and pick up some brochures?'

'Will do.' He sighs. 'Better get on with these visuals. Mind if I say goodnight?'

'No, speak soon. Love you.' I end the call.

I change into my pyjamas, thinking about what's in store. Tomorrow I must be focussed and professional. Faces swirl in my mind as I climb into bed and pull up the covers: Pierce and Mum. Dad and Carmen. Okada Atsuko. Grigor. Jonathan.

I spend a restless night tossing and turning. When the alarm blares at six, I shoot from the bed and get dressed for work. I swap out the pink striped shirt for the mumsy, floral blouse.

An envelope has been slipped under my door. Inside, I find the swipe card and a note from TJ:

1) Swipecard activated to access all areas. 2) Couldn't hack the library server. But give these a try:

TJ has added a list of logins and passwords. I fold the paper, slip it inside my wallet with the swipe card and head downstairs to the kitchen. Marshall has the coffee on but Carmen's not up yet.

'All set for today?' Marshall asks, pouring me a mug. 'Would you like toast or cereal?'

'No thanks,' I say quickly. My uneasy stomach is unable to face breakfast for the second morning in a row. 'I'd just like to go.'

At 6:50 am, Marshall pulls the car into a distant parking bay at Yoioto Corp. 'You need to eat something, Alex. I might have another muesli bar in here somewhere.' He puts his hand in his pocket.

'Don't worry. I'll get something from the canteen,' I open the car door. 'I'll call you if I have news.'

Yesterday, I dragged my clumpy heels at the thought of entering the building. Today, I stride towards the automatic doors determined to get results.

They don't open.

A security guard stares at me from behind the reception desk. I wave at him through the glass, my heart spiking.

As he approaches, I flash him my lanyard, my fingers covering the word *Visitor*.

The guard inserts a key into the lock and the doors slide open. He looks beyond my shoulder. 'Guess we're open for business. You're the second one in. Big meeting or something?'

'Something like that.'

I follow his gaze. Cars are pulling into the car park. Yoioto employees are early birds.

'Who beat me?' I ask, hoping to God it's not Okada.

'The V.P. Mr Matsuoka.'

I shrug. 'Maybe next time.' I can breathe again.

My first port of call is the library which lies in darkness. I hit the switch for the overheads and rush to the computer terminals. Their screens are dead. I follow the cables to the power strip under the desk and switch them on.

The computers chug and beep to life. I sit in front of one, tapping my fingers on the desk and throwing panicky glances at the door until it has booted up.

LOG IN > PASSWORD >

I open TJ's instructions. His suggestions are ludicrous. This has to be a joke.

LOG IN > **admin** PASSWORD > **password**

The fields go blank, which means TJ guessed wrong. I plough through the rest of his list without a smidgen of hope.

LOG IN > **admin** PASSWORD > **12345**

LOG IN > **admin** PASSWORD > **11111**

LOG IN > **admin** PASSWORD > **00000**

I change the login to **root**, and run through the passwords, then **sysadmin**, then **guest**.

LOG IN > **guest** PASSWORD > **12345**

ENTER YOUR SELECTION(S) AND PRESS <ENTER> :

I can't believe it. I'm in.

My first search is for ghost quartz but nothing comes up. I enter *Static Tape*. After much grinding and growling, a text block appears. My heart catches in my throat.

TITLE: "Static Tape in Commercial Applications, 1965-1971"
DDS: 608.13
AUTHORS: T. Matsuoka, Y. Schieder, M. Keller
ABSTRACT: "Yoioto's experimental static conductor tape does not require magnetic heads to record and overwrite data. The prototype is more robust than conventional polymer. Its thermosetting resin coating renders the tape weatherproof and scratchproof. Downsides include limited storage capacity, inflexibility and specific transmission requirements, making it unsuitable for commercial use. The format is considered obsolete."

The document proves Yoioto produced static tape around the time Dad was building the finding machine. It's a start.

I hit 'print,' but nothing happens. The laser printer is off. I crawl back under the desk, switch the printer on and try again. A figure walks up to the door as the printer whirrs to life. I grab the warm sheet of paper the moment it feeds through and shove it in my pocket.

The door opens as I log off the library computer. A woman in a burgundy skirt suit walks in.

Turning away, I duck behind a bookcase and start scouring the shelves for 608.13. I follow the ascending numbers to a shelf in the corner to the correct section.

608.13 is the second-to-bottom row. I double-check the titles with the number taped on the spine but *"Static Tape in Commercial Applications"* isn't there.

I leave the library wearing a pleasantly neutral expression as I pass the woman at the computer. I don't make eye contact because I don't want her to remember me. In the corridor, I hide the printout inside my rucksack with my heart thudding. The retro lab can wait.

I run up two flights of stairs to Okada's office and stop outside. My hand hovers over the door handle.

First, I knock. When no one answers I try the handle. The door swings open.

Ducking inside, I resist the urge to draw the blinds even though I'm visible from the car park. Okada will notice if she arrives early. She also might see me if I stand too close to the window. I can't afford to hang around.

My attempt to search her drawers fails. They're locked. Her in tray is empty apart from a schedule with team meetings for September. Address labels are stacked in the out-tray. Underneath are purchase orders from a local printing company and a letter from the Japanese branch about new appointments.

Two boxes behind her desk contain company newsletters.

My heart rate quickens. Okada's work diary sits atop her desk, unguarded.

I open it at the ribbon marker to the current week. Yesterday's box contains two entries: *am: Susan Moore, Temp. 1pm R&D team catch-up.*

Today's box contains my false name but nothing else. No meetings that might take Okada out of the office. I flick back to March and July when Jonathan visited her. There are multiple appointments and notes but no references to static tape, the League, or Jonathan.

My gaze goes to a pink snap folder nestled between her monitor and a potted bonsai bamboo tree. I ease the folder away from the plant. Inside is an American letter-sized document with lots of red print, capitals, and underlining.

US CITIZENSHIP & IMMIGRATION SERVICES. *Re: AKI ATSUKO (MRS) d.o.b. 8th October 1942*

We have identified a problem with your Certificate of Naturalization and require further information. Please send your original Certificate, USCIS/A-Number, and birth certificate. Failure to provide the required documents <u>within ninety days</u> will result in

*the revocation of your certificate, and your citizenship status deemed
null and void.*

Sincerely,

Customer Service Department 458/799

Is Aki Atsuko Okada's mother? Heat rises to my cheeks at reading her personal information. I return the official letter inside the pink folder.

The door handle creaks.

I jump in my skin. Swiftly, I slot the pink folder beside the bonsai tree, rush back to my desk and busy myself switching on my computer.

Okada Atsuko enters the office with a designer bag over her forearm and a takeaway Costa coffee in the other hand.

'You're early!' she says. Her eyes flick from me to her desk.

'I wanted to be on time. I suppose I overdid it!' My voice comes out high-pitched.

Cringing, I stare at my PC to hide my burning cheeks.

I left her diary open to the wrong week. Why, oh why, didn't I think to close it!

24

Okada places her coffee on a coaster and runs her finger down the open pages of her work diary. She flips the pages forward to the correct week. A tiny frown crosses her face.

I force a smile, rubbing my hands together. 'What would you like me to do?'

'Our monthly newsletter needs to go out.' She walks to the boxes stacked behind her desk, removes a slim, glossy brochure from the topmost one and hands it to me.

"Company Restructure, California," reads the headline, with a photo of two suited men shaking hands in front of a shiny, glass-fronted building. Beneath the photo is an upwardly trending graph that's sure to please the share holders. The rest of the brochure contains articles on magnetic drive capacity improvements, storage subsystems and disk platters. Deadly dull stuff.

Okada removes the labels I saw earlier from her in tray and places them on my desk. Each sheet contains twenty-one labels, and there's a heck of a lot of them. My fears are confirmed when Okada brings over two massive boxes of envelopes. I can see the day slipping through my fingers along with any further chances to investigate.

'I'd better get started,' I say brightly.

Ms Atsuko sips her coffee. 'I wanted to let you know, this will be your last day at Yoioto.'

'Oh?' I look up from the newsletter with a knot forming in my stomach. 'I feel like I was getting into my stride.'

I casually glance around the room, wondering if she's sussed me out. Maybe there are hidden cameras in the corners of the room or the pot plants. The security guard might have told her I was snooping around the library earlier. I suppress an urge to put my hand in my pocket to check my swipe card is still there.

Okada folds her arms, forefinger tapping her pin stripe sleeve. 'It's rare I say this but you really are too efficient for your own good. I thought the work would take you longer.' She pauses. 'I'll be sure to write you a good reference.'

'Thank you.' I grind my teeth at the thought I've curtailed my time here by being too good at my job. Or, maybe it's just her excuse.

Sending out the newsletters is probably the last thing I'll do before she sends me home. The best course of action is to continue being speedy and efficient. If I get my head down and plough through the lot before lunch, it should buy me time to investigate the retro lab.

I count the address labels, sizing up the job. There are hundreds, a regular mass mailing for a company of this size.

After an hour, I'm making good progress when my hand suddenly cramps. As I pause to flex my fingers and massage my palm, a label catches my eye:

A12 Melvyn Potter, The Analogue Laboratory, YOIOTO CORP.

Keeping my movements to a minimum, I place Melvyn's newsletter at the bottom of the pile. I search through the internal post until I see another name I recognise, Audrey Luft-Beutelspacher, the researcher who showed her findings to Okada yesterday.

Okada says over my shoulder, 'Please take a break if you want tea or coffee. You need to keep hydrated.'

'I'd rather push on,' I say, speedily slipping a newsletter into an envelope. 'These won't stuff themselves.'

'I admire your work ethic,' Okada says. 'I'll add that to your reference.'

Once Okada has returned to her desk I place Audrey's envelope with Melvyn Potter's.

By eleven o'clock I'm three-quarters through the pile. Okada makes and takes calls but they're as dull as the envelopes I'm stuffing. At eleven forty-five I've moved onto franking the external mail, when a knock comes at the door.

'Come in!' Okada calls.

The door opens and a slender, middle-aged Japanese woman enters with two white carrier bags. A delicious aroma wafts from the bags, reminiscent of my local Chinese restaurant, but with an additional savoury tang that makes my mouth water.

The woman is dressed elegantly in a white linen shirt, black trousers, and red patent penny loafers. Owl-framed glasses hang from a sparkly chain around her neck. A slick of orangey-red lipstick completes the look.

'Mom!' Okada exclaims. She slides the pink folder from her desk and tucks it away in a drawer, then hops from her chair to greet her mum with a kiss on the cheek.

'Why didn't you tell me you were coming?' Okada asks, taking the bags.

'You always too busy to take my call,' Mrs Atsuko says pointedly. Her brows rise and her forehead creases. 'I thought if you too busy to talk, maybe too busy to eat?'

Okada peers inside the packages. 'Mom, you've made enough for the entire department!'

'You need to eat more. Your legs like chopsticks.' She peers around at me for the first time. 'This the new girl? She can share, though she does not need to eat so much.'

My mouth drops.

'This is Susan.' Okada places the bags on the edge of her desk. 'She's here as a temp.'

Her mother switches to Japanese. *'Ī toshi shite jitsumu keiken nante. Kazoku ya kodomo no sewa o shite hoshīkedo nā.'*

Whatever she's saying sounds about as complimentary as her dig at my weight.

Okada places a hand on her mother's shoulder. 'Don't start, Mom. Things have moved on since your day.'

She steers her mother to the chair by her desk, but the older woman refuses to sit. Instead, she walks over to my desk and stares at my left hand. 'Women who work too much not find man.' She gives her daughter a loaded stare.

Okada holds her gaze. 'I'm happy being single.'

'Happy now. But later when you look in mirror and see old face, not so happy.' Mrs Atsuko walks to the rubber plant at the back of the room. She runs her hand over the leaf and examines her fingertips before pressing her finger into the soil.

'Small details are most important,' she tuts.

I hide a smile, amused rather than angry at her interference. She's so similar to my mum. If I substitute soda bread for sushi, they're more or less the same person.

Okada puts her hands on her hips. 'If you want to clean my office and water my plants, go ahead.'

'I am not a cleaner.' Mrs Atsuko sits and turns Okada's mouse upside down, pursing her lips at the fluff collecting around the ball before setting it down on the mat. 'You are now career woman. I have looked after you long enough. I'm ready to go home to America. I miss my friends.'

Okada's tone softens. 'I understand, Mom, and we've been through this. Just a couple more weeks, then we'll book your flight.'

'Why not book flight now?' Mrs Okada juts her chin towards the desk phone.

'It's not a good time!'

'Never good time with you!'

Feeling like a third wheel, I resume franking the external mail.

Mrs Atsuko crosses her arms and throws herself back into her chair. 'I want my apartment and my pot plants. I miss Karuta club. Most of all, I miss golf. I'm so out of practice Aiko will thrash me.'

'You'll be home doing everything you love in a few weeks. I promise.' Okada's mouth twists. 'To be honest, Mom, I don't want you to leave yet. I love having you here.'

Mrs Atsuko's eyes widen. 'Then come to America.'

I'm almost certain Okada's feigned enthusiasm concerns the notice from U.S. immigration. Unless she's sorted it already she won't want to send her mother on a five-thousand-mile journey into the arms of stern-faced officials.

Mrs Atsuko removes a tower of plastic food tubs from the bags, releasing an incredible aroma of chicken and savoury rice. She removes three cardboard bowls.

'We're eating now?' Okada says, checking her watch. 'I'm in the middle of something.'

'You always in the middle. Now we eat like family.' Her eyes flick to me. 'She can be distant cousin.'

Fulfilling my role as a long lost relative, I accept my bowl and wooden chopsticks. Lunch is a riot of colourful vegetables with a soft mound of rice and golden fried chicken cutlets with sliced eggs and spring onions.

Mrs Atsuko spies my clumsy attempts to eat with chopsticks. She digs into one of the bags and hands me a plastic spork.

'Thank you.' I smile and tuck into delicious chicken and enough vegetables to cover my five-a-day. 'This is incredible!'

Mrs Atsuko nods. She holds the bowl close to her chin. Her chopsticks move from bowl to mouth without dropping a grain of rice. Okada eats less enthusiastically. Mother and daughter chat about the weather and plans for the weekend before reverting to Japanese.

Okada speaks rapidly, repeating certain phrases. Even though I don't understand the language the two women sound like they're on different wavelengths.

Aware of passing time, I finish my meal and continue franking the post. The two women are still talking when I frank the last envelope. Gathering up both piles, I walk to the door.

'Susan, where are you going?' Okada asks.

'I'm all done. I'll take these down to the mailroom.'

Okada stares at me, her mouth a thin line. 'If you wait, I'll walk down with you.'

'Why you babysitting her?' Mrs Atsuko breaks in. 'She is grown woman.'

I grin, suppressing an urge to hug her.

'Don't worry, I know where everything is,' I say breezily.

Before Okada can protest, I slip outside and close the door behind me.

<h1 style="text-align:center">25</h1>

I descend the stairs in a rush, pushing my heels back in my shoes to keep them on my feet. I reach the ground floor and hurry to the mailroom, praying Mrs Atsuko keeps her daughter talking.

Shouldering the door open, I throw the envelopes into the Internal and External trays, keeping the two addressed to Melvyn and Audrey. I ignore the sullen look the jowly fellow gives me. His face must have stuck that way when the wind changed.

I turn my head from the receptionist as I cross the reception area towards the canteen doors, then turn down the corridor leading to the laboratory.

A red light glows on the security pad by the door down the end.

A cold sweat breaks out on my forehead as I ready the swipe card. I glance through the window to check the coast is clear, then run the card through the reader.

The light turns green. My breath releases in a shudder as I shove the card into my pocket and push through.

A technician walks towards me from the main lab. I hold the door open for him and force a smile with my heart thudding in my ears.

'Cheers,' he says as he walks past.

My arms shake as I release the door. I enter the main lab and take a second to get my bearings. There are nine or ten lab workers dotted around the spacious room. I walk past a row of booths, making a beeline for the retro lab. In my haste, my shoe comes off.

157

As I bend to slip it back on a woman says, 'Excuse me? Susan, isn't it?'

I slowly straighten at Audrey Luft-Beutelspacher's authoritative tone. She locks her gaze with mine before looking over my shoulder. Lines deepen between her brows. 'Isn't Ms Atsuko with you?'

Butterflies go into a frenzy inside my stomach.

'The mailroom made a mess of the last internal mailout and Ms Atsuko wasn't best pleased.' I pass her the envelope, hoping she doesn't notice my trembling fingers. 'She wanted me to deliver this personally.'

Audrey glances at the label. Her eyes widen. 'Is this her response to my findings? I was just about to chase her up about it.' She tears the flap open.

'Actually...it's the latest newsletter. Hot off the press.' My cheeks burn. The envelope holds nothing remotely interesting.

'Oh.' Audrey drops the partly-opened envelope on the corner of her booth. 'I'll look at it later. I'd better give Okada a call.'

My pulse thuds at my temples. 'Don't worry, I'll ask her to call you when I get back.'

Audrey smiles wryly. 'At my age, you learn to do things while they're fresh in your mind.'

My face falls as she picks up the phone. My plan's falling to pieces. I rack my brain for a reason to stall her but come up with nothing.

'Audrey?' A young lab technician approaches, his nose buried in a dot matrix printout. 'Have you got a minute? We've found anomalies within the LTO access tests. I'm not sure if it's human error or a problem with the batch results. Could you take a look?'

Audrey's gaze flicks to me. To my relief, she sets the phone down. 'Anomalies? You'd better show me how you ran the tests.'

I wave and walk away, taking a zig-zag route to the retro lab. Audrey accompanies the technician to a workstation on the opposite side of the lab. Hopefully, he'll keep her occupied long enough for me to slip in and out of the Analogue Lab unobserved.

My nerves are jangling, but I've come too far to turn back. In all probability, Audrey will call Okada when she gets back to her desk so I'm stuffed whether I stay or go.

Hurrying to the retro lab door, I peer inside. The technician from yesterday sits with his back to me wearing headphones. No one else is with him. I suppress the urge to cheer.

I rap on the door. He doesn't react. Balling my fist, I hesitate before knocking harder, unwilling to draw unwanted attention to myself.

I try the handle. The door opens and I slip inside, closing the door behind me.

The Analogue Laboratory consists of a square workspace with a double-width doorway opposite, fitted with a raised security shutter leading to a storage corridor. Strains of mellow music drift from the corridor. I recognise the female vocalist's rich, emotional tones. She was one of my father's favourites but I can't recall her name.

Above the technician, a grey metal shelf contains multicoloured Bakelite phones along with a candlestick phone straight out of a black-and-white movie. Storage racks are cluttered with old computers, monitors, and typewriters. In one corner is a wheeled metal machine with arms and claw hands that resembles a primitive robot. I look for static tape but nothing catches my eye.

The bitter odour of solder hangs in the air, transporting me back to Dad's workshop where he used to tinker with circuit boards. Mustering courage, I approach Melvyn from the side with a wave and a smile.

He jumps in his seat, bumping his *Kempton Steam Museum* mug. Tea sloshes onto the desk.

'I'm so sorry!' I rummage in my pocket for a tissue.

Melvyn waves me off and uses a stained rag to mop the spill, his brows drawing together. He throws the wet cloth in the bin, presses a button on the bank of switches in front of him and removes his headphones. His untidy hair and chunky, black-rimmed glasses give him the look of an eccentric professor.

'I really am sorry,' I say. 'I hope I didn't ruin your work.'

He leans back to study me before glancing at the closed door. 'You gave me a fright.'

'I did knock but...' I gesture to his headphones.

'Don't worry. No damage done.' Melvyn gives a rueful smile and sips from his mug. 'Most importantly, I still have most of my tea.'

I smile as relief floods through me. 'I'm Susan from Tape Storage Solutions.'

'Well, Susan, this is a first. Ms Atsuko has never sent anyone from her department to see me before.'

'I hope I'm not intruding.'

'On the contrary. It makes a nice change to have a visitor.' He smiles. 'How can I help?'

I place the envelope on his desk. 'I brought your post. And...I was actually hoping you could show me some of the old tech you're working on.'

Melvyn places his hand on an old grey typewriter with a strip of yellow tape fed through one side. 'Like this ticker tape machine?'

'Well, I was thinking more o—'

'This old thing's a museum piece.' Melvyn gives it a fond pat. 'It needs telegraph signals to function. That's the problem. Some things no longer have a place in today's world.'

My panic recedes at Melvyn's open, friendly manner.

'I'm more interested in Yoioto's older line products. Obsolete tech. Things like pagers.'

'Pagers aren't obsolete.' Melvyn's brows rise. 'The NHS still uses them, along with telex numbers.' He gives me a curious look. 'What brought about this interest? I thought you youngsters were into mobile phones and PlayStations?'

'My dad got me hooked when he built our TV. He was always replacing valves and making adjustments using the testcard. Whenever I smell lead solder or static on an old TV screen, it takes me right back.'

Melvyn laughs. 'I wouldn't advise putting your nose too close to a CRT screen. You're only half an inch away from fifty thousand volts.' He drains his tea and pushes himself to his feet. 'If you want to see a proper museum piece, follow me.'

He strides into the well-lit storage corridor. I linger a few paces behind, staring at the pre-modern electronic equipment lining the walls. I'm facing a mammoth search; there must be hundreds, if not thousands of items The music gets louder the farther we go. I recognise the theme from an animated film I saw in the '80s.

Melvyn stops by a pea-coloured behemoth covered in plastic sheeting. It's so large it takes up most of the corridor. Eight-foot-tall panels surround the central control column. Green padded seats encircle the base.

He turns the volume down on a compact music centre on a nearby shelf.

'This is a replica of the Cray-1 supercomputer.' Melvyn removes his glasses and chews on the tip. 'It's missing many components but even if we were to replace them it would never work again. The Cray requires its own refrigeration unit and uses so much power it would probably trip the breakers at the local substation.'

The phone rings out front. My mouth goes dry. I have a terrifying suspicion it's Okada.

Melvyn stares over my shoulder. 'I should get th—'

'Do you have any old tape formats?' I ask in a rush.

Melvyn drags his gaze back to the music centre and picks up a Linda Rondstadt cassette case.

'Like this?' He gazes adoringly at the singer on the cover. I wonder which he loves more, Linda, or the storage medium containing her songs. 'Nostalgia's a funny thing. Compact disks are a superior format, yet we still love our old cassettes and mixtapes.'

The phone stops ringing.

'I read about an obsolete Yoioto tape format somewhere,' I push him. 'It was called something like...I remember now...st—'

'Most tape formats will never be obsolete,' Melvyn interrupts. 'Tape is cheap and its offline nature makes it resistant to cyberattacks. It's where most of the world's data is stored.'

My attention goes to a workbench a little further down. I slip past Melvyn to the bench which contains plastic baths full of pungent liquid solvent, a stack of long, cardboard boxes and a large jar containing thin black strips that float in solution. The strips reflect the overhead lights in a distinctive green and azure bluebottle sheen.

I cover my mouth. They're the same as the contact strips on my finding machine.

'What are these?' I ask breathlessly.

His brows rise. 'They're prototypes. But they're not obsolete. They were never manufactured.'

I pick up the bottle and examine the contents. The lid on the topmost box is partially open. Inside, long strips of tape bearing the same blue-green sheen as the sample in the bottle nestle inside a foam protector.

'You'd better put that back,' Melvyn says, hand outstretched for the bottle.

'Is this static tape?'

Melvyn's mouth drops. He closes the box. 'Please, give me the bottle.'

But I can't take my eyes off the treasure in my hands. 'Who are you making this for?'

'I'm sorry, Susan. I think it's time for you to go. I have to return that phon—'

'Melvyn!'

I jump at the shrill command. The bottle slips from my grip and smashes on the floor. Acrid fumes erupt from the liquid and make my head reel.

I clamp my hand over my nose and turn from the stinging vapour.

Okada strides towards me. Her mouth drops.

'Susan? What are you doing here?'

'We were just talking.' Blinking my stinging eyes, I stare at the fragments of tape lying in a puddle on the floor. I'm itching to pick up the tape sample, but it's impossible with Melvyn and Okada staring at me.

'Sorry,' Melvyn says. 'I'll get this cleaned up.'

'Leave it for now,' Okada says. 'Melvyn, would you mind stepping outside? I need to have a word with Susan.'

'Of course.' Melvyn gives me a bewildered look through his thick lenses before leaving the storeroom.

Okada's pale face bears no trace of a smile. She stands before me with her hands on hips, blocking the way out. I stare longingly at the exit past her shoulder, dreading what's coming.

'I warned Melvyn not to talk about our project with anyone. But he doesn't get many visitors and he loves to talk.' She narrows her eyes. 'I should call security.'

My mind races. Whatever happens, I can't let her do that.

'Melvyn's a retro enthusiast like me,' I say. 'We were talking about old tech.'

Okada crosses her arms. 'Other temps, they come in, do their work and go home. But right from the get-go you showed an unusual level of interest in Yoioto's obsolete technology and this lab.' She narrows her eyes. 'I had HR do a background check on you. There's no Susan Moore with your social security number. If you're not Susan Moore, who are you?'

I press my lips together and stare at the floor. I thought Marshall would have done a better job with my alias.

Okada's lips press together. 'If you don't tell me who you are and why you're sneaking around I'll have security escort you to Mr Matsuoka. He is extremely protective of Yoioto's heritage and takes a dim view of spies.'

I straighten and take a deep breath. My new knowledge gives me leverage. If I want to get out of this mess I have to use it.

'Does Mr Matsuoka know about this?' I put my hand out to the boxes of static tape. 'Yoioto abandoned static tape years ago, so why are you manufacturing it again? If this was an official company project the technicians would be making it in the main lab. But here you are, doing it in secret.'

Red points flare on Okada's cheeks. 'This is none of your business!'

'It is when people get hurt.' I stand my ground. 'I know that Jonathan Prudente-Poulton asked you to make the tape. He's in deep trouble, Okada.'

'Jonat—' She puts her hand to her mouth, her eyes widening. 'Oh, God. You work for the League.'

She staggers over to the Cray and sinks onto the padded seat.

I stand in front of her. 'Jonathan's been abducted. It's connected to the static tape and if we don't help him he could die.'

Okada turns her cheek and brushes a tear away.

I extract a tissue from my pocket and hand it to her. 'What's going on?'

Okada dabs her eyes. 'Please go back to the League and tell them to stay out of my business.'

'I can't do that. I have to help Jonathan. Don't you want to help him, Okada? Have you betrayed him?'

'I would never do that!' She blinks rapidly. 'Jonathan started this. If it wasn't for him Mom would be safe and I wouldn't be sick to my stomach every time the phone rings or a letter drops on the mat.'

'Someone's blackmailing you? I saw the letter from U.S. Immigration.'

Okada's mouth falls open. 'You've been through my things?'

'I was trying to help. Trust me, Okada, we can work this out. My father was a member of the League. He upheld its values as do I. We need to work together.'

'Why should I trust you?' Okada presses her lips together in a tight line. 'You won't even tell me your name.'

'I'm Alexandra Martin. My friends call me Alex.'

26

— · —

'Jonathan came to visit me in April,' Okada says, one hand gripping the Cray's green seat. 'He brought a sample of static tape. It was in the jar you smashed.'

'Sorry about that.' I wince. 'You gave me such a fright I lost my grip. Can the tape be saved?'

'We'll have to see,' Okada says.

'Please, go on.'

'Jonathan asked me to manufacture static tape in our lab but refused to tell me why. I told him my bosses were unlikely to allocate a budget, technicians, or lab space to recreate an obsolete format unless he put forward a proposal showing its specific applications.' Okada's gaze shifts to the floor. 'Jonathan said if we revived the format, the League would buy as much as we could make.'

Questions bubble inside me but I keep them to myself.

'To have any chance of gaining approval, we first had to reproduce the sample,' Okada says. 'I asked Melvyn to work on the static tape as a side project. It was no easy task. He experienced multiple setbacks and failures before the reproduction passed quality control. Jonathan returned in July to check on progress. I've never seen him so happy. He offered a significant sum of money to boost production.

'My bosses still said no, though, because Jonathan refused to divulge the tape's commercial possibilities. In hindsight, I should have stopped production at that point, but the scientist in me was intrigued and Melvyn was having a field day.'

The corners of Okada's mouth turn down. 'Then, a week ago I had a call from a stranger. An American. He said he had Jonathan and threatened to harm him if I didn't do what he said.'

'I'm guessing he wanted the tape?'

Okada nods. 'I was scared for Jonathan, but terrified about what this meant for me. I said no and hung up. I rushed to a payphone and called the League but I couldn't get through. I returned to the office and tried emailing them but the systems were down. Then, the American called back.'

I lean forwards, hanging onto every word.

Okada takes in a ragged breath. 'He said I'd better not hang up this time. He had contacts in U.S. Immigration and if I didn't do as he said he'd have Mom deported. At first, I didn't believe him. The next day I received a letter by international courier.'

'The one I found? Are you sure it's the real thing?'

Okada nods. 'It has watermarks, an embossed seal, a barcode. It's real all right. The American isn't playing around. The Immigration and Naturalisation Service has threatened to revoke Mom's citizenship and send her back to Japan!' She dabs her eyes with a tissue. 'Mom left Osaka after the war with nothing except a suitcase full of clothes and an envelope full of worthless currency. She didn't have a passport or birth certificate. America gave her an identity.

'In her heart, Mom's American. She loves her life there. Since Dad died her friends have become her family. How can I break it to her that the country she loves so much wants to kick her out?'

'So you're doing what the American says?' I curl a fist, nails digging into my palms

'What choice do I have?' Okada's brows scrunch together. 'He wants every bit of static tape including the samples, then he'll call the dogs off. Mom will be free to return to America and Jonathan will be released.'

I shake my head, sickened by the idea of this villain getting what he wants. 'There's no guarantee he'll keep his word.'

'He promised.' Okada blinks rapidly.

I rub my forehead. 'Did the American give his name or who he works for? Did you get his phone number?'

Ms Atsuko's face falls. 'He withholds his number when he calls.'

'How will you deliver the static tape to him?'

Okada drops her voice. 'He hasn't told me, yet.'

I take a step closer. 'We can catch the American with your help.'

Okada's lip trembles. 'I can't risk Mom's future.'

I take her hands in mine. 'What if there's a way to help your mum and get Jonathan back?' I can't think of anything off the top of my head, but Marshall will have plenty of ideas. 'Would you help us?'

'You...as in the League?' Okada blinks rapidly and pulls her hands free. 'If I say yes, what would I have to do?'

• • • • • • • • • • •

I call Marshall from the bench in the formal garden under the cherry tree. The sounds of rustling leaves and the spluttering fountain soothes my spirits after a long, fraught day.

'It's early,' Marshall says. 'Are you in trouble?'

'No, everything's fine. Can you pick me up? I'm all done here.'

'You'll have to wait. I'm in the middle of something.'

'Be as quick as you can,' I say.

I hang up and check my phone. One missed call from Moira and a text message from Mystic Miriam:

```
Alex, it's good to hear from you. I hope
to shed light on your missing boss. I have
a free slot this evening @ 8 p.m. Mystic
Miriam. Ask & the universe will answer!
```

I text back to confirm the phone appointment before dialling Moira.

'Hello Alex,' she answers chirpily.

'Hi. I missed your call. Is everything okay? How's Mum?'

'Fine. She went to Sligo Retail Park to buy a linen suit. I needn't mention a certain someone she's trying to impress.'

'Why didn't you go with her?'

'I've been too busy investigating! I checked up on the address you gave me.'

I sit forward on the bench, clutching the phone tightly. When I forwarded Pierce's address to Moira I never thought she'd actually do anything about it. 'You found the place?'

'Easy as pie. It was clear skies and a perfect day for a drive down to Longford. I grew up around there, you know. Kennedy Drive is just around the corner from Saint Mel's Cathedral.'

'Saint Mel? I've never heard of him.'

'He's famous in these parts for being Saint Patrick's nephew, and for ploughing up a live fish from a field to prove he wasn't canoodling with his aunt. The locals needed a miracle to prove his innocence.'

I stifle a laugh. 'Something fishy was going on.'

'You know what people are like. They gossip and blow the whole thing up until it's the size of the moon.'

That's rich coming from Moira, who should win an award for spreading misinformation.

'I was tempted to nip inside the cathedral and light a quick candle for my parents, God rest their souls, but I want you to know my mind was firmly on the job.'

'Okay, so what did you find out?'

'I found the house and parked a way up the road. Sure enough, there was Pierce's car outside the house. I even made a note of the time.'

'That's very good, Moira.' I perk up, hopeful for a juicy revelation or two. 'Did you see him leave the house?'

'Well, now here's the thing. I arrived nice and early with a thermos of coffee. Investigators always have a thermos in the undercover dramas. Coffee is supposed to keep you going, but all it did was make me want to go. Before long I was in dire straits. Things got so desperate I had to leave my post in the hope of finding a public convenience, but I had to make do with a bush at the top of the rise. I thought I was hidden from the houses, only I forgot to look the other way.'

I stifle a groan.

'There was a class of schoolchildren playing rounders and they stopped to have a good gawp. Their teacher didn't look at all pleased. In my haste to restore my dignity I tripped over my trousers and tumbled back through the hedge and down the hill. Things were quite bad by now, as you can imagine. A passing woman told me that kind of behaviour could get me arrested. The cheek of her!'

I close my eyes, but the image of Moira's fall from grace is cemented in my mind. I decide this will be the last time I delegate spying to someone so incompetent.

'But don't think my mind wasn't on the job, Alexandra. I sorted myself out and returned to the house to find Pierce outside his door. There's no need to worry because I hid behind a tree.'

Slurping sounds come down the line.

'Are you all right?'

'Sorry, it's the last of the coffee. I'm gasping.'

'What happened then?'

'Pierce was embracing a woman on the doorstep. She had short ginger hair, freckles, and strong hands. The type who'd have made an excellent washer-woman back in my mother's day.'

'Were they kissing?'

'No. But she had a dewy look in her eye.'

'Dewy?'

'That's what I said. Then Pierce got in his car and drove off.

'What age was the woman?'

'Late fifties, early sixties.'

'Could she be his ex-wife?'

'You tell me,' Moira says. 'I thought exes were supposed to hate each other. Maybe she's another one of his willing women. Anyway, after she'd gone inside, I looked through the letterbox for clues. I saw a mountain bike and skateboard painted with red flames and those little wheels.'

'Skateboards tend to have wheels,' I say.

'Some don't,' Moira replies, a touch indignant.

I stare up through the cherry tree's canopy, praying for strength. 'They're snowboards.'

'Ah, so that's what they are. Well, this wasn't one of them. It was a wheelie one.'

'What else did you see in the hallway? Any photos of Pierce with the woman and the kids?'

'No, sorry. But I did look through the lounge window.'

'Moira, you could have been seen!'

'Well, I wasn't. They have a sofa, a TV, a potted cactus...and Scrabble. I didn't want to take any more risks. After what happened earlier I might have compromised myself.'

'You think?'

'What should I tell your mum?'

'Nothing! Don't tell her anything. She could be a sister or a close friend.'

'That's true. I hadn't thought of that. I should keep tracking him. Let me know where he goes next and I'll keep investigating him,' Moira says. 'All in all, it's been a grand day out for me.'

Only Moira would think that rolling down a hill and mooning the local school kids would count as a day well spent.

'I might just pop into St Mel's after all and say a few prayers before I head home. Bye, now, Alexandra. Over and out.'

Shaking my head, I change Moira's name on my phone to *IRISH_BRANCH*.

I put my phone in my pocket and sling my rucksack over my shoulder as a black Lexus turns into the car park.

27

— • —

Marshall keeps the engine running while I jump in the car. 'Are you okay?' His gaze searches mine. 'Were you compromised?'

'Yes and no.' Seeing him stiffen, I swiftly add, 'It all worked out. I'll tell you on the way.'

Marshall shifts into Drive and cruises out of the car park. I secure my seatbelt, watching the Yoioto Corporation recede in my wing mirror. I bid it farewell. With any luck, I won't be back.

Kicking off my shoes, I dig my toes into the luxurious footwell carpet. After turning the air conditioning down a notch I ask, 'What took you so long?'

'I was at Grigor's house.' He drops a TDK C-90 cassette tape in my lap. 'Recognise this?'

My mouth falls open at the label: *Rollright Stones 24th August 2000.*

'I found it in Grigor's study with two other audio cassettes. Ideally, I'd have copied it but we need the originals. With any luck, Grigor will think he's mislaid the tape under his mess.'

Curiosity burns in me regarding this experiment that started with Dad's videotapes.

'We have to find out what's on the cassettes and why the American wants them. In the meantime, TJ got the Russian translations back.'

I recall the tape recording in Grigor's study with several men talking gruffly in their mother tongue. 'What did you find out?'

'The two Russians on tape work for the American,' Marshall says. 'They begin by demanding the stone tapes. Grigor puts up a good fight but eventually agrees to hand them over. Then, they ramp up the pressure for the ghost quartz.'

'What does Grigor do?'

'Tries to stall. The Russians threaten him in no uncertain terms. Eventually, he agrees to a handover date outside the Natural History Museum.'

'Lovely people,' I say. 'No wonder Grigor was touchy when he saw you.'

Marshall glances my way. 'That's my day. How about yours?'

I fill him in on my adventures and conclude, 'The American wants Okada to hand over the static tape. She's terrified of upsetting him in case he has her mother deported.'

'I would be, too. If the American is powerful enough to get Homeland Security to do his bidding we have to take him seriously.'

I chew my lip. 'Can you get U.S. Immigration to back off Okada?'

'Are you kidding me?' Marshall's voice goes up an octave. 'They're worse than the IRS.'

'We have to help her.'

'And we will,' Marshall assures me. 'When Okada does the handover we'll be watching. I have a trick up my sleeve that should lead us to Jonathan.'

I sigh, staring out the window. Seagulls glide and swoop over a field in the wake of a tractor pulling a plough. 'Are you absolutely certain Jonathan's innocent?'

Marshall's brows rise. 'What's brought this on?'

'Do you remember Jonathan's note you found in his study?' At his nod, I continue. 'Jonathan wrote something about the genie being out of the bottle and he couldn't control it. Yet, despite his concerns, he continued reviving the stone tapes project, sourcing static tape and ghost quartz. Why didn't he involve you? You're head of security.'

We round a corner into blazing sunlight. Marshall squints and lowers the sun visor. 'Jonathan rarely goes into details about his meetings or his clients. He has his reasons.'

'Don't you think you should have known?'

Marshall mutters something.

I lunge for the grab handle as the car surges out of lane to overtake a black van. The acceleration pushes me back in my seat. An oncoming BMW zooms towards us.

Marshall tucks back into his lane a split second before the BMW speeds past.

'Jeez, that was close!' My breath explodes out.

'Nothing to it.' Marshall takes one hand from the wheel and pops a mint into his mouth. He doesn't offer me one.

'Look, if you're touchy because of what I sai—'

'Who's touchy?' Marshall says. 'The van was too slow, that's all.'

Keeping a firm grip on the door handle, I say, 'If I ask another question, promise you won't do the *Gone in 60 Seconds* thing again?'

Marshall glances my way, his shoulders dropping. 'Go on.'

'Okay. Jonathan offered Okada a significant amount of money for the static tape. Where was that money coming from?'

After a long pause, Marshall says, 'Jonathan manages all the League finances.'

'So, he's in charge of the pot?'

'Yep.'

'What if the American is a private donor? He could have given the League money in exchange for the static tape.'

Marshall shakes his head. 'Jonathan would never knowingly sell our secrets. The American hacked the League computers and compromised us. Whatever Jonathan did, he had no choice.'

I bite my lower lip. 'Jonathan disappeared without triggering the Lodge's perimeter alarm. What if he was a willing party?'

'No way. You heard the tape. It's more likely the American blackmailed him into using his keys and codes to exit the Lodge unnoticed.'

It's pointless arguing. Marshall won't allow a bad word to be said about his boss. My mind wanders to the American and the clone Drive. The boxes of static tape in Melvyn's lab will make hundreds more Drives. But I suspect those Drives won't work without one other vital, missing component.

I think back to the day I arrived at Red Croft Lodge. TJ showed me a sample of static tape and slides containing mineral particles. He was evasive when I asked what the pale specks were and I didn't push it further. I should have.

'Is ghost quartz inside my Drive?' I ask bluntly.

Marshall remains silent.

'I'm in the League, now. You can't keep secrets from me if you expect my help.'

'All right. Yeah, it is.'

'*Yeah, it is?* Is that it? Why didn't TJ tell me?' I glare at him.

Marshall sighs, 'You were a rogue operator outside the League and we couldn't keep an eye on you 24/7. We were protecting ourselves.'

'I work with you now, Marshall.'

'I'm sorry.'

I stare out of the window. 'If the American gets his hands on the ghost quartz, he can make as many Drives as he wants?'

'Looks that way.'

'We can't let that happen.' I always feared the bad guys would come after the finding machine one day. The possibility of finding anyone, anywhere, is irresistible. I clench my fists in my lap, re-envisaging a nightmare scenario of hostile countries and regimes using finding machines to track down, abduct, or eliminate enemies.

I crack open the window, inhaling the sweet smell of cut hay. *You knew this would happen, didn't you, Dad? What a mess.*

'We have a plan,' Marshall says. 'Grigor's going to the Natural History Museum tomorrow. We'll follow him using the Drive. Grigor should lead us to whoever the American's using for the handover. Then, we track the courier.'

'And the courier leads us to the American?'

'Bingo.'

Marshall pulls up outside the Lodge gates and presses the button on his key fob. The gates slowly swing inward.

Marshall drives through, parks the Lexus and cuts the engine. He turns to me, lines etched on his face.

'Are we cool?'

I nod. 'We're cool.'

············

After a swift freshen-up and a change of clothes, I join Carmen, Marshall and TJ in the Vault. I sit next to the finding machine, relieved we're back together.

'See what you can do with this,' Marshall says, handing Grigor's TDK cassette tape to TJ.

'I'll do my best, boss.' TJ takes it into the clean lab.

'Let's hope we have more luck with that than the videos.' Marshall pours coffee and sighs.

'I hear you had quite the adventure,' Carmen says, placing a mug of tea and plate of custard creams in front of me.

I update her on my day while dunking biscuits.

'Espionage appears to be your calling.' Carmen's warm smile almost makes me feel guilty for my former unpleasant thoughts regarding her.

'I'm glad you think so,' I say in a subdued voice. Over forty-eight hours have passed since I watched her and Dad on tape, yet my feelings remain raw. Her relationship with Dad is like a scab I can't help but pick at. I wonder where she's put the other videotape.

Carmen exchanges a nod with Marshall. 'If you're up for more fieldwork, Marshall and I are heading to London tomorrow.'

Marshall says, 'Carmen's mineralogy expertise will come in useful.' He stirs his coffee. 'I wouldn't know ghost quartz from a lump of sugar.'

I pause, custard cream held over my tea. 'How can I help?'

Marshall says, 'You and Carmen will be my eyes and ears inside the museum. I want you to follow Grigor using your Drive if necessary, staying out of sight. Once Grigor leaves the museum, I'll take over and follow him from there.'

I glance at Carmen. 'The Natural History Museum is enormous. Will you be able to manage the stairs?'

'I'll take my stick,' she says. 'There are lifts and ramps.'

I give Marshall a querulous look. Carmen will have a job keeping up with Grigor. And me.

A chill draft brushes my arm. I touch the finding machine's vent. 'Carmen, I know about the ghost quartz,' I say.

Her mouth falls open.

'Alex worked it out herself,' Marshall says, and gives me an appraising nod.

Carmen places her hand on her breastbone. 'Please don't think badly of us for keeping you in the dark. We did it to protect you. And us.'

'While you're on the subject, are there any other secrets you need to tell me?' I ask pointedly.

'I don't think so,' Carmen says in a small voice.

I do. You and Dad, for one.

I push the image of them from my mind. 'Does the ghost quartz inside my Drive make it cold?'

Carmen nods. 'Partly.'

'What's the other part? And don't keep anything back this time.'

'I'm afraid we don't have the answer, but that's down to our lack of knowledge.' Carmen rests her hands on the table and links her fingers. 'Ghost quartz has remarkable properties. It produces cold light at pressure as it decays, along with an exceptionally rare gas containing qualities we've barely begun to explore. We believe the interaction between the Drive's circuitry, the static tape, and the quartz has created something new and incredible.' She pauses. 'It defies science.'

'I knew Dad was clever but this is something else.' My voice drops in awe.

'He had a little help from Turing and Tesla, if Lazar's story is correct,' Carmen reminds me. 'Our problem is the gap between theory and practical application.'

'What do you mean?'

'Richard's experiments prove an eighth of a gram of ghost quartz has a useful life of five years. Therefore, the optimum amount required to power the Drive for fifty years is 1.25 grams, the amount Richard used in your Drive.'

'But that means...' I do the mental arithmetic. Dad built the original machine sometime in the '70s. If Carmen's right, it will stop working sometime around 2020. Without fresh ghost quartz it will end up as a museum piece like the ticker tape machine in Melvyn Potter's lab.

'Your Drive will eventually stop working,' Carmen confirms as though reading my mind. 'After Richard built it, there was less than 0.0025 grams of residual quartz. That's the reason we can't build more.'

'But you built the clone.'

Carmen sighs. 'We needed to prove it was possible to build another Drive even if it would only work for a few more months rather than years.'

I release a long, exasperated sigh. 'How long before it packs up?'

'Less than a month, give or take.'

'Does the American know this?'

'Your guess is as good as mine,' Carmen says. 'But he could make over eight hundred Drives with the quartz in the Natural History Museum. Their sample weighs over a kilo.'

Marshall adds, 'He could make more than eight hundred, depending on how long he wants them to last.'

'Why don't we take the quartz for ourselves?' I straighten in my chair. 'Think of all the good we could do with it.'

Carmen casts her gaze down. 'Ghost quartz is a national treasure that should be available to everyone for the benefit of mankind. The Natural History Museum's research arm is investing significant resources into determining its chemical composition. They have the resources to find a way to replicate it. That has to be better than relying on a finite amount of the original stone.'

She puts her hand on mine. 'All is not lost. Your Drive was a wonderful gift from your father. I encourage you to make the most of it while it lasts. But my opinion is, one in the world is more than enough.'

'I agree,' says Marshall. 'The risk of more Drives falling into the wrong hands is too great.'

I rest my elbows on the table and put my head in my hands, silently cursing the American.

If only I'd taken Hertfordshire Constabulary up on their offer to set up a Finding Branch. Their idea for a revolutionary new department would have prioritised finding the lost, the kidnapped, and even those who had died.

But that ship has sailed.

28

Carmen, Marshall, and I eat dinner at the kitchen table while the radio plays, *"We've only just begun,"* by The Carpenters. I'm too preoccupied with my forthcoming call with Mystic Miriam to say much beyond asking Marshall to pass the pepper and HP Sauce.

Dessert is a chocolate brownie drowned in whipped cream. I mumble my appreciation between gooey mouthfuls. No wonder Marshall has piled on the pounds. I'm in danger of turning into a waddling penguin if I stay at the Lodge much longer.

Marshall dabs his mouth with a napkin and glances at his watch. 'Seven forty. You still planning on calling the psychic, Alex?'

'I am, but there's some—'

'We should get you set up.' Marshall stands and stretches his back. 'You can use the study.'

'In private?'

'I'd better sit in.' Marshall's brows creep up. 'In case the psychic's questions cross into sensitive territory. We can't afford any more information to leak out.'

I stand and face him. 'Miriam's not a spy. I can't relax if you're looming over me.'

Plus, Marshall's scepticism will sour the call.

'It's just that we have to be extra careful right now,' Carmen says, stacking the dessert bowls and taking them to the sink.

'You can trust me,' I say.

'It's not you we don't trust.' Carmen dries her hands on a tea towel. 'But I suppose we could let you phone Miriam in private. Marshall could still join the call without being physically present.'

'That could work.' Marshall taps his finger on the table. 'We can listen in from the Vault.'

I throw my hands up. 'I said, I don't want anyone listening in!'

Marshall is adamant. 'It's non-negotiable. We're recording the call.'

'I have an idea,' Carmen moves between us. 'What if we record the call but don't listen in live? That way, Alex will be more comfortable, and we'll still have the recording if we need it.'

'That's like shutting the stable door after the horse has bolted,' Marshall says.

'Only if I divulge information which I've promised not to do!' I protest. 'I like Carmen's suggestion. I can live with it. Can you?'

'I'm putting my trust in you.' Marshall gives me a level stare. 'I'll get TJ to set it up.'

Marshall leaves to make arrangements while I help Carmen clear up.

TJ pokes his head through the door while I'm drying the last pot. 'Are you ready?'

I stack the pot in the drawer and look to Carmen.

'Good luck.' She smiles.

I nod and follow TJ from the kitchen and through the hall to a closed door opposite the TV room. Glancing back at the room where I watched Dad's Avebury video gives me an idea.

'Hey, TJ, have you finished with Dad's videos, yet?'

'No. I'm using them for comparative analyses against Grigor's recordings.'

'I'd like to watch them when you're done.'

He shrugs. 'Shouldn't be a problem. Run it by Carmen first, okay?'

'Sure thing,' I say casually, even though I have no intention of doing so.

TJ opens the door and I walk into a decadent study. The room smells of old leather and beeswax polish with a hint of expensive aftershave. A captain's chair finished in plum-coloured leather sits behind a polished walnut desk with a compact switchboard phone and a computer monitor covered by a beige dust cover. An illuminated chandelier with candle bulbs casts warm light over the room.

'Who works here?' I ask.

'This is Jonathan's office.' TJ tilts his head towards an arched doorway in the dividing wall that leads to a second, smaller office. 'Cecilia works through there.'

'I'm honoured.'

I sit in the chair, grip the padded leather arms, and swivel round. Placing a hand on the desk to arrest my spin, I survey the enormous desk inlaid with green leather. There aren't any photos of Jonathan and his family on the desk, no paperweights, calendars, or trinkets. Nothing to tell me more about the man.

While TJ concentrates on setting up a Dictaphone on the desk, I surreptitiously try the desk drawers. They're locked.

TJ asks, 'Can I have your mobile phone?'

He plugs a cable into the connector on my mobile. 'I'm going to start the recording now.' He presses 'record' and 'play' on the Dictaphone.

'Just press 'stop' when you're done.' TJ thumbs towards the door. 'I should get back.'

'Thanks.'

He leaves, closing the door behind him. I open my notepad to a fresh page and dial Miriam's number.

She picks up almost instantly. I wonder if this is a demonstration of her psychic skills or her taste for the theatrical.

'Hello, Alex, it's lovely to hear from you. Are you keeping well?'

'I am, thank you.' Her soft, grandmotherly burr is like a hug.

I rub a growing twinge at my temple. Most people who call her pay-per-minute hotline are looking for comfort after losing loved ones. But Jonathan's a completely different kettle of fish. He's still alive, and the powers concealing him are beyond the League's understanding. I hope she's up to the task. The only information she has to go on apart from his photo is his first name.

'I can sense a lot of people are worried about Jonathan,' Miriam says. 'Please try to relax and trust in the process.'

Miriam's confidence heartens me. I cross my fingers, hoping her answers will be less cryptic than her usual riddles.

'I am holding Jonathan's photo,' Miriam says. 'Don't worry if I go quiet. I'm simply interpreting the messages.'

Tingles travel up my chest bone in the silence that follows. I run my finger along the gold tracery edging the desk. My finger goes back and forth, back and forth.

I clear my throat. 'Is everything okay?'

Miriam has told me off before for interrupting as it disrupts the spiritual flow. I brace myself for more stern words.

'I'm sorry, Alex.' Miriam's voice is tight. 'Jonathan is not sending out any resonances.'

'Not anything? Is it the picture?'

'The photo isn't the problem.'

'What is, then?' A chill runs through me.

'I sense a strange barrier like...thick fog...in the way.' She pauses. 'I'm trying to find a way through.'

I press the phone to my ear, barely daring to breathe.

'I see something.' Miriam takes a sharp breath. 'A grey cube filled with mist. Inside stands a grey man. He has no...no...face.'

'Is it Jonath—'

Words spill from her. 'The cube floats in a void. Greyness pushes in like a smothering blanket.' She makes a choking sound. 'I have to put the photo down.'

'Please keep trying!'

Miriam's ragged breathing fills my ear. I feel dreadful about pushing her but I have no choice.

'Voices speak in the fog. I hear a wall of suffering.' Her voice drops until it's barely audible. 'Old souls cry out for justice. Bad deeds have gone unpunished. I can't sense their place in the universe...it's too much...forgive me.'

'Wait! What does it mean? Where's Jonathan?'

Silence.

'Miriam?'

'That's all I have,' she says. 'I'm sorry, I need to rest.'

My heart sinks. 'Thank you for trying.'

'May the universe aid your search,' she says before swiftly ending the call.

I stop the Dictaphone recording and hang my head, a bitter taste in my mouth. It sounds like Jonathan is stuck in the worst prison imaginable. I remain at the desk lost in morose thoughts as the light fades outside the window.

A soft knock comes at the door.

'Come in,' I say.

Marshall enters. 'Hey, there. You okay?'

'Miriam couldn't find Jonathan,' I blurt. 'She saw a faceless man imprisoned in a cell, protected by a strange, grey barrier. This barrier must be stopping my Drive from finding him.'

I search his eyes, expecting to see cynicism or annoyance. Instead, his gaze is sympathetic. He walks to the window and draws the curtains. 'This barrier she picked up on. Maybe it's like a Faraday cage or some kind of broad-spectrum frequency jammer.'

My brow creases. 'I thought you didn't believe in psychics?'

'I'm trying to keep an open mind.' Marshall crouches beside the desk. 'I'm actually glad you tried.'

Close-up, his eyelids are red-rimmed and the bags beneath them are droopier than ever. The bruise on his cheek has swollen and turned a mottled purplish-blue. His neglected silver and black stubble is fast becoming a beard.

I hadn't realised Jonathan's absence was taking such a toll on him.

'I gave it my best shot,' I say. 'Thanks for going along with me.'

'Hey, no problem. Let's park this for now. I don't want you losing sleep over it.' He gives a weary smile. 'That's my job.'

· · · · ● · ● · · · ·

183

I soak in the bath before bed. The lavender aroma and bubbles work their magic and ease my tension. I change into pyjamas, pack the finding machine into my rucksack, and climb into bed.

As I'm closing my eyes, my phone buzzes on the side table. I creak my eyes open and grab it, wondering if it's Antony.

IRISH_BRANCH

'Hmmm Mya,' I mumble, pulling the duvet over my head. 'Ery-thin kay?'

'Alexandra, have you been drinking?' Moira asks, just like my mother used to when I staggered in from parties as a teenager.

'No, I'm in bed.'

'Oh well, I'm sorry to disturb you but I have information. It may be something or nothing, but now that I'm a spy I'm taking note of the smallest things no matter how insignificant they appear.'

I brace myself for more skateboards, cactuses, and board games.

Moira says, 'Do you remember I popped into St Mel's Cathedral on my way home? Well, when I got there the front door was locked.'

'And?' I yawn and burrow further under the covers.

'There was a notice on the door and that's why I'm calling. Hold on. I wrote it down.' She pauses. '*Due to the recent break-in and theft, the cathedral will remain locked between services. If you want to speak to Father Sean call the Presbytery. Anyone with information on the crime should contact the Garda in Drumkeeran. God's blessings be upon you.*'

'That's terrible,' I say. 'What kind of lowlifes steal from a church?'

'The worst kind. The groundsman approached as I was leaving. We got to chatting and you'll never believe it, he knows my cousin Oona Mooney from Carrick-on-Shannon!'

I stifle a groan. I have inadvertently created a monster.

'The groundsman, Kieran, told me the thief stole the silverware, the kitty for the Senior Parishioners Christmas Dinner, the last two month's offertories, the 100 Lucky Club, and the collection for the local hospice! The burglar had keys to the front door, the sacristy, and the office. It looks like an inside job.' She pauses. 'Father Sean is devastated.'

'I'm sorry, Moira, but what has this to do with Pierce?'

'Well, lo and behold, didn't Pierce turn up out of nowhere last month and start attending services? Kieran said the ladies went googly-eyed for him. He befriended the bursar, the cleaner, and the florist. Every woman of influence with access to the church. Then, once the theft occurred, he stopped attending.'

I sit up in bed, clutching the covers. 'Hold on, Moira. Is there anything actually linking him to the crime?'

'No, but Dervla O'Hara will be doubly careful to lock up the vestry and Father's office once she hears this!'

'Please don't go spreading rumours without proof,' I caution. 'What we really need is evidence. Things like fingerprints or keys found in his possession.'

'Fingerprints!' Moira laughs. 'The parish is a thousand strong. They've put their mitts over everything.'

'What about the keys?'

'Your mum has a set. I should check with her.' She lets out a noisy sigh. 'What if Pierce has latched onto her so he can use her keys?'

'Hold on. We shouldn't jump to conclusions.'

'Well, don't you think it's odd he keeps changing churches? That's two in six months. I don't know anyone who does that.'

'You went to a different church today,' I point out.

'That's different. I was only popping in. And I'm not the only one. Dervla O'Hara is always at this church or that.'

I massage a sudden headache behind my brow. 'Let's keep following Pierce.'

'And get more intel? That's grand.' Moira's tone leaps an octave. 'Wherever Pierce goes, I'll go. Tomorrow, I'll drop in on your mother and check if she has her church keys. She often helps with the flower arranging, putting up the hymn numbers, or polishing the holy vessels. Should I warn her?'

'No!' Mum's the absolute worst at keeping secrets. 'If you tell her she'll blurt it to Pierce or Father Egan. If Pierce is guilty...and that's a big if...he'll do a runner.'

'Oh, he's guilty all right,' Moira says gleefully. 'I can't wait to see where the *hallion* goes next. Good night, Alexandra. *Slán go fóill*!

'And to you, Moira. Good night.'

29

I toss and turn for hours, and eventually drift into a series of nightmares that resemble the worst B-movie ever made. Pierce lumbers out of a dark forest like a zombie, arms held stiffly in front of him. He heads for my mother who sits on a tartan blanket beside a black lake. Mum stares across the water, oblivious to Pierce only a few steps away. I scream, but no sound comes out.

Thick fog rolls in to obliterate the scene. A man wearing a grey suit emerges from the mist. He has no face, only a shallow scoop where his mouth should be. The American whispers, "You want his blood on your hands?"

Grigor lunges from the fog, smothering me with a shovel-sized hand.

'Get off me!' I awake thrashing beneath the duvet. Casting off the covers, I gulp air while my heart pounds in my ears. I sit up and shiver in damp pyjamas, wiping cold sweat from my forehead.

Light filters through the curtains. I check the time: 06:40.

I head to the bathroom and splash water on my face. After draping my pyjamas over the heated towel rail, I have a swift wash in the bathtub and get dressed.

Then, I place Pierce's photograph into the finding machine.

5, Breffni Court, Drumkeeran, County Leitrim, Ireland, N41 CF72

Without access to a computer I can't tell if Drumkeeran is near Mum's house, Kennedy Drive, or St Mel's Cathedral. I text the location to Moira and ask her not to contact me until the evening.

The last thing I need is for her to ring me in the middle of a stakeout.

I try Jonathan's photo again, get nothing, and replace it with Grigor's.

The Old Croft, Church Lane, Tingewick, Buckingham, MK18 4RA

I tuck the finding machine inside my rucksack with Grigor's photo still in the clips, tuck the other two photos inside, and carry the bag downstairs. The kitchen's empty with the table laid for one. I pour myself a mug of freshly brewed coffee, help myself to toast from the rack, and wolf down a bowl of cereal. I'll need the energy.

After brushing my teeth I head outside. Marshall is under the bonnet of the Lexus, wiping the dipstick onto an oily rag. He raises his hand.

'Morning! Ready to leave in five?'

'I'm ready now.'

Carmen emerges from the front door. She leans on a burnished walking stick. The handle is a carved owl, inset with green glass eyes. She's wearing sensible clothes — a beige cardigan over a powder blue blouse and sensible slip-on shoes. It's a bland look but I suppose that's the point.

'Morning, Alex. Ready for the off?' Her eyes crease as she examines my face. 'You look rather pale.'

'I didn't get much sleep last night.'

'Me neither.' Carmen locks the front door and walks to the car. She opens the passenger door, slides into the leather seat, and rests her stick against the centre console.

I slip into the back seat. Marshall starts the engine and nudges the Lexus towards the entrance gates.

'Can you update me on Grigor's location?'

I check the finding machine:

Bicester North Station, Chiltern Approach, Buckingham Road, Bicester, OX26 6EF

'He's at the train station. Bicester North.'

Marshall drives through the gates onto Church Walk. 'Good. I was worried he might drive down in his old jalopy. The train from Bicester North takes about an hour to reach Marylebone. Adding in the underground journey, Grigor's looking at about a two-hour journey to the museum. We should be there way ahead of him.'

After joining the A5 past Bletchley, Marshall follows signs for the M1. Once we're on the motorway he keeps to the fast lane and engages the cruise control. The Lexus's speedometer hovers on seventy m.p.h.

'Can't you go faster?' I urge.

'We can't afford to get pulled over for speeding. Let's go over the plan. You two will be inside the museum.'

'Why can't you come in with us?' I ask.

'Grigor knows me.'

I lean forwards and grab his headrest. 'He's seen me as well.'

'Yeah, but I made more of an impression.' Marshall glances at me, the bruises from his altercation with Grigor still visible. 'You'll be with Carmen and Grigor hasn't seen her.'

'We'll look like a mother and daughter on a day trip.' Carmen looks round. 'I doubt he'll give us a second glance.'

'Grigor's ex-KGB,' I say. 'He's trained to be observant.'

'His mind will be on the ghost quartz,' Carmen insists. 'We'll be faces in the crowd, nothing more.'

She passes me a visitor's map containing a detailed floor plan. 'We'll arrive via Hintze Hall, go past Dippy the Dinosaur and up the main stairs to the first floor. The Hall of Minerals is on the right.'

I trace the route to a black box with two arrows pointing up and down at the top of the stairs. 'There's a lift if you need it, Carmen.'

'Good point,' Marshall says. 'Grigor may use it.'

'What's the plan, then?' I ask. 'I leap on top of the lift and spy on him through the roof?'

Marshall clucks his tongue. 'If Grigor takes the elevator, use the stairs to follow him.'

I memorise the location of the entrances. There are two main ones: Cromwell Road and Exhibition Road. There must be others for deliveries and staff but they're not marked on the map.

Marshall waggles his phone. 'Keep me updated. I'll be outside, ready to follow the quartz.'

'What about Grigor?'

'We won't need him after the handover,' Marshall says. 'Our focus will shift to the American's contact. I know London pretty well from chauffeuring Jonathan around. Once I'm on his tail, I won't lose him.'

'And that's us done?' I ask.

'Yep. That's it.'

My nerves build as we leave the motorway and enter the London outskirts. We join the South Circular and traffic slows to a crawl. Marshall makes slow progress down the busy Finchley Road. He brakes as a bus pulls out, swearing under his breath.

I repeatedly check my watch and Grigor's location as my stomach churns. My concerns are so numerous I don't know where to begin. Carmen's so slow she's a liability. I've had zero surveillance training and the target knows me. Grigor was furious when he rushed at me. That kind of encounter tends to cement a face in one's mind. And it's only now I realise I'm wearing the exact same outfit as when we ran into each other at The Rollright Stones.

As we pass through Chiswick, Carmen points out the townhouse where the painter and satirist William Hogarth lived. I stare grimly at the Edwardian building with its white sash windows and smoke-stained bricks.

The buildings, railings, and lampposts become smarter and grander as we enter Kensington. Cheeky cab drivers zip in front of us and dive down side streets. Motorcycle couriers zoom past.

Marshall turns onto Cromwell Road, and the unmistakable grand façade of the Natural History Museum comes into view. I'd forgotten how *large* the museum is. The Victorian grey and gold building boasts hundreds of animal and plant carvings, arched windows, statues, towers, pillars, and turrets.

Marshall pulls into a bus stop directly outside the main entrance. 'Where's Grigor?'

I check the finding machine. 'Upper Berkeley Street.'

Marshall retrieves a London A-Z book from the glovebox and opens it at a marked page. He taps the street with a pencil.

'You have around half an hour before he gets here. It's tighter than I planned but I didn't expect traffic to be this bad.' He pauses. 'Open the glovebox.'

'Okay.' Inside is a digital camera.

Marshall says, 'If the handover takes place inside, you see the American or his courier, take a picture.' He raises his phone. 'Keep me in the loop. Good luck.'

'Come on,' Carmen says. She opens the passenger door, places the tip of her walking stick on the tarmac and eases out of the car. I take the camera and my rucksack and follow her.

We join the day trippers making a beeline for the grand entrance arch and enter the cathedral-styled Hintze Hall. The buzz of voices echo in the cavernous hall. My jaw drops at the scale of Dippy the Diplodocus, who dominates the room. A sign shows him in silhouette, stretching three times the length of a London bus. I last saw him as a little girl on a primary school trip, but he still looks just as big.

Carmen purchases two tickets from the entrance booth and waves me through the turnstile.

'We need to keep a close eye on the time,' she says. Her stick taps on the mosaic stone tiles as she leads me past Dippy. The tip of his whip-thin tail points to a galleried staircase at the back of the hall.

Holding the stone rail, Carmen ascends the steps to a half-landing where a marble statue of Charles Darwin observes us with a benign expression. The staircase splits. We keep right and ascend to the first floor.

We turn the corner. Sunlight shines through skylights that run along the ceiling. I drag my gaze away from the displays containing extinct mammalian and reptilian bones, staying close to Carmen.

She picks up her pace, relying less on her stick in her eagerness to enter the Hall of Minerals a short way along.

I follow her into an exquisitely old-fashioned room. Visitors in jeans, polyester, and hi-tech trainers look strangely anachronistic in contrast to the Victorian-era vibes. Elegant pillars carved with fish and beasts support an ornate plaster ceiling. Arched windows line both sides of the hall. Light floods through, falling on rows of waist-high wood and glass cabinets separated by a central aisle.

There must be hundreds of cabinets containing thousands of exhibits. It would take years to look through them all.

Carmen touches my arm. I follow her gaze to a CCTV camera mounted in the corner near the ceiling. A second camera observes us from the opposite side of the room. Two uniformed wardens slowly patrol the hall.

'The security here is very good,' she says in a low voice. 'Grigor will know this.'

'He must have a plan. You can't steal a kilo of quartz and walk out with it.'

I stop by a cabinet containing an enormous blue gemstone, peering around an elderly couple to get a closer look.

The Ostro Stone. Flawless blue topaz. 9831 carats. The largest example in the world.

Despite the urgency of our mission I can't help but stare. Less than an inch of glass separates me from a stone that must be worth millions. Beside the topaz is a purple amethyst set into a silver, two-headed snake.

Trebly-cursed amethyst. Trail of Misfortune and Misery follows Ancient Gem.

The amethyst was looted from India. Perhaps it was karma payback.

I expected to find a load of boring old stones in the Hall of Minerals but their stories are anything but. I'm beginning to understand Carmen's fascination with minerals. I join her at another cabinet containing a display of clear gems. A teenage boy stares listlessly at two huge specimens, one slightly larger than the other.

Koh-I-Noor Diamond. Value — priceless.

'Isn't the Koh-I-Noor part of the Crown Jewels?' I whisper. 'I thought it was kept at the Tower of London?'

'It is,' Carmen says. 'These are cubic zirconia replicas showing the original diamond and the recut version. Prince Albert didn't think the gem was brilliant enough.'

Frowning, I ask, 'How do we know the ghost quartz on display is real and not fake?'

'No one's heard of ghost quartz, whereas the Koh-I-Noor is world-famous and draws thieves like flypaper.' Carmen walks on. 'Time's ticking. We need to find the quartz section. You take the right-hand cabinets. I'll take the left. Call me when you find them.'

I walk up and down the cabinets, reading the labels. All I know about ghost quartz is it's white and pale blue, and the sample is the weight and size of a kilo bag of sugar. Precious stones of that size are rare, yet the room is crammed with them.

My progress is slow. Most of the minerals are new for me: *Albite, Andesite, Howlite, Fossiliferous Limestone, Selenite, Zircon, Spinel, Melanite, Aragonite...*

By the time I reach the final cabinet my temples are twinging. I pause to stretch my back which aches from bending over the glass. A warden sits on a chair in the corner, looking into the middle distance. Before he shifts his gaze to me I make a second pass down the Hall, but I can't find the quartz section. The hall suddenly feels far too warm.

I sneak a look to a uniformed guard on the far side of the hall before ducking behind a pillar to check on Grigor.

Exhibition Road, South Kensington, London, SW7 5BD.

I stare from the window onto Exhibition Road but can't spot him.

Carmen waves from the other side of the hall. I cross the room to meet her, relief flooding through me. 'Did you find it?'

The cabinet she stands next to contains varieties of quartz in different colours. Carmen takes my arm and points to a space in the centre. Below an empty plinth is a placard.

Ghost Quartz: Tunguska, 1908. Exhibit on temporary leave.

'Where the hell is it?' I whisper, looking around. Grigor could stride through the door any moment.

'I'm trying to think,' Carmen says quietly. 'There must be store-rooms and research facilities. Goodness knows where they are.'

I guide her behind the nearest pillar. 'Let's check on Grigor.' I open my rucksack wide so Carmen can see inside.

Natural History Museum, Cromwell Road, South Kensington, London, SW7 5BD

Two lights are red, and a third is flashing. High points of colour rise on Carmen's cheekbones. She looks to the entrance doors, wide-eyed.

'Act natural and stay close,' I say. Keeping my rucksack unzipped, I loop the strap over my shoulder so I can check the display. I hurry back towards the entrance to the Hall of Minerals, using the other tourists as cover. To my chagrin the third light goes out before I reach the doors.

'He must be back the other way,' I say, retracing my steps. Carmen breaks into a limping trot to keep up.

As we exit via the Hall of Mineral's farthest door, I get four solid lights. I stop by a side corridor.

At the end is a closed door with a silver plaque: ARCHIVES. PRIVATE.

I look up and down the corridor. There are no cameras.

'Come on,' I say, boldly walking to the door. I turn the brass handle.

'Wait!' Carmen says breathlessly. 'Marshall won't like this. We're not supposed to take any risks.'

'Marshall's not here and we need to see what Grigor's doing.'

'Alex, we're too close!' Carmen squeals. 'Alex, no!'

I step to the door and open it a crack. The fifth light flashes.

30

T he heavy door opens silently on well-oiled hinges. The room inside is cavernous, on a similar scale to the Hall of Minerals, with arched windows, pillars, and a white coffered ceiling. The space is cluttered with steel lockers, wooden plan chests, and racks of shelves stacked with boxes and plastic tubs.

Conversation drifts from deep inside the room.

Grigor and a man in a lab coat have their backs to us. The two men are deep in discussion beside a huge table in the centre of the room. The Russian rests a hand on a leather satchel. Grigor wears a familiar green and brown checked shirt and combat trousers, the exact same outfit he wore at the Rollright Stones. It seems neither of us got the memo about changing our appearance.

Carmen shakes her head but I take her hand and drag her inside. She tucks her walking stick under her arm and limps behind me.

The wooden door closes silently behind us. We creep to a row of wooden filing cabinets and tuck ourselves behind them.

Carmen squeezes alongside me and shoots me a fearful look.

I put my finger to my lips, and whisper, 'Relax. We're observing, that's all.'

She nods, tight-lipped.

I peer around the cabinet. Rock samples, microscopes, analysis equipment, paperwork, and a cloth-covered lump clutter the table. I give the lump a second glance. It looks about the same size as a bag of sugar.

The young scientist's untidy black hair is cut in jags around his face. He flicks through a leather-bound notebook and nods with each turn of the page.

'...full of fascinating information, Mr Smirnov,' the scientist says. 'It's very generous of you to donate your research to the museum. The quartz is like nothing we've ever seen. Your insights will be a great help.'

'It is one in a million, Nathan.' Grigor's words come out stilted and overly formal. He's obviously trying to sound less Russian. A distorted grimace cracks his face. I think he's trying to smile. 'May I see the sample? It is a long-held dream of mine.'

Nathan tears his eyes from the notebook.

'Sorry...yes, of course.' He snaps the book shut and removes the cloth cover.

The pale crystal beneath is a rough, irregular shape and sparkles where it catches the light. Sky blue swirls are suspended at the quartz's heart like ink dipped in water.

'May I borrow your magnifier?' Grigor asks, dripping politeness.

'Sure.' Nathan sets up the equipment next to the quartz and turns on the internal light.

Grigor waits for the scientist's go-ahead before pressing his eye to the glass. He stares for a long time.

'The optical illusion is remarkable,' he eventually says. 'The blue inclusions appear to move.'

Nathan's face lights up. 'Hey, maybe we can use it to pull more visitors into the minerals gallery. Anything that drags them away from the dinosaurs gets my vote.'

'I guarantee this will bring in the crowds.' Grigor draws his head back from the magnifier and straightens his powerful frame. 'Why don't you take a look for yourself?'

'Sure.' Nathan leans forward to peer through the eyeglass.

Grigor shifts closer. 'Can you see the light moving?'

Nathan twiddles a knob on the magnifier's base. 'Just focussing. Ah, now I see the inclu—'

Grigor loops an arm around his neck and squeezes.

Nathan's groan cuts off.

Carmen lets out a horrified squeak. Her eyes widen as she stares at Grigor with a frozen expression. I press my finger to my lips and add a stern look, praying she doesn't scream.

My heart thuds like a timpani drum. I want to raise the alarm but doing so would blow our cover and ruin everything. What could I do to stop Grigor anyway?

I force myself to watch.

Grigor covers Nathan's mouth with a large hand as the scientist's legs turn to jelly. He holds the scientist upright, muttering, '*Odin Politburo, dva Politburo, tri Politburo, chetire Politburo...*'

He gently lowers Nathan to the floor and arranges him on his side with his top leg bent in the recovery position.

'Sleep well,' Grigor mutters. He gently pats Nathan's head and unclips his ID badge.

Carmen trembles violently. I catch her walking stick before she drops it and help her to sit. She sinks to the floor with her back to the cabinet and puts her head between her legs. I give her shoulder a swift squeeze before returning to my post.

Grigor strides to the bench and places the ghost quartz inside his leather satchel. The bulky stone makes the leather bulge. He slides the leather notebook alongside the quartz, swiftly latches the buckles and strides out.

I hold my breath behind the cabinet as his boots clomp on the wooden floor. Grigor walks past our hiding place. If he looks back now we're done for.

He strides to the door, opens it, and leaves without a backward glance.

Carmen gasps, rubbing her forehead. She struggles to her feet and shuffles over to Nathan, leaning heavily on her stick. 'Thank God. He's breathing.'

I glance at Nathan, then at the door. 'Can you get help? I have to follow Grigor.'

'Of course.' Carmen shoos me out. 'Make sure you call Marshall.'

I slip out of the door and run back to the Hall of Minerals, glancing at the finding machine.

Three solid reds.

I zip up the rucksack and sling it over my shoulder like a regular tourist. Anxiety grows inside my chest as I slow my pace past the security warden until I come out the other side of the hall and pass the lift.

Unzipping my rucksack again, I peer inside. The fourth light flashes.

I grab the stone railing on the top step and scour the milling people. With his height and size Grigor's easy to spot. He walks stiffly down the stairs and strides past Dippy, heading for the exit.

The sound of wailing sirens drifts through the entrance doors.

Grabbing my phone from my pocket I speed-dial Marshall as I run downstairs, weaving past sightseers. Two security guards stand by the exit turnstiles, casting their eyes over the crowds. The sirens grow louder.

'What's the news?' Marshall asks, as sirens wail in the background.

Grigor veers away from the exit and disappears down a side-corridor. *Where the hell is he going?*

'I'm following Grigor. He has the quartz,' I say breathlessly, hurrying after him. 'He took out a member of staff to get it. Carmen stayed behind to check on him.'

'Where's Grigor now? Outside?'

'No. He's heading back into the museum. I think security spooked him.'

'Keep your distance. He'll be fired up and dangerous,' Marshall advises, as a whooping alarm rushes past. 'Something big's happening out here. I'm trying to find out more. Just keep me on the line. I'm coming.'

'Understood.' I weave through the bustling crowd, crossing intersecting passages and staircases, staying as close to Grigor as I dare.

Phone in hand, I hurry along a corridor teeming with visitors, past a display board showing a flaming meteor on a collision course with a herd of dinosaurs. I duck into a dark exhibition hall.

A terrifying roar comes out of nowhere and shakes the air. A child cries in her mother's arms. I freeze, my fractured nerves jangling, until I remember what part of the museum I'm in.

I look past the mother and child but can't see Grigor.

I squeeze between loitering tourists and ascend a ramp that runs alongside skeletons of predatory Velociraptors and Allosauruses that look scarily alive despite being nothing but bones.

Panic shoots through me as I hurry beneath models of Pterosaurs suspended on wires until I spot a familiar, checked shirt.

I round a corner and leap back as an animatronic Tyrannosaurus rex lunges forwards. It releases another bone-chilling roar before its great jaws snap shut. I sneak past a group of four and five-year-olds who shriek in terror and excitement.

My frayed nerves can't take much more of this.

Ten feet ahead, Grigor descends the ramp and strides towards a curved display with grey-flippered creatures emerging from the sea onto land.

I hurry after him and nearly collide with an old man. A group of Italian teenagers engaged in a noisy debate block my way.

'Excuse me, I have to—' I give up and shove past as Grigor disappears behind the display board.

'Sei un imbicille! Scema! Cretina!' The Italians express extravagant outrage.

Ignoring them, I follow Grigor to a door marked: *RESTRICTED AREA*.

I raise my phone to my ear, 'Grigor's left the dinosaur section via a staff corridor. Where are you?'

The clamour of conversation, dinosaur roars, and screaming kids drown out Marshall's reply.

Oh, God, here we go again.

I crack the door open and step through. A service corridor lined with plain white doors leads into the distance. I spot Grigor down at the far end before he vanishes around the corner.

The door swings shut behind me, leaving my ears ringing. I break into a trot and reach the end of the corridor.

Hinges squeak behind me. 'Hey, miss? Miss? This is a restricted area.'

I glance back at a security guard wearing an earpiece with a walkie-talkie hooked on his belt. He puts his hand up and strides after me. 'I'll escort you back to the public area.'

My stomach clenches. I run for it.

'Hey! Stop!' The synthetic flooring reverberates under my feet.

The guard gives chase. His walkie-talkie clicks and releases a crackle. 'Yeah, this is Ashad. We've got an intruder in Blue Zone, utility area. You need to send someone to cut her off.'

'Roger that. I'll relay the alert. Over.'

I throw myself around the corner, my heart thumping painfully. The corridor slopes downwards to a T-junction. I glimpse a sliver of Grigor's shirt as he slips around another turn. This place is a labyrinth with more doors than Alice in Wonderland.

I race after him, bashing my shoulder as I launch myself around the bend.

'Stop!' Ashad yells.

A black figure launches from a doorway and grabs my rucksack. 'Got you!'

Twisting midstride, I yank myself free. My rucksack rips. Cradling it in one arm, I double my pace as two sets of footsteps resound behind me.

'Intruder heading towards Service Area One!' Ashad relays my position. 'Where's the backup?'

'On their way. Over.'

I'm running out of time.

I spot Grigor the same time he spots me and the guards. He runs to a fire door, shoves it open and slips through. I pump my arms, racing to put space between me and my pursuers even though I'm terrified of catching Grigor up.

I burst through the fire door into a warehouse barely two seconds behind the Russian.

SERVICE AREA ONE is stencilled in black on the wall. Thankfully, my fear of running into a wall of guards with riot shields and truncheons is unfounded.

A beeping forklift truck carrying a pallet of boxes wrapped in clingfilm drives straight for me. A red light on its roof flashes.

The crackling burble of walkie-talkies is a worryingly short distance behind.

Grigor turns mid-stride. He locks eyes with me before increasing his speed towards the exit. I jump out of the way of the forklift, ripping my shirt on a sharp metal edge.

'I'm in Service Area One!' I yell into the phone. 'I'm not going to make it!'

'Hang in there!' Marshall says.

The Russian breaks into a galumphing run towards a raised metal roller shutter leading to an external concrete ramp. Sunlight streams inside, reflecting off three workers' fluorescent jackets.

'Close the shutter!' Ashad yells out, waving his arms at the workers.

The workers look round and see Grigor pounding towards them. One drops his cigarette and hits a red button beside the door.

Metal slats slowly descend from the roof with a screeching rattle, cutting out the sunlight and my sole chance of escape.

I sprint flat out towards the shrinking rectangle of light. A guy in a hi-vis vest rushes at me and tries to grab me. I don't spare a breath to scream as I dodge around him.

The workers stand back from Grigor as he ducks under the rattling barrier.

One of them reaches for me.

'Stop! You'll get yourself killed!' he yells, grabbing my forearm.

I wrench free and throw myself the final few feet, sliding underneath the descending shutter, clutching my rucksack. I pull my feet through just before the shutter door hits the concrete with a resounding clang.

31

— · —

I push myself to my feet and look up the service ramp, squinting under harsh sunlight. Steep concrete walls flank the ramp, muffling the sound of wailing sirens and honking horns up ahead.

One of my rucksack straps hangs by a thread and my red, denim shirt has a triangular piece ripped from it.

As I switch the bag to my other shoulder Grigor turns from the top of the ramp and glares at me.

I freeze, all pretence of subterfuge gone.

Grigor's brow lowers. He shakes his head and strides off.

'Marshall?' I hiss breathlessly into my phone. 'Grigor's outside the museum. Where are you?'

'Stuck in traffic,' Marshall replies. 'Damn truckers have blocked the road with a go-slow protest. I'm trying to find a way around, but you'll have to track Gri—' His voice turns muffled. *'What's up, officer? Yeah, I'm on a call but it's hands-free, I'm not touching my phone. What's the problem?* Sorry, Alex, I have to clear this up. I'll get back to you.'

Great. I grit my teeth and push on to the top of the ramp.

The way ahead is blocked by a red-and-white automatic barrier with a guard booth wedged beside it.

Inside the booth, a guard speaks into a walkie-talkie. He stares through the window at Grigor and mouths, *'I see him,'* before lunging for the door.

Grigor sprints to the half-open door and hurls himself against it. The door slams into the guard, sending him crashing into the back wall. He swipes for his chair which tips over. Grigor ducks under the barrier arm and strides up the access road, forcing an oncoming delivery truck to hit the brakes. Tyres screech as the truck judders to a halt.

The driver leans from the window, angrily waving his arm. 'Oi! Get out of the way!'

Grigor ignores him and keeps walking.

I whip round at a rattling shriek behind me. The metal shutter rises, revealing several pairs of legs. Four are coated in fur. Growling escapes through the gap.

My mouth goes dry. I race up to the barrier's long arm, duck underneath and run along the far side of the delivery truck, using the long trailer as cover. I emerge at the top of the ramp and glance back.

Ashad and two guards emerge from the warehouse. One holds a straining German Shepherd on a lead. The dog sniffs a scrap of material in its handler's hand — the same colour as the piece missing from my shirt — and strains at its lead, pointing towards the security booth.

The guard staggers from his post, red-faced. He keeps his distance from the dog and points up the ramp with his other hand clamped to his head.

I run up the access ramp. There's no way I'm ending up chased by a dog again. I shrug off the red denim shirt I'm wearing over a white T-shirt, and scrunch it into a ball.

Grigor jogs down a narrow road shadowed by office blocks. He passes a billboard advertising leather sofas and heads to a T-junction before darting across the road, weaving through a jam of cars, cabs, and buses. A motorcycle courier snaking through tiny gaps in the traffic suddenly brakes and beeps his high-pitched horn. Grigor barely reacts to the near-miss and continues to the far side.

Exhaust fumes hang over four lanes of stationary traffic. I cover my nose and mouth, my gaze darting from one black saloon to another.

Marshall, where are you?

I look both ways before squeezing between vehicles. Halfway across, I duck behind a flat-bed truck and chuck my shirt into the cargo bay. Fingers crossed, that's enough to flummox the dog.

Grigor lopes ahead and disappears down a grand avenue flanked by white-porticoed mansion blocks.

I make it safely across the road and dare a look back. Ashad, the museum guard and his colleagues gesticulate wildly on the other side. The dog sniffs the ground and swivels its ears in my direction.

Battling a stitch in my side, I tuck myself behind passers-by and force my wobbly legs to follow in Grigor's footsteps to the next street.

Grigor marches past millionaire mansions and high-end cars lining the kerb. He looks seriously out of place in one of the poshest postcodes in London.

I raise my mobile to my ear. 'I'm following Grigor down...' I scour the side of the buildings until I spot a sign. '...Queen's Gate Place. How close are you?'

No reply.

'Marshall? You there?'

I check my phone. *Damn!* I've accidentally terminated the call. I lose precious moments speed-dialling Marshall on the move, huffing and puffing with each step.

Grigor looks back. He gives me a hostile glare.

I check my backtrail for a snarling German Shepherd. Still clear.

The Russian walks on. A suited passer-by eyes up his rough appearance and gives him a wide berth. A smartly dressed lady with a chihuahua lifts the dog into her arms and takes refuge under a porch.

A tinny voice comes from the phone. *'Alex, hey, you there?'*

I raise my phone. 'Just about! I'm heading down Queen's Gate Place. Hold on. Grigor's gone again.'

Grigor has ducked down a side street. He's slower and drags his leg every few steps but I'm also dropping behind. My stitch is getting worse and every breath's a struggle. Nausea builds under my ribs as I push my beleaguered body on.

He disappears under a sandstone archway. I break into a sham-bling run, desperate not to let him out of my sight. The archway leads to a narrow, cobbled street lined with Georgian townhouses.

A white BMW saloon waits with its engine idling in the middle of the street. Grey puffs chug from its exhaust.

Grigor halts behind the car.

I duck behind a Ford Fiesta. Swiftly, I check my finding ma-chine.

5, Petersham Mews, South Kensington, London, SW7 5NR

After whispering the address to Marshall, I say, 'The handover's about to take place. Look for a white BMW. You can't miss it.'

'Got it,' Marshall says. 'I'm almost there.'

I slink from the Fiesta to a Range Rover and crawl underneath its raised wheelbase, dragging my rucksack behind me. I watch Grigor and the BMW from the shadows.

The BMW's doors open. I hold my breath as two men step out, leaving the engine running.

The first brute rolls his massive shoulders. He's taller than Grig-or, with short-cropped hair that emphasises his broad, lantern jaw. He wears black combat trousers, grey T-shirt, and a black leather jacket. The other guy has a military buzzcut. He's average-sized with a wiry frame and craggy lines etched on his face. He takes a deep drag on a cigarette before flicking it onto the cobbles.

I scrabble for my rucksack and yank at the zip. Thrusting my hand in, I feel around for the camera.

'*Oo vas eto yest?*' The giant approaches with his hand out.

Grigor peers into the BMW's back seat. His gaze travels to the boot. 'Where is Jonathan?'

'You two are friends, *da*?' The giant grins, showing glints of metal. 'Jonathan is not here. He is in safe place. We release him when we have the stone.'

'That was not the deal.' Grigor straightens, the satchel pressed close to his hip. He thrusts his index finger towards the giant. 'Jonathan should be *here*.'

'We keep promise.' The giant holds up a phone. 'I make call. Jonathan goes free.'

'No.' Grigor glances to the archway and steps back to a red Jeep, clutching his satchel. His gaze flicks from one man to the other as he puts his back against the Jeep's door.

Finally, I drag the camera from the rucksack and feel in the dark for the 'on' button. The lens cover retracts with a *whirr*.

The giant closes the gap until he's within spitting distance of Grigor. 'You speak to Jonathan on phone. That is the new deal.' He puts his hand out. 'Give me the stone.'

'*Nyet!*' Grigor lashes out, his fist crunching against the giant's nose.

The giant rocks on his feet, blood streaming from his nose. His wiry comrade launches at Grigor, slamming him against the Jeep. The wing mirror snaps and clatters on the cobbles. The Jeep's car alarm erupts in piercing squeals. Hazard lights flash, and the horn blares.

I huddle on cold cobbles, my gaze fixed on the unravelling disaster. I aim the camera at the blur of moving bodies and arms and click away.

'Not wise move, comrade,' says the wiry man, and gut-punches Grigor.

Grigor grunts and retaliates by driving his fist into the wiry man's stomach. The Russian reels back a few steps.

The giant wipes blood from his face and joins the fight, pummelling Grigor with massive square fists while his wiry colleague yanks and twists on the satchel. The giant swings a muscled arm at Grigor, who ducks to avoid the blow. His fist punches through the Jeep's side-window.

I cower and tuck the camera away as glass shatters into a thousand tiny pieces and cascades onto the cobbles.

'Get back,' the giant orders the wiry man. He grabs Grigor by his checked shirt and slams him onto the Jeep's bonnet. The chassis rocks as the giant hauls him up and throws him down again with a roar. The pummelled metal crunches under the impact.

'*Quickly! In here!*' a woman hisses behind me, crouching beside her open door to see under the car. An old man stands at the first-floor window, speaking into a telephone. Curtains twitch along the street.

'*I'm okay!*' I hiss back, waving off her offer of help until she retreats inside.

The giant pins Grigor down while his wiry comrade wrenches the satchel from his grip, unbuckles the straps and removes the quartz. He throws the satchel aside.

The smaller Russian says, 'Yury, we have it.'

A dog barks nearby.

The Jeep's suspension creaks as the giant removes his weight from Grigor.

'*Spasibo*, Grigor,' he chuckles through bloodstained teeth.

I fumble for the camera and aim at him, but he turns away before I can take a picture.

Both men run to the BMW. Car doors slam. The engine roars.

I crawl from under the car and stand on shaky legs as the BMW screeches to the end of the lane and turns right. Grigor lies spread-eagled in a metal crater on the Jeep's bonnet, his face bruised and swollen. He looks dead.

Cautiously, I approach him, and lean over to check his chest is moving.

Grigor's eyes pop open. His hand shoots out to grab my wrist. He sits up in one fluid move like a reanimated vampire and fixes me with a manic stare.

I gasp as he pulls me close.

'I remember you,' he says. 'You are with the League.'

'I...I...' Terror stills the words in my throat. The barking dog sounds horribly loud.

His eyes bore into me. 'You must find Jonathan.'

I nod emphatically.

'The American has my stone receiver and my modulator. Get them back. Promise me.' His grip tightens around my wrist until my bones creak.

'I promise.'

Grigor swings his legs to the cobbles, dragging me with him. He bends to retrieve his discarded satchel and presses it into my aching hand.

'Take this. Keep it safe.' He releases me. 'Now, go!'

A fast-moving blur moves in the periphery of my vision. A black and tan furry missile baring sharp canines drags its handler under the arch. Ashad and his colleagues survey the scene in open-mouthed astonishment, looking from Grigor to me. I hope they don't think I caused all this.

Grigor faces the guard and the German Shepherd.

'Davai!' he roars, arms outstretched

'Lie down or the dog will attack!' yells the handler. He spots me over Grigor's shoulder. 'You! Don't move!'

I make a run for it with Grigor's satchel, praying the handler sticks with Grigor instead of coming after me.

Adrenaline surges through me as I attempt to put as much distance between myself, Grigor, and the ravening dog as possible.

The road adjoining the mews is chock-a-block with slow-moving traffic. I spot the white Beamer fifty yards down the road.

Deep breath, Alex. Traffic is backed up. You can follow them on foot.

An arm lands on my shoulder. I curtail a scream, recognising Marshall. 'You nearly gave me a heart attack!'

'Sorry.' He points up the road to the BMW. 'That the car?'

I nod, dizzy and trembling.

'Come on, I got you,' Marshall puts his arm around me, guiding me to the Lexus parked on the kerb with its hazard lights flashing.

I stumble to the passenger door, fling myself inside and collapse on the soft leather. The Russians are stuck behind two lorries driving side-by-side. They inch forwards slower than the original horse-drawn hackney cabs.

Marshall presses the ignition button, puts his arm out the window and nudges the Lexus into traffic. 'Sorry I took so long. The police pulled me over for using my phone.'

'I was nearly beaten up by Russians and eaten by a dog. I don't think I want to be a spy anymore.'

'You did great.' Marshall looks my way and nods. 'Really great. If I swear I won't let you out of my sight again would that make a difference?'

'Ask me again in an hour,' I sigh.

Marshall taps the steering wheel, glaring at the crawling lorries. 'Why are you British always protesting?'

'It's what we do.'

'This one's about the price of fuel.' Marshall rolls his eyes. 'Seems counterintuitive to waste it by going one mile an hour.'

Ashad appears at the end of the mews. I slide down in the seat and turn my head away.

Once Marshall assures me we're safely past the canine squad I sit up and relay my story.

'You do not want to mess with the Russians,' I say. 'The big one totalled the Jeep with his fists and flung Grigor around like a rag doll.'

'Point taken.'

'I tried to take pictures of the Russians but I don't think they'll come out.'

'Well done for trying.' Marshall glances at the leather satchel beside my rucksack. 'That Grigor's bag?'

I quickly tell him about the notebook. 'Grigor trusts me. He trusts the League.'

'That's too bad.' Marshall shakes his head. 'As of today, I've officially terminated his membership.'

32

We crawl along in traffic six cars behind the white BMW. Police cars blockade a side street, holding back protestors waving banners: *Fair Fuel for Folks Sake!*

Marshall raps the steering wheel as we wait at a set of red lights. The lights go green. Two lorries at the front cross the junction. The BMW turns right without indicating.

Marshall accelerates and makes the turn as the lights change from amber to red. Finally, we're moving, although this being London I reckon I could still run faster than the car.

'Alex, you've got sharp eyes. Can you note down the BMW's registration?'

I unzip my rucksack's side pocket and remove my notebook and pen and jot down the details while Marshall calls TJ on the hands-free car phone.

'Yes, boss,' the teenager says.

'Okay, TJ, it's your time to shine. I want everything on a car we're tailing. Registered owner, parking violations, the lot.'

'Give me the details,' he asks.

I raise my voice. 'Hi, TJ. It's a BMW 5-series saloon, registration W533 LMG.'

'Got it,' TJ says.

'Another thing, TJ,' Marshall adds. 'Can you call Carmen? We left her at the Natural History Museum. I need you to check she's okay.'

'No problem. Anything else?'

'That's it for now. Call me once you have news on the car.'

Marshall follows the Russians at a safe distance through Central London, past Green Park, Buckingham Palace, and up the Mall towards the Strand.

'Fine time for them to be sightseeing,' I mutter as we pass The Savoy Hotel. 'They should have taken a Hop-on-Hop-off bus.'

Twenty minutes passes, then half an hour. I stare out the window as adrenaline leaches from me, replaced by growing tension.

The BMW joins a road running alongside the Thames. Beyond the concrete balustrades pleasure boats and Thames Clippers cut frothy wakes through the water. I envy the tourists and office workers strolling along the riverside, seemingly without a care in the world beyond what to have for lunch.

We tail the Russians through London's outskirts. Terraces of rundown Victorian houses, factories, offices, and advertising billboards replace the historic landmarks and manicured parks.

'We're heading towards Woolwich,' I say, as we descend through a three-lane underpass snarled with traffic. 'Where on earth are they going?'

Marshall shrugs.

Traffic moves at a crawl through the sprawling, industrial landscape of the East India Dockyards. We pass construction workers, concrete silos, mountains of aggregate, and billboards advertising swanky new riverside flats.

The car phone rings. Marshall presses a button on the steering wheel. 'Yeah, TJ, what've you got?'

'The BMW's a Hertz rental,' TJ says. 'Hertz operate from twelve locations throughout London. The cars bounce between pickup and drop off points like pinballs. I can't narrow it down any more.'

'Who rented the car? Have you got a company name, anything?'

'That information's on Hertz's booking system. Accessing it will take time.'

'Do your best. Any news on Carmen?'

'She's giving a statement to the museum's head of security while they wait for the police.'

'Good job, TJ,' says Marshall, ending the call.

'Will Carmen be okay handling the police by herself?' I ask.

Marshall grins. 'Don't worry. She's very good at playing the kind old lady who just happened to be passing by.'

I slump in my seat as we follow the BMW under a gantry marked Isle of Dogs, Royal Docks, and a plane symbol next to City Airport.

'Oh, God.' I throw Marshall a panicked look. 'What if they get on a plane?'

'There is that possibility,' he says resignedly. 'We may lose the Russians, but my gut feeling is the American won't leave without the static tape.'

'What about the quartz? Once it leaves the country it's gone forever.'

Marshall sighs. 'Our focus has to stay on the American. Once we learn his identity we can follow him anywhere.'

He hangs back as the traffic thins, tucking in behind a white van, then a lorry carrying aggregate. We tail the BMW around three bleak looking roundabouts, past a long-stay car park and a Travelodge hotel.

We drive past a metal banner anchored to the pavement: *Welcome to London City Airport.* The roar of jet engines makes my jaw tingle. I peer upwards at the underbelly of a plane taking off overhead.

The BMW exits another roundabout by a second banner: PRIVATE JET CENTRE.

I always thought private jets equalled glamour but this place is a windowless grey and white building, bounded on all sides by a chain-link fence topped with razor wire, surveillance cameras, and security lights. It looks anything but glamorous.

A plane taxis on the runway less than forty feet away. Whining jet engines fill the air.

The Russians stop at a yellow and black barrier. Two security guards in navy uniforms and peaked caps approach the car.

Marshall drives past and pulls up on the pavement that circles the roundabout.

I turn in my seat, digital camera in hand, as a guard approaches the Beamer. I take a picture of Yury extending his arm through the car window. He hands the guard some papers. The guard nods to his colleague and the barrier rises. The BMW drives into a small car park and pulls into a bay.

A rumble vibrates the Lexus's floorpan as another jet takes off.

'You okay to wait here while I take a look?' Marshall asks.

'Absolutely.' I pass him the digital camera and watch from my comfortable seat as he leaves the car.

He strolls along the perimeter fence to the airport entrance, then crosses the road to a bus stop opposite. He stands under the awning, surreptitiously watching the airport and occasionally glancing at his watch.

I chew on my fingernails, willing the Russians to exit the airport and return to the BMW. If they've boarded a plane our chances of finding the American drop considerably.

Shortly afterwards Marshall returns to the Lexus and sinks into the driver's seat.

'Well?' I prompt.

'Both Russians went into the private terminal. The smaller one carried an aluminium case. It was big enough for the quartz.'

'Did you get a picture?'

'Only of the back of their heads,' Marshall sighs.

'Couldn't you follow them in?'

'This isn't Gatwick or Heathrow. Security's tight. Let's wait. The Russians might return to the car. I'll call TJ for an update.'

The phone rings through the speakers.

TJ picks up. 'I don't have anything new on the car rental.'

Marshall clears his throat. 'Forget the car for now. I need passenger rosters for private jets leaving London City Airport from midday onwards. Also, who chartered the flights and where they're going.'

'That's a tricky one, boss.' TJ sucks in breath.

'What's the problem?'

'Private charters aren't like mainstream flights. Schedules and passenger lists are tightly guarded and the same goes for whoever charters the flight. Jet owners are notorious for hiding beneath subsidiaries, umbrella corporations, consortiums, non-profits, NGOs, you name it.'

I break in. 'In other words, private jets are the perfect vehicle for rich criminals.'

'Yep,' TJ confirms.

Marshall hangs his head, pinching the bridge of his nose. 'All right. Change of plan. Call our League contact and tell him we've followed the quartz to the private jet centre at City Airport. Pass on details of the car and the Russians. See if they can get things moving.'

'Will do.'

Marshall cuts the call and meets my gaze. 'At least we're causing trouble for the American. Once the police start combing the airport he'll think twice about using it again.' He checks his rear view mirror. 'The police can access plane rosters and schedules. They may be able to recover the quartz wherever it ends up.'

Engines whine as a small jet aircraft slowly taxis down the runway. I check my watch: 12:45 a.m. It's frustrating to sit here twiddling our thumbs while the Russians take the quartz out of the country.

The aircraft takes off. 'I doubt they're coming back.'

'Let's give it a few more minutes.' Marshall flicks through the London A-Z to a double-page spread showing City Airport and studies the routes in and out.

I glance in the wing mirror. A yellow and orange chequered car with SECURITY emblazoned on the side is coming our way.

'We've got company,' I alert Marshall.

'I see them.' He turns on the ignition and drives away. 'It could be a routine sweep.'

The security car follows at a distance. A pit opens in my stomach at the thought of more trouble.

'They should be after the Russians,' I mutter. 'Not wasting time following us.'

Marshall turns down a wide, exposed industrial road lined with warehouses.

The security car follows.

I bite my nails for several nerve-jittering minutes, eyes fixed to the mirror while the security car tails us. At the next roundabout orange lights flare into life on its roof.

My mouth drops open.

'Stay cool,' Marshall says, taking the first exit.

The security car circles the roundabout and doubles back towards the airport with its sirens blaring.

Marshall drives down a side street and parks next to the kerb.

'I thought those sirens were for us!' I release a pent-up breath. 'Do you think the police gave them a heads-up about the quartz?'

Marshall shrugs. 'Whatever the reason, we should head back. There's nothing more we can do here.'

I clench my hands in my lap and close my eyes, the bitter taste of failure rising in my throat.

'Don't give up.' Marshall gives me a sympathetic look. 'We still have Okada Atsuko, Grigor's stone tapes, and the rental car records to go on.'

Despite his reassurances, it's galling to have gained so little for our hard work. The Russians have the quartz and we aren't a single step closer to finding Jonathan.

33

Marshall tunes the car radio to Classic FM for the drive home. The mellow orchestral music, comfy seats and smooth-as-silk ride act like a warm hug, and my eyelids start to droop.

It seems I've only just closed my eyes when Marshall touches my shoulder. 'Alex, we're here.'

I blink awake. The bustle of London has been replaced by birdsong, trees, and the familiar sight of Red Croft Lodge.

Marshall leaves the car and walks round to the passenger door. He opens it and extends his hand. Stifling a yawn, I gather my torn rucksack and Grigor's satchel and allow him to assist me from the car.

'I don't know whether to eat something, have a bath, or go to bed,' I say, shielding my eyes from the brilliant afternoon sunlight.

'How about a late lunch?' Marshall suggests, locking the car. He opens the front door and leads me through to the kitchen. 'Give me ten minutes? TJ needs to download the photographs and my police contact might be able to push some buttons regarding the stolen quartz. I also need to check on Carmen.'

'Sure. Take these down to the Vault for me?' I hand him the rucksack and the satchel before heading to the kitchen.

I slice and butter a baguette from the bread bin then add cheese, ham, tomatoes, and piccalilli, and arrange the impromptu Ploughman's on a tray with two slices of coffee cake.

Marshall finds me in the garden setting out plates and cutlery on the patio table.

'Looks good,' he says, taking a seat and tucking a serviette into his collar.

'Any news?' I ask.

'The police are still interviewing Carmen at the museum and TJ's finishing his research. He needs more time.'

I pass Marshall a plate. 'Did she mention how Nathan's doing?'

'That the scientist Grigor took out?' At my nod, he says, 'He's pretty shocked but doing okay. As for Grigor, the police have charged him with theft, actual bodily harm, assault, and reckless damage.'

I speak through a mouthful of bread and cheese. 'He won't be doing fieldwork for the foreseeable future.'

'There's more,' Marshall adds. 'My contact told me the police are on scene at London City Airport. Hopefully, they'll find the quartz.'

'That is good news.' I grin.

A warm breeze bends the knee-high grass and rustles the apple leaves overhead. Marshall nips into the kitchen and returns with a tray containing mugs, a cafetière, and a milk jug. He pours us coffee before plunging his fork into the rich sponge cake.

'Have you told Antony any of this?' he asks casually.

I shake my head. 'I don't want to worry him. He thinks my field work consists of visiting standing stones and museums. If I told him we're running down Russian gangs he'd be down here in a flash.' I give a shaky laugh.

'Sounds like you two are close.' Marshall sips his coffee. 'My wife and I used to be like that. It's a good way to be.' He stretches back in the patio chair. 'Today was tough. If you want out I'll understand.'

I put down my fork. 'I'm in the League. You need my help.'

'We do. But things are getting serious and you've already put yourself in danger.'

I shake my head, unsure if Marshall wants to protect me or is simply testing my resolve. 'We have to find Jonathan. I can't let the American steal my father's legacy. No way.'

Marshall places his empty mug on the tray and gives me a level look. 'As long as you're sure.'

'I'm sure.'

After our late lunch we descend to the Vault. TJ glances up from a neat pile of paper on the table and raises his hand in greeting.

'Hi, TJ,' I wave back. 'Any luck with the photos?'

The teenager shakes his head. 'There were no clear shots of the Russians' faces, I'm afraid.'

'I thought as much.' I remove the leather notebook from the satchel and hand it over. 'Grigor donated his research on ghost quartz to the League.'

TJ flicks through the pages, rubbing his chin. 'Mineralogy is more Carmen's speciality than mine.' He sets the notebook down. 'I'll show it to her as soon as she gets back.'

Marshall joins us at the table. 'What have you got?'

TJ retrieves a sheet from the pile. 'I'll start with the BMW. The car was rented from Hertz in Milton Keynes first thing this morning.'

'Milton Keynes? That's less than five miles from here.' Marshall frowns, glancing at the live-feed CCTV showing the exterior of Red Croft Lodge.

'Yep. The car was signed out under a company account, Champion Micro.' He shows us a car rental contract and points to the bottom of the page. An illegible squiggle sits above the company name. 'Champion is a Silicon Valley tech startup. The company was formed in 1998. It has less than twenty permanent employees.'

I pass the printout to Marshall. 'Who's the boss?'

TJ says, 'A woman named Laura Harris.'

'Are there any American men on the board?'

TJ looks down, biting his lip. 'Give me a second to process my tasks.'

'Sorry,' I say, swallowing my next question.

Marshall turns his back on the teenager and crosses his arms, giving him time to reset. I walk around the lab, praying the police have found the quartz.

'Champion Micro is a small company,' TJ resumes. 'It's a subsidiary of Data Foundries, another Silicon Valley start-up. The companies are stacked on top of each other in layers like this.'

TJ draws ten small boxes at the bottom of a blank sheet of paper, then five boxes above them, three boxes above that, ending with one at the top. He connects the boxes via lines from the top down until it looks like a pyramid. 'All these companies are owned by one big one. All Tech Corp.'

'The name sounds familiar,' I say.

TJ nods. 'They're the biggest company you've never heard of.' He shows me the company logo: a blue square with the letters ATC inside it. It vaguely rings a bell. 'All Tech is a mega funded U.S. corporation that exploded from a medium-sized business into a multinational in the '90s. The company aggressively buys up smaller microelectronic industries, especially those specialising in firmware and miniaturisation.'

Marshall raises a brow. 'They sound like IBM.'

'Up to a point. All Tech pumps millions into advertising their products worldwide. Then things start to get more sinister,' TJ says. 'There are rumours All Tech markets its products on the dark web to the Middle East, Nigeria, China, and Russia. Even North Korea.'

Marshall taps the ATC logo. 'Who's the big boss?'

TJ points to the stacks of paper. 'I've only skimmed the surface of this megacorp. They have a board of directors one hundred strong as well as a president, stockholders, executive officers...'

'Have you checked beneficial ownership information?' Marshall asks. 'That should state All Tech's owners.'

TJ ruffles through papers. 'I did check. Major Buchanan Quinn owns the whole kit and kaboodle. He was All Tech's CEO for twenty years.'

Marshall presses his fist into his palm. 'Do you have a photo?'

TJ hands Marshall an image of an old man in swimshorts leaning on the deck-rail of a yacht with a glass of champagne in hand. 'The photo's from 1995. Major Quinn's in his nineties now. He lives in a luxury retirement facility in Palm Springs. I can't see him running the operation.'

'Let me try his photo in the Drive,' I say.

'Be my guest.' TJ hands it over.

I grab the picture, rush back into the Vault, and use scissors to cut it out. I slip the small image into the finding machine's clips and turn it on.

26.860776, -80.111769

3000, Central Gardens Cir., Palm Beach Gardens, FL. USA

With a sigh, I remove the photo and return to the others.

'Guess that's a no,' Marshall says, seeing my glum expression.

'The American could be any of several hundred employees,' TJ says. He gestures to his diagram. 'Or he might not work for any of these companies. More importantly, we don't have time to obtain pictures of every person we're interested in.'

Marshall scratches his brow. 'If that's a dead end, what's next?'

'We wait for Ms Atsuko to hand over the static tape.' TJ shrugs. 'Then hunt these guys down.'

Silence falls as we mull over the facts.

Marshall eventually says. 'I don't suppose you have any good news?'

'Actually, I do,' TJ says. 'I had a breakthrough with Grigor's stone tape.'

Marshall and I stare at the teenager.

'What?' I exclaim. 'You made sense of that noise?'

'You should have said so straightaway!' Marshall stands. 'This is huge. I have to call Carmen right away.' He backs towards the door. 'Give me five minutes.'

I sidle alongside TJ. 'If you've cracked the stone tape, I guess you don't need my dad's videos anymore.'

'Guess not.'

'Please can I could borrow the Stonehenge one?'

TJ removes the video cassette tape from a drawer. He hesitates. 'I should ask Carmen.'

'I already have! She says it's okay.' Hopefully, she'll be so pleased about TJ's breakthrough she won't ask where it's gone. 'I'm not taking the video from the building. I only want to watch it in the TV room.'

'I've made copies so I suppose it's okay, but I'll need it back.'

'No problem.' I tuck the video into my rucksack's internal pocket, zip up the bag and place it under the table beside Grigor's empty satchel.

'I've set everything up in the clean lab,' TJ says. 'You want to come through?'

I follow him through the door and we don plastic hair caps and shoe covers. 'This isn't necessary for the stone tapes,' he says. 'It's to preserve other ongoing experiments.'

Once we're suitably attired, TJ leads me to a table cluttered with audio equipment. A cassette player is wired to two large speakers, headphones, and a digital audio mixer with multiple banks of sliders. The set-up looks like a mini sound production studio.

Tingles run through me as TJ puts on the headphones and rewinds the tape.

'How did you do make sense of the noise?' I ask, remembering the discordant clashing booms and whistles on the Avebury video.

'Grigor did most of the work,' TJ generously admits. 'The rest was trial and error using enhanced noise-cancelling and cleanup software and digital signal processing. It's still not perfect by any means.'

Marshall enters the lab, looking ridiculous in his blue plastic cap, white shirt, tie, and suit. I turn away so he can't see me smile.

I ask Marshall, 'Shouldn't we wait for Carmen? She'd hate to miss this.'

'Carmen's just left the museum,' Marshall says. 'She told us to go ahead. TJ can repeat the demo when she gets here.'

He nods to TJ who presses a button. Static hiss fills the room.

My heart speeds up as a voice comes through the speakers.

It's impossible to tell if it's a man or woman beneath the hissing. TJ leans over the audio mixer and adjusts some sliders and the interference fades into the background. The voice sounds muffled, as though it's coming from behind a heavy curtain.

A man speaks with a rural burr. His unusual cadence makes me feel peculiar, off-balance.

'...lament my daughters' deaths every day I linger upon this earth...[crackle]...hath dealt me four cruel blows...[crackle]...called to heaven stricken with the sleeping sickness. I bore my suffering alone...[crackle]... approaches. I take a rope into the woods, Mary, to the tree where I kissed you first...pray we may be...'

The voice fades out. I stare at the cassette player, entranced by the voice's spell.

'Who was that?' I whisper. 'He sounded like a ye olde actor.'

TJ says, 'We know he lived near the Rollright Stones a long time ago.'

'How long ago?' I ask.

TJ flicks through his notes. 'After the Great Vowel Shift, when the long vowel sounds changed. That puts the earliest date at 1400, but the inclusion of more modern words makes me think it's later, maybe sixteenth or seventeenth century.'

Marshall's incredulous gaze meets mine. 'But that's over two hundred years before the first voice recording.'

'Thomas Edison's phonograph recording. 1870,' TJ confirms.

'It can't be...it's impossible,' I whisper. The strength runs from my legs and I collapse into a plastic chair. The concept of hearing voices from the past, hundreds of years before the invention of audio recorders, leaves me momentarily speechless.

'This is like finding Shakespeare's DVD collection!' I say, wild-eyed.

I try to get my head around the sheer out-of-left-field-ness of rocks being ambient recorders. I'm no scientist but if TJ says it's a five-hundred-year-old recording then it's a five-hundred-year-old recording.

This is as big as Dad's finding machine.

'Congratulations, TJ,' Marshall says. 'This is one of the League's finest breakthroughs.'

'Thanks,' TJ manages, his face flushing.

'It is amazing.' I meet Marshall's gaze. 'But if the American has Grigor's stone tapes, receiver, and modulator, what does he want them for? Why would anyone need the voices of the dead?'

34

'We don't know why the American needs these old voices,' Marshall says, staring at the cassette-recorder. 'And I'm not sure it will help us find Jonathan.' He flicks through the Hertz rental documents. 'We're better off tracking down the American the old-fashioned way. Unpicking ATC's company structure is a good place to start.'

A twinge flares across my temple when he mentions subsidiaries, overseas branches and conglomerates. It's impossible to concentrate after hearing the stone tape.

'I'm really sorry. I have a headache,' I interrupt. 'Can I take a break?'

Marshall looks at his watch. 'Yeah, sure. We'll call you if we need you.'

'Thanks.' I hop up from my chair, lifting my rucksack by its one good strap. 'Do you know where I can find a sewing kit?'

TJ says, 'In the kitchen, the cupboard above the toaster.'

'Thanks.'

I escape the Vault, rucksack on my shoulder, and head for the kitchen where I find an old Quality Street tin in the cupboard TJ mentioned. The tin is full of cotton reels, scissors, needles and buttons. I tuck it under one arm, take it to the TV room and close the door behind me.

Amber light filters through the windows. I draw the curtains to cut out the glare. After removing the *STONEHENGE 1970* video from my rucksack, I kneel before the VCR, insert the video and rewind it.

Ensuring the volume is turned down low, I press 'play'.

White specks dance across the screen, accompanied by crackling sounds. I fast forward until an image appears. A beam of white torchlight shines in an arc across grass tussocks. Elephantine sarsen stones topped with horizontal capstones loom un the distance. The world-famous historical site is unmistakable even in the dead of night.

A campfire flickers outside the stone circle, sending up a stream of pale smoke. Shadowy figures sway and dance around the fire. They raise their arms to the skies, moving to the beat of a drum.

The torch, probably held by Carmen, shines on Dad. He puts on headphones and faces the camera. The stark light deepens the hollows beneath Dad's eyes. There's a grey cast across his jaw where he hasn't shaved.

Static dances across my fingertips when I reach out to touch his face.

Dad clears his throat, a habit of his whenever he had something important to say. I turn up the volume.

'We're at Stonehenge for the final day of the stone tape experiment,' Dad says. 'It's an hour before dawn on the summer solstice, believed by many to be an auspicious time. For this reason we're recording both video and audio, in case we discover a correlation between light levels, visual events, and the sound dynamics.' He pauses. 'We've placed the recorder on the outer stone and run out a cable as far back from the other people as we can. Hopefully, their noise won't contaminate the recording.'

His use of the word '*we*' grates on my nerves and my irritation doubles when Carmen hands the torch to Dad and he shines the light on her. She wears a red and ochre woollen tasselled cape with a repeating design of alpacas. My mum had a shoulder bag with the same design.

Carmen unscrews the cap of a tartan thermos flask. She pours coffee into the lid before offering it to Dad. They take turns drinking from it.

I put my hand up to block her. They must have shared hundreds of moments like this. I thought Mum's domineering behaviour was to blame for the fault lines in the marriage, but now I wonder if Carmen was the catalyst.

I tell myself the past is a different country.

Reluctantly, I lower my hand. Dad moves behind the camera and adjusts the angle on the tripod, bringing the horizon perfectly level. Carmen joins him off-screen. I bite my lip, trying not to think about what they're up to.

The chanting and drums suddenly cut out, replaced by the ghoulish sounds I heard on the Avebury tape. The discordant mix of roaring wind, eerie whistles and dull booms chills my bones. If anything, it sounds worse than before. I turn down the volume.

The solstice worshippers continue swaying. The sky stays dark. As the minutes roll on my brain adjusts to the background white noise.

I retreat to the Chesterfield with the remote control, open the Quality Street tin and choose a needle stuck in a pincushion. I use backstitch — the only stitch I know — to reattach my rucksack's damaged strap.

I regularly glance at the screen but dawn is a long time coming. By the time I've completed the repair, tiny dots of pink lighten the sky. The cloudless horizon behind Stonehenge grows lighter.

I double knot the thread, cut it, and test the strap. Not bad.

My phone buzzes in my pocket. I retrieve my mobile and check the display: *IRISH_BRANCH.*

I sink into the cushions and stare at the ceiling. Do I really want more drama after the day I've had? I steel myself for another dose of Moira, vowing to cut her off if she starts jabbering about unusual saints or other irrelevancies.

'Hello, Moira.'

'You said not to call, but you have to hear this!' Moira dives in headfirst. 'I've just been to Drumkeeran on the hunt for Pierce. On the way I popped into McColl's for a pint of milk for my mouth ulcer. And who was there but my old neighbour—'

'Moira, can you please stick to Pierce?'

'I am! Didn't your mother ever say, "a handful of patience is worth more than a bushel of brains?"'

I roll my eyes. 'Strangely enough, no she didn't.'

'Well, you've made me lose my train of thought. Where was I? Ah, yes, I showed Mary the address you sent me and asked if she could point me in the right direction. She said, "*That's Fiona Creedy's place. She hasn't been up to visitors since the break-in.*" What do you think of that?'

'What break-in?'

'Last Wednesday at St Brigid's Church. Fiona's the bursar and she was first on the scene. It was another insider job. And wouldn't you know, a certain someone has recently started attending services.'

I grab a cushion and squeeze it. 'Is his name Pierce, by any chance?'

'First prize to you, Alexandra.'

I throttle the cushion. County Leitrim has turned into holy crime central since the day he moved in.

Moira continues, 'It's only a matter of time before he strikes at St Ignatius's. Father Egan has hundreds of Euros for the car park extension stashed away in the office safe. The silverware in the tabernacle and the vestry is worth a queen's ransom. Even the processional cross is gold-plated. We have to do something!'

'We will. Just let me think.'

The sad thing about stealing from church is it's not just about losing valuables or money. The church ends up locking their doors when they're supposed to be open to all.

'We need to analyse Pierce's modus operandi. Look for weaknesses,' I say. 'He turns up in church as an eligible bachelor and latches onto the older women volunteers.'

Moira adds, 'Then he targets anyone with keys like the cleaner, florist, bursar, or the organist. He professes an interest in the parish so he can ask lots of questions without sounding suspicious.'

'When the opportunity presents itself, he borrows a set of keys and makes copies,' I take up the story. 'You can get that done on any high street.'

'Your mother has a set.' Moira reminds me.

On TV, the sky behind Stonehenge gradually lightens to a soft velvet grey. I press 'pause' on the remote.

'I think it's time to go to the police,' I say. 'We don't have solid evidence but if you tell them about Pierce they can look into him.'

Moira says, 'The Drumkeeran Garda have asked anyone with information to come forward. I'll tell them everything. Let's put him in the frame.'

'Before you do, go to Father Egan. Persuade him to hide the silver.'

'He can't do that. The church silver's used every day except Monday.'

'Then he can take it all home after Mass.'

'How long will he have to do that for?'

'I don't know! Until the thief is caught?' I clench my teeth and take a steadying breath. 'First things first, let's deal with the money. Father Egan has to go to the bank today.'

'That won't fly. It's not a Friday.'

'So?'

Moira sighs. 'Friday's banking day. Father and Dervla O'Hara take the 563 bus to Sligo and make a morning of it. It's the only day Father can go because of his responsibilities.'

'Dervla can go without him. You could offer to drive her.'

'That's a grand plan. Oh, wait...Father Egan's a signatory. He has to be there.'

I fling myself on the sofa. What will it take before anyone does anything?

'I've an idea.' Moira's voice rises. 'Why don't we persuade Brigid to join our spy network? It would give her something useful to do and might make her feel better after acting like such an eejit.'

'That won't work,' I say instantly. Mum would have to admit to being duped and she'll never do that.

My gaze lands on the finding machine. I retrieve Pierce's photograph from the side pocket and slide it between the clips.

I switch on: **6, Castle Court, Dromahaire, Co. Leitrim, Ireland.**

My breath catches.

'Alexandra, what is it?'

I double-check. 'Pierce is with Mum!'

'The absolute cheek of him! Shall I run down there with my rolling pin and give him what for?'

'No! We need to handle this carefully. We don't want Pierce to run or do something worse. I'll call her...' I curse under my breath. My burner phone doesn't have her numbers stored on it. 'You need to give me Mum's home and mobile numbers.'

'How can you not have them?' Moira harrumphs. 'I'll text them to you.'

'Good. Once you've done that, go to Mum's house and ring the doorbell. Say you wanted to drop by and see how she is. Then, you need to get Pierce out of the house.'

Moira says, 'I could call him a thief and a trickster to his face. Get him riled up and make him chase me.'

'Don't do that! Make up some emergency like your car's broken down and ask him to take a look. Once Mum's alone I'll try and talk some sense into her.'

'All right. Give me ten minutes to text you the numbers and get to Brigid's.'

'Good luck.'

Moira's true to her word. A text arrives within a minute.

I push up from the sofa and dial Mum's landline, walking back and forth on the Persian rug with my gaze switching between the finding machine's reading and the frozen image on TV.

Mum answers in an upbeat voice. 'Well, hello, Alexandra! I was only just talking about you. You'll never guess who's here with me.'

I speak in a rush. 'I need to speak to you in private. Can you move to another room where he can't hea—'

'PIERCE! It's Alexandra herself! Come and say hello!'

'Mum, I don't want t—'

A mellow voice with a refined Irish accent says, 'Good afternoon to you, young lady! Brigid's told me so much about you. She was only saying it's a shame you and your brother live so far away.'

Hurry up, Moira!

'I wish I was closer,' I say coldly. 'I want to speak to her if that's okay.'

Instead of saying yes and passing the phone over, he lowers his voice. 'You may have heard rumours about strange goings-on in the area. I understand that Moira's been giving you her take on things. She's been a good friend to your mum in the past but you mustn't believe everything she says.'

I bite back a spirited defence of Mum's best friend. 'Moira just wants to know Mum's okay.'

'Don't worry about your mum. She and I have been taking time to work on a special project together.'

'What kind of project?' Gloves, masks, and church heists come to mind, with my mum pushed forwards as the fall-guy.

'If I told you, I'd have to kill you!' Pierce laughs, setting my teeth on edge. 'Don't worry about your Mum. I want you to know I'm taking very good care of her.'

His smooth and controlled delivery reminds me of Michael Corleone from The Godfather.

'What does that mean?'

Pierce sighs. 'Brigid can be a tiny bit too trusting. She doesn't realise there are unscrupulous people around who would try and take advantage. It's important we keep her away from them.'

Every word comes across as a barely concealed threat. A shiver goes through me. He sounds like he's controlling her.

A bell shrills in the background.

'You should get the door.' My voice rises. I clench my fist and pace the carpet faster, my plans in pieces.

'Your mum's going,' Pierce says. 'You take care now.'

'No! Pass me over to Mu—'

The line goes dead.

35

I redial Mum. The ring tone repeats six or seven times. I kill the call and try her mobile as a knot grows in my stomach.

Finally, she answers.

'Oh, it's you again.' She sounds strained.

Her voice goes muffled. I catch the odd snippet. '*...what do you expect Pierce to do? He doesn't go around with spark plugs in his pocket!*' before she resumes the conversation. 'Sorry about that. Pierce is helping Moira. She can't seem to stay away.'

'I really need to talk to you alone,' I plead. 'Can you go into the lounge?'

'If you insist.' Seconds pass. 'What is it? Are you in trouble?'

'No, you are! Moira's at your door because she's worried about you. So am I. This will probably come as a shock, but Pierce isn't the man he says he is.'

'Did you hear this from Moira?' Mum responds warily.

'Please hear me out. Pierce has recently started attending two churches in Drumkeeran and Longford as well as yours. Both have suffered thefts in the last month. We believe he's now planning on robbing St Ignatius's.'

Mum lowers her voice. 'You and Moira are obviously in cahoots but you've got the wrong end of the stick. If you don't mind, I'd like to make the most of Pierce's company before he has to go.'

'Go where?'

Her voice catches. 'Not that it's your business, but his work called and he has to leave for Dublin tomorrow evening. He won't be back any time soon.'

My stomach twists. If Pierce is going to skip town it seems even more likely that he's planning to rob the church.

'Mum, do me a favour and check you still have your set of keys to the church.'

'Why are you asking?'

'Humour me, please.'

After a long pause, she says, 'They're on the peg in the kitchen where they always are.'

Pierce could still have made copies.

Mum huffs. 'Forgive me for saying this, but you are starting to sound hysterical. Ring me tomorrow night when you're calmer and we'll talk.'

'This can't wait!' I hiss. 'Pierce is going to run off with the church funds and the silver.'

'You couldn't be further from the truth.' Mum's voice turns hard. 'Now, I'd be obliged if you'd both stop interfering.'

Casting a desperate glance to the ceiling, I say, 'Can't you see what's going on under your nose?'

'I know what to believe.' Mum's voice brooks no refusal. 'And I won't be convinced otherwise, Alexandra. If you'll excuse me, I have to go. God bless.'

The line goes dead. I sink on the sofa and groan as I run over the conversation. I gave it my best shot. What more could I do?

My phone rings.

Hurriedly, I answer.

'Mum?'

'No, it's Moira.'

'Is Pierce still with you?'

'No.' Her tone is mournful. 'He was too smooth for me. I said I had car trouble, thinking he'd take a look and I could keep him talking. But he wouldn't leave the house. He offered to call me a taxi and have the car towed to a garage. I couldn't think of anything to say, so now I'm fleeing the scene before the taxi and the tow truck arrive.' She pauses. 'Did you do any better?'

'Not really.' A short laugh escapes me. 'Mum's a law unto herself. She won't listen to a word I say.'

Moira's voice rises. 'I'm not letting him get away with this. I'll go to the police in Drumkeeran.'

'But we don't have any evidence!'

'All the same, I feel it's my duty. After that, I'll go to church, say a few rosaries and keep an eye on the silver until tomorrow night. I'll take a sleeping bag and camp under one of the pews. Pierce can't steal anything if I'm there the whole time.'

'He can if he turns nasty!' I warn. 'I'll track Pierce and tell you if he goes to the church. The police will have to do something then.'

'I'll be waiting, Alexandra.' She ends the call.

I drop the phone on the table, press the cushion to my face, and yell at the top of my voice until I can't yell any more.

I sink onto the sofa. The frozen image on TV catches my eye. I reach for the remote control and press play, hoping the summer solstice will take my mind off the Irish problem. The peaceful scene, lightening sky, and white noise in the background combine to calm me down.

On TV, the sky's pinkish haze slowly brightens to amber. Solstice celebrants garbed in white and brown robes rise and link hands to greet the start of summer, no doubt chanting and praising the sunrise to the beat of a drum. The sun breaches the horizon as dawn arrives. Fiery rays light the land and turn the stones blood-red.

The discordant sound leaps in volume.

I crawl to the TV and put my ear to the speaker. Deep booms and whistles send curious tingles along my limbs as the sun climbs higher into the morning sky. Light floods the stone circle and the surrounding fields. The volume drops again.

I kneel back and stare at a dark shape on one side of the screen.

Dad's arm is around Carmen's waist. She leans her head on his shoulder as they watch the dawn.

Something dies inside me. My problems with Mum fade away. The perfect picture I've built of Dad is a lie. He and Mum had their problems but I thought his solution was tinkering with electronics in his workshop.

Dad kisses the top of Carmen's head. I squeeze my eyes shut, my gall rising.

'Alex, here you are! I wanted to see how you w—'

I jam my finger on the remote control. In my haste, instead of pressing 'stop', I hit 'pause'. White bands shimmer on screen, partially obscuring the image.

Carmen stands in the doorway, leaning on the owl-handle of her walking stick. Her gaze flicks to the image frozen on the TV screen, then to me. She misses a step and stumbles, grabbing onto the sofa to steady herself.

For a second I feel sympathy for this old woman with her grey hair, lopsided stance, and glasses. But then my vitriol returns.

'I'm just watching Dad's video,' I say. 'Do you remember it?'

Carmen nods and says softly, 'The summer solstice at Stonehenge. The morning was unusually bitter.'

She softly closes the door behind her and gestures towards the armchair. 'Do you mind?'

I direct my glare to the floor.

Carmen sinks into the armchair and rests the stick across her knees. 'I felt bad about everything afterwards.'

Goosebumps rise on my arms. I hug myself. 'You admit you feel bad about Dad?'

Carmen nods. 'I pushed Richard on the stone tape experiments. He wanted to give up after Avebury but I was blinded by enthusiasm. I believed we would eventually succeed. All we had to do was keep going.' She smiles. 'And now, TJ has finally got a result from the stone tapes. Isn't it marvellous?'

Her smile fades when she catches sight of my expression.

My stare bores into her. 'Why did Dad listen to you? He was the lead scientist on this project. You were his assistant.'

Carmen blinks, looking stunned. 'Richard did it to please me. I was young. I thought we had all the time in the world.'

Narrowing my eyes, I ask, 'Did he ever mention his family?'

'Of course.' Her eyes widen. 'He often mentioned you and Matthew. He constantly referred to you as the technical one. I think he was a little disappointed you chose a career in art rather than science but he never said so in front of you. He didn't want to put pressure on you.'

That sounds fair enough. Mum was the one who did that.

In a small voice, I ask, 'Did Dad ever mention my mum?'

Carmen's lips press together. 'We tended to leave our day-to-day lives behind when we were in the field.'

'Did you forget he was married?' The words slip out.

A horrible silence descends. An ugly red flush blooms on Carmen's neck and rises to her cheeks.

'I can see you're upset.' Carmen falters. 'You should know that with your father his family came first. Always.'

'Except when he was with you.'

'I...I was fond of Richard, I admit,' Carmen says falteringly. 'But I would never have done anything to break up his marriage.'

'How can you know what damage you caused?' I drive the nail in. 'You thought you could do what you liked because no one was watching.'

Carmen turns to me, removes her glasses and wipes her eyes. 'Please, Alex. It was a very long time ago.'

'That doesn't make it right!' I shoot up, fury burning a line across my shoulders. I cross my arms and look down at her. 'Admit it, you were having an affair.'

She looks into her lap, her red face displaying her guilt.

'Say it.' I stand over her like a playground bully. My gall shocks me, but I have to know.

'Richard and I...we had a brief relationship. It was my fault. I was young and foolish and somewhat star-struck. I had a huge crush on him.'

Her admission hits me like a stinging slap. I turn away, fighting tears. My mental image of Mum and Dad rips apart, leaving hot anger in its place.

Carmen dabs her cheeks with a tissue and balls it up in her fist.

'If you want to blame someone, blame me.'

I do.

'I had no idea what I was doing,' she continues. 'Your family, I never gave them a second thought. It was the ignorance of youth, Alex. That's the only excuse I can give.' She blinks back tears. 'Richard ended it if that helps at all. He knew what we were doing was doomed. You and Matthew were his life.'

Carmen doesn't even mention my mother. Did she even know? I stare at dust clinging to the frill on the lamp.

Poor Mum.

'If I could take it back I would.' Carmen's face is a blotchy mess. Her mouth tugs down at the corners. 'I judge that girl on the video too.'

'A bit late in the day for that,' I snap.

'If you can't forgive me, forgive your father. Don't let me spoil your memories of him.' Carmen reaches out and grabs my hand. 'Please, don't hate us.'

I drag my hand free and back away to the door.

'I can't help how I feel.'

36

I spend the next hour in my room crying into my pillow. I desperately need Antony's take on things, but I'm in no fit state to talk so I ask him to text me instead. We go back and forth multiple times, constrained by the 160 character limit until he finally calls.

'Just talk to me,' he says.

'It's so awkward with Carmen.' The moment I speak, I start welling up. 'I don't know what to do!'

'Are you sure you should do anything? The videos are ancient history.'

'That's not exactly helpful, Antony. I can't unsee them now!'

Antony speaks calmly. 'It seems like you and Carmen were getting on well. Do you really want to ruin that?'

'How can I forgive her? Or Dad?' My indignation rises. 'He used to be my hero until I watched those videos!'

'I get that. But he didn't split the family. He never left you.'

'That doesn't make it okay.'

'What I'm saying is, no one's perfect.' Antony sighs. 'It sucks, but it could be worse. I've never forgiven my father for leaving. I'm still bitter about it twenty years later. You don't want to carry that inside you. Try and let it go, babe.'

I swallow, my thumb brushing a tear from my cheek. 'He was a brilliant dad.'

'He was. I wish my dad had been half as good.'

Antony's mum had to bring him and his sister up alone. It makes me realise, although Dad was away from home a lot we always knew he'd return.

A knock comes at the bedroom door.

'Hold on!' I call out, turning away from the door and lowering my voice. 'I have to go. I love you.'

'When you get back, we'll open a bottle of wine and talk it out. Love you too.'

I sit up, sniffing and wiping my eyes. 'Who is it?'

'It's Marshall. Mind if I come in?'

Forcing myself from bed, I walk to the door and open it.

'Room service,' Marshall says with a small smile. The unmistakable aroma of hot pepperoni drifts from the Domino's pizza box under his arm. In his other hand is a bottle of Labatt's lager, condensation forming on the glass.

'That looks great,' I mumble.

Marshall carries the pizza and lager to the dresser and sets them down. He glances from my phone to the rumpled counterpane before facing me, hands on his hips.

'I've got an idea about what's going on. This isn't my business but I wish you two would make up. I've never seen Carmen so upset.'

'The past came back to bite her,' I say sullenly. 'That's not my fault.'

Marshall leans back on the dresser. 'She thinks the world of you.'

I keep my mouth shut, aware of how bitter I sound.

Marshall folds his arms. 'When I first told Carmen you were coming, I may as well have said it was the Queen. She made such a fuss over everything, making up your room, baking cakes, shopping for things she thought you'd like. She even made me clean the car.'

I sink onto the bed and scrunch the blankets.

'She said you reminded her of Richard.'

A jab of pain spikes my ribs.

'Carmen treats you like a daughter, Alex. Think about that for a moment.'

I look down at my feet. 'I already have a mother.'

Marshall raises his hands. 'Eat something. Sleep on it. Things should look different in the morning. I know you're finding this difficult but try and be kind to her.'

'All right,' I concede, closing my eyes and releasing a tense breath. 'I'll try my best.'

'Good.' Marshall blows out a long breath. 'I have other news. Okada Atsuko called. The handover for the static tape is going ahead tomorrow morning at nine. If you feel up to it, I'd really like your help.'

'Of course,' I answer swiftly. Anything that puts distance between me and Carmen gets my vote.

'This is our last chance to find the American.' Marshall's brows draw together. 'I'll see you first thing in the morning.'

· · · • · • · · · ·

I manage eight hours of half-decent, dreamless sleep before my alarm goes off at 6.30 a.m. My feelings regarding Carmen are far from resolved. It makes me even more determined to help Mum.

I place Pierce's photo into the finding machine's clips and turn it on:

6, Castle Court, Dromahaire, Co. Leitrim, Ireland.

Looks like the smooth criminal stayed the night round Mum's. I text the news to Moira, adding:

`Did you go to the police?`

Hopefully, she'll take the hint to get down to Drumkeeran police station if she hasn't already done so.

I tuck the finding machine into my mended rucksack and head down to the kitchen to recycle my bottle and empty pizza box. To my relief, Carmen's nowhere in sight.

I push my jumbled emotions to the back of my mind, make coffee and slip bread into the toaster.

Marshall turns up as the last drip of coffee falls into the percolator jug. He appears to have a sixth sense for when his next caffeine fix is ready.

'Morning,' he says, pouring coffee into two mugs. 'Sleep well?'

'All right,' I say noncommittally, hoping he doesn't mention Carmen.

'I've had news from my police contact,' Marshall says, handing me a mug. He stirs sugar into his coffee. 'The police examined the CCTV footage from City Airport yesterday. The two Russians never boarded a flight. They handed the aluminium case to another man. The police don't know where he went and the Russians left soon after.'

'If the Russians didn't get on a plane, where did they go?' I ask, buttering toast.

'CCTV footage shows them walking out of the car park. It's anyone's guess where they went after that.'

I drop my toast. 'If we'd stayed longer we could have followed them.'

'Yeah. I know. But we were drawing unwanted attention.'

'What about the man they handed the case to?'

'He bypassed security and evaded the cameras. Gave everyone the slip.' Marshall gives me a world-weary look. 'The police think he took the quartz onboard a flight as hand luggage, but getting information out of the private jet companies is like pulling teeth. Four planes left from City Airport that afternoon. Three flew to the U.S. and one to Moscow. The police have permits to search the planes but Moscow isn't cooperating.'

'I'm not surprised,' I say. 'The quartz came from Tunguska. Russia probably wants it back.'

Marshall drains his mug and stands. 'Let's hope it's gone to the States. We have strong ties with the Transport Security Administration over there. My contact will call me when he has news.'

We leave the house after breakfast. Grey tinged clouds roll in overhead. It's the first overcast day we've had in weeks. Marshall places a black sports bag in the footwell behind his seat. I slip into the front passenger seat, secure my seatbelt and push up the sun visor.

As we drive away from Red Croft Lodge, something releases inside me — relief, no doubt — at leaving my family troubles behind.

The route Marshall follows is familiar. After twenty minutes the Yoioto Corporation building looms into view. My palms go clammy as I stare at the ornamental garden and water sputtering from the fountain.

I sigh with relief once we've driven past. 'Where's the handover taking place?'

'A place five minutes away called Pages Park. Should be just ahead.' Marshall turns up Eden Way, a road lined with beech trees that cuts through a business park. He follows the road to a T-junction and turns left onto Billington Road.

Marshall cruises slowly up the road, glancing into every car we pass.

A flash of green grass catches my eye. A sign on the verge reads: *PAGES PARK.* Beyond, a half empty car park faces a playground. Teenagers play football in large fields edged by trees.

Marshall drives to the next side street, turns the Lexus around and returns towards the park. A Vauxhall Corsa sits in the shade of an expansive oak tree opposite. He pulls in behind it. Our vantage point gives us a clear view of the car park, the playground, and passing traffic.

Marshall cuts the engine and checks his watch. 'An hour to go. As stakeouts go this is pretty good.'

'What do you mean?'

'This is a safe neighbourhood,' he explains. 'We don't have to wait up all night for a mark who doesn't turn up. We're not freezing in an unheated car or baking alive in the sun.'

'I don't think I'll take it up as a career, then.'

'Wise choice.' Marshall winks. He reaches behind his seat, unzips his sports bag and removes a high-end Nikon digital camera with a large zoom lens. He switches the Nikon on and cycles through the illuminated display.

'The flash is off,' he informs me, passing the camera over. 'Are you happy to be my nominated photographer?'

'My pleasure.' The Nikon is a world away from my old Kodak but the basic principle's the same. I put the viewfinder to my eye, getting a feel for the camera's weight, and aim at the playground in the distance.

'The automatic focus does the work for you,' Marshall says. 'Press the button halfway to focus, then take the picture. Don't worry about taking too many photos. The memory card can hold hundreds of images.'

In the playground, young children clamber up playframes, shoot down slides, and run around shrieking. A few wear sunhats despite the cloudy conditions. I apply gentle pressure to the button, zooming on a child sitting on a swing, scissor-kicking her feet. Her T-shirt's Pokémon logo is easily legible, with, *"Gotta Catch 'Em All!"* below.

I switch my aim to a distant sycamore tree and depress the button halfway again. Individual leaves come into crisp focus.

'Easy enough,' I say, training the camera on the car park and then the road. I take a few practice shots. Happy with the results, I sit back and count the minutes. Marshall plays the radio on low volume.

My phone buzzes. A text from Moira:

`I saw the Garda yesterday! They agreed to interview Pierce but couldn't say when. They need an independent witness to confirm our suspicions. Looks like it's just you and me.`

Marshall glances my way. 'Everything okay?'

I explain the Pierce situation, while checking his location with the finding machine. 'The police aren't interested. They won't act until a crime is in progress or they have concrete evidence.'

Marshall nods. 'The police are spread thin these days. I imagine it's the same in Ireland.'

Pierce is still at Mum's house. I update Moira and add:

`Sit tight for now and don't do anything rash.`

At 08:53, a red VW Polo approaches the entrance to Pages Park.

'We're on,' Marshall warns.

'I'm ready.'

The Polo's orange indicator flashes. I zoom in on Ms Atsuko as she turns the wheel with white knuckles, her lips a thin line. I track her through the viewfinder as she parks in a bay facing the playground. Glare from the windows prevents me seeing in.

I aim the camera at the road as a silver Audi cruises towards us. The wiry Russian is behind the wheel.

Click. Click.

Marshall scribbles down the registration and calls TJ. The Audi turns into the car park and reverses into a space opposite the Polo.

'Yep, I'm here,' TJ answers.

'TJ, can you run this car? It's a silver Audi A4, registration T351 AFC.'

'Got it. Anything else?'

'Just stay by the phone.'

The Russian speaks on a mobile phone before getting out of the car. I click away. He stands by the rear of the Polo and raps on the roof.

Ms Atsuko rolls down her window and holds out a sheet of paper. I zoom in on a blue circular logo in the corner of the page with an eagle and a shield, and read the banner underneath. I recognise the logo from the papers I found on her desk.

'The letter's from U.S. Immigration,' I tell Marshall. 'I bet it's the one the American sent Okada's mum, threatening to pull her citizenship.'

The Russian smiles, displaying metal-capped teeth. He shakes his head and extends his hand towards the window.

Ms Atsuko hesitates before passing him a stack of slim cardboard boxes. The same ones I saw in Melvyn's retro lab at Yoioto.

Click. Click. Click.

The Russian checks the contents of each box before resting them on the Polo's roof. He turns his back on her and puts his mobile phone to his ear. After a short conversation he nods and ends the call.

He takes the sheet of paper from Okada and rips it into small pieces. He pushes the fragments into her hand.

Ms Atsuko wipes her eyes. I read her lips: '*That's it? Are you sure?*'

Another nod. The Russian makes the OK symbol with his thumb and forefinger, picks up the boxes and walks towards the Audi.

I lower the camera. 'Can the American really call the dogs off Okada's mother just like that?'

'I guess so.' Marshall peers past me at the Russian. 'The American has everything he wants. Let's see what his next move is.'

'Won't he release Jonathan, now?'

'I hope so.'

Marshall presses the Lexus's ignition button as the Russian drives from the car park. He tails the Audi along quiet roads to a set of double roundabouts. A van and a people carrier have right of way and insert themselves between us and our target.

Marshall drops farther back at the next junction until we're five cars behind.

'We'll lose him if we're not careful,' I warn.

'Relax,' Marshall says. 'I've got this.'

At the next roundabout the Audi takes the exit for the A4146 and disappears around a bend. Traffic builds with commuters and mums returning from the school run. The single carriageway gives Marshall no opportunity to overtake and we lose sight of the Audi until the car reappears as a silver dot in the distance, barely distinguishable from the grey skies.

Marshall checks his mirrors and moves out of his lane. The powerful engine gives a low-throated growl and the sudden acceleration pushes me into my seat. I grip the door handle as the Lexus surges past a white van, a Saab, and a bus.

An oncoming lorry flashes its lights. I grit my teeth, the gap between us closing fast. Suppressing a scream, I count my last moments on earth.

Marshall jerks the wheel. The Lexus slips back into the left lane mere seconds before the lorry blasts past.

'See. Easy.'

We crest a hill. The Audi's much closer. Four cars ahead.

I force my fingers to let go of the door handle. 'You've taken years off me! Could you possibly warn me next time?'

'Sure,' says Marshall.

We follow the Audi for several miles, returning along the same route we took this morning. Our target takes the third exit off the next roundabout onto Stoke Road.

I mutter, 'Are you thinking what I'm thinking?'

'Yep.' Marshall's expression is grim as the Audi continues onto Manor Road and drives past a green sign with white letters.

Welcome to BLETCHLEY, home of the Codebreakers.

Marshall presses a button on the steering wheel. 'What's the news, TJ?'

'The Audi's another Hertz rental, signed out of London City Airport yesterday,' TJ says. 'The name on the paperwork was Horizon Data which is another subsidiary of All Tech.'

'The Russians switched cars,' I say, again regretting we hadn't stayed longer to track them.

'There's something else,' TJ adds. 'Your contact ran a check on small airfields near Bletchley and found something interesting. A company called VikingAir has a small fleet of private planes for hire. They operate out of Cranfield Airport, ten miles from here. Horizon Data has has chartered a plane from them, tonight.'

'The American is planning his getaway,' Marshall says. 'What time is he flying out?'

'Ten past ten this evening,' TJ says. 'Your contact's happy to assemble a team to intercept the American before he gets on the plane, as long as he gets the credit.'

'Fine.' Marshall rolls his eyes. 'Tell him it's a go.'

A sudden, horrible thought hits me as the roads become ever more familiar. My heart quickens as I recognise a road near the turn off for Church Walk. I shoot Marshall a worried look.

'By the way,' Marshall says to TJ, 'We've tailed the Audi to Bletchley and there's a chance he might pay you a visit at the Lodge. Lock down the place and watch the cameras. And look after Carmen.'

'Will do, boss.'

I grip the door handle. The next road is Church Walk which leads straight to the Lodge.

The Audi continues past.

I sink back in my seat and exhale loudly. 'That was close.'

'These guys took Jonathan from under our noses,' Marshall says. 'I've got to hand it to them. I never thought they could be operating close by.'

I bite my lip, tormented by the thought of Jonathan being held hostage near the Lodge.

A drop of rain splats on the windscreen as we turn onto Sherwood Drive.

Marshall says, 'I knew it.'

The Audi turns down a side road and drives past a black monolithic sign: WELCOME TO BLETCHLEY PARK.

37

— · —

The Russian drives to Bletchley Park's main entrance, lowers his window and speaks to the security guard on duty. Marshall hangs back and parks the Lexus in the shade of a sweet chestnut tree.

The security guard waves the Russian through the raised red and white striped barrier. He drives past a white concrete building and a sign pointing to the visitors car park and disappears from view.

'You're going to follow him in, right?' I ask. 'This place is open to the public.'

'Slight problem.' Marshall points at two CCTV cameras mounted on the concrete building aimed towards the car park and entrance gates. 'I don't want my plates on camera if the American's involved somehow. I know another way in via an old access road. We can leave the car and go on foot.'

'We'll lose him if we do that.' I cradle the Nikon in my hands, wishing we could instantly print the photos I took earlier so I could track the Russian. I secure the camera strap across my shoulder. 'I'll go.'

'Wait a sec.' Marshall holds my arm. 'We should stick together.'

'I'll be fine. The Russian doesn't know about me. I'll text you once I've spotted him.' I gently pull my arm free and glance at the rucksack in the footwell. 'Lock my Drive in the boot, would you?'

I slip out of the car and walk towards the entrance without a backward glance. Spits of rain hit my shoulders as I approach the guard.

I give him a rueful smile. 'Typical. My first time here and it's raining.'

The guard smiles. 'You'll be fine. The main exhibits are under cover.' He points to the concrete building. 'The entrance is the green door on the left.'

'Thanks.'

I walk to the green door and glance back as a coach pulls up to the barrier and the guard approaches the driver. While he's occupied, I walk down the side of the building towards the car park. I round the corner and stop short, narrowly avoiding a collision with the Russian who is walking towards me.

His brows draw together.

'Sorry, sorry.' I throw up my hands and hurry past before he gets a good look at me.

After a few seconds I glance back. The Russian strides to the green door carrying an orange Sainsbury's bag. I wait for him to go inside before following him.

The Russian strides past the ticket counter to a wall of glass doors and shows a white card to a female staff member checking tickets. Maybe the Russian has a season pass, even if he's not here for the culture.

She waves him through.

I choose the shortest queue for tickets behind an elderly couple, biting my lip as they pick up their change one coin at a time. I glance constantly at the glass doors. After a minute, which feels like an hour, I reach the counter.

'One adult,' I say, sliding a ten-pound note under the glass partition.

The lady prints out a ticket and unfolds a map showing individual buildings, green areas, a lake, and a mansion. She points to a white C in a blue circle. 'This is where we are now, the visitor's centre. The main complex is over h—'

'Got it!' I cut her off, grabbing the ticket and hurrying over to the attendant who punches it. I push through the doors into the main visitor's centre and spot the Russian down the far end as he exits the building. An old woman gives me a curious look as I rush past interactive displays containing decoding machines, weird-looking typewriters, and primitive computers.

Throwing open the door, I step outside. Rain falls onto the parched grass and bounces off the concrete path. I look everywhere for my target but the Russian has gone again.

Tucking the Nikon beneath my shirt I duck my head, following the path to a dark grey hut with a placard stuck on the verge: *National Radio Centre.* I stick my head through the door, wrinkling my nose at the smell of static, burnt metal, and old carpet. A photograph of Nikola Tesla catches my eye beside a display of old valves and wireless sets. The only other people in here are two staff members with headphones, demonstrating the working radio station to a family.

Leaving the building, I swiftly check my map before continuing along the path. Visitors hurry past me for shelter. I pass Block B, a pink 1920s museum, and glimpse the main complex of huts farther down.

A flash of orange catches my eye.

The Russian tucks the carrier bag under his jacket and enters a long hut with a tin roof.

I jog past a sign: *HUT 8, Centre of Naval Codebreaking,* and crack open the door. A central corridor with a wooden floor runs the length of the hut with green doors to either side. I peek past three wet Japanese tourists unfolding plastic rain macs.

The Russian is by the exit door at the end. He leans against the wall with his mobile to his ear. I can't hear him over the tourists' excited babble.

The Japanese tourists head left and I duck into the room opposite. Blinds are drawn over the windows. Anglepoise lamps and ceiling lights provide low lighting. A projector suspended from the ceiling casts life-sized images of British servicemen and service-women onto the wall. The wartime personnel pore over maps and discuss cryptanalysis, as I extract my phone from my pocket and text Marshall:

I creep to the doorway down the other end, pausing beside a wooden desk with an inkwell. A cardboard cut-out of Alan Turing stands behind the chair. A placard declares this is his desk.

I touch the wood and offer up an impassioned plea.

Mr Turing, I'd really appreciate your help here.

I stand by the doorway pretending to study the desk as the Russian's phone conversation drifts through from the corridor.

'...if the boss is happy he will release our guest and we crack open the vodka.' The Russian breaks into laughter. 'No, don't tell him yet, Yury. Not until he has checked the goods.' He pauses. 'Meet me at the bunker.'

Moments later, footsteps resound on the wooden floor and a door hinge squeaks.

I slip into the corridor and through the door before it swings shut, then follow the Russian past an ornamental lake. Rain hammers the water's surface and soaks my shirt.

I tuck the camera under my arm and slip between people carrying umbrellas. My target runs in the direction of a fancy red brick building with plaster façades and a green copper roof. That must be Bletchley Mansion.

The Russian veers down a service road running down the side. I run to keep up, overtaking a young couple with a toddler. He heads for a long garage with open corrugated metal doors, containing restored wartime cars and motorcycles and ducks inside.

He walks past a bedraggled-looking tour group, gathered around a large cream-coloured ambulance with massive headlights.

I tag myself onto the back of the tour group. The young family joins me.

'...Austin 18 ambulance is a fully restored and working example.' The guide says, tapping the chrome front bumper. 'I was lucky enough to have a drive in it today! The vehicle has starred in several films including 'Goodnight, Mr Tom', and a little bird tells me it will soon be appearing in a new film, 'Enigma,' about cryptographers at Bletchley during the war.'

The Russian heads for a door a few paces behind the ambulance's rear bumper. A CCTV camera with a red blinking light is mounted above it. The door bears a metal plate with red letters: *PRIVATE: NO ENTRY.*

I raise my Nikon.

Click.

The Russian presses his thumb against a security pad. The door clicks open. I catch a glimpse of grey walls before he slips inside and the door closes.

Is that the bunker? Is the American inside, holding Jonathan hostage?

I zoom in through the viewfinder at the illuminated security panel with a keypad, scanner, and blue light.

Click. Click.

Tucking behind the group, I text Marshall my location, keeping a surreptitious eye on the door.

The toddler breaks free from his father, races to the ambulance and clambers onto the step board. He grabs the door handle and peers inside.

'Wanna go in da car, Daddee! Me go in and press buttons!'

'It's not a toy.' The father tries and fails to disengage his son's death grip on the handle. He grabs him around his waist and hoists him up, but his chubby hand remains anchored to the handle.

The door opens with a loud creak.

'Uh-oh!' the mum exclaims.

The toddler lets go and wriggles in his father's grip. 'Drive da car, NOW!'

The giant Russian, Yury, strides past me from the direction of the mansion. With his grim expression, square jaw, and flinty look in his eye, he's every bit as terrifying as I remember. He looms behind the father and child and I have a terrifying image of him punching them both to the ground while he roars with laughter.

Yury gently reaches past the man and closes the door.

The toddler's gaze rises to the Russian's full height. He freezes and falls silent, his jaw dropping open.

Yury's mouth cracks into a terrifying grin. He ruffles the boy's hair. 'Good boy.'

I raise the camera and aim at the Russian's face.

Click.

The toddler retracts his neck into his shoulders and clings to his father.

Yury takes three steps to the security door on the back wall and swipes a card through the reader. I hear a beep and he slips inside.

My phone buzzes with a text from Marshall.

`Alex, leave NOW. We may have been compromised. I'm outside the main gates.`

My finger hovers over the buttons. I want to tell him about the bunker and that Jonathan could be on the other side of that door. But Marshall's relying on me.

`On my way.`

Biting back frustration, I leave the garages and retrace my steps past the lake. Rain plasters my hair to my forehead. Tucking the camera beneath my shirt again, I skirt the visitor's centre and walk out of Bletchley Park.

The guard spots me and waves. 'Leaving already?'

'Rain spoiled play!' I wave as I run past, all the way to the black entrance sign. I push my wet fringe out of my eyes and look up and down Sherwood Drive.

After a few minutes I spot the Lexus approaching. Marshall pulls into the turn off and performs a U-turn around the central island.

I jump in and he drives off before I've properly closed the door. He takes a sharp right and races to the next roundabout.

'What's going on?' I ask.

'We have a problem.' Marshall's forehead creases. 'Did the Russian see you?'

'I don't think so.' I wipe water droplets from the camera lens with my shirt. 'What is it?'

'While you were inside I drove to one of Bletchley's old access roads. Someone's replaced the old padlock with an armoured anti-drill lock and heavy chains. There's a CCTV camera and a 24-hour video surveillance warning on the gate. The company running security is ATC.'

'ATC? As in All Tech Corp?' My breath stills in my throat.

'Yep.' Marshall's shoulders drop. 'There's a chance they got me on camera.'

Swiftly, I tell him what I found. 'The Russian mentioned a bunker, then he went through a security door. Jonathan could be inside. Maybe the American, too.'

Marshall nods quickly. 'We can't do any more on foot.'

'What about the League?' I lean towards him. 'Wasn't it formed after the war? It must still have contacts in Bletchley. Can't you find out?'

'The League might have had links to Bletchley Park, but that was over fifty years ago. Any connections we once had no longer exist.'

'Then call the police. Hand over the evidence and let them go in and rescue Jonathan.'

'Did you see Jonathan? Or the American?'

'No.'

'Then we have no evidence.'

'What about the static tape? Ms Atsuko can verify she handed it over. Melvyn Potter also knows, if push comes to shove.'

'I doubt she'll admit to stealing the tape from Yoioto when her bosses don't even know she manufactured it or it's missing,' Marshall says. 'Until we have evidence it's up to us. And your Drive.'

38

Marshall calls Carmen on the short drive back to the Lodge. 'We may have a problem. Lock up the house and get into the Vault.'

Minutes later, he guns the Lexus through the Lodge gates. My seatbelt jerks tight against my chest as he slams on the brakes. I grab my rucksack and jump out. I've never seen him so rattled.

Marshall locks the Lexus, abandoning the car at an awkward angle on the drive. He ushers me through the front door and bolts it behind us. Once we've descended to the Vault, he resets the secret staircase and locks us inside.

He straightens his tie and releases an immense sigh.

'Are you all right?' I ask, touching his arm.

'All good.'

Carmen raises her hand in greeting, the phone to her ear.

I return the wave. I might not be ready to forgive her, but in the time we've spent apart my resentment has started to fade. At the very least I'm determined to be polite.

A platter of sandwiches, a tea service, and slices of chocolate and coffee cake sit on the table. Carmen's clearly on autopilot despite her stressful day. Nevertheless, I'm touched by her efforts.

Marshall hands the Nikon to TJ who removes the SD card and slots it into his PC.

I peer over TJ's shoulder as he flicks through the photographs. 'Any good?'

'Not bad.' TJ examines a picture of the security door inside the wartime garages and enlarges the security pad beside the door. A blue logo on the corner of the plastic housing bears the letters ATC.

'The security pad looks the same as the one at Yoioto.' I comment. 'The only difference is the logo.'

TJ leans back in his chair. 'That doesn't surprise me. China manufactures the bulk of these RFID units. Companies around the globe plonk customised housings on top and call them theirs. Looks like ATC has done the same.'

'If Yoioto's unit is the same as ATC's, could you reprogram my swipe card to get past the door?'

TJ's frowns. 'The card you took from Yoioto already worked within the building. All I did was change the access privileges. We know nothing about ATC's swipe card tag information or facility codes.' TJ peers closer at the screen, his eyebrows drawing together. 'There are other ways to get past the door. My primary concern is the camera.'

He zooms in on the CCTV unit which also bears an ATC logo. On the camera's side is a sticker containing serial numbers and a barcode. 'It's high-res, digital, colour.'

'Made by ATC?'

'Appropriated by them,' TJ says. 'The camera and keypad are Chinese. Rebranded, I suspect. ATC buys them cheaply in bulk and sells them on at a hefty profit.'

'Is that what the American plans to do with my Drive?' I ask mournfully. 'Mass-manufacture it with an ATC logo on the side?'

'Guess so,' TJ says. 'He'll probably patent the units, too.'

'Great!' I give a bitter laugh. 'Just what Dad would have wanted.'

Marshall comes alongside, 'Sorry to interrupt, but I need print outs of the Russians so we can track them. I also want to know why ATC is in bed with Bletchley.'

I return to the table, overhearing snippets of Carmen's phone conversation.

'Yes, I understand,' she says. 'Could you spell his name? And where have they taken him?'

At a loose end, I retrieve the finding machine from my rucksack. It's been hours since I last checked on Pierce's location. I insert the rogue's photo into the clips.

Sligo Garda Station, Pearse Road, Sligo, Co. Sligo F91 E372

Stifling an exclamation, I text Moira.

```
Pierce is at Sligo Police Station! Hope-
fully it's all over for him! :)
```

Shortly after, Moira texts back.

```
I'll check on your mum while he's out of
the way. Maybe now she'll believe us.
```

It's a relief to know Moira might actually have a handle on the situation. I replace Pierce's photo for Jonathan's and get nothing.

Putting the finding machine aside, I help myself to sandwiches while staring dolefully into space. I'm on my third cucumber and cream cheese triangle when TJ hands me printouts of the two Russians.

I jolt into action, slipping Yury between the clips.

51.997089, -0.743627

Bletchley Park, Bletchley, Milton Keynes, MK3 6EB

'Yury's still at Bletchley,' I tell Marshall and write down the co-ordinates for TJ so he can pinpoint his location. I swap out Yury for his comrade.

Nothing.

'That's weird.' I swap out his photo for Jonathan's.

Nothing.

'When the Russian went inside the bunker, it was like he stepped into the Twilight Zone,' I say. '*Poof!* He disappeared.'

Mystic Miriam's vision comes to mind, with a faceless Jonathan floating in a cube through the mist.

'They might be inside a secure vault like this one.' Marshall picks up a sandwich and peers at the display. 'Bletchley Park has bunkers and air raid shelters dotted about the site.'

'But my Drive works down here,' I point out. 'It has to be something else.'

'Their bunker might be encased in six feet of concrete or lead-lined in case of nuclear attack,' Marshall suggests. 'It might go so deep underground the location signals are unable to reach the Drive. We never had time to properly test its limitations.'

I switch photos again. 'I think the wiry Russian is inside the bunker and Yury's outside. I'll tell you when the vanished Russian pops up again.'

Carmen puts the phone down and raises her hand. 'I have news,' she says breathlessly. 'The police retrieved the quartz!'

'Wow! That's fantastic!' I grin and pump my fist before I remember we're not friends. I shutter my smile. 'Where was it?'

'Tampa Airport.' Carmen walks towards the table, leaning on her walking stick, and lowers herself into her chair with a wince. 'Federal Air Marshals searched a jet inbound from London City Airport and confiscated an aluminium case matching Marshall's description. It was in the possession of an American scientist, Jared Ferreira, who works for All Tech Corporation. They've detained him.'

She leans her arms on the table. 'All Tech sent Ferreira on a round trip to pick up the quartz, and it gets better. Ferreira gave up a name.'

'Go on,' Marshall says. TJ peeks around his computer monitor as I lean forward in my seat.

'Ferreira's boss is Nathaniel Quinn, CEO of All Tech Corp, second son of Major Buchanan Quinn. Nathaniel stepped into his father's shoes upon his retirement. When the police checked Nathaniel's passport, they discovered he flew to the UK in June on the same jet where the police found the quartz. He hasn't re-entered the States since.'

'So, he is at Bletchley!' I bang the table with my fist. 'He's down in that bunker with Jonathan!'

'We don't know that for sure,' Marshall cautions.

'The police can't question Nathaniel if they don't know where he is.' Carmen gives the finding machine a meaningful stare. 'If only we had a photo.'

Marshall rests his hands on the small of his back and stretches. 'That shouldn't be a problem. TJ?'

'I'll find one,' TJ says. Keys rattle as he searches the internet.

Carmen shifts on her chair and closes her eyes, drawing a sharp breath.

I sit opposite, my bitterness fading at her drawn expression. 'Are you okay? Is it your leg?'

She exhales, shifting position. 'The chair in the police interview room was the most uncomfortable I've ever sat on.'

'I'm sorry,' I say. 'Can I get you anything?'

'No, it's fine. Please have another sandwich. You've had a long day, too.'

Marshall returns to the table with a bottle of Highland Park Scotch Whisky, four crystal tumblers and three cans of Diet Coke. He pours three fingers of whisky into three of the tumblers and Coke in the fourth, which he passes to TJ.

'Would you add some Coke to mine?' Carmen asks. 'I'm not sure whisky and sandwiches mix.'

'Get it down you. It'll do you good,' Marshall says, raising his glass. He swigs his measure back.

Carmen screws up her eyes and forces the golden liquid down her throat.

I raise the glass to my lips. The whisky has a smoky aroma and burns a fiery line down my throat. The alcohol kicks in nicely after the first gulp. By the third, my stress levels have receded, replaced by a growing conviction we're on the right track.

Marshall, Carmen and I eat sandwiches and cake in near silence. I start to feel a little sozzled and pour myself a cup of tea.

The League landline rings. TJ answers it, straggles of hair falling across his face. He looks up and his face turns ashen.

'Guys,' he whispers, covering the mouthpiece with his hand. 'I think it's Quinn, the American!'

'Maybe he's calling to say he's releasing Jonathan,' I say, barely daring to hope.

Carmen's hands shake. She drops her fork.

Marshall stands and pushes his chair back with an ugly, scraping sound. His serviette falls to the floor. He stares at the beige receiver in TJ's hand.

'Record the call. Get a trace on him,' he whispers.

TJ nods.

Marshall takes the receiver from TJ and puts the call on speakerphone. 'Who's this?'

'You can call me sir.' The American sounds upbeat. Arrogant. 'You must be James Marshall Jones. Jonathan's head of security.'

'I prefer Marshall.' He glares at the phone. 'You must be Nathaniel Quinn.'

'You've been a busy boy.' Quinn's tone hardens. 'I warned you to stay out of my business. You lost me the quartz.'

'What makes you think it was me?' Marshall asks.

'Let's say, my reach is wide.'

'Do you mean your CCTV?' Marshall shakes his head. 'Are you accessing your consumers' live feeds and recordings?'

'Every technology has its security flaws, Marshall.'

'Like our League servers?' Marshall shakes his head. 'Sounds like a serious invasion of privacy. Maybe even a breach of national security. I'll add that to my file.'

Quinn laughs. 'Funny thing is, I was planning on releasing Jonathan until you stuck your nose in. Now, I'm thinking of delivering him to your front door in a suitcase.'

Silence falls into the Vault.

Quinn breaks it. 'I'm leaving tonight. If I see a police car, suspicious vehicle, or anyone sneaking around you'll never see Jonathan again. Just sit tight and you'll have him back by dawn.'

'How do I know he's not already dead?' Marshall says tightly. 'I want to speak with him. Put him on.'

'You can have a few seconds. I'll be listening.'

Marshall's head dips. He stares at the floor.

'Hello, old friend.' Jonathan Prudente-Poulton sounds far more world-weary than in the previous recording. His voice is nothing like his former confident and debonair self.

A lump sticks in my throat.

Marshall says between gritted teeth, 'We'll get you out, I pro—'

'No. This is the end of the line. Promise me you'll back down. You're not dealing with some Tom, Dick, or Harry. These people are out of our league.'

Jonathan sounds utterly beaten which is so unlike him. I always thought him the epitome of the stiff upper lip and British bulldog spirit.

'Take his advice,' Quinn breaks in.

I scribble on a piece of paper. *Tell the American his Drive will soon stop working.* I wave it under Marshall's nose.

Marshall glances at my note and says, 'If you harm Jonathan you'll face life behind bars. And for what? A few strips of obsolete tape and a Drive that will stop functioning in a few weeks? Is that worth giving up your freedom, money, and privilege for?'

Quinn says, 'I'll get more quartz. The Russians catalogued multiple fragments around Tunguska. And you're mistaken about the Drive. My scientists say it's good for another twenty years.'

Carmen pushes herself from her chair and passes Marshall another scrap of paper.

'You should fire your scientists,' Marshall says, reading the note. 'Your Drive contains 0.002 grams of quartz. Sorry, buddy, but it's about to fail.'

'I don't think so. Your decimal point's in the wrong place.'

Marshall goes rigid and shoots a glance at Carmen. A queasy feeling goes through me. I place my hand on the finding machine as sick realisation drags my mouth down.

'I'm not wasting time talking math,' continues Quinn.

The line goes dead.

Fury courses through me as I stand and jab my finger at the phone. 'The absolute bastard! How could he!'

Carmen leans back in her chair, knitting her brow. 'I know Quinn's a corrupt individ—'

'Not him. Jonathan!' I spit out my words like venom. 'He must have switched the Drives! After the upgrades he gave me the clone and kept Dad's finding machine for himself! I'll never forgive him. Never!'

39

Hauling in an unsteady breath, I stare at Marshall. 'Did you know?'

Marshall raises his hands in surrender. 'I want it on the record that I knew nothing about the Drives being switched. Besides, Quinn could be lying.'

'Why would he?' I spit the words out.

Carmen looks at me wide-eyed.

'You're the mineralogist,' I round on her. 'You must have known which Drive was which.'

'Jonathan never mentioned anything to me.' Carmen's lips tremble. 'If I'd known I would have said something. Your father's Drive belongs with you.'

'She's right,' Marshall intercedes. 'None of us knew.'

I cross my arms and glare at Carmen. Her cagey behaviour around the stone tapes, my father, and the Drive makes it impossible not to suspect her of interfering. First, her betrayal with Dad, and now this. It makes me wonder what else she's hiding.

I round on TJ. 'When you showed me the leftover Drive parts, I asked about the mineral sample between the slides. You fobbed me off. *"It's a rare mineral. A form of silicon dioxide,"* you said.'

'That is technically correct,' TJ says, squeezing a stress ball.

'You knew it was ghost quartz. And just like the others, you kept it from me!'

TJ flinches and shoots Marshall a guilty look. 'It was secret information and I wasn't sure how much I could tell you,' he mumbles. 'After what happened with Jonathan, we were concerned about information leaking out. Marshall said you might be a liability.'

I glare at Marshall. 'You said what?'

'I said, *might be.*' Marshall frowns at the teenager before facing me. 'This was right after we had a major breach and before we started working together. Security is my responsibility, remember? We were only trying to protect the League's secrets.'

'At least I know why Jonathan never got back to me about the job,' I say, unable to control my seething temper. 'We were supposed to work together, but that went out of the window once the clone Drive was ready. He must have thought, *why not keep the Drive that's got twenty years of life left in it, and give her the one that's about to fail?* Both machines look identical with their new cases. He probably thought I'd never find out.' I haul in a shuddery breath. 'How smug he must have felt to get the upper hand.'

'Jonathan's not like that,' Marshall cuts in.

'Really?' I round on him. 'You told me yourself, he's a closed book. He had meetings in private, made calls when you weren't there. You didn't know a thing about his dealings with Grigor and Okada Atsuko.'

'I've known Jonathan for years.' Marshall stands his ground. 'All that time he's been a man of his word.'

A sour taste comes into my mouth. 'He never wanted me in the League. All he wanted was Dad's machine. Turns out, the weakest link isn't me. It's him.' My anger hangs between us like a prickly wall. 'I want to look him in the eye before I punch his lights out.'

'I get it.' Marshall puts both hands up. 'I understand you're mad.'

His reaction gives me pause. I stare at the floor, shocked by my own anger.

Marshall speaks softly. 'No matter how Jonathan acted or whatever you think of the League, none of this helps us now. Quinn's the one using dirty tactics. We have to rescue Jonathan and make Quinn pay.'

I cast a sorrowful look towards the clone finding machine and focus on my breathing. The printer chugs in the background. The mundane sounds help my vitriol subside. Forcing my bitter thoughts aside, I move to the line of photographs on the wall. Alan Turing, Nikola Tesla and my father gaze upon me with a benevolent eye.

Whatever happens, I can't let Quinn walk away. It will destroy the League. It will destroy me.

'Let's refocus.' Marshall faces me. 'You want your Drive back. I want Jonathan back, the static tape, Grigor's research, everything. We're on the same page.'

'I'm with you.' I nod. A fragile truce. 'But what if Quinn has twenty goons inside his bunker?'

'From what we know, Quinn's no criminal mastermind,' Marshall says. 'He's a businessman who's trying to capture intellectual property. He'll want to keep things quiet, control every aspect of his scheme. That won't involve killing Jonathan. I have a hunch the two Russians are the only muscle he has on site.'

'Yury and his mate are serious characters,' I mutter.

'We'll worry about that later.' Marshall waves me over to TJ's workstation. 'Any news on ATC's involvement with Bletchley?'

'It's public knowledge online that ATC is working in partnership with Bletchley Park. Quinn's company recently upgraded their CCTV systems, network servers and computers, and threw in a hefty donation to the Trust, too.' He bites his lower lip, looking glum. 'I couldn't access their servers. ATC has patched up the back door I created two years ago. The system's sealed tight.'

'And I guess Quinn wanted more than his name on a silver plaque in return for ATC's generous donation,' Marshall says. 'We need ground plans of Bletchley's premises and facilities, especially the garages.'

'Slight problem with that. Bletchley Park is a government classified site,' TJ says, as the printer kicks into action again. 'The building works and site plans have a 100-year seal on them.'

'What do we do?' Carmen breaks in. Her face has turned deathly pale. She shakily pours herself a generous measure of whisky and gulps it down.

'Track the boss.' TJ removes a paper sheet from the printer and places it on the table. 'Nathaniel Quinn. He goes by Nate.'

Quinn's professional portrait shows a plump-faced man in his late thirties clad in a sharply cut business suit. His bright pink tie bows out over his expansive chest. His receding hairline exposes a gleaming forehead with a smattering of bristling, black hair. Beetling brows overhang sunken eyes. Sharp white glints shine from the pupils.

The intensity of Nathaniel's stare burns through the page. His fleshy half-smile look more like a sneer. He's probably enjoying a victory at the expense of someone.

Marshall reaches for the photo before drawing his hand back. 'You do it, Alex.'

I take the sheet, tearing the page around the photo so it fits into the finding machine. Prickles run down my spine. When I think of how little time I have left before the machine fails, I want to throw up.

I push down resentment at using the Drive on such a lowlife and secure Quinn photo between the clips.

51.99639. -0.74302

Hut 4 Café, Bletchley Park, Sherwood Drive, Bletchley, MK3 6EB

While we've been pulling our hair out, fighting amongst ourselves and desperately watching our backs, Nate's probably been enjoying a Bletchley Park cream tea! I swiftly write down the co-ordinates before switching Quinn for Jonathan.

It's a forlorn hope. There's no reading.

'Marshall, you have to contact your police guy and get a team inside Bletchley,' I plead. 'Everything's right there. We can guide the police from the Vault. They could break into the bunker and rescue Jonathan. This could be over without any risk to us.'

'I'll pass on the information.' Marshall glances at his watch. 'But without concrete evidence on Quinn, the police won't organise a response. All we have on him is a connection to the stolen quartz and a missing man. It's not enough. In a few hours, he'll be gone.' He taps the desk and glances at the League landline. 'Something else is bugging me. About what Jonathan said on the phone.'

'What is it?' I ask.

'The way he folded. It's not like him. It sounded hokey.'

'I agree,' Carmen adds, sipping water. 'Jonathan would never back down like that. The League is everything to him and he would die to protect it. He'd want us to fight, not give in.'

'Can you replay the recording?' Marshall asks TJ.

TJ presses 'play' and Jonathan Prudente-Poulton's voice drifts into the Vault.

"This is the end of the line. Promise me you'll back down. You're not dealing with some Tom, Dick, or Harry. These people, they're out of our league."

'He says, "League," I point out. 'Could that be deliberate?'

Marshall traces his forefinger in a circle. 'Run it again, TJ.'

I write Jonathan's words down on the second playback. Reading them through again, something jumps out.

'That's odd.' I beckon the others to gather round. 'Does the phrase "the end of the line" mean anything to you? What about "back down?" They sound like directions.'

Carmen adds, 'So does "out of our league."'

'The end of the line could be a telephone or road,' Marshall suggests.

Carmen stares at my writing. 'You back down from an argument. But Jonathan doesn't mean that. You go back down something deep. Like a bunker.'

'The phrase "out of our League."' Marshall pushes his jacket back and hooks his fingers over his belt. 'Could Jonathan mean out of the Lodge?'

'Let's say he does.' I run my pencil along the message. 'So, we go out of the Lodge, down somewhere, to the end of the line.'

Marshall points to the third line of text. 'Tom, Dick and Harry. Isn't that from a film?'

'It's from The Great Escape,' Carmen pipes up. 'Tom, Dick, and Harry were three tunnels the prisoners of war dug to escape the German camp.' She pauses. 'Could there be an old tunnel from the Lodge that runs to Bletchley Park?'

I stand, my trembling hands gripping the table.

'I have an idea,' I say. 'Unlock the Vault.'

40

— · —

As soon as Marshall opens the Vault door I rush outside, relieved to leave the half-lies and secrets behind.

The door clicks closed behind me. I cross the chequerboard hall as the grandfather clock gently bongs the quarter hour: 5:45 p.m.

Bletchley Park will have closed for the day. I run up the red-carpeted stairs to the first-floor landing and down the hall to the attic door.

The narrow staircase creaks underfoot as I ascend to the top. I switch on the light. The air is stale and musty, and I stop to catch my breath. I walk to the nearest dormer window, push up the sash, and breathe in cool air laced with wet earth and damp grass. The rain has stopped, leaving banks of lead-coloured clouds overhead.

My gaze goes to the driveway, the locked gates, and the perimeter wall. All looks quiet.

Turning my back on the view I head to the wardrobe, praying my hunch is correct. I pull open the bottom drawer, yank out the scarves and remove the GPO satchel.

Unbuckling it, I empty out the contents. Black and white photos of postal workers and dispatch riders spill across the floor, but I'm only interested in the Ordnance Survey map.

Yellowed sticking tape holds the map's worn folds together. I carefully unfold it, praying my memory's correct and I'm not mistaken in what I saw before.

Red Croft Lodge is near the bottom of the map, at the end of Church Walk. The two sycamore trees are drawn in outline. A faint grey line I previously assumed was a path leads northeast from the Lodge to a grand building called Wilton Hall, then to The Old Rectory. From there, the line runs to St Mary's Church and to Bletchley Park. A bubbling sensation rises in me.

Could the line possibly be an underground tunnel?

I'm refolding the map when my phone buzzes in my pocket, making me jump.

I glance at the green screen: *IRISH_BRANCH.*

My thumb presses the *Accept Call* button. I send up a fervent plea that Moira's resolved the Pierce problem.

'Hello, Moira.' I walk to the sash window and close it. 'Has Mum finally come to her senses?'

'In your dreams,' Moira whispers.

'Why are you whispering?'

'Because I don't want Dervla O'Hara to hear me. She just popped into Father Egan's office.'

'You're in church? Didn't you go and see Mum?'

'I did, and what a waste of time that was. Your mum couldn't wait to tell me the police are following up other lines of enquiry. The police don't consider Pierce a person of interest!'

'But he's connected to two burglaries!'

'Alexandra, it gets worse,' Moira says. 'He's going ahead with his plans to rob the church.'

'How do you know that?'

'The first clue was when your mum answered the front door holding the church keys. When I asked if she was going somewhere, she replied, *'Oh, no, I was just dusting them.'* She told me she was very busy and would I mind coming back tomorrow, as if I were the gardener.'

'Any other clues?' I tuck the map in my pocket and walk to the top of the stairs.

'Well, Brigid and Pierce are parked under the yew tree where the car park extension's going. I can see them perfectly well through my binoculars.'

'You might have mentioned that first!' I clench my fist. 'Where exactly are you?'

'I'm up on the choir balcony. I sneaked past Mr McGuigan as he was going in for confession. He couldn't have been inside the box more than five minutes. It's all very well wanting to feel righteous, but he should save up his sins so as not to waste the priest's tim—'

'Is anything happening?' I interrupt in exasperation. Marshall must be wondering where the hell I am. 'I can't stay here chatting.'

'All right, keep your hair on,' Moira says, affronted. 'Father Egan left with Mr McGuigan and locked up the church. Ten minutes later Dervla O'Hara let herself in. She's still here, opening all the doors. She must have lost something, although you're hardly likely to lose your car keys or your phone inside a tabernacle! Pierce and your mum will have to wait until she's gone before they can thieve the place.'

Something's bugging me about Moira's account, but I can't put my finger on it.

'Sit tight,' I say. 'I have to go.'

I'm about to terminate the call when Moira says, 'That's odd. Dervla's gone but she hasn't locked up. She must be coming back.'

I glance at my watch. How long can this saga last?

'Whatever happens, don't confront Pierce,' I say. 'If he feels cornered he could turn nasty.'

'I'm only looking out for Brigid. If she touches the silver she's an accessory.'

I'm unable to conceive the thought of Mum stealing from the church. Surely Pierce's hold over her isn't that strong?

Moira's tone turns solemn. 'If the worst comes to the worst I'll visit Brigid in prison every Monday and second Saturday, depending on my Irish Dancing class.'

'She won't go to prison!' I bite my lip at Moira's catastrophising.

'God willing.' A pause. 'Hold on. A black van's pulling up. It's a little late for deliveries. Maybe it's the cleaner, but she usually walks to work.'

'Alex?' Marshall calls up the attic stairs. 'You up there?'

Covering the phone, I say to Moira, 'Hold on a sec!'

I cup my hand over my phone and call down to him. 'I need five minutes! Family problems.'

'Don't be long. We need you down here.'

'Moira!' I hiss into the phone. 'What's going on?'

'Two masked men have entered the church!' she whispers. 'They've gone into the vestry. I can't believe it. They're burgling the church before Pierce has his chance. What are the odds?'

My heart pounds. 'Stay on the balcony. Don't let them see you.'

'They're looting the place!' Her whisper sounds strangled. 'They've put the gold and silver into a black bin liner. They've even taken the ciborium from the tabernacle.'

'Just stay out of sight.' I gnaw the inside of my cheek, praying she won't do anything rash.

'It's no use. I can't stand by,' Moira whispers. She suddenly yells, 'Stop, you heathen hallions!'

I can only listen in horror as she clatters down the stairs, muttering, *Steal from the Lord, would you? He helps those who helps themselves, but not when they're helping themselves to the church silver!'*

Moira raises her voice. 'Your mothers would be ashamed of ye! Hiding behind masks!' She pauses. 'Show your faces!'

'Get out of my way, you ole bag,' orders a gruff, male voice.

'Never in a month of Sundays. You'll not get past me!'

'Moira, no!' I yell.

A man curses.

'I threw the binoculars,' she hisses down the line. 'Caught one of them bang on the head!'

'Please get out of there!'

'Don't worry, Alex. I have everything under control.' She shouts, 'Think you're leaving with that? Over my dead body!'

'If that's how you want it,' says the gruff man.

A succession of groans and thumps ends with a clatter that sounds like the phone hitting the floor.

My mouth goes dry. I clench my eyes shut, leaning forward with my finger in my other ear to catch the slightest noise.

'You've only gone and killed her!' hisses the second man.

'I barely touched her. You saw.'

'Freeze! Police!' a man shouts. His voice sounds familiar. 'I have a taser aimed on you! Drop the bags and get on the floor, or I will taser you!'

In the background is the sound of approaching sirens.

'Moira!' I shout. 'Moira!'

'Is that you, Alexandra? It's me. Mum.'

'Mum? What are you doing there?' I gasp.

'Just listen. Moira's taken a bit of a tumble and we're looking after her. Don't worry. We've called an ambulance.'

'Ambulance? Mum? What's going on?'

'I've got to go.' The line goes dead.

I hit redial but no one answers. I call Mum's mobile number with no luck.

What on earth's going on? Was that Pierce with a taser?

Moira's out cold in the aisle. There are robbers in the church. If Pierce is a policeman, why didn't Mum just bloody tell me? And sainted Dervla O'Hara is clearly up to her neck in it.

Mum told me I'd got the wrong end of the stick. How could I have been so wrong? I hate it when she's right.

'Alex!' Marshall yells up the stairs.

'Coming!' I slide my phone into my pocket and run downstairs with my head spinning.

'All sorted with your family?' Marshall asks.

As I struggle to come up with an answer, he hurries me down to the Vault.

On the threshold, he turns and fixes me with a stare. 'Alex, are you with me?'

'Yes...sorry, I'm here.'

Marshall waves me inside. 'We've lost the reading on Quinn. And the Russians. Our police contact's waiting at Cranfield Airport in case Quinn makes a run for it.'

My thoughts turn dark, imagining Nate Quinn and the Russians sipping champagne on a private jet as they fly across the North Atlantic with Dad's Drive and the League's secrets.

'You need to see this. I think there's a path leading from here to Bletchley Park.'

TJ and Carmen gather around the table as I open out the map. I stare at it, unable to stop worrying about Moira.

'Alex?' Carmen gingerly touches my arm. 'Are you all right?'

'Yes. Fine.' I snap myself back to business and point to the grey line. 'There.'

'That's interesting,' Carmen says. 'See those little crossing lines?'

I peer closer at tiny cross marks drawn at regular intervals along the grey line. They're so faint I never noticed them before.

'That represents a narrow-gauge railway,' she says. 'Richard taught me that.'

A pang hits me at the mention of my father. I push it aside. 'If there was a railway nearby we'd know about it.'

'Not if it runs underground,' Carmen says. 'Bletchley Park may have built an underground railway to move important people about in secret, or to ferry supplies and information between themselves and the Lodge.'

'Not just the Lodge,' TJ adds. 'Wilton Hall was used as an assembly hall for the Government Code and Cipher School. Top officials from the UK, France, and Russia stayed there including Winston Churchill.'

'Maybe it's a postal line,' I say. 'I found a post bag in the attic with wartime photos taken outside this building. I thought the workers might have been billeted here.' A light goes on in my mind. 'If there is a trainline on the property, it would explain how Jonathan vanished under your noses without you knowing. The perimeter alarm didn't go off because he never left by the main gate.'

Marshall places a ruler against the line and compares it to the scale on the map. 'The line's a mile long. That's some feat of engineering. I can't understand why we haven't stumbled across it. The builders would have found something when they excavated the Vault.'

'Do you have the plans?' I ask.

Marshall shakes his head. 'They were shredded once it was built.'

'What about the cellar?' TJ suggests. 'Or the garage? That's outside the main footprint of the house.'

'The cellar was dug out and damp-proofed the same time the Vault was built,' Marshall says. 'There's no access through the floor to any train line.'

'The garage, then,' I say. 'Or what about the air raid shelter? I'm happy to check them out as long as I have a torch and something to defend myself against spiders.'

Marshall shakes his head. 'I've been inside the garage a thousand times. There's no train line there. The air raid shelter's built on solid concrete. We're wasting our time.'

'It must be somewhere.' My brow arches. 'We can't get past ATC's cameras. That tunnel is the only route in to rescue Jonathan.'

'I'll help Alex look for it,' TJ says, putting his hand out. 'Give me the keys to the garage.'

Marshall shoves his hand into his pocket and hands his key fob over. 'Be careful.'

41

I follow TJ to the kitchen. He opens a cupboard behind the bin and removes a large flashlight and two pairs of gardening gloves.

'In case of spiders,' he says, passing me a pair. 'They creep me out, too.'

He unlocks the back door and swings it open. The rain has stopped. Goosebumps rise on my arms in the fresh, chilly air. It appears the long heatwave is finally over.

Outside, birds sing a subdued evening chorus under dark clouds.

TJ follows a shingle path leading around the house to the double garage, which is a self-contained block tucked behind the house. I walk all the way around it, pushing through holly bushes and encroaching viburnums, but there are no hidden doors or signs of disturbance.

I rejoin TJ as he raises the metal up-and-over door. Inside, a dusty Model T-Ford sits forlornly with wooden wedges behind the perished tyres. A clutter of irregular dark shapes fills the space behind.

I flick the switch on the wall. A fluorescent strip light blinks into life overhead, illuminating a boarded floor.

I walk past a torn oil painting, dusty bookcases, a mirrored armoire, tarnished bedsteads, suitcases, and an upright piano with candelabras fixed to the front. Rolls of carpets lean like fallen towers against the wall. Everything in here looks to have been abandoned decades ago.

'Search for hatches or trapdoors,' TJ instructs, sweeping the torch underneath the furniture. 'Don't get too excited if you see footsteps in the dust. They're probably Marshall's.'

A large metal shelving rack stands at an angle away from the wall. Its flat base conceals a large rectangular section of floorboards.

'Did you check under there?' I point to the rack.

TJ goes up to it, examining the floor. 'If there's a tunnel underneath the intruder would have had to move this out of the way then back again. It's too heavy. And, there are no scrape marks or signs of movement.'

'I'll check the back wall.' I edge through gaps in furniture, working my way down the garage. Old spiderwebs hang in the corners, reaching from the floor to the rafters. Thank God for my gloves.

TJ joins me at the back wall. 'Anything?'

I shake my head. The wall is solidly constructed. So are the floorboards.

'I can't think where else to look except the air raid shelter,' I sigh. 'I was in there a few days ago and saw nothing unusual.'

'Let's check again.' TJ walks outside and locks the garage.

I follow him down the garden, wondering if the train line was nothing more than an architect's proposal that never made the leap from design to reality. Maybe I was completely wrong about Jonathan's message.

I wade through wet grass, nettles, and bracken. Water drips from the apple trees and pools at the centre of the patio table. The bottom of my jeans are soaked through by the time we reach the concrete steps leading down to the air raid shelter.

I shove against the recessed door. It squeaks open on rusty hinges.

'Some light, please,' I call over my shoulder.

TJ hands over the flashlight. I play the light over the wooden bench and table, cast iron stove, and posters scattered across the floor.

DON'T RUN. DON'T SCREAM.
PREVENT DISORDER. OBEY ALL INSTRUCTIONS.

'It's creepy,' I mutter.

TJ follows me inside, stooping to pick up the fallen posters. 'It's quiet. I like it. '

The concrete floor is solid without drains or plumbing. Two air bricks are set into one wall above ground level. The stove is a black metal lump. Above the single hot plate a flue runs vertically into the brickwork.

'We should look behind here,' I say.

TJ examines the stone slabs beneath the cast iron feet. He tugs at the stove and one of the slabs before stepping back. 'The stove is too heavy to access from underneath or behind. It's a no.'

The coal scuttle is sunk into the floor with the lid askew on top. I left it that way on my first afternoon when Carmen called me for lunch.

I aim the light at the large lid, which measures around three feet square. TJ lifts it and flips it over, examining the underside.

The interior face has a handle welded onto it. My heart picks up pace. Why hadn't I noticed that before?

I aim the flashlight inside the blackened metal container. TJ reaches inside.

'There's a seam running around the bottom. Hang on. These could be hinges at the end.' He shuffles awkwardly. 'Found a recessed handle.'

I jump at a metallic screech and a bang.

TJ meets my eye. 'Trap door.'

I shine the light on the void. Three feet down, the topmost rung of a ladder is anchored to the wall with grabrails either side. I lower myself to the ground and peer over the rim, coughing as dislodged coal dust goes up my nose. A faint breath of warm wind brushes my face, laced with an old, limestone smell.

Far below, is a grey patch of ground. I take a two pence coin from my pocket and drop it. It takes less than a second for it to hit the ground with a *chink*.

'See that?' TJ points to a scrap of fabric clinging to a rusty rung.

'I'll get it.' I pass him the torch then shuffle forwards until I'm bent at the waist and stretch my arm down, wary of tipping in head-first.

My fingers pinch hold of the fabric and I tug it free, holding my breath until I've brought it to safety.

The torn triangle is wine-coloured silk. The paisley design of curved teardrops is the kind you'd find on a silk handkerchief or the lining of an expensive suit jacket, worn by someone who champions traditional British fashion.

I meet TJ's eye. 'Get the others.'

• • • • • • • • • •

I wait by the hole until TJ returns with Marshall, Carmen, and my rucksack. The teenager wears a workman's belt around his waist with Velcro pockets and slotted holders.

Marshall approaches the coal scuttle, clicks on a slim LED Maglite torch, and shines light down the ladder.

'How ingenious.' Carmen peers over the container's edge, using her stick for support. 'To think this has been beneath our feet all these years.'

Marshall has the grace to look contrite when he meets my eye. 'Well done, both of you.'

Carmen keeps a tight grip on her cane's owl handle. 'I'm sorry, but I don't think I can manage the climb down. I'd hate to hold you up.'

'You can help us more by staying back,' Marshall says. 'Watch the cameras, answer the phone, remain in contact.'

Carmen meets my eye. 'I'm happy to keep the Drive with me if you don't want to risk taking it.'

I say coolly, 'The Drive comes with me.'

Marshall glances at the two of us. 'If the tunnel's useable we'll need the Drive to check on Quinn and the Russians. Alex should bring it.'

'Thanks,' I say, grateful he's playing peacemaker.

280

Carmen's says, 'Promise me you'll be careful.'

'If it looks too dangerous we'll turn back,' Marshall assures her, accompanying her to the stairs leading outside. 'Lock up the Lodge. I want you to stay inside the Vault until we're back.'

'I will.'

He assists her up the stairs and keeps a watchful eye as she makes her way across the garden to the house.

While I wait, I unzip my rucksack to check on Quinn and the two Russians.

'No reading on our friends at Bletchley,' I inform Marshall, zipping up the bag with a sick feeling. 'I don't know if that's good or bad.'

'Let's say it's good,' says Marshall. 'It means they're not near us or on their way out of the country.' He stares at his mobile. 'The phone signal's pretty poor. We may lose contact once we go underground. You two ready?'

'One sec.' TJ rearranges bits and bobs in the various pockets on his work belt, including a pair of latex gloves, batteries, string, and a stick of plasticine. 'I'm ready.'

Marshall sits on the edge of the aperture, his feet feeling for the top rung. As he starts to descend, the metal edges of the opening dig into his stomach. Whether the original coal-scuttle was converted into a passageway after being built, or was purpose-built from the start, it's painfully clear Marshall does not fit the demographic of a time when rationing was in effect.

He breathes in and drops a few inches lower, his jacket bunching beneath his arms. Something rips. Stuck half in, half out, he braces his hands on the floor and hauls himself back up.

TJ and I lend him a hand.

Marshall brushes soot from his shirt. Black smudges run across his ribs. 'Dammit. This was a good suit!' He strips off his jacket. 'One of you go first.'

'I will.' I crouch by the coal scuttle, hand TJ my rucksack, and lower myself down the hole. My foot brushes the top rung. Resting my elbows on the stone floor, I lower both feet onto the ladder.

Marshall watches with a furrowed brow as I remove one hand from the scuttle lip and reach down for the grab rail. I descend a rung and drop my other hand to the rail.

TJ aims his flashlight at the floor.

'My rucksack,' I call up.

TJ lowers the bag. I spend a few awkward moments swapping arms on the rungs to secure it on my back. Flakes of rust shift beneath my gardening gloves as I continue my descent. The last rung is bolted to bare brickwork.

I dangle my legs into space. Torch light hits grey concrete a few feet below and the copper coin.

I let go and thud onto hard ground, flexing my knees to soften the impact. Immediately, I spring up, looking in all directions.

The torchlight reveals a code — A104 — stencilled in dark grey paint on the wall by the ladder. The ever-shrinking circle of light meets complete darkness.

Silence surrounds me.

I remove the map and secure my rucksack over my shoulders as TJ starts his descent, the flashlight clipped to his belt.

His weedy appearance is deceiving. He shins down the ladder and lands beside me like a cat, torch in hand. TJ picks up the coin and puts it in his pocket, then turns in a circle with the flashlight.

An arched corridor about eight feet wide and fifteen feet high ends at a blank wall just past the ladder. In the other direction, metal gleams. Narrow parallel rails curve ahead and are swallowed by the dark. On either side are narrow walkways.

'It's a narrow-gauge railway,' I say. Dad taught me well.

'Somebody catch this,' Marshall calls down. He throws down his jacket.

It lands on the floor.

'Thanks, guys,' Marshall mutters as he makes his second attempt down. He squeezes past the trap door's constricting lip and feels for the ladder with his feet. He swiftly descends, pausing three rungs from the bottom to brush rust flakes from his hands.

The metal rung he's standing on snaps.

Marshall's feet land on the rung below which also gives way. He lets go and plummets onto concrete, rolling unceremoniously onto his side.

Carmen definitely made the right decision to stay behind.

'Let me help.' I take Marshall's arm and pass him his jacket.

'I'm fine.' He gains his feet and glares at the broken ladder before brushing himself down and slipping his jacket on.

'Found something,' TJ mutters. His flashlight illuminates a grey metal box on the opposite wall. Cables run from the box and continue along the wall, following the rail tracks.

TJ pulls the cover open. Inside is a bundle of wires and two levers with the positions, 'on' and 'off'. One is labelled 'Train,' the other 'Lights'.

'The system's a mess,' he mutters. 'Bakelite fuse housings. Vulcanised rubber wiring. I've only seen that stuff in text books. The consumer unit doesn't even have a circuit breaker.'

I eye the cracked insulation around the tangle of wires inside the fuse box. 'Looks like a fire hazard.'

'The fuses should blow before it catches fire.' He examines the wires. 'Two mains, no ground, 100 amps...let's see...'

TJ grips both levers and pushes them up.

A light blinks on in the distance, then another and another, until a row of lights is marching towards us. The dim light reveals a forgotten tunnel stretching ahead. A deep whirring starts up, farther down the tunnel.

'What the hell!' Marshall slams both levers down.

The lights go out. The whirring stops.

'Sorry, boss.' TJ raises his hands and steps away from the fuse box. 'I didn't think it would work!'

Marshall stabs his finger at him. 'You'd better pray Quinn didn't see those lights on camera.'

TJ sweeps the flashlight along the walls. 'There's no CCTV down here, no exterior-mounted cables. I doubt Quinn would run a mile of cable just to spy on a deserted tunnel, especially when he's the only one using it.'

Marshall says, 'If Quinn has any sense he'll have installed a camera down the other end.'

'The lights were only on for a second,' I say, chewing the inside of my cheek. 'Do you have any night-vision goggles?'

'We'll have to manage with torches.' Marshall shines his Maglite into the distance.

Nothing moves in either direction. The way ahead lies dark and silent.

'We'd better get going.'

I place a hand on his arm. 'You told me the rail line is over a mile long. It'll take us at least twenty minutes to walk that far and that's with the lights on. It's too dangerous to do it in the dark. We should take the train.'

'It's probably down the Bletchley end of the tunnel,' TJ says. 'We could call it though, and walk to meet it.'

'The train might not come,' Marshall says. 'Even if it does, I don't fancy meeting it head-on in the dark.'

'We can walk along the platform,' TJ says. 'With the state of the power supply, I very much doubt the train will be fast.'

I eye him dubiously. 'How will we stop it and get onboard?'

'Leave that to me,' TJ says.

Marshall checks his watch. 'All right. Do it.'

TJ flicks the *TRAIN* lever in the fusebox. The whirring noise starts up again. He presses a green button on the wall.

Marshall shines his light on my rucksack. 'Check on Quinn and the others.'

I swiftly unzip my rucksack and check the three photos. Quinn and the second Russian yield nothing, but I get a hit with Yury's photo:

51.99722, -0.74336

The Stable Yard, Bletchley Park, Bletchley, Milton Keynes, MK3 6EB

None of the LED indicator lights are flashing. 'We're good for now,' I say.

'Keep your eyes and ears open,' Marshall says, leading the way into the dark. 'Let's go.'

42

—·—

Marshall marches forward and shines the Maglite along the rails while TJ sweeps his flashlight around the curved walls.

I swallow a sudden lump in my throat and glance back, but the ladder to Red Croft Lodge has been swallowed by the dark.

I walk quickly along the side of the tracks to catch up with Marshall, and follow him around the first bend. After a few minutes' walking TJ aims his flashlight on a ladder bolted to the wall. The set-up looks identical to one we left behind except for the stencil: A105.

Great Britain removed its road signs during the war to confuse enemy spies. Maybe they did the same down here. I open out the map as I trudge along, pull my mobile from my pocket, and turn on the torch.

'If Red Croft Lodge is A104, could A105 be Wilton Hall?' I ask.

Marshall hangs back to examine the map. 'I think so. A106 should be The Old Rectory. The distance looks about right.'

A mouldy, metallic breeze courses through the tunnel and tousles my hair, accompanied by a strange tingling that tightens the nape of my neck and makes the hairs on my arms stand up.

Marshall squints into the darkness as a faint hum starts up in the distance, accompanied by an echoing, metallic whine.

I stop dead and whisper, 'Can you hear that?'

A blocky shape appears around the curve in the distance and trundles rapidly towards us.

I jump back, bumping my head against the curved brick wall. My stomach knots at the sight of the train rushing from the dark without lights or a driver. The train consists of four open carriages with a compact locomotive at the back. The vehicle is of the most basic construction; black painted rectangles with rusty sills and crudely welded seams. There are no doors.

'I've got this,' TJ says, standing close to the rails. He waits until the carriages rattle by before grabbing the lip of the locomotive and swinging himself inside. He presses a red button on a control panel welded up front and the train judders to a halt.

I climb in alongside him on the hard bench seat and Marshall clambers into the carriage behind.

'All right, let's go,' Marshall says. 'Keep your eyes open.'

'You got it, boss,' TJ says. He pulls a lever and presses a green button on the control panel.

The train lurches back the way it came, picking up speed. My heart drums a panicky tempo as it trundles towards another dimly lit curve. Beyond our bubble of light I swear I see movement in the darkness, but whenever TJ or Marshall's torch light hits the spot there's nothing there.

The crudely welded seat vibrates uncomfortably and shakes the map on my lap. My tiny phone light makes it a struggle to read. This is nothing like the fun miniature railways Dad and I used to visit, with their upholstered seats, cheerily painted carriages, and waving conductors.

'Dang it!' Marshall hisses from the carriage behind. He stares at his open hand. 'The cart zapped me! What the hell is that? Static?'

'Yep,' TJ says. 'Don't touch the bare metal.'

'I could have done with that information a minute ago,' Marshall says dryly.

I draw my elbows in and squeeze my knees together as the train chugs past ladder A106. Empty postal sacks, hessian bags covered in black smudges, wooden boxes, and pallets with mouldering mattresses litter the narrow platform. It looks like the railway line served several purposes during the war by providing emergency shelter during aerial bombardments.

We turn another bend. The view's exactly the same. I'd suspect we were going around in a circle if it weren't for my map and the letters on the walls.

Another ladder appears ahead. A107.

I struggle to control my shaking voice. 'One more stop then it's Bletchley.'

I fold back the flap on my rucksack to check on our suspects. I get nothing on Quinn and Yury. The second Russian is more or less in the same spot as before.

'Yury's friend is sticking close to the old garages,' I say. 'Let's hope he stays there.'

Minutes later, we pass ladder A108. If I'm right – and I really, really hope I am – the next stop is the end of the line.

Ahead, the track straightens and runs a further hundred feet before terminating at rubber buffers. TJ shines his light on another fuse box hanging on the wall. A thick cable runs underneath to a large black box on the ground.

Beyond the buffers, the platform continues to a concrete staircase that cuts through the rear wall. The limited light reveals a set of stairs ascending to a landing illuminated by a caged light. A metal door with a blue-lit security pad stands at the top.

A red LED light flashes on the finding machine. Yury's friend has moved.

51.997091, -0.743634
Bletchley Park, Bletchley, Milton Keynes
There's no postcode. I guess underground tunnels don't have them

'Uh-oh. The second Russian is coming.' I throw a wide-eyed look back at Marshall. 'What do we do?'

'I know how to deal with him.' TJ keeps the torch on the fuse box. 'Does it matter if he dies?'

'Yes. It does!' Marshall gives him a sharp stare.

'Okay, non-lethal force only,' TJ says breezily as the train continues towards the buffers. 'My plan is to connect the d—'

'Just do it,' Marshall orders. 'Stop the train.'

TJ hits the red button on the console. A high-pitched squeal hurts my ears. The buffers are thirty feet away, then ten.

I brace myself as we rush towards the wall, praying the brakes still work.

The train comes to a shuddering halt, the whirring noise fades and falls silent.

I release a pent-up breath. The black box on the floor ahead buzzes loudly. I suspect it's a very old transformer.

I check the finding machine. Two solid reds and the third is flashing.

'The Russian's getting closer.'

'That's what we want.' TJ removes a spool of black wire and pliers from his tool belt. He swiftly strips the insulation from both ends, vaults from the locomotive and races up the stairs.

I hop from the train. Marshall takes my arm and shines his Maglite, hurrying me to the rear of the carriage. We peer around as TJ wraps bare wire around the door handle, then unspools the reel of wire on the way back to the fuse box.

'He's messing with the electrics,' Marshall whispers, turning the torch off. 'Don't touch anything.'

TJ flings open the fuse box door, flashlight in hand. He removes a metal cover and drops it.

I check the finding machine. Three solid lights. The fourth light flashes.

'Hurry up!' My voice comes out as a nervous squeak.

'Ssshh,' Marshall hisses. 'Let him concentrate.'

As TJ fiddles with the fuse box wiring, my eyes dart between the finding machine reading and the illuminated stairwell. A leaden sensation drags at my guts.

A muffled voice comes from the other side of the door.

'The power is on,' says the Russian. 'Did you leave it on? Over.'

Four solids. The fifth light flashes. My heart hammers, matching the blinking light.

A tinny voice answers, too faint to hear.

'Okay, I will check it out,' the Russian says. 'It must be the fuse box playing up again. Or ghost. There are many ghosts down here.'

TJ inserts the end of the black wire inside the fuse box, raises his hands and takes a large step back.

Several things happen at once. The door handle depresses. A loud pop precedes a flash of light inside the fuse box. Flames rush across the panel. Then silence.

'Sorry.' TJ's voice comes through the dark. 'I think I killed the train.'

'Pray you haven't killed anything else,' mutters Marshall. He clicks his torch on and hurries to the stairs.

I follow him to the door at the top. The blue security pad is identical to the one inside the Wartime Garages. Silence comes from the other side.

I wedge myself in a corner and check the finding machine. All five lights are solid. The Russian is a few feet away, most likely on the other side of the door, but the machine can't tell if he's alive or dead.

'You can touch the door,' TJ says, removing the wire from the door handle.

Marshall gestures to the glowing security panel. 'Why's this still on?'

'The current went through the Russian, not the pad,' TJ says, removing a paperclip from his tool belt. 'It must be on a different circuit.'

'Get it open.'

TJ straightens the paperclip and uses a screwdriver to loosen a screw beneath the security pad housing. He inserts the paperclip beneath the housing and lifts the cover away.

I cringe, anticipating a screaming alarm followed by pounding feet. But nothing happens.

'The tamper's not wired in,' TJ informs us, removing the paperclip. 'Quinn's getting sloppy.'

The circuit board inside the housing is a jumble of coloured wires running to plastic connectors. TJ bends the paperclip into a U shape. Using insulated pliers, he pushes the clip onto two connectors to bridge the gap.

The door emits a *beep* and clicks open.

I stare at TJ in open-eyed wonder. Marshall grabs the handle and opens it. The door opens an inch before catching on something.

'Damn, he's in the way,' Marshall says. He puts his shoulder to the door and gives several hard shoves.

The door opens enough to allow him to squeeze through, into a rundown corridor. The wiry Russian lies in a trembling heap on the floor.

The Russian groans, his body twitching, as Marshall crouches and touches two fingers to his neck.

'Good pulse. He'll live. Let's tuck him up. Hand me the electrical tape.'

Marshall rolls him on his side and pulls his arms behind him. TJ binds the Russian's wrists and ankles with the tape, rolling it round multiple times before tearing the end off. He stuffs a handkerchief in his mouth for good measure.

'Wait,' I say, swiftly searching his pockets. I retrieve a white security card with a black strip and tuck it into my jeans pocket. 'Bingo.'

The Russian's walkie-talkie crackles into life. *Aleksei. What is happening?*

Yury.

Marshall silently lifts the communicator.

'Aleksei, give me an update,' Yury says. *'Is there a problem?'*

Marshall presses the button and covers his mouth. 'No problem.'

It's not a bad impression, all things considered.

'No problem? Ya pridu. Over.'

I meet Marshall's gaze. 'What does "Ya pridu" mean?'

'It means we need to get out of here. Keep tracking Yury.' He strides to the nearest door and cracks it open, shining his light on a clutter of boxes, bottles, and large plastic containers. 'We'll put Aleksei in here.'

Aleksei wriggles and grunts against his bonds as TJ and Marshall drag him inside and tuck him beneath a shelf. Marshall shines his light on a large wooden crate with rope handles.

He freezes. 'Look at this.'

I peer around the door. Large red letters down the side of the crate spell out: *High Explosives.*

'Maybe they store bleach in there,' I mutter. 'Or tea. You know, to keep it dry.'

Marshall levers up the lid. The crate is crammed full of clay-like rectangles wrapped in dark green paper sleeves. He releases a low whistle. 'This ain't tea.'

'Could it be old explosives from the war?' I ask.

'Afraid not.' TJ points to a date stamp on the corner of the crate. 12/97.

'There's enough C-4 in there to blow up Bedfordshire,' Marshall mutters. He swiftly searches the surrounding shelves and rummages in boxes. He steps back, rubbing his forehead. 'Detonators, timers, wire.'

Swiftly, I switch out Aleksei's photo for Yury's in the finding machine.

51.99713, -0.74362

The Wartime Garages, Bletchley Park, Bletchley, Milton Keynes, MK3 6EB

No lights flash.

'Yury's still upstairs,' I tell the others.

'Keep checking,' Marshall says. He closes the door on Aleksei and heads down the corridor. Security lights mounted to the wall illuminate a concrete path scattered with chunks of broken mortar. Hairline cracks run haphazardly across the surface and water drips from the ceiling.

Marshall leads us to a T-junction. A sign hangs from chains, blocking the left-hand passageway:

DANGER. NO ENTRY.

Beyond, a staircase has collapsed. Only the top step remains hanging in space. Rubble and sheared off concrete slabs form a pile below.

'I can see why they haven't bothered with security down here,' Marshall mutters. He checks his phone. 'The place is falling apart. No phone signal, either.'

My gaze travels up the broken staircase. That can't be the only way out or the Russian would be stuck down here, too. I check on Yury.

51.997102, -0.743488

Bletchley Park, Bletchley, Milton Keynes

One red light is on. 'He's on his way down.'

I switch to Jonathan's photo.

??.??????, -?.??????

??

It's gibberish. I try Quinn's photo.

??.??????, -?.??????

???

'We're close,' Marshall says. 'Let's push on.'

We walk twenty yards. Another tunnel branches off to the right.

'Maybe it's time to split up,' I suggest, taking a step down the branching passageway.

TJ snorts, 'Only if you want your chances of failure to rise stratospherically.'

I concede the point. I've seen enough Scooby Doo episodes to know that dividing the group rarely ends well.

'Hold on.' I raise my hand. 'Can you hear that?'

A dull murmur comes from farther down the tunnel. It sounds like people talking.

Marshall nods and takes the lead down the dimly lit corridor which gradually slopes downwards. The odour of wet limestone and musty air is stronger here. As I pick my way along, the concrete floor turns to packed earth and the walls become bedrock.

Darting, furtive movement catches my eye. I stop dead and stifle a squeal as a swarm of small shadows skitter past with tiny pattering feet and long tails.

'Ssssh!' Marshall glares at me. He stops suddenly and shines the Maglite ahead.

The passageway ends at a studded wooden door with a closed metal observation hatch at eye level. It looks like an old prison door. Red lights shine like beacons on either side. A dull thrum travels through the floor, sending vibrations along my legs. Long throw bolts secure the door at the top and bottom and run into holes drilled into the rock.

Marshall and TJ click off their torches. Marshall slides the hatch open, revealing iron bars. Beyond lies a dimly-lit, deserted corridor.

Voices drift through the open hatch. For some reason they give me the heebie-jeebies.

Marshall grabs the top bolt and wiggles it open.

I yank the bottom one. The door has swollen from the damp air and the bolt scrapes and squeals as I slide it. Gritting my teeth, I work the bolt back to the stop plate at the same time as Marshall.

Marshall turns the iron handle and puts his shoulder to the door. He glances at me and TJ.

'Be ready for anything.'

43

The door opens into a roughly hewn rock corridor covered in old toolmarks. If we end up trapped down here no one will ever find us.

A cacophony of voices criss-crosses the dimly lit and empty space. The nearest voice, amidst the confusion of noise, is a woman with a thick, rural accent.

'T'was thee. I saw it! Sweet Mary did not deserve to die so young. Thou tookest her life out of jealousy! I kept thy secret to my grave, for none wouldst heed the word of a midwife against a village elder.'

A chill goes through me which increases when I spot a loudspeaker mounted on the wall. A second is farther down the corridor projecting a man's voice.

'You durst not, Alaric. If they discover us, we'll hang. Stay back. I'll take no part of your diabolical scheme.'

TJ halts on the threshold and covers his ears, shrinking in on himself. 'I don't like it.'

'It's okay,' I say, touching his arm.

A jittery look comes into his eye.

'Take a deep breath,' I say calmly. 'Remember, we're here for Jonathan.'

Marshall walks forward, finger to his lips. TJ lowers his head and trudges after him. I stay at the back, glancing nervously around.

Our progress along the winding corridor is accompanied by heartfelt monologues in strange dialects. I catch words like *'brabble,' 'andswarian,' 'dreogan,'* that sound like a foreign language.

The voices transport me back to the Vault and the stone tape recording of a sixteenth century man who lost his family. Demands, accusations and sadness echo in the tunnel. My spine tingles and my throat dries up.

The voices have a natural, unselfconscious quality, unlike any historical TV show, play, or re-enactment. These men and women aren't actors. They've lived these words.

If these are Grigor's stone tapes, why is Quinn playing them through the loudspeakers? I have a horrible feeling this is another League technology Quinn has stolen for himself.

Cold unease fills me as I step further into the corridor.

'Al be that they fire the keep to trappe us, forthy the sotte King John not shaltow tek us.'

The corridor opens out into a roughly circular cavern around twenty foot in diameter. Marshall signals a halt and surveys the space from the shadowy corridor.

Tin pendant lights bolted to the rock ceiling cast a feeble light that fails to reach the outskirts of the cavern. There could be CCTV cameras in every corner watching us from the dark.

Taking up much of the floorspace is a ten-foot-square plexiglass cube. The side facing me contains a door made from the same material. The cube is reinforced with metal strips at each corner and is bolted to the floor. Air holes have been drilled on each side. A phone receiver is mounted beside the door, with another mirroring it on the inside.

'Heo læg on þære flor mid blōde on hyrre hæð. Hē þæt sæde hē lufode hīe, stōd ofer hīe mid ān pytce.'

Inside the cube, a man lies on a camp bed with his back to us. His arm, draped across the blankets, is clad in paisley patterned wine-coloured fabric. The cube contains a plastic stool, a lamp with a bendy neck, a small wooden coffee table with a stack of books and a camping toilet.

Mystic Miriam's vision floods into my head. *A grey cube filled with mist. Inside, a grey man with no face.*

Marshall rushes to the cube and yanks on the door handle. 'Jonathan! Wake up, it's Marshall!'

The figure in bed doesn't stir.

'Hey, come on! Jonathan!' Marshall moves around the cube, banging on the plexiglass.

He waves TJ over. 'Get this open.'

'Please stop hitting that!' TJ walks to the cube, face etched with anxiety. He examines the metal handle and lock assembly and runs his fingers around the doorframe.

Marshall drops his hand, glares at the teenager. 'Well?'

'It's an electromagnetic lock. We need something like a Neodymium rare earth magnet to get past it. Before you ask, I never carry one. The magnetic field kills electronics and erases data. Not great for the League or the Drive.'

Marshall puffs out a breath. 'What about rigging up an electromagnet?'

'It will take time and I doubt it'll be strong enough.' TJ squeezes his eyes shut and covers his ears. 'I need quiet. I can't think in here…I'm sorry!'

He turns and runs from the cube, back down the corridor.

'TJ, come back!' Marshall yells. 'Get back and help us!'

I make a grab for his arm but he dodges past and disappears around the corner.

Marshall curses and runs over.

'Shall I go after him?' I ask.

'Better if I do it. I know his triggers. Wait here.' Marshall runs back down the corridor.

'…the birth of these children which were his own and of the death of such of them as deceast, and that having estranged her affection to her husband…'

Jonathan's only ten feet away. I rub my clammy hands against my jeans, staring at him.

'…she contrived his Murder, and for that end employed a servant to buy poison…'

I run to the cube and bang on the outside. 'Jonathan! Jonathan!'

Through the see-through walls, I spot yellow foam plugs protruding from his ears. No wonder he won't wake.

The metal door lock and grab handle are a single unit with an indent below the handle with a red light. The indent must be for a key fob. The lock engages into a metal receiver fixed on the adjoining plexiglass panel.

Grabbing Aleksei's card from my pocket, I tap the indent but it doesn't work.

Pocketing the card, I lift the phone receiver attached to the bracket on the outside, covering my other ear to block out the voices.

'Jonathan!' I yell. 'Jonathan!' I bang on the door.

Jonathan Prudente-Poulton finally stirs. He sits up and looks round.

His formerly sleek hair is unkempt, his jawline coated with untidy silver stubble. With his hollowed eyes and haggard expression he looks more like an old man in need of respite care than the Director of Operations.

His mouth drops open. Throwing off the covers, he discards the foam earplugs, lurches towards me and picks up his phone.

'Alex!' His voice is crystal clear. 'Where's Marshall?'

'He's coming,' I say, casting a nervous glance behind me. 'How can we get you out?'

'The Russians have release fobs. They come down here on regular patrol.' He stares at the back wall. 'They're watching. Listening.'

I follow his gaze. A faint glimmer catches my eye. A reflection from the pendant lights overhead.

A ball settles in my guts. The back wall contains a black plate glass set of doors. I was so focussed on waking Jonathan that I never noticed it.

Quinn could be on the other side of the window. He could be watching from a hidden camera.

'You'd better hide until Marshall and TJ get here,' Jonathan urges.

'We've come too far to turn back now,' I say, ignoring the prickles marching up my back. 'What's with these voices? Are they Grigor's stone tape recordings?'

'You know about that?' Jonathan sags forward and closes his eyes. 'These voices are my prison. As much as this box and the cave.' His brows draw together. 'Quinn calls it a soul cage. The voices of the dead bind together to form a protective barrier around me and the lab. They interfere with the Drive and render it useless.'

'So that's why we couldn't find you!' I gasp. 'The soul cage is a…a counter-measure to the Drive. Why does Quinn need it?'

'For anonymity. He plans to make and sell hundreds of Drives but doesn't want anyone to be able to find him. His soul cage means he can never be found.'

'But how can that possibly work?' I frown. 'He can't stay inside a box, bombarded with voices twenty-four hours a day.'

'What you're hearing is Version One.' Jonathan lets out a mirthless laugh. 'Quinn's technicians have already refined it. It's probably portable by now.'

I blink and look down at my feet. Quinn's soul cage cancels out my finding machine. It renders it useless. If Quinn rolls out his invention it will destroy everything my father worked for.

Jonathan places his hand on the door, his face ashen. 'Please forgive me for compromising your safety, and for my weakness in giving up the Lodge's master codes. I held out as long as possible. I'm sorry.'

'And my Drive? Are you sorry about that, too?' My tone hardens. 'I know you swapped it for the clone. I suppose you're going to say Quinn made you do that, too?'

'I didn't swap your Drive. You still have your father's original invention. I swapped the quartz.'

My jaw clenches. 'How is that better? If anything, it's worse! You took advantage of my trust.'

'I'm sorry your feelings are hurt. But I assure you I had your best interests at heart.'

'No, you served your own!'

I'm so close to hanging up and walking away. But I don't want to let Marshall down.

Jonathan says, 'I believed in my actions, and still d—' His eyes widen. 'Look out!'

I spin round.

The phone drops from my hand and clatters against the side of the box. I lurch sideways a split second before TJ crashes into the plexiglass door.

'Get out of the way!' Marshall yells. He rushes from the corridor with one arm clutching his ribs.

A mountain of a man charges after him.

I grab TJ and yank him out of Yury's path. TJ scrambles into the gap behind the cube, slides down the wall and clamps his hands over his ears.

Marshall swivels and punches Yury in the stomach, then strikes at his face. Yury ducks and leads with his elbow, catching Marshall's brow.

As Marshall staggers, dropping the Maglite, Yury looms close, grabs his throat and slams him against the plexiglass. He locks his huge hands around Marshall's neck and starts throttling him.

Jonathan's tinny voice yells through the phone receiver dangling by my feet. 'Let him go, you blockheaded oaf!'

Marshall splutters as he struggles to break free.

'You hurt Aleksei. I hurt you.' A demented gleam comes into Yury's eyes. Tendons stand out on his neck as he applies more pressure to Marshall's throat.

'You have what you want. Stop this nonsense!' Jonathan implores.

I dive for the Maglite and swing it at Yury, catching him on the temple. He curses and looks around.

I shine the light into his eyes.

The Russian squeezes his eyes shut and flinches. He loosens his grip on Marshall with one arm and lunges for me.

Marshall moves faster than I thought possible. In a fraction of a second he wrenches free of Yury's grip, twists his body and drives the heel of his palm into Yury's chin.

The Russian crashes against the wall with a grunt, visibly stunned.

For a second – maybe two – my hopes soar.

Yury smacks his huge mitt against Marshall's face – an open-handed slap that sends Marshall twisting sideways. Yury advances and kicks him in the back of the knee.

Marshall folds to the ground with an, *'Oof!'* Yury rests a giant boot on his neck.

I rush the giant and grab his arm.

He swats me away like an annoying fly. I land hard on my backside and the Maglite skitters from my hand.

I scramble to my feet. My eyes flick to the corridor, the only way out.

Yury follows my glance. A gleam comes into his eye. 'Try it, *devochka*. Please.'

He puts one knee on Marshall's back and removes his burner phone and keys. Yury pockets the keys and stamps on the phone, shattering the case. Then, he touches a round metal tab to the door handle.

The lock clicks.

Yury opens the door and shoves a still-struggling Marshall inside like a piece of airport baggage.

Jonathan catches Marshall before he goes headfirst into the acrylic wall and helps him onto the bed. Marshall grimaces, holding his ribs.

'Aleksei will soon be here,' Yury tells Marshall, locking the door. 'I am sorry.'

Marshall coughs and rubs his throat. 'Go to hell.'

'You.' Yury gestures to me. 'Come.'

He has a wonderfully persuasive way about him. Yury's the best security measure ATC ever came up with and it'll take a hell of a lot more than a pair of pliers and a paperclip to get past him. What choice do I have but to obey?

Yury grabs my rucksack. His other hand shoots for my wrist, squeezing until my bones creak. Stitches tear as he rips the bag from my shoulders.

'No! Please!' I cry.

Marshall's wide-eyed glance meets mine. He shakes his head.

Yury shoves me inside the prison and locks the door. TJ cowers behind the cage. My hopes that Yury can't reach him are short-lived.

The Russian thrusts his arm behind the plexiglass prison, looping his thick fingers around the teenager's tool belt. He drags him out, stamps on his phone, unclips his tool belt and chucks it aside.

Yury unlocks the door again. TJ scrabbles for the doorframe, throwing his arms and legs out in a star shape, but it's no use. Yury manhandles the teenager inside and locks the door.

The stone tape voices suddenly cut out. After the constant jumble of noise, the silence comes as a welcome relief.

Yury unzips my bag and removes the finding machine.

His brow rises. He raises the walkie-talkie to his mouth. 'I have them. And a gift. From the League.'

'You've done well,' the American says through the walkie-talkie.

A rectangle of harsh white light spills into the cavern as the plate glass doors slide apart.

Nate Quinn's voice comes at us from multiple directions.

'Don't you just show up in the damnedest places?'

44

—·—

T J slumps against the prison door, his forehead knocking against the plexiglass. I lean across and gently rub his shoulder.

Yury leers through the see-through door. 'Don't worry. Soon, it will be over.'

'He's wrong,' I whisper to TJ. 'We're not done, yet.'

Marshall rises from the cot bed. He draws in a sharp breath and cradles his ribs.

'How are you holding up?' I ask.

'Ask me in an hour.'

'No talking!' Yury slams his hand on the side of the cube. The plexiglass shivers. He fixes Marshall with a brutal glare.

Four of us are stuffed inside a prison built for one with ten drilled airholes for ventilation. The walls and roof trap our shared body heat as effectively as a greenhouse. With every passing minute it's growing warmer and stuffier.

I'm squeezed between TJ and the phone, squinting against the bright light streaming through the open glass doors. Jonathan watches from the corner, mopping his brow with a silk handkerchief.

Once my eyes adjust to the light I look beyond the glass doors to a laboratory. Fluorescent strip lights are suspended from the ceiling by wires. In contrast to the ochre rock walls the floor is shiny, grey, and perfectly level. A row of lightweight aluminium tables contains computers, monitoring equipment and black box-

303

es with switches. Discarded lab coats hang over empty chairs and disconnected wires snake from the tables to the floor.

A blue light catches my eye. At the centre of the lab's back wall is a metal door fitted with a security pad. If we can escape from the cube Aleksei's card might just open it.

Monitors mounted in the far corner display black and white CCTV images which are impossible to make out from this distance.

Nate Quinn sits on a swivel office chair under the CCTV screens, polishing a pair of black-rimmed spectacles with a yellow cloth. The chair's plastic arms sink into his well-padded torso like foam wadding. His blue shirt's top two buttons are unfastened, revealing pasty white skin.

Quinn replaces his spectacles and heaves himself to his feet. He strides towards us at a surprisingly spritely pace considering his bulk. He halts a few feet away, close enough for me to see individual sweat beads on his brow and dark stains spreading beneath his arms like a Rorschach pattern.

He performs a lengthy slow clap which sounds muffled inside our plastic prison.

'Jonathan's true and loyal servants.' A grin spreads across his face. 'All that dashing around searching for your master like a faithful dog. Have to say, the cameras love you!'

Marshall glowers, one arm pressed against the plexiglass. 'I'll see you in prison!'

'Looks to me like you got there first.' Quinn takes the finding machine from Yury and tips his head towards the Russian's photo between the clips. 'That's a good one of you, Yury.'

Yury rubs his jaw. 'Not good. I am smiling.'

Quinn turns on my finding machine. Five solid LED lights run across the top.

'Excellent. This is a very fine gift from the League.' He gazes adoringly at the display. 'I had a suspicion there was more than one Drive. Jonathan wasn't forthcoming when questioned but I know how you scientists work. You always have prototypes, backups, and copies.'

'It's not yours,' I mutter.

'What? Sorry?' Quinn puts his hand to his ear. 'I can't quite hear you. You'll have to use the phone. Press the button.'

I raise the receiver and jab a red button beside it. 'I said, it's not yours, you thieving bastard!' My voice echoes through the loudspeakers. 'The Drive is mine!'

Quinn smirks. 'Susan Moore, isn't it?'

I bite my tongue, my heart pounding.

Quinn saunters closer. 'The League's secret weapon. A nobody. A girl who does not exist.' He grins. 'It's a shame the Drive's inventor is dead. I had questions for him. Apparently, he had a daughter called Alex Martin.' He shrugs. 'Turns out she's thousands of miles away in the middle of a rainforest.' He leans closer. 'Do you know her, Susan? Maybe I should let Yury loose on you to find out if that really is your name.'

'You'll miss your flight,' Marshall breaks in, pointedly tapping his watch.

Quinn's smile drops from his face. 'Don't worry about me. I have plenty of time.'

Jonathan steps close to me and puts his hand out. I pass him the receiver, keeping my finger on the button.

'You have what you came for,' Jonathan says. 'Let us go.'

Quinn glares back. 'You're wrong. I *don't* have what I want. Marshall took my quartz. He needs to pay.'

Marshall steps towards Jonathan and snatches the receiver from his hand.

'Cut the crap, Quinn. You're finished. Try and run, our contacts will scoop you up. You and your thugs are wanted for assault, kidnapping, and murder threats. You'll spend thirty years behind bars for running the damn show.'

'You've got nothing on me.' Quinn folds his arms. 'Just remember this. You could have avoided all this nastiness back in March when I asked to join the League.'

Marshall pauses, frowning. 'I don't recall any requests from a slimeball like you.'

Quinn's gaze flicks to Jonathan. 'I offered your boss a hundred thousand dollars but he still wouldn't have me.'

'If you don't mind.' Jonathan extends his hand and Marshall passes him the handset. 'I was very clear on the subject, Mr Quinn. Your ethics and moral code fell short of those required to join the League. I'm astonished you made it past Bletchley's rigorous scrutiny.'

'Why don't you take off those rose-tinted glasses?' Quinn sneers. 'ATC's donation enabled the Bletchley Trust to become a major online presence with a state of the art interactive website and top of the line computers, protected by the latest security systems. We add value, and could have done the same for the League.'

Jonathan's tone turns curt. 'You would have corrupted our projects and stolen our research. You're the antithesis of everything we stand for.'

'Better than being a relic!' Quinn laughs. 'Your organisation is dead in the water. You're running projects thirty years out of date with a stiff upper lip that went out with the ark. You're obsessed with science over enterprise.'

'If you had done your research, you'd know profit is not our guiding principle,' Jonathan says tightly.

Quinn retorts. 'Your *old guard* reserve would have served you well during the war, but no one does business like that now.'

'As I have said repeatedly, we are not a business.' Jonathan's tone is barely civil.

'And *that's* why you failed.' Quinn puts his face close to the plastic. 'It's time for the League to roll over.'

Aleksei emerges from the gloomy corridor. He carries a black plastic square with switches. His glower is darker than the shadows.

Yury strides over and claps him around the shoulders. 'All done?'

Aleksei nods. His head twitches as his gaze roves over me, Jonathan, and TJ, then settles on Marshall.

He grins and taps the box. 'For you!'

Quinn chuckles to himself. 'All in good time, Aleksei.'

Aleksei paces back and forth in front of the cube, shooting us evil looks and scratching his arms like mites are crawling over him. I guess the electrical jolt must have left him with a few unexpected aftereffects.

Quinn says. 'I should mention, my boys have had, how shall we say, troubled upbringings. As a child, Aleksei used to blow things up for fun and Yury was a notorious pyromaniac. I wouldn't trust him around an old pile of tinder like Red Croft Lodge.'

A chill rushes through me. Carmen's still inside.

Jonathan barks down the phone. 'Don't even think about it.'

'You just can't help yourself, can you?' Quinn snaps. He grabs a tissue from his pocket and dabs sweat from his brow. 'I'm blowing the tunnel. It's outlived its purpose. The same goes for the Lodge. It's an old, shoddy building. A faulty fuse, a leaking gas pipe, one small spark, and *Kaboom*!'

'You're mad to think you can get away with this,' Jonathan seethes.

'Reality check, Jonathan. I already have.' Quinn gives him a pitying look. 'There's nothing linking me to you, the League, or the ghost quartz. The cops can chase their tails trying to unpick ATC and the Trustees at Bletchley will be none the wiser.' He gives the finding machine a loving look. 'Meanwhile, we're creating a new buzz. I'm thinking of calling this, The ATC Soul Engine. What d'ya think?'

Jonathan's frown deepens.

'I haven't nailed down the price, though a million sounds about right,' Quinn continues. 'Then again, Russia, China, and the Middle East would pay ten times that to get their hands on one. Fact is, the Soul Engine takes surveillance and information trading to a new level. Information's the new currency, but I doubt you'd know that with your head buried in the sand.'

I snatch the phone from Jonathan's hand.

'Those people will use it for all the wrong reasons!'

Quinn's brow creases. 'What people do with my products is none of my business. I don't discriminate. I sell to anybody. Do-gooders, arms manufacturers, information brokers, the police. They're simply customers. What's so villainous about that?'

I slam my hand against the plexiglass. 'Only the rich will be able to afford one!'

'Welcome to free enterprise.' Quinn shakes his head. 'I've got major interest from all over, so I must be doing something right.'

Suddenly, I feel very small. Could Quinn possibly have a point? If every police department bought a finding machine a huge amount of good would come out of it. But I also know the deepest pockets often belong to the most ill-intentioned and greedy individuals.

'If you exploit my Drive, the most dangerous men in the world will be able to find their enemies,' I mutter darkly, foreseeing an unfolding nightmare. 'They'll start wars.'

'I have an answer to that,' Quinn says smugly. 'The ATC Soul Cage. For consumers needing protection from the Soul Engine. In the last few weeks my guys have refined the technology so the soul cage operates in silence. Turns out, the volume is unimportant. What matters is the energy, frequency, and vib—'

'Don't say it!' Jonathan takes the phone from me. 'I won't let you sully Nikola Tesla's good name by quoting him. He'd turn in his grave if he knew what you've done.'

'I believe Tesla would salute me,' Quinn says. 'The jammer's portable. It fits in your pocket. That's progress!'

Dad knew the downsides of his invention. He knew there'd be Nathan Quinns in the world. That's why he kept it secret. The thought of Quinn commodifying the voices of the dead makes me nauseous. I lower my head and take deep breaths.

'Let the people decide.' Quinn folds his arms. 'Let market forces decide.'

'You've forgotten something,' I say. 'You need more quartz.'

'Not a problem. I'll auction off one of the machines. It must be worth millions to the right buyer. With that kind of money, finding more ghost quartz will not be a problem!'

Quinn's grin stretches from ear to ear. I can almost see dollar signs in his eyes.

'Is there anything you won't box up and sell?' I ask bitterly, even though there's no point arguing with the money-grabbing snake.

'My genius?' Quinn gives me a smug smile and passes Yury my finding machine. 'Put it in the case and wait for me.'

I watch forlornly as Yury carries the finding machine into the lab. He walks to a large aluminium case open on the table and tucks my machine inside. He carries the case to the metal exit door, swipes his card through the reader and shoulders the door open.

I catch a glimpse of a lit passageway with a criss-cross metal stairway before the door swings shut.

Aleksei stares at Marshall, his fingers twitching. 'How long, boss?'

'Set it for ten minutes.' Quinn checks his watch. 'Our ride will be here soon. Be quick.'

Aleksei turns a dial on the controller and shoves it towards Marshall.

'Soon, it is all over for you!' He releases a manic laugh as he backs away and slips past Yury.

Quinn waves. '*Adios amigos*. I guarantee you'll never find me again.' He glances briefly at us before retreating to the lab.

He hits a switch, and the CCTV screens and computers go dead.

Another flick of a switch.

The lights go out.

45

— · —

Apart from the glowing security pad in Quinn's lab the cavern and our prison lie in darkness.

I hear rustling, then a click. A small beam of torchlight pierces the gloom. I make out TJ holding a mini keyring torch.

'Thank God,' Marshall says. 'I won't ask where you hid that.'

'In my sock.'

'We need to come up with a plan,' Marshall says. 'We have less than ten minutes before Aleksei blows the tunnel. This whole place could come down on our heads.'

I press a button on my watch, struggling to calm my racing heart. The display lights up: *21:50*. I shine my watch around but the backlit LCD screen is too weak to pierce the darkness.

TJ's keyring light shines through our prison and lands on a dark, snaking shape a few feet outside the door.

'Your tool belt!' I say. 'If we could find some way of hooking it, we could drag your tools through the air holes.'

'None of my tools will work on this lock.' TJ gives the door a shove.

I pick up the phone receiver and press the button.

'Hello? Hello?' My panicking voice echoes off the rock walls. I turn to Jonathan. 'Is there any way we can dial out on this?'

Jonathan says ruefully, 'The phone's connected to the speakers and the lab. It's not an external line.'

'How are we going to call Carmen? We have to tell her to get out of the Lodge!' I struggle to control my rising terror. 'Once she spots Yury on the CCTV she'll lock herself inside the Vault. It's the worst possible place!'

'Let's not panic,' Marshall says. 'The Vault is fireproof and Carmen can close off the ventilation valves if she smells smoke. She should be safe for an hour, at least.'

'But what if the house burns down on top of her? She'll be trapped!'

'We need to get out of here first.' Marshall looks at each of us in turn. 'Any ideas?'

'I've thought of nothing else for weeks,' Jonathan says. 'This plexiglass cube is securely bolted to the floor. It's made from multiple bonded layers. Each pane is tough as an aeroplane window.'

'Even so, this is a prison built for one,' Marshall points out. 'It was never meant to hold four people. I doubt it's been stressed tested against 650, maybe 700 pounds of combined force.' He nods to TJ. 'Have you spotted any vulnerabilities?'

'Not the lock.' TJ moves his light from the solid metal block securing the door to the two metal hinges on the other side of the panel. The hinges span a tiny gap, a millimetre or so wide, running up the side of the door.

'The hinges.'

Marshall knocks books off the small coffee table and picks it up.

'Get back,' he warns. He smashes the table against the hinges.

The plexiglass wobbles slightly. Marshall repeatedly slams the table into the door but the hinges hold. He drops the table onto the floor.

'It's not going to be enough,' he says, gasping and wiping sweat from his brow.

He steps to the cot bed and shoves the pillows and blankets off and chucks the thin mattress aside. The metal-framed bed hinges in the middle. He folds the bed in half and tucks in the legs.

'Everyone grab a corner,' he orders. 'We'll ram the hinges until they break.'

TJ rests the keyring by the door, directing the light onto the hinges.

'If this doesn't work what's Plan B?' I ask.

'There isn't one.' Marshall adjusts his grip on the bed. 'Back up so we can take a proper swing at it.'

Jonathan and I raise the cot bed by its rear corners while TJ and Marshall take the front. I shuffle back to the plastic wall.

'On three, give it all you've got,' Marshall orders. 'One, two, three!'

Together, we ram the door for all we're worth.

Whamm! The bed slams into the hinges, jarring my wrists and elbows.

'Go again!' Marshall says, breathing heavily

Whamm! We repeatedly ram the door until my arms go numb.

I grit my teeth. A deep-seated fury rises inside: part terror at our predicament, part anger at losing the finding machine and Quinn getting away scot-free. In my mind's eye a ticking clock counts down the seconds to detonation. It feels like we've wasted eight minutes already.

I check my watch. I'm not far off; there can't be more than a minute left. My head starts to spin as the air inside the cube becomes harder to breathe.

'Keep going!' Marshall orders.

Whamm! Whamm! Whamm!

The plexiglass wobbles. Metal clatters to the floor.

'Wait!' Marshall calls a halt.

'Have we done it!' I peer into the gloom.

TJ shines the torch on a broken piece of metal. 'It's the hinge cover.'

'We're close!' Marshall wheezes. 'One, two, three!'

Whamm! We hit the door for the umpteenth time.

WHOOOMMM...RRR! Thunder shakes the floor. A roar fills the cavern along with a powerful, rolling rumble that resounds through the walls.

I scream and stumble over discarded books. The back of my head bangs against the cube. Tin lights rattle and swing above as dust hisses from the ceiling.

Inside the lab, fluorescent lights shatter. Sparks flash, illuminating the computers for a split second. Lab tables skitter around on the smooth floor, sending equipment crashing down.

Repeating shudders rattle my teeth and reverberate beneath my feet. I cover my mouth against thick dust as stones slam onto the prison roof.

'Keep going!' Marshall yells.

I can barely hear him but I know what to do. I ram the door.

Metal snaps and clinks onto the floor.

Marshall shouts. 'One down!'

Renewed hope surges through me. I dig deep into my final reserves of strength and slam the bed against the door.

The second hinge clatters onto the ground. TJ grabs his torch and shoulder-barges the door which falls outwards and bangs on the ground.

Marshall, TJ and I spill out of the cube, coughing in the dust-laden air.

Jonathan turns to stare at his prison. By the light of TJ's torch I see him flex and clench his hands into fists before slowly straightening.

TJ shines the light around. Plastic shards and splinters lie amongst fallen stones — all that remains of our mobile phones. TJ swiftly retrieves the SIMS from the debris along with his toolbelt, the flashlight, and Marshall's Maglite.

Streams of dust clog the air. I glance back to the tunnel. A rockfall blocks the entrance.

I mutter, 'My God, how much C-4 did Aleksei use?'

'The whole place is unstable! Come on!' Marshall grabs the Maglite and weaves his way around a pile of rock where the ceiling has collapsed and through the shattered glass doors. He kicks a toppled chair out of the way then grabs the nearest landline.

'Hello? Hello?' He rattles the switch hook, then slams the receiver down. 'Damn. Line's dead.'

He strides to the security door. 'TJ, get this open.'

I wave Aleksei's card in the air. 'Let me try.'

I swipe the plastic card through the reader. The lock beeps.

'Yes!' I pump my fist and push the door open.

A dark passageway leads to a shiny, switchback staircase. I run to the base and shine my torch up to the first turning.

'Alex, wait!' Marshall warns.

Without heeding his warning I run to a tiny landing where the staircase turns back on itself. Taking the lead, I race up one more switchback to reach the top. A security door blocks my way.

'Please, please work,' I pray, swiping Aleksei's card.

Beep.

I open the door. Fresh air hits me in the face along with the smell of petrol and old engine oil. Five feet away is the Austin 18 ambulance I saw earlier today. Two other classic vehicles and a dispatch bike sit further back in the gloom.

Relief floods me. We've made it to the surface.

The Wartime Garages are deserted. One of the corrugated garage doors has been left open to the night air.

In the distance I hear a faint *chupp-chupp-chupp-chupp* sound that's getting louder.

'Wait here.' Marshall runs outside onto dark tarmac.

Jonathan stumbles to the ambulance and leans one arm on the roof. He closes his eyes and takes deep breaths of fresh air.

'We have to call Carmen,' I say, looking for a phone. I throw my hands up, finding nothing. 'What about a public callbox? Or, we can knock on someone's door!'

TJ says, 'There aren't any callboxes on Sherwood Drive. We're on an industrial estate. Everywhere's closed.'

'It's over a mile to Red Croft Lodge,' Jonathan says. 'We'll need a car if we're to reach Carmen in time.'

His eyes alight on the display board in front of the WW2 Ambulance. 'Shame this doesn't run.'

'But...it does!' I exclaim. The tour guide's words from earlier come back to me: *"This Austin 18 ambulance is a fully restored and working example. I was lucky enough to have a drive in it today!"*

I rush to the driver's door. It opens with a mournful creak. 'TJ, start her up.'

'Are you crazy?' The teenager leans inside the compartment. 'This vehicle's a relic.'

I put my hands on my hips. 'No, it's a film star.'

Jonathan peers inside the passenger compartment.

'My father had an Austin 18. She'll be easy to hotwire.' Seat springs squeak as he slips inside and sidles across the bench to the driver's side. 'Hold the torch for me and pass me a flathead screwdriver.'

Jonathan uses TJ's screwdriver to lever off the steering column panel. A spaghetti bundle of wires falls out.

'We need three wires. The battery, starter, and—'

'Ignition,' TJ interjects. 'I'll strip the ends.'

I leave them to it and run to the garage doors to tell Marshall. The service road outside runs up the side of Bletchley Mansion and intersects with a wide road that runs past the lake, huts and visitor's centre. Overhead, the whirring noise fills the sky accompanied by a blinding white searchlight.

A helicopter hovers far above. Orange and green lights blink on and off by the main blades and rear rotors as it slowly descends.

I look for the word *POLICE* on the side. Instead, I see *VIKINGAIR*.

Marshall appears around the corner of the Mansion and runs towards me. 'Quinn must have chartered that helicopter! He's waiting by the lake with Aleksei.'

'You said they were going from Cranfield Airport!'

'I assumed they hired a plane!' Marshall says between gasps. 'Our contacts are at Cranfield and there's no way to let them know.' He shakes his head. 'Quinn can hop over to France, then take a plane back to the States.'

'We can't stop the helicopter from landing,' I say, 'but we can get to the Lodge and save Carmen.'

Marshall raises his arms. 'How?'

The ambulance's engine chokes and splutters.

Marshall turns and stares at the car. 'Are you serious?'

'Come on, my beauty.' Jonathan crouches by the open driver's door, fiddling with a bundle of exposed wires. The engine gives a high-pitched whine, splutters again, then catches with a four-star petrol roar. A black cloud spills from the exhaust.

'Get in!' I tug Marshall's sleeve and run to the ambulance.

Jonathan waves me behind the wheel. 'You'd better drive, Alex.'

I take a step back. 'Me?'

'It's been thirty years since I was behind the wheel,' Jonathan says blithely. 'Marshall chauffeurs me everywhere.'

TJ raises his hands. 'I don't have a driving licence.'

I stare at Marshall.

'I can't drive a stick shift,' he says. 'You do, Alex.'

'Oh, God,' I say, sinking into the driver's seat.

Jonathan climbs in next to me with Marshall alongside, leaving TJ squeezed against the passenger door like a tinned sardine.

Everything inside the vehicle is massive. The steering wheel's big enough for a boat. The clock is larger than the speedometer. There's a dial for Ampères and mysterious knobs and switches on the steering wheel and dashboard, but I haven't a clue what they're for.

'This is an emergency vehicle,' I say. 'Shouldn't there be a radio to call for help?'

'This vehicle was built in the thirties,' Jonathan informs me. 'Emergency vehicles weren't fitted with radios back then.'

'Where are the lights?'

'We don't want lights,' Marshall orders. 'Just drive!'

46

The Austin ambulance is a beast, made from twice the steel as a modern car, supported on enormous enamelled wheels. Visibility is appalling, especially without the headlights on. The bonnet stretches ahead forever and the bulky ambulance compartment blocks my rear view.

'One small thing,' Jonathan says as I depress the clutch and shove the gearstick into first. 'The Austin doesn't have a modern synchromesh gearbox. You'll need to double declutch.'

I shoot him a panicked look. 'What the hell does that mean?'

Jonathan gestures to the gearstick. 'All you need do is match the rotational speed of the input shaft to the rotational speed of the gea—'

He sounds just like Dad when he gave me driving lessons!

'Get on with it!' Marshall yells over Jonathan's shoulder.

The clutch squeaks as I let it out. The ambulance jolts forward. I rev the accelerator and slam the clutch in before the engine stalls; no easy task with a pedal as stiff as a rusty spring. The clutch bites and we lurch forward, bouncing up and down on heavily sprung leather.

I aim for the gap in the garage doors and squeeze the ambulance through with inches to spare.

The descending helicopter casts an ever-widening circle of light onto a large lawned area in front of the Mansion. The deafening sound of the rotors drowns out the Austin's rumbling engine as I surge forward.

The speedometer gauge reaches ten miles per hour which feels like warp speed for this bus.

Jonathan braces himself against the dashboard. 'Put it in neutral, rev the engine, then slip it in second.'

'I barely got it into first!' I protest.

'Look out!' Marshall leans across Jonathan and stabs his finger at a giant redwood tree lurking on the verge. I scrabble for my seatbelt, then realise there isn't one.

I wrench the steering wheel round. My old Mini was basic but at least it was easy to steer. The Austin's as responsive as an oil tanker.

The redwood looms through the windscreen.

'Hold on!' I yell, as the front fender scrapes bark with a horrendous grinding sound.

'Accelerate!' Jonathan orders. He yanks on the wheel.

I shove my right foot on the accelerator. The ambulance breaks free of the tree and lurches forward.

Off to my right, a lawned area dotted with picnic tables runs down to the lake. The grass is lit up like daytime under the helicopter's landing lights. Four signal flares fizz and spit orange sparks under the rotors' downdraft.

Nate Quinn and Aleksei stand at the far edge of the green with the lake at their backs, staring upwards. Aleksei holds the aluminium case.

'Cut across the lawn,' Marshall hisses. 'Drive at them!'

'What?' My mouth drops open. 'No!'

'Aim at Quinn and put your foot down,' Marshall urges. He shoves the steering wheel over. The ambulance bounces up the kerb and onto the lawn. 'Stamp on it!'

'I'm not driving into anyone!'

'Trust me!' His tone brooks no refusal.

TJ clings to the door strap. 'This can't be legal!'

I slip into neutral and rev the engine. The engine whines as I ram the gearstick into second and thump my right foot down.

The ambulance shoots across the grass.

'Don't brake until I tell you,' Marshall orders, holding his hand up.

Jonathan loops his arm around the back of the seat, eyes fixed on our targets as we hurtle forward. A hedge smacks against my wing mirror. The ground dips a little and the ambulance picks up speed, clipping a picnic table with a *bang*.

Fifteen miles per hour. Twenty.

Jonathan stares at Quinn with fevered intensity. I can't work out whether he's terrified or relishes the idea of ploughing into him.

Quinn looks down and spots us. His face blanches as I aim the Austin's nose towards him. He yells and staggers backwards, waving his arms like he's about to fall off a tightrope.

The old Austin barrels forwards enthusiastically. Aleksei throws the aluminium case out of the ambulance's path and dives to the side.

'Brake, brake, brake!' Marshall chops his hand down.

I slam my foot on the spongy pedal. The Austin is slow to respond. Too slow.

Quinn's horrified expression looms in the windscreen. His mouth falls open, his screams drowned out by the roaring engine.

I hit him.

He tumbles backwards and hits the water with a splash.

The Austin slows to a halt with its nose over the water's edge.

'Look out!' Marshall barks as Aleksei rushes the passenger door.

TJ twists the handle and kicks the door open. The lump of solid steel smacks the Russian in the face. He stumbles backwards and collapses on the grass.

'Go! Go!' Marshall shoves past the teenager and throws himself on Aleksei. The door blocks most of my view, but through a tiny gap I see Marshall throw his fist and the Russian stops moving.

Jonathan dashes from the car and grabs the aluminium case.

I peer through the windscreen at the helicopter hovering above the lake. The searchlight illuminates Quinn thrashing in the water as though sharks are attacking him. God knows what the pilot's thinking.

'Hurry! Bring the electrical tape!' Marshall barks at TJ, as he sits on Aleksei.

Aleksei moans as TJ winds electrical tape around his wrists and ankles for the second time this evening.

Quinn splashes about in the water, his face barely above the surface. I jump from the ambulance, leaving the engine running. His panicked gaze meets mine.

Jonathan slides the aluminium case into the deep passenger footwell.

'Shouldn't we help him?' I ask.

'I suppose we'd better.' Jonathan runs to Marshall's aid and holds Aleksei down. 'I've got him, Marshall. Get that idiot out of the water.' He glances my way. 'Alex, open up the back of the ambulance.'

Marshall hurries towards the bank of the lake, as I run to the rear of the vehicle and yank on the handles, praying they're not locked. The doors creak open, revealing a cavernous interior with canvas webbing running down the sides.

Jonathan grabs Aleksei's belt. 'TJ, you take his shoulders. Alex, hold his legs.'

On Jonathan's count we heave Aleksei's dead weight off the ground. He mumbles and groans. His legs give an involuntary twitch and he boots me in the ribs.

I stagger back, gasping for breath.

TJ and Jonathan manage to dump Aleksei in the back of the ambulance. Jonathan clambers inside and drags him to the metal bulkhead. TJ hooks him to the webbing using the fixed canvas straps until he's trussed up like a Christmas turkey.

Aleksei wriggles and curses as he comes to his senses.

Leaving the angry Russian, I run to the lake. Marshall has waded out waist-deep. He loops an arm around Quinn and drags him from the water.

Quinn flops onto the bank like a dead seal.

'Wake up!' Marshall slaps him heavily between the shoulder blades. Quinn rolls onto his side and vomits water. He gives a desperate wheeze then vomits some more. Jonathan and TJ heave Quinn to his feet and drag him to the back of the ambulance.

Quinn yells hoarsely, 'You ran me down! I think you broke my ribs! I'll sue your asses! My lawyers will rip you apart!'

Relief washes over me despite his threats. If he has the strength to shout after being hit by an ambulance and half-drowned, he'll probably be all right.

'Give it up, Quinn,' Marshall snaps. 'It's over.'

Blinding light turns to darkness as the helicopter banks sharply across the lake and rapidly ascends into the night sky.

Marshall and the others shove Quinn unceremoniously inside the load area, his wrists and ankles taped together. TJ straps him to the webbing opposite Aleksei.

Quinn slumps against the side of the ambulance, glaring at the Russian. 'Thanks for your help back there,' he snaps. 'I'll remember that.'

Aleksei sneers. 'You are welcome.'

'Hold tight. It'll be a bumpy ride,' Marshall says, slamming the back doors. He climbs into the car with Jonathan and TJ.

I slip behind the wheel and stare at the flashing lights swiftly shrinking in the night sky. 'What will the pilot do?'

'Depends on his involvement. If he has any sense he'll radio the police,' Marshall says. 'Speaking of calling for help....' He passes a mobile phone to TJ. 'Aleksei kindly donated this. Call Carmen, then the police.' He points in the direction of Bletchley's main entrance. 'Alex, drive us to the Lodge.'

Jonathan winces as I grind the gearstick into reverse. The wheels spin on wet grass but I persevere, backing the beast away from the lake. I slip into first gear and follow the road running between the brick huts, around a curve to the main entrance.

This time I brake early and cruise to a stop by the unmanned sentry post and striped barrier. A black box bearing ATC's logo is mounted to a metal post. A blue light shines by a card reader.

I roll down the window and swipe Aleksei's card, an old hand at this game by now. The red and white striped barrier arm rises and I drive through. It makes a welcome change from ramming things.

The gears slip in nicely as I change up to second. Finally, I'm getting the hang of it.

'Aleksei's phone's locked,' TJ says. 'I can dial emergency services but not Carmen. Not without the code.'

Marshall twists in his seat and slides open a hatch that allows a direct view into the loading bay. 'Aleksei, give me the code for your phone!'

Aleksei spits at him.

'Like he's gonna tell you,' Quinn adds. 'You're too late, anyway. The Lodge is history.'

Marshall slams the hatch and wipes his face. 'Alex, step on it. TJ, call the police.'

Cool air streams into the cabin as I speed to the junction with Sherwood Drive. My nerves frazzle at the sight of passing head-lights. The idea of turning right across oncoming traffic without lights or indicators gives me palpitations.

'Police. Fire brigade,' TJ says into the phone. He glances at me. 'Ambulance.' Another pause. 'The address is Red Croft Lodge, Church Walk, Bletchley. An armed and dangerous intruder has set fire to the house.' Another pause. 'My name?' He turns his head aside and drops his voice. 'It's—'

'Marshall, I need lights now!' I yell.

'Try this.' Marshall flicks a lever on the dashboard.

A bell dings away like we're on the mother of all emergency missions.

'That's helpful!' I shoot him a glare.

Marshall turns off the alarm bell. 'How about this?' He twists a knob by the steering wheel. Weak cones of light spill onto the road ahead.

'Better.'

I search for a gap in the traffic as we reach the junction, . A lorry shoots past, spiking my heartrate.

'After the white taxi,' Marshall says.

The taxi speeds past. I stomp on the accelerator and yank the wheel. We shoot from the junction as a ten-ton juggernaut appears around the corner. I overcompensate with the steering wheel and we clip the far kerb, causing my teeth to clack together. I straighten in lane as blazing headlights blind me in the rear view mirror.

The juggernaut's horn blasts from behind. TJ clings to the passenger door strap, humming tunelessly.

'Don't spare the horses,' Marshall urges. 'All the way to the roundabout.'

I floor it, putting space between us and the lorry. Sherwood Drive winds its way to the roundabout. A car is coming round.

'Let them go first,' Marshall warns.

But panic overtakes me, thinking of Carmen stuck in the Lodge.

I put my foot to the floor and the Austin shoots in front of the car with inches to spare. The engine screams as I accelerate away. Marshall helps turn the steering wheel to keep us tight to the grassy centre island. The tyres release a low howling sound that drills into my head.

'What the hell are you doing, trying to kill us?' Quinn yells from the back.

I exit the roundabout and slip the vehicle into fourth gear. My driving has improved enough that I no longer need Marshall's help. If only this beast weren't so slow!

Marshall directs me up Church Green Road. I squeeze past parked cars in the narrow road, clipping a few wing mirrors on the way.

I take the tight turn into Church Walk as fast as I dare. The Austin's headlights are so weak I can barely see ten feet ahead. The suspension bounces on the uneven track and the ride becomes so bone-rattling I fear the seat springs will twang free. Twigs snap and branches whack the side windows as I guide the bulky ambulance to the end of the lane.

Marshall leans forward. 'The gates are open!'

I screech to a halt in the driveway, inches from the back bumper of a white Audi — the same car we tailed this afternoon.

Yury's nowhere in sight.

I stick my head out of the window, staring at Red Croft Lodge. The house looks quiet and the windows lie dark. For a second, I dare to hope.

Then I catch the smell of acrid smoke.

47

I peer through the windscreen at Red Croft Lodge, my hands gripping the steering wheel. Lights are on all over the house. My heart quickens at the bitter smell coming through the open driver's window.

Jonathan retrieves the aluminium case from the passenger footwell and leaves the vehicle.

As TJ goes to follow him, Marshall puts his hand out. 'Give me your toolbelt.'

TJ unclicks the belt and hands it over before hopping out.

A leaden weight settles in my guts as Marshall loosens the elastic waistband and straps the belt around his waist.

'What are you doing?'

'I'm going in for Carmen.'

I tug on his arm. 'Shouldn't we wait for the fire br—'

'There's no time. Back up this bus to the wall so our guests can't escape. Then, hide in the lane. You've done your bit.'

Marshall slips from the vehicle and slams the passenger door, cutting off my protests. I watch dry-mouthed as he strides to the porch, pushes the door open, and disappears inside.

Cursing, I reverse the Austin towards the perimeter wall. The vehicle bumps over grass and picks up speed. I hit the brakes, too late. The Austin comes to an abrupt halt with a horrible crunch of metal on stone.

I wrench the ignition wires apart and the engine cuts out.

'What the hell?' Quinn yells from the back. 'Put the light on! We can't see a damn thing back here!'

I turn in my seat, staring at the closed hatch.

'Tough luck, Quinn!'

It's about time he tasted his own medicine. Leaving the ambulance, I look from the Lodge to the lane, torn between following Marshall and running to safety.

Jonathan and TJ are beneath a giant sycamore tree outside the gates. Jonathan stands ramrod straight, punctuating his words with precise gestures and radiating authority despite his unusual getup of paisley pyjamas and slippers.

I run over.

'—tell the emergency services exactly what I told you,' Jonathan says, handing TJ the aluminium case. 'Hide this well away from the Lodge. We'll retrieve it later.'

'Got it, boss.' TJ hurries across the lane with the case and disappears into the darkness.

Jonathan glances my way. 'Ah, Alex. You have my sincerest thanks for your help. Best if you go with TJ. Stay out of sight.'

I take a hesitant step after TJ, but something makes me turn. 'What about you?'

'I have to ensure the future of the League. Please, stay with TJ.' He returns through the gates and hurries towards the Lodge's front door.

Pushing reason and better judgement aside, I run after Jonathan and catch up with him on the porch.

'Jonathan, this is madness!' I say. 'Yury's still here! Not to mention, the building's on fire.'

His eyebrows draw together. 'I need a few moments to make a phone call.'

'Use someone else's phone! The police will be here any minute.'

'I have to take care of this.'

'Open the Vault and I can get Carmen!'

'Carmen is safer staying in the Vault until Marshall takes care of Yury.' Jonathan covers his lower face with his handkerchief and slips inside the building. 'I'll do my best for her, don't worry.'

'You can't leave her in there!' I yell, following him into the chequerboard hallway.

A wall of heat hits me along with the bitter stink of burning plastic, acrid rubber, and old wood. I cover my nose and mouth. The door across from me leading to the Vault hallway is closed.

Jonathan heads down the other hallway through a haze of smoke. Dark clouds billow from the kitchen at the end. A furious orange glow as bright as lava pulses at the kitchen's heart.

For one terrible moment I think Jonathan's about to rush head-first into the inferno. Instead, he halts outside his study, wraps his handkerchief around his hand and tests the brass knob. He opens the door and disappears inside.

Beyond the heavy tick of the grandfather clock, crackling and snapping sounds come from upstairs. My room — my father's room — is probably ablaze. Scraps of charred paper fall like black rain down the stairwell, drifting past my father's seven-foot Oxford varsity oar.

What if Marshall hasn't taken care of Yury?

The dreadful thought spurs me to dash up the stairs and wrench Dad's oar from its mountings. I'd have preferred a hockey stick or cricket bat as a weapon, but beggars can't be choosers. Returning downstairs, I hurry to the closed door leading to the Vault corridor.

I remove my glove and touch the brass handle. It feels cool. Muffled noises come from the other side. I swing open the door.

The Vault staircase hasn't been activated. The floorboards run straight and true to the end of the hallway.

Shouts, thumps, and the sound of breaking glass reach me through the first door on the left.

'It's over, Yury!' Marshall shouts. 'The police will be here any minute!'

'Too late for you!' Yury bellows back.

My hopes that Marshall has rescued Carmen and taken her from the building die a swift death. The thought of her trapped underground while the fire takes hold makes my heart wrench. All my previous grievances shrink to nothing.

I'll forgive her everything if only she makes it out alive.

I jump at another loud crash. Beside the door is the FIRE switch that operates the secret staircase down to the Vault. I need Marshall's thumb to operate it, but his thumb has other things to worry about right now.

I creep to the doorway and peer round.

Yury and Marshall face off in front of a snooker table. Behind them is a well stocked bar, a Wurlitzer jukebox, and a set of French doors framed by red velvet curtains.

The Russian has his fists clenched in a pugilist stance. Marshall wields a snooker cue two handed.

I flinch as Marshall takes a swing at Yury's head, catching him a glancing blow across the temple. Yury roars. Shaking his head, he grabs the cue and jerks it towards him, yanking Marshall within grabbing distance. Marshall releases his grip and staggers back, banging into the snooker table.

Yury lunges, jabbing the cue into Marshall's belly. 'You are getting soft, old man!'

'Ooof!' Marshall folds over, gasping for breath. Yury grabs him by his tie and belt and slams him onto the green baize, sending coloured balls rolling and clacking. Yury puts his hands around Marshall's neck and squeezes. Marshall fights to push him off but it's a wrestling match he can't win.

I grit my teeth and run at Yury, swinging Dad's oar with all my might. The paddle catches the Russian squarely between the shoulders with a satisfying *smack.*

Yury releases his grip on Marshall and staggers sideways into the bar. His eyes lock onto me.

'You!' He makes a swipe for the oar. I jerk it out of his reach and back away to the door, terrified he'll drag me into his grip.

Yury grabs a whisky bottle from the bar and hurls it at me.

I duck. The bottle smashes against the doorframe, releasing the sharp smell of liquor. From the corner of my eye, I spot Marshall sliding to the floor and crawling under the snooker table.

Yury hurls a crystal carafe at me followed by a gold-plated bottle. I knock the carafe aside with the oar. Bottles smash against the wall, spraying port, brandy, and glass everywhere.

An insane gleam comes into Yury's eye as he stares at the alcohol pooling on the floorboards. He flicks open a Zippo lighter, strikes a flame and tosses it at my feet.

I yell and jump back as the alcohol bursts into flame by my feet, igniting a sheet of flame that expands across the floorboards.

Yury's triumphant grin is suddenly wiped from his face as Marshall grabs his legs and yanks him off his feet. The Russian topples like a demolished chimney, striking his head on the corner of the pool table on his way down.

Marshall wastes no time in throwing himself onto the stunned Russian. He locks his arms around Yury's thick neck. The Russian rolls violently from side to side, bashing Marshall into the snooker table and then the wall. His face turns red under Marshall's chokehold as he fights to stay conscious.

Fire licks up the legs of the snooker table and climbs up an armchair. My heart pounds as orange tongues leap up the curtains, across the pelmets and ignite the fringed canopy lights. I retreat to the hallway with sweat trickling down my neck, coughing under thick and foul-smelling smoke.

A figure stands by the *FIRE* switch, his thumb under the cover.

A frightened cry escapes me as I swing the oar. I pull back a split second before I hit Jonathan.

Clunk. Clunk. Clunk. Clunk.

The hidden staircase descends.

I throw a panicked glance in the direction of the front door. The raging conflagration is eating the stair spindles and the grandfather clock.

'Go down and get Carmen,' Jonathan says. 'She won't leave on her own.' He yanks the fire extinguisher from its bracket and pulls out the retaining pin. 'I need to help Marshall. Quickly, now!'

He strides to the open doorway and depresses the lever. Foam shoots out and extinguishes the flaming floorboards.

Jonathan approaches the struggling men. 'Need a hand, Marshall?' he says, before neatly clonking Yury on the head with the fire extinguisher.

Wrenching my gaze away, I race downstairs to the metal door and bang on it for all I'm worth.

'Carmen! It's Alex! Open up!'

I pound and pound on the Vault door until it opens inwards. Carmen lets out a horrified gasp and coughs in the sharp heat. A sheen of sweat coats her ghost-white face.

'We have to go! Now!'

I grab her arm and haul her up the stairs. Her limp is worse than ever but I refuse to slow down. At the top, I pull her away from the Vault stairwell, keeping a tight hold around her waist. My nose and eyes sting from the heat as smoke rolls up to the ceiling.

'Are you okay?' I ask.

'I think s—' She dissolves into a coughing fit.

Inside the snooker room, Marshall kneels on Yury's back. The Russian lies motionless on the floor, blood trickling from a welt on his forehead.

Marshall removes the electrical tape from TJ's toolbelt and binds long strips around Yury's wrists and ankles while Jonathan extinguishes the last of the fire, leaving the curtains and furniture coated in so much foam it looks like Narnia.

I hold Carmen tight, shifting my gaze from the snooker room to the raging inferno in the hallway. The smoke is so thick it covers the black-and-white squares. I shield my lower face with my sleeve but it's too hot to bear.

Jonathan steps into the hallway. 'Inside, you two!'

He waves us into the snooker room, pausing to press his thumb to the sensor pad beneath the *FIRE* switch before closing the cover.

The staircase rises and the treads lock into place, leaving the Vault's secret location safe once more.

Jonathan closes the door behind us, cutting out the worst of the smoke.

Carmen takes a tentative step towards Yury. 'I saw him on the camera creeping up to the front door. Is he dead?'

'Sadly not,' Marshall says, throwing Jonathan a set of keys. 'Found these on him.'

'Ah, thank goodness,' Jonathan says, giving Marshall a sardonic look. 'Far easier than breaking these lovely doors down.'

He walks to the French doors and unlocks them. As he pushes them open, cool air streams in along with the sound of sirens.

'You first, Carmen,' Marshall orders, double-checking Yury's bonds.

She stumbles outside and stops on the grass, heaving in lungfuls of fresh air.

Yury stirs and groans.

'I know he's a monster, but we can't leave him in a burning building,' I say.

'It's your lucky day, comrade,' Marshall says, grabbing Yury's ankles. 'Someone give me a hand.'

Jonathan, Marshall and I drag Yury outside feet first like a sack of grain. His head bangs unceremoniously on the door ledge on his way out. Marshall orders us to haul him along the grass and dump him on the lawn.

'Quickly.' Jonathan herds me and Carmen past the Austin ambulance and out of the gates.

Safe at last, I turn to Carmen. She moves towards me at the same time.

'You came for me.' Carmen blinks up at me. 'Thank you.'

'I'm sorry! So sorry!' I hug her, tears rolling down my cheeks. 'I kept thinking we were too late. We tried to warn you but we couldn't find a phone.' I wipe my eyes. 'Please forgive me.'

Carmen draws back, her eyes watery. She squeezes my forearm. 'There's nothing to forgive.'

I smile through my tears. How could I have blamed her so harshly?

'It's all right, about you and Dad,' I say, close to blubbing. 'It's all right.'

She gives me a wavering smile. 'I'm so sorry, Alex. I loved him.'

'I know.'

'You made it!' TJ rushes over and gives her a swift hug. 'Are you all right?'

'I'm fine,' she says hoarsely. 'I want everyone to stop fussing. You've all been through far more than me.'

We retreat to the sycamore tree and watch the inferno. Fire engulfs the roof, sending orange tongues and sparks into the night sky. The ruined building groans and spits and splutters. A window explodes, sending shards of glass across the lawn.

Jonathan shakes his head. 'I thought we could save the old pile.'

Multiple sirens and blue and red lights pierce the night. A fire engine roars up Church Lane, closely followed by an armed response van and two police cars that screech to a halt on the drive. An ambulance arrives moments later.

Marshall directs the police to the figure on the lawn as firefighters equipped with oxygen tanks, face shields and protective suits reel out yellow hoses. They stand with legs braced, sending powerful jets of water arcing onto the roof and through the smashed window.

The police lug Yury to their van. A paramedic secures an oxygen mask over his face. Armed officers with tasers stand to either side while they replace Marshall's tape with handcuffs.

Police officers run to the Austin ambulance. They wrench the driver and passenger's doors open and heave the vehicle away from the wall.

A shout of alarm goes up from the fire crew as the roof sags. The chimney caves in with a colossal smash, sending orange embers shooting into the sky like fireworks. Despite the firefighters' best efforts, flames continue to shoot from the giant cavity.

'Alex,' Jonathan says. 'May I have a word?'

He walks me across the lane. Across the verge is a small gate I never noticed before. Moonlight shines on a narrow path.

'What is it?' I ask.

'I'm proud of you. Your father would be, too. But it is imperative you leave immediately. If I am to protect you, it must be as though you were never here.' He puts his hand in the direction of the path. 'Follow the path to the next road. My contact is waiting to take you home.'

'But...but...' Questions jumble in my mind as I stare at the burning building. 'What about the League? And Quinn?'

'Trust me. Everything will be taken care of. I'll be in touch.'

'But I'm one of you, now.' I shake my head. 'At least let me say goodbye.'

'I will pass on your sentiments to the others.'

My hands fly to my face. 'My God! The finding machine!'

'It's safe. I will return it to you. I promise.' Jonathan opens the gate. 'But now, you *must* go.'

The Lodge lets out an almighty groan. Tiles fall from the roof. The house leans over and cracks appear. The red bricks that gave the Lodge its name turn black.

I tell myself it's only bricks and mortar. It's not the sum of the League.

Turning my back on the Lodge, I follow the path to the waiting car.

48

TWO DAYS LATER

"*And that's all from the BBC news. We'll pass you over to Sue for the weather which looks distinctly autumnal after all the sunshine. Good night.*"

I switch off the TV and drop the remote onto the coffee table. Since my return to Birmingham I've been channel surfing national news and the internet like a woman possessed. So far, there's been nothing on Bletchley's underground explosion, the Lodge fire, or Quinn's arrest. Somehow, Jonathan managed to sweep everything under the rug.

I should be thankful he delivered on his promise to keep me safe, but my relief is tempered with misgivings. Jonathan remains a mystery, a man who serves the League above everything.

Antony sinks onto the sofa and passes me a glass of wine. He slips two glossy brochures onto my lap.

'These made the shortlist,' he says.

I sip Merlot and snuggle into him, relishing his warmth. The weather turned as soon as I returned to Birmingham, raining solidly overnight until the following afternoon. Today, there's a chill in the air. The summer heatwave is fast becoming a distant memory.

'Perhaps we should put on the heating,' I say, dragging a zebra-striped throw over my legs.

Antony rolls his eyes. 'Are you nuts? It's September!'

I flick through the top brochure. The glossy pages are filled with villas, beaches, and sun-kissed models laughing and running into the sea. Each page offers an escape from dull, damp England. My eyes widen at a spectacular buffet with huge prawns, lobsters, carved fruit and ice sculptures. Attentive waiters serve wine from ice buckets while chefs pour chocolate sauce onto ice cream sundaes, and sear steak over flames.

'It's an all-inclusive place in Majorca,' Antony says. 'Fancy it?'

'You bet!' I grin. 'I'm happy anywhere with sun and unlimited ice cream.'

'You'd better check out option two,' Antony says.

I set my wine glass down and take a look at the second, thinner brochure. The cover shows a young couple walking hand in hand along a cliff path. They're wearing rain coats and scarves, but their smiles are as broad as the Majorca sun worshippers.

WILD ATLANTIC WAY ~ Slí an Atlantaigh Fhiáin

'Ireland.' I shiver.

'You keep saying we'll meet your mum. Why not now? We could make a proper holiday of it. Hire a car, see your family and the sights,' he adds. 'If we go over, your mum might open up about Pierce. Maybe share some memories about your dad.'

Mum and I still have a lot to catch up on. She's only given me the bare bones over the phone. Moira's in hospital under observation after taking a blow to the head. Pierce is indeed a policeman and will be off to Dublin on a new assignment any day now. The saintly Dervla O'Hara has been arrested with two local wrong 'uns.

As for Mum opening up about Dad, I can only hope.

I open the Irish brochure. Pub-goers in fisherman's jumpers enjoy pints of Guinness inside a traditional bar while an Irish Folk Band entertains them on the accordion and Bodhrán.

My gaze flicks to the Majorca brochure. Large prawns. Sun.

'Can't we do both?' I suggest. 'Go to Ireland and Spain?'

'I don't know if I can take two weeks off.' Antony rubs his chin. 'Saskia would have to push back my deadlines and you know we're flat out.'

The Edinburgh Expo was so successful that Antony returned to Birmingham with more work than his design cooperative could handle. There's talk of hiring new creatives and partnering with a design company in Surrey.

'You don't want to burn out like you did at Apex.' I add a kiss to soften my point. 'We both deserve a break.'

'I'll see what I can do.' He returns the kiss and grins. 'We have to do Ireland. I'll finally get to meet your mum.'

'I'd rein in that enthusiasm if I were you,' I mutter.

'What about Moira?' Antony laughs. 'She's got to be worth the price of the airfare alone, if she's as bonkers as you make out.'

He leans close again for a longer kiss. Satisfaction buzzes through me. This is what I love. Our simple life. The two of us in our tiny flat. Antony's next to me and that's the only thing that matters.

I've told him the story. Or rather, the edited highlights. I left out the bit about being imprisoned in a plastic cube and Aleksei blowing the tunnel, and I seriously downplayed the fire at the Lodge. With each day that passes without seeing anything on the news, the more I can relax.

I spent less than a week at Bletchley. But in that short time I broke the law enough times to fill a phone book: breaking and entering, using a false name, theft, hacking, joy riding, and assault with a Varsity oar.

After my adventures, I'm perfectly happy to put my finding machine in a box and hide it at the back of a cupboard.

That is, if I ever get it back.

Antony claps his hands on his thighs. 'I'll call Saskia right now. If she agrees I can have the time off I'll check dates with you, then shoot down to the travel agents and book everything.'

We chink glasses. 'I'll check if Moira's out of hospital and see how she's getting on.'

'Remember, meeting Moira is non-negotiable.' Antony winks, before heading across the hall to his studio.

I wrap the throw around me, feeling a twinge in my ribs. Aleksei left me with a memento: a footprint-shaped bruise from where he kicked me by the Lake at Bletchley. Antony wasn't at all happy about that.

I grab my mobile and dial: *IRISH_BRANCH.*

Anticipation worms through me. You never know what you're going to get with Moira. Still, it's wonderful to make a call without worrying about being bugged, tracked, or recorded. Things would be better if I could get the latest from Marshall, but his burner phone's toast. There's no point calling the League, as it's nothing but ashes.

'Hello from Fowleys Bar!' Moira says against the sound of revellers. A cheer goes up behind her, followed by a chant. 'Moy-ra, Moy-ra, Moy-ra!'

'Hi Moira!' I say loudly. 'You're out of hospital?'

'Oh, yes. Thanks to my big, thick skull. That's what Doctor Dooley said, and he's a man who knows what he's about.' Another cheer goes up in the background.

'Have you entered a drinking competition?' I ask.

'Indeed, I have not! You know I only take a half of lager now and then. I asked the landlord to switch from Sky Sports to the news because I'm on TV! I'll read you the headline. *Dromahair churchgoer helps foil criminal gang.* I'm famous! You should be too, only you're not from around here and—'

'It's perfectly fine, you enjoy your moment in the spotlight,' I assure her.

The last thing I want is my name bandied about. I'm still on tenterhooks every time the front door bell goes in case the police turn up.

'There's the bad egg herself, getting out of the back of a police van!' Moira exclaims. 'Don't bother covering your face, Dervla O'Hara! We know who you are!'

The other patrons let out long boos.

'And here come Dervla's partners in crime,' Moira adds. 'Two ne'er-do-wells from Sligo. Those boys were born with their fingers in the till. To think we suspected Pierce!'

I cringe, recollecting how we suspected the man of being a romance scammer, con artist, thief, and fraudster. Although, in our defence, Pierce's guarded behaviour did him no favours.

More cheers go up in the pub.

'That's the football back on, now,' Moira says. 'Your mum's here and wants a word.'

'Mum's in the pub?' My eyebrows shoot up. As far as I know, Mum's never visited a pub in her life. 'All right, pass her over.'

'Goodbye, Alex. Call me if you need me again. I'll be standing by.'

'Sure.' *Not in this lifetime!*

'Alexandra?' I struggle to hear Mum's strident tones amidst the cheers and yells. 'I'm moving into the private lounge.' The background noise cuts out. 'That's better.'

'It's great to hear Moira's on the mend,' I say. 'She's the best friend you could ever wish for.'

'She is, even if she does get the wrong end of the stick sometimes.' Mum pauses. 'She can be so easily influenced.'

My cheeks burn as I read between the lines.

'If you'd been in our shoes you'd have been worried, too,' I say. 'We weren't sure if Pierce was out to marry you or murder you!'

'I told you very clearly, everything was in hand. You shouldn't have been so swift to jump to conclusions.'

'Why didn't you just tell us Pierce worked for the police?'

Mum sighs. 'I promised Pierce I wouldn't say a word about his mission in case Dervla O'Hara got wind of it. Then Moira started sneaking around asking questions. I was at my wit's end. She could have ruined all our hard work.'

'Well, everything turned out well,' I remind her. 'Has Pierce gone off now?'

'Yes, to Dublin.' Mum sighs. 'He's on his next assignment for the Garda Síochána.'

'What's that?'

'It's a surveillance unit. But that information is strictly between you and me. Pierce did mention he'd pop back to see me in a few months,' she says guardedly. 'We got on extremely well. He brought the house to life while he stayed here.'

'Sounds like there could be something more there, Mum. A new boyfriend on the horizon.'

'Women in their sixties do not have boyfriends, Alexandra.'

'Suitor, then. Partner. Paramour. Does it matter?'

'He's divorced, you know.'

'That doesn't bother me and it shouldn't bother you.' My voice rises. 'It's been seven years since Dad died. You deserve to be happy.'

'Let's not get ahead of ourselves.' Mum bristles. 'Can we please change the subject?'

Taking a deep breath, I say, 'You can tell me more about him when I see you, if it's okay to come for a visit?'

'You're coming over?' Mum's voice brightens immediately. 'Oh, that's grand! I'll make your room up just the way you like it.'

'Antony's coming too.'

In the pause that follows, my heart races in anticipation of judgement, silence, or a lecture.

'Well, now,' Mum says. 'It's about time.'

49

I follow the path curving around the edge of Longmoor Pool. Swans cruise past, preening their feathers. Moorhens and coots make clicking sounds on the water.

I tear up a bread crust and toss the pieces to a group of squabbling ducks.

The pool lies in the southwest corner of Sutton Park. Only fifty yards from here is a concrete culvert covered in brambles.

Last winter, I found and rescued a boy who took shelter there against the cold. That was the first time the League stepped in to keep my name away from the authorities.

Back then, it was dark and freezing. Now, late summer sunshine reflects off the water and bathes the surrounding countryside in a golden glow.

I walk around the bend. A majestic oak tree overhangs the path and a wooden bench.

Shading my eyes against the sun, I squint at the figure sitting on the bench. Even though I've arrived twenty minutes early, he's already here.

I hurry across the grass.

Marshall stands and smiles. Instead of his usual suit, he's wearing a Chicago Bears sweatshirt, beige chinos, and Timberland boots.

I do a double take.

'Yeah, it's me,' he says, drawing me in for a hug.

'Where's the suit?'

'The suits have had their day.' He gestures to the bench and takes a seat.

I sit, staring at a butterfly closure strip on his temple and his grazed and swollen cheek. 'How are you doing?'

'I've had worse.' Marshall touches his face. 'Still, I'm getting too old for this game.'

I give a half grin. 'I think you do just fine for an old man.'

Marshall shakes his head, smiling.

I close my eyes, tipping my head back to the sun's warmth. The temperature's a far cry from the August heatwave but it still feels good. Oak leaves rustle overhead, stirred by a breeze.

'First things first.' Marshall removes a black rucksack from a gym bag and passes it over.

The rucksack is brand new with the tags still on. The lump inside feels the correct weight and size. I set it on my lap, reassured by the familiar chill seeping through the fabric.

I tug the zip open and peer inside.

'We swapped the quartz back. TJ, Carmen, and me,' Marshall says. 'It's just as it was before. One hundred percent.'

'I believe you.'

'There's cash in the front pocket to cover the clothes and other stuff you lost in the fire.'

'Thanks.' Reaching inside the rucksack, I flick the switch and Dad's dot appears. 'What happened to the other Drive?'

'Jonathan has put it into storage until the Lodge is rebuilt.'

The last time I looked, Red Croft Lodge was a smouldering pile of rubble. Jonathan's machine will be in storage for many, many months.

Marshall crosses his leg over one knee. 'Jonathan's planning substantial security upgrades for the new Lodge. The League's systems will be watertight. If he does it right, nothing like Quinn can ever happen again.'

I give him a dubious look. The Lodge may rise again like a phoenix from the ashes, but I don't share Jonathan's confidence about security. If there's one thing I've learnt over the last week, it's that someone will always find a way in.

I switch off the finding machine and zip up the bag. 'How does Jonathan feel, knowing my machine will work another twenty years while his won't last the month?'

'Not as bad as you felt about it.' A glint comes into Marshall's eye. 'The ghost quartz Grigor stole has been returned to the Natural History Museum. If Jonathan wants to extend the clone Drive's life, he'll have to locate more ghost quartz from somewhere else. He's mothballed that idea for now to focus on other League projects that are just as revolutionary.'

'Like the stone tapes?'

Marshall looks away.

'Can't you tell me?'

'I'm sure Jonathan would be happy to, but I'm out of the loop.' Marshall sighs. 'I've left the League, Alex. I'm heading back to the States to be with my family. My grandchildren.'

'But you'll be back,' I say, unable to separate Marshall from the League. 'This is just a sabbatical, right?'

'No, I've left for good.' He pauses. 'Jonathan's headhunting a new head of security. Someone younger.'

'They won't be as good as you,' I say.

Marshall hides a smile.

'Is TJ leaving?' I remember his distress at the soul cage voices.

'Yes and no. Jonathan found him a role with one of his contacts until the new Lodge is rebuilt. TJ's happy with the arrangement. It's flexible hours, he can fix his own routine, and he gets his own office.'

'Hopefully, in the quietest corner of the building.' I smile.

'Guess so.'

I link my hands around the rucksack. 'And Carmen? How is she?'

'Carmen's good.' He pauses. 'She's left the League, too. She told Jonathan she'd had more than enough excitement for one lifetime.

But it was more than that. The fire really shook her up. It shook us all up.'

'Didn't seem to shake Jonathan up,' I say.

'He hides his feelings, but you're wrong to think he doesn't care.'

'If you say so,' I mutter.

'He risked his life going into a burning building,' Marshall argues. 'He did it to save the League and protect its people. Including you, remember?'

'Jonathan's priority was certainly to protect the League,' I say tightly. 'Maybe more than its people. Saving Carmen seemed to come second.'

'Getting Carmen out was my job.' Marshall gives me a sharp look. He clenches his hands in his lap. 'Jonathan's a good man. He thinks highly of you.'

Before Marshall asked for my help I was desperate to work for Jonathan and the League. But knowing he switched the quartz in my machine and witnessing his priorities firsthand makes it impossible to fully trust him.

Biting my tongue, I stare at the reflections of clouds scudding over the water. I decide it best to change the subject.

'What's the situation with Quinn and the Russians?'

Marshall's hands relax. 'Quinn, Yury, and Aleksei are in custody facing a barrage of charges. Abduction, assault, fraud, illegal use of explosives, destruction of commercial and private property. I'm sure there's more.' He pauses for breath. 'Quinn's boasting about how his lawyers will get him off. He has no idea about Jonathan's connections.'

'None of us do,' I mutter under my breath.

'Quinn's problems don't end there,' Marshall adds. 'The Bletchley Trust has dropped him as a donor. They're suing him for fraud, malpractice, and property damage. The U.S. Department of Justice has frozen Quinn's assets. ATC's share price is bound to tank when word gets out. He's screwed.'

'Couldn't happen to a nicer guy.' I shade my eyes as a ray of sunlight breaks through the clouds. 'What about Grigor?'

Marshall nods. 'He's agreed to give evidence against Quinn. Jonathan will see to it he gets a lighter sentence.'

'I suppose I'd better resign from the League, too,' I say. 'It won't be the same without you and Carmen. I don't see how I'd fit in.'

'Give it some thought before you make your decision. Jonathan wants you as a consultant on your dad's projects. Like an overseer.'

'I don't know. I need time out.' I close my eyes and stretch my back, desperate to resume my regular life with Antony. 'I'm going on holiday.'

'You need breathing space. I get it,' Marshall says. 'You might think differently in six months, by which time Jonathan should have everything back up and running.'

I suppose he's right. I could stay part of the League. Then I'd know if they made more finding machines and what they were doing with them.

Marshall reaches into his gym bag and passes me an envelope with my name in blue ink and a shoebox-sized package wrapped in floral paper.

'This is from Carmen. She wants you to destroy the letter as soon as you've read it.'

Marshall checks his watch. He gets to his feet and stares across the lake. 'It's a shame summer's over.'

I smile. 'We had a blast, didn't we?'

'We did.' He grins. 'Good luck, Alex.'

'Goodbye, Marshall.'

A lump comes to my throat as he walks away.

For a long moment I stare at the water. A child laughs in the distance. Cyclists ride past on the path, chatting.

I set the package on the bench beside the rucksack and tear open the envelope.

A lavender aroma drifts from a single sheet of writing paper. The blue ink has smudged in places.

Dear Alex,

By the time you read this, you'll have heard that I left the League. I'm staying with my sister in the countryside while I consider my future. Marshall thinks I left because my recent ordeal was too much for me.

In fact, it was meeting you that spurred my decision.

Over the years, I slipped into a routine that made me feel useful, that I believed honoured Richard's legacy. I realise now I was holding onto the past when I should have let go, years before.

In mentioning this, the last thing I want to do is upset you or bring up any more sadness or bad feelings. I can only apologise again with all my heart. I am moving on and I hope you can, too.

I have no doubt you will continue to honour your father's legacy. I think there is a certain irony that Jonathan didn't trust you with your father's machine. And yet you were the one who kept it safe while he was compromised.

The League will attract enemies and face external threats as long as it exists. You are free of that now, should you choose to be.

As far as the authorities are concerned, the contents of this package burned in the fire along with your finding machine. No one is looking for it because it doesn't exist.

Love and best wishes, as ever,

Carmen.'

I breathe in lavender, fighting a welling sadness. I hope Carmen finds peace and happiness. If she'd left a return address I would have written back to tell her all is forgiven. Even though I'm pretty sure she already knows.

I tear the paper and open the box. Inside is a small cassette recorder with a tangle of wires and two black boxes with switches and lights. I remove an A5 sheet of paper with technical diagrams and printed text and read the title:

STONE TAPE MODULATOR AND RECEIVER:
USER INSTRUCTIONS.

ALEX MARTIN COZY MYSTERY SERIES:

THE FINDING MACHINE
THE MILLENNIUM AFFAIR
THE NOUGHTY SPY
THE STONE TAPE HOUSE

Thank you for reading! Please take a moment to leave me a review — no matter how short — you won't believe the difference it makes, plus, it's so helpful for other readers. If you enjoyed my book, please recommend me to your bookish friends! To keep in the loop about my latest projects, exclusive content, sneak peeks and other random cool stuff, sign up for my newsletter on my website and receive a **FREE** book of short stories!

Come find me at lucylyonswrites.com
Facebook and Instagram under lucylyonswrites

ACKNOWLEDGEMENTS

As ever, I had an incredible amount of help and technical input from many people all over the world. Thank you to my test readers, John J. Delaney, Isobel Peters, Peter Berriman, and W.K. Greyling, and to my international critiquers at Scribophile. Special mention goes to Jim Moran, L.N. Hunter, Nate Stonecypher, Sonny Kohet, and Jed Winter. Translation credits go to Yuko Burge for the Japanese, and Angela Sawyer for the Russian. Thanks to Audrey for the loan of your name, and thank you to hubbie, Carl, for cozying everything up for the final draft. As ever, If I have missed anyone out, forgive me. The legend of The Rollright Stones is truly magical and well worth a visit. If you are ever in the Milton Keynes area, I recommend a day out to Bletchley Park. There may not be an underground train line, but there are many amazing attractions including the Austin 18 ambulance stored in the Wartime Garages. If you see her, please give her a pat from me!

www.ingramcontent.com/pod-product-compliance
Lightning Source LLC
Chambersburg PA
CBHW020350220726

48290CB00014B/1482